Barb

Shakespeare's True Love
By
Helen E. Burton

Cover photo Anne Hathaway's Cottage
iStockphoto #158882373

Author's photo
Alisha Keezer-Lewis

ISBN 9781546337645
Printed in the United States of America

Acknowledgements

I am extremely grateful to my early readers: Rob and Lauren Kirkham, Francie Stephens, Doris Autenrieth, Ramona Hazlett, and Barb and Dave Bishop for their support and friendship. Thank you Dr. Cheryl Callaghan for your expertise on delivering twins; thankfully, you weren't a midwife in the 16th Century! I would also like to thank the Morro Bay Writers' Group for listening to my early drafts and answering endless publishing questions.

My children have always believed in me, and I could not have finished this novel without their encouragement and suggestions. Amy, Nathan, Natalie, and Alisha you are and always will be my finest creations. Aiden, my dear grandson, I hope you will want to read this when you are older.

I especially want to thank the National Endowment for the Humanities. The two summer seminars on Shakespeare sponsored by the NEH which I was fortunate to attend allowed me to spend quality time in Stratford-upon-Avon and at the Folger Library in Washington, D.C. These academic experiences enriched my knowledge of and love for William Shakespeare.

To my husband, Gary, I can't thank you enough for reading each chapter with a critical eye and sharpening your editing pencil on my rough drafts. I knew I was making progress when you handed back a chapter and said, "You are getting better." High praise from my favorite CPA!

Chapter One
Spring 1582 Stratford-upon-Avon England

Anne strode down the street, a million thoughts raging in her head. Why must she be so misunderstood? Her brother, Bartholomew, insists she be married. Her stepmother Joan constantly compares her to the Larrington girl next door. *Beatrice dresses modestly, smiles demurely, and remains silent around men. Beatrice has countless suitors and will make a good marriage.* Anne could hear her stepmother's voice in her mind, *Beatrice is younger than you, Anne, but she has already had three good offers of marriage.* Humph! Her stepmother's idea of a good marriage was laughable. Should Beatrice accept the hand of seventy-year-old Frederick the sheep merchant, or cold, calculating Mr. Cole the arrogant businessman from Cambridge? Perhaps Peter was a better match as he was closer to Beatrice's age, but Peter could be smelled two streets away and loved mead more than work.

Anne's thoughts flew from Beatrice to her brother's constant warnings, "You will be a spinster, Anne. The neighbors have stopped asking me when you will marry, and now they just pat me on the back and shake their heads when I mention your name." Should she be forced to marry to leave the discomfort of her home life in Shottery? What a pathetic reason for marriage! Yet, a single woman living on her own was unthinkable in Warwickshire.

Anne's fury began to assuage, and she realized that she had been walking at such a furious pace that she was already in the center of Stratford-upon-Avon in Henley Street. She heard a strange noise which sounded like choking coming from behind her and turned to see a young man leaning casually against the glover's home. He was chortling. Anne looked around her, but she could see nothing to induce his laughter. He seemed to be looking at her. "What's wrong with you, you gleeking fool-born oaf?" Anne demanded.

At that, the young man increased the volume of his laughter and smiled merrily at her. "I only laugh to think that if you keep up the pace at which you are walking, you will soon be in London!"

"And what if I am?" hurled Anne. "What is it to you how fast or slow I walk? At least in London I might encounter those who have a brain and are not idle, lop-eared nutsops like you!"

"My, my! Your tongue is as fast as your legs! Begone then. I will not delay you from your journey to London to visit the Queen," he said with merriment in his eyes.

"Humph!" was all Anne could manage as she turned on her heel and continued down Henley Street. She soon discovered, however, that she could not return to her former state of anger and frustration with her home life. Much to her dismay, she could not get the young man's laughing eyes out of her mind. It wasn't just his eyes that she replayed in her mind. It was his attitude toward her speech and demeanor. He had not cowered from her as most young men did when she gave them a tongue lashing. No, just the opposite, he seemed to enjoy sparring with her. What a peculiar young man.

Well, Anne contemplated, he is, after all, just another young man, and as with all young men, he is interested in only one thing. In fairness to Stratford men, Anne had to concede that they were interested in two things: passion and dowry. Unfortunately, the men her brother introduced her to seemed primarily enchanted by the dowry her father had provided for her in his will and most of them seemed bereft of passion.

In contrast, the stranger she had just accosted in the street seemed full of humor and passion. He was about her height and had looked her directly in the eye with no embarrassment or apparent malice. She could not shake the memory of his eyes. They were deep brown pools which seemed to reveal great depth of soul and intellect. He had a strong, thin face, and his pale complexion was highlighted by ruddy cheeks. His hair was as black as a raven but curly like a young lamb's wool. It framed his face and hung down his back, shimmering in the sun. He smelled of soap and leather and his apparel was well-fitted. Though Anne could normally think of a dozen criticisms of the men she met, she could think of but one for this mystery man: his fingers were blackened at the tips and stained with what she thought must be the dye of the glover's trade.

The young man in front of his home watched the churlish woman continue her rant down Henley Street. She was unlike any woman he had ever met--so outspoken and bold. Why, he had never been so upbraided. Even his school fellows who teased him for his bookish ways had never unleashed such disdainful words upon him. He smiled to himself remembering her outlandish torrent of epithets. As he watched her proud back disappear from view, head held high, never looking back towards him, he couldn't get the vision of her eyes out of his head. She had the greenest, most mischievous, and most intelligent eyes he had ever seen. If not for the deep furrow of anger on her forehead, he would declare that she was the most beautiful woman he had ever seen. Her hair was a radiant auburn, long and flowing down her back. She did not sweep it up on her head like most of the young women who came into the shop. Rather, she pulled back a few tendrils from her face and fastened them with a simple ribbon in the back. She was nearly as tall as he and carried herself with confidence and pride. Her shoulders were broad, chest heavenly, waist small, and her delicate ankles belied her physical strength.

William wandered across Henley Street to the bake shop. As he opened the door, the warmth and aroma of freshly baked bread stirred him from his daze. He stepped inside and heard his friend Hamnet Sadler welcome him. Hamnet was nearly as wide as he was tall with a balding pate and an enormous smile.

"Good morning, William. I was beginning to think you had forgotten about us," Hamnet smiled at his best friend. "I don't suppose I could interest you in a fresh bun just out of the oven."

"Hamnet, your buns, as good as they are, pale in comparison to the sweetest of sweets I just saw in the street. I am in love!"

"This may be a record even for you William. Not yet ten in the morning and you have fallen in love this day."

"This girl is different, Hamnet."

"Let's see. Is she different from the butcher's daughter who you fell in love with on Monday or the merchant's cousin you fell in love with on Tuesday?"

"She is superior to any girl that I have ever seen. She is perfect."

"Oh, William, there is no such thing as a perfect woman."

Just as Hamnet said this, a slight dark-haired woman with a pan of fresh buns passed through from the kitchen and stopped in mid stride, staring at Hamnet. The robust young man rested his hands on his ample belly, blushed, and hesitantly said, "Look who's come to visit us, wife dear."

"Don't wife dear me Hamnet Sadler. I have ears. I heard you telling William big as brass and twice as cocky that there is no such thing as a perfect woman."

"Judith dear, you didn't hear what I told William right before that which was that I had already married the one perfect woman and so, unfortunately, none were left for him."

The three friends laughed together and Judith said, "Husband if you keep up those stories, you will become the writer, and William here will have to be the baker. Pull up a stool and join us for some fresh baked bread, William."

William eagerly accepted their offer and soon he was telling his friends about the mystery woman that had approached him in the street. Hamnet and Judith laughed at his description and both agreed that the outspoken young woman would be a good character for him to write about but not a good match for him.

"Why wouldn't she be a match for me?"

Hamnet glanced at Judith, and she just shrugged, so Hamnet tentatively said, "You need a quiet, proper wife to fit your place in business here in Stratford. Think of your mother, Mary. She is the perfect example of a wife and helpmate who has supported your father and gained him the respect of the entire village. Don't you think your mother and the Arden name helped your father climb the social ladder in Stratford? His business and his political life have been helped by your mother's quiet dignity. I don't recall her ever calling anyone an idle, lop-eared nutsop!"

William had to smile at the thought of those words coming out of his mother's mouth, but he wasn't pleased with his friend's obviously well-intended advice. He had felt the tension in his home between his parents, and he knew that though to the outside world, John and Mary Shakespeare had made a proper match, in William's romantic view, their marriage was missing one very important component: love. Since John's fall in political stature (he was no longer mayor of Stratford-Upon-Avon) and the decline in the glove business, his parents seemed to barely tolerate each other. William felt that his mother was deeply unhappy, and he didn't know what to do to help her.

William quietly confided in his dear friends, "You know that's not what I want in life. I don't have any interest in the glove business or in the baking business for that matter. It was easy for you, Hamnet. You have loved baking since you were just a lad, right?"

"Well, yes, Will," Hamnet replied. "I guess it never occurred to me to do anything else. I was only fifteen when father passed away, and mother needed my help, and I was happy to do it. Then when Judith and I married, it became our business, and we like working together as a team."

"I'm the perfect woman and wife and baker," Judith chimed in.

"Is it too much for me to have what you two have? To be in love and to love what I am doing with my life?"

"No, it isn't too much, William. But we worry that you don't really know what you want. You are in love with being in love. Your romantic poetry has tainted your brain, and you think every girl you see is the girl of your dreams. The girl you met today sounds more like someone out of a nightmare, not a dream. You might wake up married to an outspoken, shrewish wife."

"If I do, Hamnet, it is all your fault! After all, you married the last perfect woman on earth."

Judith gave William a fond embrace and said, "Be patient, Will. You will find what you are looking for soon enough. You are only eighteen. Hamnet was twenty-two when he found me. That gives you four years of getting to know many a maid before you make one your wife!"

Will gave Hamnet a wink and said, "I must admit that getting to know girls is my favorite part of the sport of courting."

Judith pushed herself away from Will and said, "William Shakespeare, you are awful. You know perfectly well that I meant you should get to know their personality and character, not what is under their nickers."

Hamnet and William enjoyed a laugh together as Judith returned to the ovens to check on the bread. "Will, you have a real advantage over the average man looking to impress a woman. The words just roll off your lips, and the girls swoon. You make it sound so sincere and pure."

"You are a fine one to talk, Hamnet. Your golden voice lured Judith to your side. When you strum your lute and sing your beautiful songs all the women's hearts melt. You make the lyrics of others sound like your own heart's desire. My words, as humble as they are, always come straight from my heart. I really do love women. Short ones, tall ones, skinny ones, plump ones. I love them all until the next one comes along, and then I love her too!"

"William!" His father's shout could be heard inside the bakery. William jumped from his stool embarrassed by his father's commanding tone and uttered apologies to Hamnet as he hurriedly left the bakery and headed for the leather shop to see what his father required.

"William, it is bad enough that you spend every spare moment of the day scribbling away with pen and ink. Now you are idling about with your friends when there is work to be done."

"I'm sorry father. What do you need me to do?"

"The young lad who does the deliveries is down with a sickness, and I need you to take this order of gloves to an important customer."

William was relieved it was a simple delivery his father needed done. He had tried as a young boy to follow in his father's trade, but he had no interest in tanning hide, cutting patterns, and sewing gloves. Not only had he no interest in the trade, he was bad at it! He marred the leather as it cured; he miss cut the patterns and wasted precious resources. Worst of all, he hated the idea that the leather had once been part of a living, breathing animal. His tender heart couldn't reconcile the cruelty of the slaughter of innocent lambs to fashion expensive gloves for selfish gentlemen and women. He just wasn't meant to be a glover, and he felt his father was beginning to come to terms with that. What his father couldn't reconcile was William's desire to be a writer.

"So you want to be a solicitor and write up people's legal documents?" his father would question.

"No, not that type of writer, father," William would patiently answer.

"So you want to be a curate or the paster of a parish and write sermons and such?" his father pursued.

"No, no, father. I want to write poems and plays, and I want someday to perform in those plays on a big stage in London," William would eagerly explain.

His father, John, would simply shake his head at this and mutter something about not knowing what he and his good wife had done to ruin the boy.

Lately, William had given up trying to explain his ambitions. He just wrote whenever he had time, helped his father around the shop as much as he could without doing damage, and managed to keep peace in the family.

William started out at a brisk pace for the cottage at Hewlands Farm in Shottery where the gloves were to be delivered. He had never been to the Hathaway's home, but he had walked by it many times and admired the fine garden and the neat and tidy look of the thatched house. It was less than two miles from his home, the leather shop on Henley Street, and William looked forward to the peaceful walk. It gave him time to think about the sonnets on which he was working. He would work out the meter and beat as he walked along, substituting one word and then another, sometimes speaking the lines out loud to hear how they sounded. Finding natural rhymes was the key to a good sonnet, William thought; that and an important idea. Of course, the theme of love was already set with the form, but the variety of ideas about love seemed boundless, and though he knew little of real love yet, he felt passionately about the idea of love.

With these thoughts filling his mind, William soon arrived at the Hathaway home and knocked soundly on the door. Presently, a matron opened the low door slowly and asked, "What is your business here?"

"I have a delivery for Mr. Bartholomew Hathaway from Mr. John Shakespeare on Henley Street," William answered, rather amused by the woman's abrupt greeting.

"Oh, thanks be to God. It's just the gloves Mr. Hathaway ordered. I thought mistress Anne had gotten herself into a scrape again," Joan Hathaway gushed as she took the package from William. "Thank you." With that, she shut the door and left William wondering who Anne was and in what sort of scrapes she usually found herself.

William shrugged and bethought to retrace his steps back to Stratford, but he was drawn to the Hathaway's garden and began to wander through it admiring the roses, hollyhocks, and lilies. He thought about incorporating flowers into his next sonnet and using the meanings of the flowers to evoke an encrypted message to readers. What had he read? Rosemary is for remembrance; pansies are for thoughts; columbine signifies thanklessness. He was concentrating so

9

deeply on remembering the language of flowers that he did not hear the footsteps approaching him until a shadow moved across the daisies he was admiring, and he looked to see a familiar face directly in front of him.

"What are you doing in my garden? If you have come to complain to Bartholomew about my behavior earlier today, you need not waste your breath. My brother has heard from everyone in the neighborhood that I do not conduct myself the way a young woman ought."

William recovered his speech enough to sputter, "I was just delivering some gloves from my father's shop."

"The son of Mr. Shakespeare making deliveries. I doubt that. You are the errand boy and no more. You still have not told me what you are doing in my garden." Anne could not believe that the young man she could not get out of her mind was standing amongst the daisies in her own garden.

Anne's condescending tone towards him helped William regain his equilibrium, and he smiled widely at her. "You must be Anne Hathaway. The famous Anne that gets herself into one scrape after another."

Anne blushed at these candid remarks, and in one of the rare moments of her young life, was speechless. "You don't know me!" she finally managed to blurt.

"Not yet," William replied with a wink. Then he walked toward the garden gate without looking back at the amazed young woman standing amid the daisies. Daisy. Daisy. Ah yes, daisy signifies the light of love. He mused, *This bud of love, by summer's ripening breath, may prove a beauteous flower when next we meet"* (Romeo & Juliet, 2.2).

Chapter Two

Anne watched in amazement as the audacious young man walked away from her. Then she hurried into the house, through the main room, past the hearth, and up the narrow stairs to her little refuge among the eaves. She hurled herself upon the straw-filled mattress and sobbed. She didn't know what was wrong with her. She lost her temper at the least provocation, and she couldn't stop herself from crying. She had always thought crying was a sign of weakness, and she had sworn no one would ever see her cry. Why had the young man in her garden caused such a rush of emotions in her?

Anne missed her father so much. He had been dead for nearly nine months now and still she ached to speak to him and to ask his advice. He knew how to calm her tempestuous spirit without breaking it. Richard Hathaway was the kindest, smartest, and strongest father a girl could have. Anne was only eight when her mother died, and she didn't really understand the permanence of death. Of course, she had sad memories of the loss of her younger brother, Richard and the baby, Catherine, but she was just a child then and death and loss was something she thought was simply a part of life. Though Anne loved her mother dearly, the pain she felt at losing her was amplified when she saw her father's grief at losing the woman he loved. She watched her father care for her mother the last days of her life. She saw the tenderness and love in his eyes, and she vowed that someday someone would love her that much.

Her father's love for her helped shape Anne's confident, self-assured poise. Richard Hathaway's loving nature extended to all seven of his surviving children. Anne was not necessarily his favorite child, but he made her feel special by finding time for her. When Richard came in from the fields, he would settle by the fire and tell Anne that he needed her to help him sort through his day's work. She would climb upon his knee, and he would tell her in which fields he had worked that day and what he had accomplished. She would listen carefully and take her duty as record keeper seriously because sometimes he would first ask her questions about what he had done the day before. "Did I get the sheep moved from the lower meadow to the upper yesterday, Anne dear?"

"No, father," she would giggle. Don't you remember that it was the other way around? The upper meadow needed a rest, so you moved the sheep to the lower meadow."

"Oh goodness! You've saved me again from starving the poor sheep to death. Is it time to hoe the peas?"

"You finished three acres yesterday."

"So I did, but how many acres of peas do we have?"

"We have seventeen full acres of the best peas in Warwickshire!"

"Well-spoken, my little Anne. I don't suppose you know how many acres I have left to tend starting tomorrow."

"Fourteen," her older brother, Bartholomew, shouted before Anne could say a word. Because he had started grammar school, Bartholomew had to practice his numbers, and he was proud of his ability to figure the simple problems his father gave him. He often joined Anne and their father in the game of managing Hewlands Farm. Bartholomew had the more difficult job of writing down the number of sheep in the meadow and the measurements of the barley and pea fields. Richard called him his little bookkeeper, and he helped Bartholomew record the numbers accurately and checked his sums. Richard also corrected any errors he made in the written log Bartholomew kept of the activities on Hewlands Farm. Anne always watched carefully and admired the way Bartholomew could form the letters so perfectly and create words that his father would then read out loud to her. Anne couldn't remember how old she was when it happened, but she was still very young as her mother was still alive the day Bartholomew wrote "sheeq" instead of "sheep," and she laughed and said, "No, silly. You need a "p" not a "q."

Her father turned to her and said, "Why, Anne, you are correct. Do you know the letters?"

Anne was suddenly embarrassed and said, "I don't know, father."

"Well, don't be ashamed. Let's just see what you have learned." He gave her Bartholomew's slate and asked her to write the alphabet. With just a bit of help from Bartholomew, she successfully wrote all the letters.

Even Bartholomew was engaged in this new game, and he said, "Now tell us the names and sounds they make." To Anne's own amazement, she knew all of them. "What about the numbers, Anne? Do you know them too?" Bartholomew wanted to know. She did. All three Hathaways were delighted. Her father and Bartholomew helped her write a little sentence about the sheep, and that evening as they sat around the table, Anne read it to her mother. Mrs. Hathaway clapped her hands and hugged her sweet daughter. Anne had never felt so loved.

Those warm feelings which filled her breast with such pride from just the smallest intellectual accomplishments spurred Anne forward with a desire to learn more and more. Though educating girls was not a part of the culture of Stratford, at Hewlands Farm it became the norm, and every evening Bartholomew would share what he had learned at school with Anne, and he would bring her small paperback chapbooks to read. Anne would sit in the security of her father's lap and read to him.

Anne roused herself from her daydreaming. How long had she been hiding in her little loft feeling sorry for herself? She couldn't understand what had prompted these tender memories and the tears she was shedding. Why would the sight of the young man she had met in Stratford and then again in her own garden cause such an outburst? Lately, she longed for those happier days when she and her father would sit before the fire together and share the activities of each other's days and read to each other. Even when Richard Hathaway remarried, and he and his new wife, Joan, started their family together, Anne and her father remained close. He was what made Anne's life bearable. She didn't mind helping her stepmother with each of the five babies as they came along because her father still took the time to make Anne feel loved and worthwhile.

Since her father's death, everything had changed. Joan, with the help of Bartholomew, had taken over the operation of Hewlands Farm. Anne suddenly felt awkward and out of place without her father there. She loved her half siblings, Joan, 16; Thomas, 13; Margaret, 11; John, 8; and William, 5; but they were growing up. Joan, christened with her mother's name but always called Jo in the Hathaway household and Margaret were able to help by gathering the eggs, milking the goats, and sweeping the floors. Anne spent her days washing clothes and cooking meals, jobs that Jo and the younger girls could handle on their own, now that William was old enough to entertain himself. Jo and Margaret were so different from Anne. Though Richard Hathaway tried to teach his younger girls the things that Anne had been so delighted to learn, they weren't interested and thought it was strange that their father encouraged them in this odd exercise. This made Anne feel even more alienated and alone.

As Anne stared up at the beams of her beloved cottage, she wondered what was to become of her. Had her love of learning ruined her chances of ever having romantic love? She wasn't like the other young women in and around Stratford. She had opinions about everything; she had ideas of how to make the household run more smoothly. She even counseled Bartholomew on the operation of the farm. She tried to be quiet and demure and listen while the men talked, but she just couldn't. No man wanted a churlish wife. No one would ever want her.

Anne knew she needed company to improve her mood. She left her tiny loft and went to the garden, her favorite place at Shottery. She carefully selected several of the biggest stalks of bright orange and white gladiolas. The sturdy flowers exhumed strength and beauty, the traits she was struggling to find today. She gathered five stalks of the striking glads into a bouquet and walked hastily out the gate and down the lane towards the Larrington farm.

She found Beatrice Larrington tossing feed to the chickens in the barnyard behind their large rough hewn farm house. Masses of curly blonde hair billowed around Beatrice's finely featured face and caressed her porcelain complexion. She was delighted to see her friend, Anne.

"Oh, Anne. Those flowers are beautiful. Thank you for thinking of me! As you can see," Beatrice gestured around her, "father does not think flowers are a good use of land."

Anne looked from the dilapidated chicken coop, to the muddy pig sty, to the large vegetable garden which occupied all the space between the Larrington farm house and the fields. Not a flower was in sight. She couldn't imagine Shottery without the gorgeous flowers surrounding it. Her spirits lifted, and she scolded herself for ever feeling so low and unhappy.

"I've finished my chores, Anne. Let's put these flowers in some water and take them to my little attic room so we can talk," Beatrice said as she tossed the last of the grain to the hens gathered around her.

Beatrice had her own space in the Larrington home, but unfortunately it had such low ceilings that she and Anne had to do a duck walk through the door to sit on her bed. They set the pitcher of gladiolas on the floor and the long stalks brushed the roof.

Tiny Beatrice was about a head shorter than Anne, and Anne teased, "I never thought I would see you have to stoop. I'm always hitting my head at Shottery because I'm so horribly tall."

"Anne, don't you ever complain about your height," Beatrice scolded. "I am so jealous of you. You are tall and dignified, and I am just a dwarf."

"What? You jealous of me!" Anne fell back on Beatrice's bed and laughed.

"What's so humorous about that?" Beatrice demanded.

"I'm sorry, Beatrice, but my stepmother is constantly comparing me to you. In her opinion, you are perfect. That you are jealous of me is absurd!"

Beatrice gaped at Anne and started giggling. "All I think about is how I can be more like you!"

"My stepmother would not be happy to have two of me, so you need to stay your quiet, sweet self!"

"I hate being quiet and sweet!" Beatrice said forcefully.

Anne was shocked at her friend's outburst. "You are just the type of girl that all the men in Warwickshire want to marry. You are petite, beautiful, and modest. Why Beatrice, you can have any man you want!" Anne gushed.

"I don't want any man!" Beatrice shouted.

Anne laughed and said, "You want a man, all right. You just don't want the ones your father picks out."

"No, Anne! I don't want a man period. I don't ever want to get married. You'll never get married, and you are just fine."

Anne was taken back by Beatrice's honest appraisal of her as a life-long spinster. She hesitated and said, "I met a very interesting young man today."

"You did?" Beatrice raised her eyebrows and studied Anne's face. "Did you hurt him very badly?"

"Beatrice! I didn't hurt him at all. Well, I didn't hit him with anything, but I did insult him just a little."

"Uh huh. You just insulted him a little," Beatrice said skeptically.

"Really! The strange part is that he just smiled at me. It didn't bother him at all that I spoke rudely to him."

"Is he simple minded?" Beatrice asked seriously.

"No! Now you are being ridiculous. He seems very intelligent, and he is extremely nice looking."

Beatrice declared, "Anne Hathaway, you are smitten! I didn't think you had any interest in courting."

"Don't jump to any conclusions, Beatrice. Just because I met a tolerable young man does not mean we are courting." Secretly, she had to admit that she hoped Beatrice was right. "Why don't you want to marry? Don't you want to have children?"

"I do want to have children. I just don't want a husband!" Beatrice said adamantly.

Anne giggled, "It probably isn't a good idea for you to have children without being married. I have a feeling your father would not be happy."

"It doesn't matter what I want anyway," Beatrice said sadly. "My father is looking for the highest bidder, and then my fate is sealed."

Anne hugged Beatrice tightly and said, "I'm sorry, sweetie. It might not be as bad as you think. Perhaps he will find someone who wants nine children and loves flowers."

Beatrice welcomed Anne's embrace and comforting words, but when the visit ended and Anne left, she had tears in her eyes.

Chapter Three

William Shakespeare was only eighteen years old on that fateful day in April when he first met Anne Hathaway, but he was a young man filled with passion and dreams of a life beyond Stratford. He knew from a very young age that writing was his destiny. Could it be that part of his destiny was to make the head strong Anne Hathaway his wife? As Hamnet had teasingly reminded William, he did fall in love often, but Anne was like no woman William had ever met. He knew she wasn't perfect; she was honest and outspoken. Most of the girls he met were instantly charmed by his intense brown eyes and sweet words, but Anne didn't seem to notice. She was a challenge!

Over the course of the next two weeks, William found ways to "accidentally" be where Anne was. He happened to be passing by Hewlands Farm when Anne was hanging out the wash. He mysteriously appeared as she was leaving the parish church. He encountered her at the market place in Stratford. He was outside the grammar school when she went to meet her young brothers. Each time he saw her, he would introduce himself, "Hello, I'm William Shakespeare. I don't believe we have had the pleasure of meeting."

Each time this happened, Anne would unleash a torrent of insults on him. "You fly-bitten, nut-hook! You just introduced yourself to me yesterday."

"Why, Miss Hathaway, you mean to say that you have been thinking about me since yesterday," William would pronounce with a large smile.

By the end of the first week of these social "attacks," Anne found herself watching for William, but he always managed to appear when she least expected it. One day, he didn't appear at all, and to her great surprise, she felt disappointment. How could she possibly be disappointed in not seeing an annoying beef-witted lout? To her further consternation, she found herself looking forward to seeing the irrepressible young man.

It wasn't long before she gave up the pretense of avoiding William and soon they were arranging to meet. They would talk for hours as they walked in the beautiful meadows and forests around Stratford. They spent lazy afternoons rowing on the Avon by Trinity Church admiring the swans and laughing at the ducks and geese who dipped their heads underwater for lunch and bobbed their bottoms straight up in the air. William took Anne out into the country to the home of his godparents, Richard and Sarah Spencer, who lived on a farm near Wilmcote and the Ardens, his mother's parents. Since his grandparent's deaths, William had become even closer to his godparents, the Spencers. They were the only ones with whom he could share his dreams for the future. They believed in him and his talent. Much to William's delight, they liked Anne from the first moment they met her, and they could see she was good for William. Grandfather Arden had given William two horses which the Spencers stabled for him. Anne loved Barbary and Dobbin on first sight, and Dobbin adopted Anne after the first apple was offered him from her soft hand. Anne's first ride on Dobbin was much more eventful! They had been standing in the stable yard brushing the horses, when William disappeared inside and came back through the stable door and out into the sunshine carrying a dusty, awkward looking object which he started to place on Dobbin's back. While Dobbin careened his neck around to see what was going on, Anne just burst into laughter.

"What are you doing?" Anne asked through her laughter.

"I'm saddling Dobbin with Grandmother's side saddle, why?" William asked quizzically.

"I'm not riding on that thing. Here give me a hand up."

Amazed, William put the old saddle down, put his hands together as a mock stirrup and gave Anne a lift up onto Dobbin's back. Anne simply bunched her skirts around her legs, clutched Dobbin's mane in her hands, gave him a gentle kick in the side, and Dobbin and Anne trotted off toward the meadow. It took a few minutes for William to grab the reins and mount Barbary to follow his impetuous Anne.

****

Anne was twenty-six years old on that fateful day in April when she first met William on Henley Street; she was older and seemingly wiser than young William, yet he fascinated her. She treated him with contempt, and he only smiled and met her contempt with kindness. She railed at him about his youth, his hopeless occupation, and his ink-stained fingers. He told her he admired her loveliness, her gentleness, and her modest wit. Was he a madman? No. He wrote the most beautiful poetry she had ever read. Early in their courtship, he even wrote a poem for her:

Those lips that Love's own hand did make
Breathed forth the sound that said 'I hate,'
To me that languish'd for her sake:
But when she saw my woeful state,
Straight in her heart did mercy come,
Chiding that tongue that ever sweet
Was used in giving gentle doom,
And taught it thus anew to greet:
'I hate' she alter'd with an end,
That follow'd it as gentle day
Doth follow night, who like a fiend
From heaven to hell is flown away;

Helen E. Burton

'I hate' from hate away she threw,
And saved my life, saying -- 'not you.' (Sonnet 145)

Anne loved the double pun William had made on her name--
hate away, instead of Hathaway; Anne saved my life. She
knew that he was right. She didn't hate him, not at all.

His intellect was amazing; it seemed he could read something once, grasp its meaning, and remember it forever. He
never forgot the things she told him either. He listened to her
and was interested in what she had to say. Anne began to forget her former self; she smiled more and laughed at Will's
quick wit. She found herself agreeing with Will more often
than criticizing him.

When they walked together through the countryside near
Stratford-upon-Avon, they spoke as equals, and they never
ran out of things to discuss. He loved mythology, and it
seemed to Anne that he had memorized Ovid's *Metamorphoses* from cover to cover. Anne told William how her father and brother helped her discover the joy of reading and
introduced her to the transportive powers of books. She loved
philosophy and psychology; human behavior intrigued her,
and she longed to learn more about the mercurial ways of
men.

When William had first returned to the Hathaway cottage,
not as a delivery boy, but as a young man asking permission
to take a walk about the garden with Anne, Bartholomew
Hathaway was skeptical. As anxious as he was to have his
sister married, he hardly thought an errand boy for John
Shakespeare's leather shop a suitable match. William admit-
ted that he at times felt like the errand boy, but he explained
that he was John's oldest son and heir to the business. In a sin
of omission, he did not further explain that he had no interest
in leather, gloves, or the business. He thought there would be

22

plenty of time later to attempt to explain his writing and ambition to be on the stage in London. If William's own father could not understand his career choice, how could Anne's puritan brother possibly grasp it?

At first, the couple seemed a strange pair as they walked along Henley Street arguing amiably about the topic of the day. These topics varied from which English Kings were the most effective leaders to women's proper role in British society. William thought he was making great headway in convincing Anne that by studying English history, she could learn all she needed to know about human suffering, ambition, and greed. Anne felt confident that William was beginning to see the great waste of resources the nation was inflicting upon itself by keeping women voiceless and primarily uneducated.

"William, instead of spending hours reading about Henry VI and Richard III and other Kings of the past, why don't you devote equal time to our current royal? Is it because she is a woman and thus a Queen rather than a self-indulgent King?"

"I do admire Queen Elizabeth," William responded. Then with a sly grin he added, "She's a spinster just like you, and she puts the fear of God into the men around her, just like you! And someday, my plays will be performed for her!"

"William, you are impossible," Anne gave him a gentle shove on the arm, but in her heart, she felt happy to have been compared to a woman she admired so much. With Queen Elizabeth on the throne, the treatment of women in England was destined to improve. Someday, young women in Warwickshire and all of England would make their own decisions about who or if they would marry, and perhaps they would eventually be afforded public education and be free to pursue careers as freely as men had always done.

Anne was feeling particularly emotional about this issue because she had spent the morning with her young neighbor Beatrice Larrington. As Beatrice predicted, after months of resisting her father's request, she finally had to consent to a loveless marriage which her father had arranged, and he disposed of her like any other piece of his property. Now she had gone from belonging to her father to belonging to her husband, a stranger to her. Mr. Cole and his new bride Beatrice left immediately after the wedding at the parish church in Stratford-upon Avon for Cambridge where she would live among his family and rarely see her parents or siblings. As the carriage rolled away, Anne waved and tried to smile encouragement while she watched the tears roll down Beatrice's face.

In contrast to unhappy Beatrice, Anne was the happiest she had ever been in the summer of 1582, and she knew it was because of William. He made her laugh; he made her cry; he made her feel alive. His touch was like a salve to her tender skin. The more time they spent together, the more desperate she was when they were apart. The age difference seemed to have disappeared or more accurately, it never appeared. William, Anne thought, was an old soul and was like no eighteen-year-old she had ever known.

One beautiful day in July, after an enjoyable morning riding Barbary and Dobbin, Sarah Spencer offered to prepare a picnic lunch for the young couple. While the basket of food was being prepared, William showed Anne the Spencer's falconry. Richard Spencer had several hawks, falcons, and even an eagle. William explained how the birds were trained to return to the glove and take only food from their trainer's hand rather than eating their own kill. Those who enjoyed the sport of hawking had their magnificent birds hunt for them. Once the trained birds had prey in their talons, they would either fly back to their master, or the master would send his hunting dogs to retrieve the prey from the place the birds dropped it.

Anne thought the birds were incredibly beautiful, but she felt sorry for them. They were forced to live a life completely alien to the life they were meant to live, and yet, they were beautiful to watch.

"Would you like to hold one?" William asked as he saw Anne admiring the birds.

"Do you think I can?" Anne gasped.

"Yes. If Master Spencer trusts you with his favorite young writer, I'm sure he will trust you with his favorite falcon, Edgar."

William put the heavy leather glove on Anne's hand and carefully placed Edgar on the glove. Anne was in awe of the weight and power of the bird. William told Anne to raise her arm as high as she could in the air and away from her body, and then he gave Edgar the signal to fly. As Edgar's weight left her hand and he spread his majestic wings, Anne uttered a gasp. She could understand more clearly the allure of falconry. Watching the bird reach for the sky was one of the most amazing experiences of her life.

"William, will he come back?" Anne asked with concern in her voice.

"Yes, Anne. Edgar is a very obedient falcon. He always returns to the glove."

"How did Master Spencer train him so well?"

"Falconry is the art of making the bird exclusively dependent upon his master. Spencer placed hoods on the wild birds, so they were blind. He told me a blind bird does not resist handling. Each day he would keep the bird on the glove, not allowing it to eat or sleep. When the bird becomes completely exhausted, it will do as the master wishes. Even after he is trained, the bird is never allowed to eat the prey he captures with his talons. He must only take the food offered him by his master. His hunger brings him to the glove to eat and fill his stomach.

"Have you ever wanted to train a falcon, William?" Anne asked.

"No. I must confess that though I love watching the birds and feeling their power, their captive state makes me melancholy, and I long for them to have the freedom to soar in the skies as nature intended." Then to lighten the serious tone of their conversation, William laughed and said, "Besides, I have a more beautiful creature to tame." He smiled at Anne and pulled her into his arms.

Anne broke from their embrace and said earnestly, "You don't seriously think that you can train me to come and go as the Spencer's falcons! Would you keep me from eating and sleeping so I would be dependent upon you for my every need?" She was appalled at his audacity, but she knew in her heart that he was only teasing. Her thoughts were confirmed when he drew her into his arms and kissed her passionately.

"Oh, Anne, you know that I am drawn to you because of your strong will and independence. Why would I want to rob you of that? Why would any rational man think that he could rob you of that?"

They left the magnificent birds of prey in the able hands of Richard Spencer's falconer, and Anne took William's hand as they walked back to the house to retrieve their picnic lunch. They found a lovely picnic spot under an elegant willow tree on the edge of the farm. William spread a colorful quilt on the ground while Anne removed bread and cheese from the basket. They enjoyed the trilling of a song bird as they sipped their wine beneath the weeping willow.

Shakespeare's True Love

The setting was beautiful, the peace so complete, that William felt his heart swell with love for his dear Anne. "You know, my dearest, I have composed many a poem for you. I have compared you to a summer's day such as this. I have praised your voice which is as melodious as the birds' sweet songs which surround us. I find the passion in your blood as rich as this wine which we sip. I love to caress your beautiful auburn hair which flows like a crimson river down your back. I see the red of prize roses in your lips, and melt in the nearness of your perfumed breath. But, dear Anne, I want you to know that all my poetic comparisons aside, I see you for who you really are. I know that you speak in a human voice, that your lips are not as red as a rose, and that after you have a garlic and onion sandwich, your breath does not smell like perfume, and I love you even more because of these things. You are my precious Anne, as human as I am, as flawed as I am, and yet I love you more each day."

Anne felt her heart begin to swell with the love she felt for her dear, dear William, and tears began to form in her eyes. William brushed the tears gently aside and kissed her tenderly. "Anne, will you marry me? I promise that I shall not be foolish enough to try to tame you. I will love you and treat you as the equal you are. I want to share my life with you. I promise that I will not tear you from your family and friends. We shall live here in Stratford-upon-Avon, the little village you love so much."

Anne could not stem the tears which were flowing from her eyes as she listened to her dear William's long proposal. When she recovered her voice, she sobbed, "Yes, yes, a million times yes, I will marry you!"

Chapter Four

True love overcomes all obstacles and knows no impediments; however, William and Anne were faced with one, seemingly unmovable force: John Shakespeare. Anne's brother, Bartholomew, was glad to learn of William's intent to marry his outspoken sister. He had grown to love and respect William, and he thought Anne had finally found someone she could not so easily outwit. Of course, it also pleased Bartholomew that with Anne married and one less person at Hewlands Farm, he could pursue his own desire to marry. Anne's stepmother, Joan, was sad to lose Anne's help with her large family, but she didn't begrudge Anne finally starting her own family.

John Shakespeare, on the other hand, saw William's desire to marry Anne Hathaway as just one more bad decision by his irresponsible son. William had no profession beyond the rudiments of the glove business which was on the decline. What was worse, in John's opinion, was that William had no interest in obtaining a sensible position. He spoke only of his foolish dreams of being a writer--a writer of poems for pity sake. How could he possibly support himself, much less a wife?

Then there was the matter of Anne Hathaway herself. Though she came from a respectable family and had a small dowry, she was eight years older than his son--the age of being left on the shelf, not married to a respectable businessman's son! She had already helped raise her five younger half brothers and sisters. Would she even want to bear her own children? Could she even bear children at her age? Not only was she old, she had a reputation in Stratford of being outspoken. What was William thinking?

"Absolutely not! I will not consent to this marriage," John Shakespeare bellowed at his son. "You are only eighteen, and you need my permission to obtain a marriage license. Instead of spending your time walking in the country with this woman, why don't you find work that would contribute to the family budget. Haven't you noticed the difficulty I am having in making ends meet? Now go away and don't bother me about this outrageous idea again."

William was disappointed at his father's attitude, but he was not surprised by it. He knew there must be some way for him to make dear Anne his wife. As he left the house on Henley, his feet seemed to automatically take him out of Stratford toward the Spencer's farm. If anyone could help him find a solution to his heartache, they could.

Sarah Spencer greeted William warmly and had him take a comfortable chair near the hearth while she went to get him a cool glass of cider. Presently, Richard Spencer joined William and when Sarah returned with the cider, William told his godparents about his desire to marry Anne Hathaway and his father's strong objections to the match. Sarah clicked her tongue softly and twiddled her thumbs as she listened to Will's sad situation. "William, dear boy, you are not the first young person to face challenges in love. Richard had to move mountains to obtain my father's permission for our union. Within a year of our marriage, my parents were both bragging to all who would listen what a good match they had arranged for me!"

"Yes! Yes!" declared Richard. "When your father gets to know Anne, he will love her and tell everyone the marriage was his idea. We just need to find a way to convince him now, so you can get on with your plans."

"You said one of your father's objections," Richard continued, "is that you don't have a position which brings any money into the household. What could you do to show your father that you are able to support both yourself and Anne?"

" To be honest, I didn't realize that our household situation was becoming a burden to my father. We've always done well, and when he was the High Bailiff of Stratford, he had so many contacts that we couldn't keep up with the orders. Since he left the Village Council, the business has been less prosperous. I'm just not sure what I can do to help."

"William," interjected Sarah, "I know several families who would love to have someone of your great intellect and knowledge tutor their sons. You are a gifted writer, but you can also help the children with their Latin and elocution. So many of the boys cannot speak a word of Latin without fear of reprobation from their school master. You could help them love to speak out loud and perhaps, even perform simple productions."

"I'm not trained as a teacher. Do you think fathers would really pay me to work with their sons?" Will asked in a hopeful tone.

"Absolutely, William! I think my Sarah has hit on just the right solution. We will spread the word in the neighborhood and at Church that you are available, and you will soon have a dozen eager young souls waiting to be tutored by you!" Richard declared.

"Now Richard dear, finding money to support Anne is only one obstacle William has to overcome. How can we convince John Shakespeare that Anne will be a wonderful wife to William and a suitable mother to his future grandchildren?" Sarah asked.

"Yes. You are right as usual dear wife. William, you say your father even doubts whether Anne can bear children at her age."

"Yes he ...."

But before he could finish his sentence, Sarah interrupted, "That is the most ridiculous thing I have ever heard. How old does he think his own wife was when she had your baby brother Edmund. Why, I was thirty when I had our dear Timothy, and it was perfectly natural. If your father is worried about not having grandchildren, we should just show him how easily that can be accomplished!"

"My dear, Sarah!" exclaimed Richard. "Whatever do you mean by that?"

Sarah just ignored her husband and turned to William, "Do you think Anne would trust us if we came up with a plan which would mean she would consummate her marriage, not on the night of her wedding in the Church, but on the evening of her betrothal?"

"I, ah, I don't know. Just what do you mean?" William asked incredulously.

"The contract of marriage or betrothal doesn't require the signature of your father, just the marriage license requires his permission. To be legally bound and betrothed to Anne, you just need two witnesses. If Anne has faith in you and us, we can legally bind you to marriage in a hand fast ceremony, you and Anne can live as husband and wife, and let nature take its course. Once Anne is pregnant, you can tell your father what has happened, and he will have no choice but to sign the marriage license. He would never risk having his grandchild born without the sanction of the Church."

William and Richard just stared at Sarah. What a devious and wonderful plan she had devised. William knew that Anne loved him and trusted him. Would she agree to this plot?

"Sarah, what if Anne doesn't become pregnant?" Will asked.

"Don't you worry about that William. We women have our ways of knowing when the time is right to conceive a baby, and I will help Anne with everything she needs to know."

"I can't thank you both enough. I came here *beweeping my outcast state*, and I leave *like the lark at break of day singing hymns at heaven's gate*,"(Sonnet 29) William declared.

"How can your father not appreciate the poetry that falls from your lips so easily?" laughed Richard.

Chapter Five

True to his word, Richard Spencer walked with William to several neighbors who might be interested in hiring a tutor for their young boys. William's refined manner and ready wit impressed the fathers of the house. The young boys were charmed by his sense of humor and warmth. After only three days of introductions, William had secured five young lads to instruct in Latin.

William, with the help of his godfather Richard Spencer, settled on a plan to both satisfy his father on Henley Street and expedite the hand fast ceremony. "Father, I have found a way to contribute to the family income," William spoke to John and Mary Shakespeare as they sat by the fire that evening. William knew it was better to explain his idea with his mother present because though John made the final decisions, William knew that his mother held great influence over his father. After all, it was the Arden money, his mother's dowry and inheritance, that had allowed John Shakespeare to climb socially in Stratford.

"What half-cocked idea do you have now?" John demanded.

"Richard Spencer has helped me find five families in the Wilmcote neighborhood who will pay me to tutor their sons. Richard believes, and I agree, that as those five boys begin to achieve success at the grammar school, more families will be interested in hiring me."

"So you are completely turning your back on my business, now while I am struggling," John accused his son.

"No father. The tutoring will be a second job for me. I will still work here every morning and as late in the after-noon as I can," explained William.

It's quite a walk to Wilmcote and the Spencers. You won't get back home here until late, and you'll be worth nothing to me in the morning, " John complained.

"I've thought about that, and Richard and Sarah have made me a very generous offer. Since their children have all grown and are established in their own homes, the Spencers have reduced the number of servants they keep at the farm. A small thatched cottage that once housed their kitchen helpers now stands empty. They've offered to let me stay there at no charge. I can tutor my students in the late after-noon and early evening, get a good night's sleep, awaken ready for a brisk ride on Babary to Henley Street, and be here to help with the business as early as you need me," William explained.

"You'll no longer be living here on Henley Street?" his father asked.

William hesitated slightly and then forged on with his plan, "That's true, but it means you can lodge one of our workers here. I overheard our cutter, Simon, saying that he is being asked to move from the Pulliam home because an in-law is moving into his space. By allowing him to sleep here, you can deduct his food and lodging from his pay and lower our costs, thus improving our cash flow."

"You are willing to leave your mother and brothers and sister and allow Simon to take your place?" John asked.

William laughed, "I will never let Simon take my rightful place in this family. I will be here every day working beside all of you and loving you the same as always. Simon gets my bed only, not my family."

Shakespeare's True Love

Mary Shakespeare smiled quietly to herself as she listened to her husband and son's discussion. She admired her son's pluck in speaking to his father, and she thought his ideas made very good sense. She had felt the tension growing between her husband and her eldest son. Their recent financial problems had exacerbated the problem, and she was worried it would cause a permanent rift between father and son. Though she hated to have her son move out of her home, she agreed with William that it was a good solution.

John Shakespeare didn't know how to respond to his son. William was the apple of his mother's eye, and though Mary had nothing to say about the way the business was run, John didn't want to have to deal with her anger in addition to his financial stress. When he looked at his wife, he saw a slight smile on her face. Could she be okay with William's plan? He refused to ask her opinion, and she knew better than to speak without being asked. After a few minutes of silence, John declared, "If I need you to work on orders for my customers, you will be here and not out tutoring, understand?"

"Yes, of course, I know my first duty is to you and mother," William answered.

William felt a great sense of relief that he had successfully overcome the first obstacle in his quest to marry Anne. He had obtained his father's permission to leave Henley Street and live at the Spencer's. However, he knew he must be very careful as he explained to Anne, his father's objections to their marriage, and Sarah and Richard Spencer's idea of the hand fast ceremony. Would she think he was trying to take advantage of her? He must make sure that she understood his honorable intentions.

Chapter Six

After much thought, William decided the best way to approach Anne with his unusual proposal was to talk it over in the presence of her brother, Bartholomew. With Bartholomew privy to the plan from the very beginning, Anne would have less fear of her reputation being destroyed. If either Bartholomew or Anne objected, William would have to work out another way to make Anne his wife.

William attempted to gather his thoughts by walking in the beautiful garden at Hewlands Farm. He remembered that day in April when he first met Anne, and she told him he was an errand boy and nothing more! Oh, how he loved her. She would always speak truth to him and never fear offending him. What more could an author want in life than an honest critic who loved him? When he was with Anne, the ideas for his poems flowed with ease. She was his muse, and she must be his wife.

His nerves calmed and his resolve strengthened, William knocked on the Hathaway's cottage door. Thirteen-year-old Thomas Hathaway opened the door, and with a large grin on his face, invited William inside. Thomas wanted to ask if Will had any new verses to share with him, but he could see by the expression on Will's face that his favorite storyteller had serious things on his mind, so he said, "I'll just run and fetch Anne." William had been a frequent and welcome visitor to the cottage for the past four months, and he was well-liked by the Hathaway family, especially the young children.

"Thank you, Thomas. Could you ask Bartholomew to join us as well?"

"Yes, Will," Thomas nodded and hurried from the room.

William sat on the stiff, wooden settee by the large stone fireplace and thought of the evenings Anne and he had passed telling stories and sharing their lives with each other on that very settee. Tonight William had the most important and extraordinary story to tell Bartholomew and Anne, and he hoped with all of his heart it would be well received.

Anne rushed into the room, and William stood to embrace her. "Oh, William, how good of you to come this evening. I was afraid I would have to wait until tomorrow night to see you. Darling, you look pale. Is everything all right?"

At that moment, Bartholomew entered the room and said, "You wanted to speak with me, William?"

Anne's concern increased as William gently bade her sit by him on the settee, and her brother pulled a stool near them. "William, please. What is it? What is wrong?"

"Nothing is wrong dear Anne. Things could be oh so right, but you must trust me."

He began by telling them that when he had spoken to his father about his desire to marry Anne, John Shakespeare had objected. Anne began to cry softly, but William put his arm around her and told her that all would yet be well. He told them that he too had been very upset at his father, but he had gone to his godparents, the Spencers, and they had given him wise advice. It was easy to explain the Spencer's idea of him being a tutor and earning the money to support Anne. Bartholomew applauded the plan as an excellent one, and Anne began to dry her eyes.

William continued hesitantly, "Unfortunately, my lack of financial means to marry is not my father's only concern. He is worried about our future children, his grandchildren." He felt Anne stiffen next to him.

"What? Does he think I would be a bad mother?" Anne shrieked.

"Stay calm sister; let William explain," Bartholomew encouraged.

"Anne, it's not that. He has never met a woman like you before. You must admit, Anne, you are not like most of the young women in and around Stratford. Your father taught you to read and write, and speak your mind. The things I love about you make my father think you may not be interested in being a mother and a helpmate. I think, also, he is worried about our age difference, and you know how many babies are lost in childbirth or in early infancy."

"So I shan't even be given the chance to prove to him that I am as capable of having healthy children as any eighteen-year-old girl! I probably have a better chance of successfully raising children than a mousy, milk toast woman because I have a brain in my head. I won't traipse my babies around out in the cold with only a nappie on them." Contrary to Bartholomew's advice, Anne was not remaining calm.

William held her close and shushed her tenderly. "Listen to the rest of the Spencer's plan, and you will see that you shall definitely be given the chance to show what a good mother we both know you will be."

Now it was Bartholomew's turn to be agitated, "What are you suggesting, Will Shakespeare?"

William explained the rest of the Spencer's plan as carefully as he could. He was interrupted many times by questions, first from Anne and then from Bartholomew. After what seemed liked hours of explanation, even William, the man of words, was unable to think of anything else to say.

"It is up to you, my dear Anne. If you agree to the plan, and your brother concurs, we will be betrothed with Richard Spencer and Bartholomew as our legal witnesses. Then we will pray for a quick pregnancy, so we can tell father that he is to be a grandfather. Once he understands that we are be-trothed, he must agree to the reading of the Banns, and we will be married in the Church at Luddington." William looked into Anne's eyes and asked, "Do you trust me?" Before she could answer, he continued, "*Doubt thou the stars are fire; doubt that the sun doth move; doubt truth to be a liar, but never doubt I love*" (Hamlet, 2.2).

"William, you know I trust you, and I love you. I want to be your wife. Though I am frightened, I agree that Sarah Spencer's plan is our best chance for a happy ending. Bartholomew, will you support us in this decision?" Anne asked her brother.

Bartholomew hesitated and then said, "It took a great deal of courage for you to come here this evening, William, and present this preposterous scheme. I realize that you and Anne could have decided on your own to carry out this plan with the help of Master Spencer, leaving me completely uninformed. It is for that reason, your straight forward honesty, that I support you in your quest to make Anne your lawful wife."

Anne jumped from the settee and threw her arms around her brother. "Thank you, brother. You won't be sorry. We will be the happiest couple in Stratford."

Bartholomew extended his hand to William and said, "Take good care of my sister, or I will be sitting on the front row with a bushel of rotten tomatoes at any production of which you are a part!" They laughed together and embraced.

Anne walked out to the garden with William to say good night. "Oh, Anne, *the very instant that I saw you, did my heart fly to your service* (Tempest, 3.1). You have made me the happiest man in all of Warwickshire. No! I am the happiest man in all of England tonight." He held her close, and they embraced under the stars, by the lovely purple violets, the flowers of faithfulness.

Chapter Seven

Anne awoke on the morning of the hand fast ceremony with nervous energy and excitement coursing through her body. Her younger sisters were nearly as excited as she was, and they each were enthusiastic about helping Anne prepare to meet William at the Spencer home. Ten-year old Margaret mused that she couldn't wait for her own wedding day, and she began to describe what her true love would be like. Her description sounded very much like William, and Anne had to smile and hug her little sister close.

"Do you think I have made a good choice, Margaret?" Anne asked her.

"Oh, yes, Anne. William is perfectly lovely. He tells me the sweetest stories, and he acts all the parts when we are playing in the garden. He lets me ride on his back when we need a pony for the princess to ride, and then he becomes the prince and escorts me to my throne. You will never be bored with William as your husband, and he knows how to treat a princess!"

"Margaret, you must let me plait Anne's hair, so she can be beautiful for William," sixteen-year-old Jo insisted. "Do you think you could find some delicate lily of the valley in the garden, so we can weave it into Anne's hair?"

"I know where to find the freshest ones!" Margaret declared, happy to be able to help her dear sisters. She hurried from the tiny room, down the stairs, and out into the garden.

"What about you, Jo? Do you think William is a good match?" Anne asked.

"I think he is a perfect match for you, Anne," Jo answered carefully.

"I see," Anne tried not to sound hurt, "but you would not choose him for yourself."

"Oh, Anne. Don't take what I am saying wrong. You love poetry and literature and the theatre. You have as vivid an imagination as William. You are able to tell the difference between make believe and real life. I don't think I can. When I watch the players that come to Stratford, I fall in love with their bold speeches, and their confident manner on stage stirs excitement inside me. I don't even know them, but I want to be with them. Does that make sense to you?"

"Yes, Jo. That is part of the magic of theatre. You can forget who you are and be swept away to another place and time. It's one of the things I love about the players."

"I know it is okay to be swept away for an evening and pretend life is different, but William speaks sweet words and acts out scenes so smoothly every day. How do you know he isn't just acting a part with you?"

"You are wise beyond your years sweet Jo. I did worry about that at first, but we know each other so well now, I can tell the difference between when he is just telling me what he knows I want to hear and when he is being completely honest with me. Our love is strong enough to keep us together forever."

"I'm glad you have thought about that Anne. I just want you to be happy. If my husband were on the stage with all the young women in the audience hoping for a glance from him, I would be so jealous I couldn't stand it!"

"Well, luckily, I'm not the jealous type, and if he makes young women swoon while he is on the stage, it is okay because I know when the play is over, he will be coming home with me! Is there anything else you find lacking in Will?"

"Oh, no, Anne, Will is wonderful and luckily, you care little for material things. He is perfect for you, but he would not be a good match for me because, though I hate to admit it, I want expensive things, not stories. I want the latest dresses and bonnets. I want to live in a grand house and have lovely pewter and china. Where will William get the money to buy those things? When will you have a house of your own? Don't you ever worry about those things?"

Anne laughed and held Jo close to her. "I'm so glad you know what you want in life, Jo. You deserve all the things you just described to me. Perhaps William and I can move into your manor house if he can't make a living from his writing! But you see, Jo, I believe in William. When he tells me that someday his plays will be performed for the Queen, I believe him! I think I can have both my wonderfully romantic William and a set of fine pewter!"

Jo was impressed by her sister's faith in William, but she continued in her own resolve to make a match with a wealthy young man. She worked three days a week at the haberdashery in Stratford, and she had met someone special. He was a mercer from Scotland who dealt in fine silk, velvet, and other luxurious fabrics. At the young age of sixteen, Jo was falling in love with the dashing and rich Angus Macloed from Edinburgh. She wasn't ready to risk her dream of beautiful frocks on the mere *belief* that her husband would be successful.

Margaret returned with fragrant lily of the valley, and both sisters delicately wove the flowers into Anne's long, wavy hair. They plaited a braid to form a band across the crown of her head and then tied curled tendrils of her hair with ribbons to frame her face. They stood back to admire their accomplishment. Anne studied herself in the hand mirror and was pleased. She stood to retrieve her best cotton dress which she had carefully draped at the foot of the bed. It wasn't new, but it was her favorite, and she knew William liked it. "Will you girls help me slip my dress over my head, so I don't muss my beautiful hair?" Anne asked. When neither girl answered, she turned back to where they had been fixing her hair a moment before, but they were both gone. They had slipped out of the room without her hearing them leave. "Now, what are they up to?" Anne wondered aloud.

She took a moment to check herself again in the hand mirror, and then she heard soft footsteps behind her. She turned to see her stepmother, Joan, entering her little alcove with a bundle, loosely wrapped in brown paper and tied with string.

"The girls have done a beautiful job with your hair, Anne," Joan smiled as she admired her oldest and most challenging daughter.

"Thank you, mother. They have made me feel so loved this morning," Anne said softly.

"I would like to contribute something for your special day as well. Here, open it," she said quickly as she handed Anne the wrapped bundle.

Anne placed the package on her bed and carefully removed the string. When she folded back the brown paper, she gasped and turned to look at her stepmother with amazement and joy in her eyes.

Joan simply said, "Go ahead, take it out of the package so you can see if you like it."

Anne could not believe what she was seeing. Folded in the brown paper was a gown of emerald green silk. She gently lifted the dress by the shoulders and held it out so she could admire its beauty. The material was smooth, rich, and delicate. She caressed her cheek with one of the sleeves, and it felt like a rose petal on her skin. Anne never imagined material could be so luxurious. The pattern was simple but elegant, just what Anne would have chosen for herself. It had a square neckline, long sleeves that puffed at the shoulders but narrowed at the wrist, and an empire waist with a full skirt falling in perfect gathers. A delicate white lace edged the neckline and the sleeves at the wrists. Anne thought it was the most beautiful dress she had ever seen. She couldn't stop the tears from flowing as she hugged her stepmother and thanked her repeatedly.

"Now, Anne dear, don't carry on so. You can't have puffy eyes on your big day. Sit here by me for a while so we can talk before your sisters come back. I asked them to give us at least ten minutes, but you know how excited they are today!"

Anne dabbed at her eyes with her handkerchief and sat next to her stepmother. "Where did you find this gorgeous dress?"

"I made it for you, Anne."

"You made it!" Anne knew her stepmother was an excellent seamstress, but Anne had only seen her mending her brothers' work shirts or altering Jo's outgrown dresses for Margaret. "How did you find time?"

"The same way you always found time to help me with the children and the household work. When you love some-one, you find the time."

Tears flowed down Anne's cheeks again, and she choked, "I have been so difficult. I'm sorry."

"No, Anne, I'm the one who is sorry. I knew how much your father loved you when he married me, and I moved in with you and your brother. I was a little jealous of you. I know it sounds daft, but there it is. So I was hard on you, and I didn't do much to make things easy between us. I'm sorry for being so distant. Now that I am about to lose you, it is breaking my heart. The dress is an attempt to make amends."

"Mother, you don't need to make amends," Anne sniffed.

"Oh, but I do. I feel especially guilty about constantly bringing Beatrice Larrington up as an example of how a young woman should behave. Her mother tells me that Beatrice is so unhappy in Cambridge with Mr. Cole that she has threatened to run away or worse, throw herself under a moving carriage. Her mother is worried sick about her. I'm so glad you had the sense to ignore me and make your own match. You and William will be as poor as church mice but as happy as lambs in a fresh spring meadow!"

Anne had to smile at her stepmother's frankness. She was never afraid to speak her mind. As Anne and her stepmother embraced, the younger girls shouted from the stairwell, "Can we come up now?"

Nothing could have kept the girls from bursting in on Joan and Anne. They couldn't wait to see Anne in her dress.

"Do you like it? Do you?" Margaret asked as she danced around Anne.

"I love it!"

"Put it on, Anne," her sister, Jo, implored.

With the help of her stepmother and enthusiastic instructions from her sisters, Anne managed to slip the beautiful gown over her head without destroying her lovely hair. The dress's square neckline and empire waist meant no laces were needed in the back to cinch Anne tightly, and the dress could simply be slipped over her head. The dress was light and free flowing, just what Anne wanted. She hated the restriction of whale bone corsets and heavy draped fabric.

Anne twirled with delight and the beautiful green fabric sailed out around her and then came to rest again perfectly caressing her body. "Mother, how on earth did you create this magnificent gown?"

"Your sister, Jo, was a tremendous help. She has learned much about fabrics at the haberdasher's shop, and you have no idea how much she knows about dresses." Anne and Jo shared a conspiratorial smile as Joan continued, "Fitting it was easy. I just used your favorite cotton dress as a pattern of sorts. I had a much different fabric and design in mind, but Jo would have none of it. She said you needed a continental look and sketched the design for me. I must admit, seeing it on you, it is more lovely than I ever imagined it could be."

Anne had never felt so beautiful! The most important day of her life had started out better than she could ever have imagined. She just hoped William would be as pleased and excited as she was.

As Anne was preparing for the hand fast ceremony at Hewlands Farm in Shottery, the Spencer home in Wilmcote was being decorated with fragrant, fresh cut lilacs, lilies, violets, and irises. The aroma of freshly baked cakes and puddings warmed the home and created the perfect scene for the happy event. William awoke early to put the finishing touches on the sonnet he was preparing to recite for Anne as part of his vows at the ceremony. He had written much since he had moved into the quiet little cottage behind the Spencer's manor house. He hadn't realized how busy and noisy the house on Henley Street in Stratford had been, until he experienced the contrast in Wilmcote. Here he could hear no crying babies, loud customers, or banging workmen tanning leather. The comfortable little two room cottage had a large stone fireplace in the main room which provided both a place for cooking and for heat. The lath and plaster walls were freshly white washed and helped brighten the room despite the few small windows. The rough hewn stone floor was covered by several small rag rugs provided by Sarah. The cottage's simplicity made it the perfect spot for William to concentrate on just the right words and phrasing for his poetry. William only hoped that Anne would like it as much as he did, for this is where he would bring her to start their life together.

Bartholomew Hathaway had surprised William the week before by arriving at Wilmcote in a horse drawn cart with a heavy load in the back. William asked, "What have you brought me, Bartholomew?"

"It is not a part of Anne's dowry in my father's will, but her stepmother and I both want you and Anne to have this bed to start your life together. Joan says it makes her sad to be in the wedding bed she shared with father, now that he is gone. She claims she will be fine in the bed Anne will leave behind at Shottery. We thought you could use it in your little cottage."

"Thank you, Bartholomew. Sarah and Richard have been helping me get the cottage ready for Anne's arrival, but we had not figured out a solution to replace the narrow cots the servants used. Our best plan was to push them together and hope neither Anne nor I fell through the gap between them caused by the frames! This bed is perfect. Now I am ready to set up my first household."

William read over his newest sonnet carefully, made the last few changes, and then walked out into the early morning sunshine to the Spencer's rose garden. Sarah told him the day before he was welcome to cut as many of the blossoms as he wanted. He walked from rose bush to rose bush admiring the pink, red, yellow, pale peach, and white blossoms. He planned carefully in his mind before he took his knife and cut blossom after blossom, removing the long thorns from the stems after he cut each rose. He held the roses tightly in his fist until the bouquet he had created was just the right size and the right combination of colors. Then he went back to his little cottage and carefully wrapped the stems together with a wide, pure-white satin ribbon. When he was finished, he held the beautiful bouquet to his nose, closed his eyes, and breathed in the glorious scent of the flowers while he pic-

tured his beautiful Anne holding the bouquet at their wedding. "Today, my true love becomes my wife." William
could not wait to see sweet Anne.

William prepared himself to meet his bride by carefully
trimming his mustache, scrubbing away the ink stains from
his fingers, and donning a white blouse-sleeved shirt and
leather doublet. He wore new white hose and his black
leather boots came to his knees. He walked the short distance
to the Spencer home and knocked. When Sarah opened the
door, he couldn't believe how busy she had been. "Oh, Sarah,
the flowers are beautiful and what are those enticing aromas
coming from the hall?"

"You look wonderful, Will. How are you feeling? Come
with me and try the cake. I need an appreciative opinion!"

"I'll be happy to help you out. You know I've never met a
cake I didn't like!"

As William ate his cake, Sarah went through a checklist
of things that must be completed before Anne and her family
arrived. "Richard has gone to fetch fresh cream from the
neighbors. Do you have the cottage ready for Anne?"

"Yes."

"Do you have your vows ready?"

"Yes."

"Do you have a gift for Anne?"

"Yes."

"You must thank Bartholomew again for Anne's hand and
the bed."

"Yes."

"Are you upset that your family won't be here today?"

"No."

"You know they will all be with you at the Church in a
couple of months."

"Yes."

"You still feel good about this plan?"

"Yes."

"You love Anne."

"Yes."

William Shakespeare, don't try to tell me that everything is okay! I've never in my life heard you say so little."

William laughed, "It's the cake, Sarah. I've never tasted such good cake. And it's you. I've never seen you so nervous before."

"Of course, I'm nervous. I came up with this crazy plan, and now I'm worried I've interfered in your life and caused irreparable damage. Oh, William, do tell me you are happy!"

"Sarah, I could not be more happy if I were just about to be crowned King of England. Here's a better comparison. I couldn't be happier if I was promised a plate of your cake every day for the rest of my life."

Sarah clapped her hands and declared, "Now I know you are serious, boy. Thank goodness!" Just then they heard a commotion in the other room, and they knew that the Hathaways had arrived. William nearly dropped the plate of cake as he jumped to his feet. "Calmly, William. You must be calm for your dear Anne."

William was not to be delayed from seeing his love. He entered the great hall just as Anne came through the front door. He gasped and all eyes turned to him. He had never seen Anne look so beautiful. He moved toward her as if in a dream, his eyes never wavering from her face. He stopped a foot from her and took both of her hands in his. He studied her from the top of her head to the tip of her toe. He had never seen anyone so beautiful in his life. Her hair was plaited with flowers and fell softly on her shoulders, her eyes were like emeralds shining on him, her smile warmed him entirely, and her gown was stunning.

Anne finally broke the silence by saying, "Good morning, William. Shall we get married today?"

William found his voice and said, "Oh, yes, dear Anne. I would love to marry you today!"

Sarah and Richard welcomed the Hathaway family to their home, and Sarah asked Anne's stepmother Joan to sit next to her. William, still reeling from the beauty of the woman he was about to marry, didn't move when Hamnet and Judith Sadler arrived with fresh bread from their bakery and huge smiles on their faces to see their good friend William so bedazzled by his bride to be.

"My goodness, Judith," Hamnet laughed. "William has accomplished the impossible by finding his own perfect wife. How can that be?"

Judith quickly moved into the room and embraced Anne. "For once my husband is correct, Anne. You are per-fect and a beautiful bride."

"Thank you, Judith and thank you both for coming. It is wonderful to have someone here to support William--and it looks like he needs all the support he can get!"

Poor William was standing like a statue staring at Anne from across the room. As if awakening from a dream, William shouted, "Thanks for coming Judith and Hamnet. I have to go now!" He ran out the front door.

Bartholomew laughed and said, "Our reserved, well-spoken William seems a bit nervous today."

Sarah Spencer said, "I certainly hope he is coming back! If not, I've really mucked things up!"

The guests laughed and visited until William returned. He walked with his hands behind his back straight to Anne, "I made you something special for this day." Anne knew that traditionally young men gave their brides gloves for the wed-ding day, but she knew how much Will hated the glovery business, and she couldn't imagine Will would think it an appropriate gift today, especially with the absence of the entire Shakespeare family.

"What have you done, Will?" she asked suspiciously. "Please don't make me guess?"

Will smiled a beaming smile and pulled the bouquet from behind his back and presented it to Anne. She admired each blossom and raised it to her face to inhale its lovely fragrance. "It is beautiful, Will. It is the perfect gift for me."

"Shall we begin?" Richard Spencer asked.

"Yes," William and Anne responded in unison.

Hamnet quickly produced his lute and played a lilting melody to set the tone for the ceremony.

William and Anne faced each other holding hands. William cleared his throat to gain his composure and said, "I have another gift for you, Anne. I wrote a sonnet for you on this special day. It can't convey all that I feel in my heart for you, but it is a beginning."

When, in disgrace with fortune and men's eyes,
I all alone beweep my outcast state,
And trouble deaf heaven with my bootless cries,
And look upon myself, and curse my fate,

Wishing me like to one more rich in hope,
Featur'd like him, like him with friends possess'd,
Desiring this man's art and that man's scope,
With what I most enjoy contented least;

Yet in these thoughts myself almost despising,
Haply I think on thee, and then my state,
Like to the lark at break of day arising
From sullen earth, sings hymns at heaven's gate;

Helen E. Burton

For thy sweet love remember'd such wealth brings
That then I scorn to change my state with kings.
(Sonnet 29)

Anne fought back tears as she confessed her true love for William. "I will never be the poet that you are William but I have tried a sonnet of my own."

> That I could show the level of my love
> But when I try, words vanish in cruel air.
> Your words seem to fall from heaven above
> Sweet patience and belief in me you bear

> Fearful sweet love will turn itself to hate,
> Drives my tormented soul into the sea
> Repenting misunderstanding too late,
> Finding I do not want to be set free.

> For when I think on thee, I gently smile.
> Before we met, my lonely heart was poor.
> Though opening my soul was for me a trial
> You gently walked through the unlocked door.

> And now I feel the height and breadth of cheer
> As I breathe sweet, rich kisses in thy ear.

William, you are my heart, my soul, my very life, and I will cherish you forever."

The Spencer home was filled with love and emotion and even Richard Spencer had to gather himself a little before he said, "William hold Anne's right hand in yours and repeat after me. I, William, take thee Anne to be my wife."

William held Anne's hand gently and looked into her eyes as he said, "I, William, take thee Anne to be my wife."

"Now, Anne," Richard Spencer said, "You repeat after me. I, Anne, take you William to be my husband."

Anne smiled at William and said, "I, Anne, take you William to be my husband."

Richard Spencer said, "We should seal this with a kiss," but William and Anne were already embracing and the guests were applauding with happiness.

Judith and Hamnet surprised the couple with a beautiful love song, and then Hamnet asked the wedding guests to join him in serenading the happy couple. The Spencer home was full of beautiful music, fragrant flowers, and delicious food!

Though the simple ceremony took only a few minutes, August 17, 1582, would live in Anne and William's memory all of their days together. Later, William and Anne would go to the chapel in Luddington to solemnize their marriage with the sanction of the Church, but for the young lovers, their betrothal at the Spencer home that day was the true beginning of their lives together. With Richard Spencer and Bartholomew Hathaway as their witnesses, and Anne's entire family there to join in the celebration, it was a memorable day. They enjoyed delicious cake and wine and conversation.

When the Hathaways and Sadlers left, Anne and William thanked Richard and Sarah for the wonderful celebration and then William lead his bride to the little cottage he had pre-pared for them. Anne was as pleased as William hoped she would be. It certainly wasn't large or fancy, but it was all theirs with no parents or brothers or sisters with which to share. They could be alone.

As a couple, they felt so comfortable with each other that being together in the little cottage seemed the most natural thing possible. At times during their courtship, they nearly had to walk away from each other to rein in their passion, but now they were betrothed, and they could express the full love and passion they had felt for so long. They fell into each other's arms, Anne's breast heaving as William stooped to kiss her. The kisses seemed to ignite a fire burning deep within each of them, and William carefully lifted Anne's gown and pulled it over her head. The joy they had felt at the hand fast ceremony still welled in their hearts as their bodies came together as husband and wife.

Chapter Eight

Marriage completed William and Anne. They reveled in every aspect of their lives together. They awakened in each other's arms, teased each other as they prepared for the day, and longed for each other when William was working on Henley Street and Anne was alone in their little cottage in Wilmcote. Though they both loved their families dearly, the freedom they felt living on their own was exhilarating. They felt for the first time that they were in control of their own destinies. They were no longer children living under their parents' roofs; they knew what it was like to put all their energy into building their new lives together.

William, despite the hours he spent working on Henley Street and tutoring, wrote more than he had ever written before. He was inspired with creative ideas wherever he turned. He worked tirelessly on a historical play about King Henry VI and wrote long romantic poems. Richard Spencer had been correct when he said that other parents would want their sons to be tutored by William, and he now had fifteen students. He insisted on paying the Spencers a small rent on their little cottage with the extra money he was earning. He felt proud that he was able to take care of Anne.

One evening as he entered the little cottage in Wilmcote and put his arms around Anne, he delighted her by looking into her eyes and saying, *"My bounty is as boundless as the sea, / My love as deep; the more I give to thee, / The more I have, for both are infinite"* (Romeo and Juliet, 2.2).

Anne echoed the sentiment in William's words. It seemed impossible, but it was true that the more love they gave to each other, the more love they felt. Anne had experienced this paradox with each of her siblings as they came into her life. She loved them the first time she held them in her arms, but somehow that love grew even stronger as she watched them grow into children and then young adults. Anne was beginning to understand the love she had seen in her father's eyes as he held her mother for the last time. Love is infinite. She also realized she saw infinite love for her in William's eyes. She couldn't believe her good fortune.

Anne found much to keep her occupied during the first few weeks of her new life with William. Though she had worked hard in Shottery and helped her stepmother with all the tasks she was given, Anne soon discovered that being in charge of the household and being a helper were very different. Sarah Spencer became her mentor, and Anne spent hours learning the basics of how to keep the fire in the hearth always burning and how to bring in household water in large wooden buckets from the well, to the finer things like making the cake that William loved and making tallow candles. Anne gained a newfound respect for the work women performed day after day to maintain a comfortable household.

One day over a glass of cider, Sarah told Anne, "Being married to William Shakespeare, you will have to befriend bees. You will need their honey for the cakes he loves and their wax for candles which burn brighter and longer, so William can write his poetry late into the night."

Fortunately, the woods around Wilmcote were a favorite place for bees to build their hives, and Anne agreed with Sarah and wanted to learn all she could about these industrious creatures, and the bounteous honey they produced. She spent hours wandering through the woods near her cottage to find bee hives. She enjoyed the fresh air and peace of the forest and felt a kinship with the creatures who lived there. Often she would pause and listen for the hum of the bees and their buzzing and fluttering would lead her to their hives. Some hives were built in fallen logs, others in the crook of a tree trunk. Once she located a healthy hive, she would establish her bearings and look for distinguishing landmarks so she could take a direct route from the farm back to the hive. Then she would alert Richard and Sarah to her find, and the three of them would go on their quest for honey and beeswax. Anne was their guide, Richard carried a smoking green grass torch, and Sarah followed behind with a large crock to catch the honey.

Anne quickly learned the value of beeswax candles. William was using the tallow candles almost faster than she could make them, and the smell of the burning tallow was beginning to make her feel ill. One evening in early October as William scratched away at the table on his latest sonnet, Anne found her herself having to concentrate to settle her stomach. When William looked up from his page to read a verse to Anne, he was shocked to see how pale she looked. "Are you all right, Anne?" he asked with concern.

"Yes, Will dear," she answered bravely, "I'm just a little tired today." They went to bed early that night, and William held her close until she fell asleep.

William woke early the next morning, dressed quietly, and slipped out of the cottage hoping that Anne would be able to sleep longer and feel better. Unfortunately, Anne awoke soon after he left and felt queasy and faint. She ate small crusts of bread and slowly felt strong enough to get dressed. She had so many things to accomplish. The straw mats needed to be aired and the floors swept. She and Sarah had planned to bake bread together, but Anne was already tired without having done any work, and she felt sick to her stomach all day long. She managed to eat small crusts of bread but very little else. William was extremely alarmed when he returned home and found Anne as pale as she had been the evening before. He was concerned that Anne had contracted a serious illness, and he went quickly to Sarah Spencer with his fears. She only smiled and said, "It sounds like it is time for us to have the reading of the banns and get you two to the Church."

William was confused at first and then he understood. "Do you think it is possible? Could Anne really be pregnant?" he couldn't stop grinning, and he couldn't stop asking questions. "When will the baby come? Is it normal for Anne to be so sick? Is everything all right?"

Sarah just patted the exuberant William on the shoulder and said, "I was the same way with my first child. I couldn't eat anything for the first three months of the pregnancy and then I ate everything in sight for the next six months."

William ran back to their little cottage, paused at the threshold to catch his breath, and walked quickly to Anne. Anne had never seen such an odd expression on William's face, "Will, what is it? What has happened?"

"Only the most wonderful miracle," William could not keep the emotion from his words.

Anne stood quietly, and William took her in his arms in a tender embrace. "Sarah thinks the reason you haven't been feeling well is because you are with child."

Anne gasped and leaned away from Will to look into his eyes, "Could it be?"

William laughed and said, "We have been trying for that exact result, my dear!"

"Oh, Will, I want to believe it is true, but I feel so sick that I just can't blame it on our child! Surely, no baby can be so cruel to its mother."

William laughed again, "Sarah said it happened to her, and her daughter Betsy is the sweetest young woman we know. Once Sarah told me what she thought was wrong with you, I remembered how sick my mother was with my younger sister."

Anne slipped onto the chair in disbelief and joy. She and Will were going to have a baby. It was extraordinary. She couldn't stop smiling, and when she looked at her dear William, she saw that he had a matching grin on his face that would not go away.

As the couple stared at each other in love and amazement, they heard a light knock at the cottage door. William went quickly and opened the door to Sarah Spencer. "Come in, come in. We are just trying to comprehend the magnificent news."

Sarah went straight to Anne and gently hugged her tight. "I am so happy for you both. I just couldn't stay away, even though I know I am interrupting your precious family time together. I'll only stay a minute. William have you thought about how you are going to tell your parents about this blessed event?"

Sarah's question wiped the happy smile from William's face, and he shook his head sadly.

"Don't despair William," Sarah said cheerfully. "It seems I have become the busiest busy body in the shire."

"I don't understand," William said with some confusion.

"A fortnight ago," Sarah continued, "I was in Stratford at the market, and your mother, Mary, saw me there. She thanked me most sincerely for allowing you to live here and asked me home to Henley Street for a cup of spiced cider. I was afraid your father was waiting there to give me a piece of his mind, but it was just the two of us by the hearth. A very fine cider indeed. Your mother makes the nicest biscuits. A bit dry though, I must remember to send some honey with you tomorrow."

"Sarah," William interrupted. "What did my mother want to talk to you about?"

"Oh, yes. She just raved on and on about what a changed young man you are and how pleased your father is with your work and how happy you seem. She said your father was proud he had set you straight by demanding you stop courting that Hathaway woman, but she suspected just the opposite was true."

"What?" William and Anne both gasped at the same time.

"Oh, yes William, A mother knows her son, and your mother suspected the reason for your change in temperament had everything to do with Anne Hathaway. She recognized how much you loved her long before your father declared her unsuitable. She asked me straight out whether you were living alone in this cottage."

"What did you say?" William asked as Anne held his hand tightly.

"What do you think I said? Of course, I told her the truth. I knew she would be happy to hear the news, and she was."

Anne and William were both struck dumb. They just stared at Sarah as she continued to explain how she had told Mary all about the hand fast ceremony and how much we were all looking forward to the Church wedding when the entire Shakespeare family would be present. Sarah continued, "Mary insisted that she make the wedding feast, and I tried to convince her that I could at least help out with the biscuits, but she wouldn't hear of it, so we will have to provide a crock of honey."

When William was finally able to speak, he asked, "What about Father?"

"Don't you worry about your father, William. The reason I came running right back here to talk to you even though I knew you needed time alone to savor the news is I promised

Mary I would let her know the minute I knew Anne was with child. Then she will break the news gently to John. She has an amazing way of making him think all important decisions are made by him. She will have no problem helping him see how good Anne has been for you, William. Then John will decide you two should be married!"

William and Anne both went to Sarah and hugged her and thanked her. Anne hurried out of the cottage while William and Sarah looked at each other puzzled. Soon Anne was back with a small crock full of fresh honey. Anne handed it to Sarah and said, "Hurry and take this to Mary along with our news!"

William and Sarah laughed at Anne's insistence that she go to Stratford immediately, but Sarah told them she was glad to go and wished them good day.

Chapter Nine

Sarah Spencer was as good as her word, and before William and Anne could humble themselves before John and Mary Shakespeare to ask their permission to marry, John took his son William aside and advised him to make Anne Hathaway his wife. Customarily, Will and Anne would have had to wait three weeks to be married, with a reading of the banns each Sunday, announcing their intended marriage. However, as no reading of the banns or wedding ceremonies could take place in December and January, Anne and William were granted a special license, a common practice at the time in England, which allowed them to announce the wedding and marry on the same day. Thus on a cloudy Sunday, November 28, 1582, William and Anne reconfirmed their vows- -this time in the Church with both the Shakespeare and Hathaway families present.

Despite no early announcements of the marriage in the little parish, the Shakespeare, Hathaway, Spencer, and Sadler families had all spread the happy news to their neighbors, and the Church was crowded with friends and family on that chilly November day. Anne and William wore the same finery they had for their hand fast ceremony, and Anne received many compliments on her elegant green gown. John and Mary Shakespeare were proud to host the wedding feast at their home and thankful the couple were going home to their little cottage in Wilmcote rather than moving into crowded Henley Street with them. Hamnet Sadler provided music for the happy occasion and everyone joined in a sing along. It was a joyous day for all!

The days that followed were happy ones for William and Anne. William was gradually spending more time on his tutoring and writing and less time on Henley Street. As the glove business declined, John Shakespeare looked more to leasing his space and securing a steady income from lodgers. He felt some gratitude to his son William for steering him in that direction by moving to Wilmcote and freeing up space in Henley Street for his first paying lodger. With the business waning, John eased his pressure on William to become a glover, and he was relieved that William was finding his own means of supporting himself and Anne. John and Mary Shakespeare found it a pleasure to walk out to Wilmcote and visit their son and daughter-in-law. Just as Sarah Spencer had predicted, they were soon singing Anne's praises and found her industrious and supportive of their son.

Anne found renewed energy from her pregnancy once her initial stomach issues passed. She was invigorated by the new purpose in her life and made the most of every day. However, she missed her long walks in the woods to find her friends the bees. As the days grow shorter and colder, the bees needed to consume their honey to live through the winter, and Anne needed another activity to help her feel productive. One evening in early December when Anne and William were enjoying a cup of cider with the Spencers, Richard said, "Anne, my dear, did you happen to notice how far we had to tromp through the woods to find the last bee hive of the season? I am afraid I am getting too old for these long ramblings in the woods. The other day at the Black Swan, I met a fellow, Lawrence Pulliam, who said he had skeps on his farm to keep bees right in his backyard. If I find out how to make skeps, would you be willing to spend the time you are waiting for your child to arrive weaving skeps instead of dragging an old man through the forest and marshes in search of honey?"

Anne was ashamed she had not considered Richard and Mary's age in her quest for beeswax for William's candles and honey for cakes. "I am so sorry! Since the nausea of my pregnancy has ebbed, my energy just flows, and I forget my-self."

Sarah laughed and said, "Enjoy that newfound energy while you can dear. Soon that child of yours will take every bit of your strength, and you will rejoice when you can stand up from the stool and walk to the hearth across the room!"

A fortnight later, Richard Spencer knocked at Anne and William's cottage door with a strange, hat shaped object in his hand. "What have you there, Richard? Is this the latest style come straight from London to Wilmcote?" William joked.

Anne arose unsteadily from the stool by the hearth and joined the two men by the door. "My goodness, Anne!" Richard exclaimed. "You and the baby are blossoming."

Anne blushed and said, "Your dear wife was so right about the fleeting energy burst this dear little one gave me! Now I just want to sit by the fire and imagine the baby grow-ing perfect little fingers and toes." Suddenly becoming em-barrassed about discussing her changing body with William and Richard, she changed the subject. "Is that the skep you told me about?"

"Yes! It is so simple, but it will save us from tromping through the woods searching for bee hives. It will also help the bees as they look for a place to deposit their nectar." Richard turned the skep over so both Anne and William could examine its simple construction. It was like a basket woven from coils of grass with an open bottom for the bees to use to enter and exit. Once Richard had explained what the mysteri-ous object was used for, both Anne and William could see that turned with its wide side down, the skep very much re-sembled the natural hives found hanging in the trees around their home.

"How did Mr. Pulliam get the size of the coils of grass so uniform?" Anne quizzed, her mind already racing to imagine if she could successfully make skeps.

"It's quite ingenious actually," replied Richard. "He cut a slice of a cow's horn the exact diameter he wanted the coils to be, and as he wove the grass, he slid the slice of horn over the weave checking the girth as he worked."

"I could do that," Anne declared. "How are the coils attached to each other?"

"I'm sure your stepmother could help you with that, Anne. Lawrence Pulliam said he just gave the coils to his wife, and she stitched them together to form the cone shape. It looks like she used something stronger than thread, perhaps a twine of some sort."

"Joan will be glad to help me find the right materials," Anne declared. The thought of occupying her idle hands as she sat by the fire worrying about the child growing inside of her warmed her. Not only would she be busy, she could be contributing to their meager income. Perhaps she could earn enough to help clothe their new little one. "Is it all right if I keep this skep to use as a model and to show to my stepmother?"

Richard smiled, "That's why I brought it, Anne! Well, that and my little scheme to keep both of us inside by the fire this winter instead of traipsing through the woods trying to find hives for you to raid!"

William and Anne both laughed and thanked Richard as he turned to leave. Once he had left the cottage, William hugged Anne close to him. "I am the luckiest man in the world! I am married to a woman who understands my need for honey cakes and my love of beeswax candles!"

"Don't you have that backwards, dear?" Anne teased. "You *need* the candles to write your great verses, but you *love* the honey cakes for your insatiable sweet tooth!"

"What me insatiable? The only thing I cannot get enough of is you, my dear!" Will declared as he kissed his sweet wife, and all thoughts of honey cakes vanished.

Chapter Ten

Winter came to Wilmcote, and the short days and long nights made William and Anne even more grateful to have each other. William helped Anne find tall, strong rushes along the marsh that she could use to weave skeps. They cut them and carried them back to the cottage before the snow would make it too difficult. Joan had shown Anne a thread of briar that was strong enough to stitch the coils of grass into the hive shape needed for a good skep.

It was time for the young couple to prepare for their first Christmas together. Family meant so much to them this year, and they felt the true spirit of the season. They bundled up one day and went into the woods in search of their Yule log. Anne remembered seeing a fallen tree on one of her many honey-seeking adventures, and she was sure it would make the perfect Yule log for them. When she lead William to the spot and pointed at the tree with pride, William began to laugh.

"Why are you laughing?" Anne demanded.

"You do know we are not yet living in the biggest house in Stratford, don't you? If we could manage to get this huge tree home, we would have to leave the door to our cottage open for all twelve days of Christmas to make room for the log!" William exclaimed.

Anne looked more closely at the fallen tree and realized William was right. It hadn't seemed so big in the forest with all the grand trees surrounding it, but now as she pictured their tiny cottage and hearth, she realized her mistake.

"Could we cut part of it?" she inquired.

"I am afraid you married the wrong fellow, dear Anne. I do not want to stand out here in the freezing cold chopping this giant tree for the rest of the winter. Could we find a smaller Yule log?"

Anne, who was nearly frozen, quickly agreed, and they started back towards the cottage. Along the way, they nearly tripped over the perfect log for their first Christmas! It was even close to the cottage, and William could drag it by himself by using one of the dead branches as a handle.

Once they had warmed up by the fire, William trimmed the branches from the log, throwing them on the fire as he worked. The log was nearly five feet long and ten inches in diameter. Anne produced the ribbon and fabric her stepmother had given her, and they began to plan how they would decorate their first Yule log together on Christmas Eve.

On Christmas Eve, Mary and John Shakespeare, Joan Hathaway and family, the Spencers, and the Sadlers all squeezed themselves into Anne and William's tiny cottage to help them celebrate their first Christmas together. The men brought the Yule log in from its resting place beside the cottage and managed to fit one end inside the hearth with the other end extending to the door. Hamnet joked, "You couldn't find a longer Yule log, could you, Anne?"

"Actually," Will started to speak, but the look Anne gave him froze him in mid sentence. "Ah, we thought this one was perfect."

The women quickly decorated it as it would be the centerpiece of the holiday and burn for the twelve days of the holiday celebration. Then John Shakespeare and Joan Hathaway stepped forward with scorched slivers of wood they had saved from their Yule logs of 1581, the logs Anne and William had helped light when they were single and living at home, and together their parents lit Anne and William's first Yule log. Now the couple was officially autonomous!

Once the Yule log was lit, Anne's favorite Christmas tradition began as each guest took a seat on the end of the log by the door and sang their favorite Christmas Carol. Mary and John Shakespeare sang, "The Cherry Tree Carol" which told the story of Mary and Joseph on their journey to Bethlehem. They stopped to rest by a cherry tree, and Mary asked Joseph to pick her some cherries. Joseph was tired from the journey and said, "Let your baby's father pick the fruit." The limbs of the cherry tree lowered themselves in front of Mary and presented her with luscious ripe cherries.

Jo and Margaret Hathaway sang a beautiful duet of "The Coventry Carol," and their younger brothers sang the sad lullaby which recounted the story of King Herod ordering all the babies killed. "Herod the king, in his raging Charged he hath this day His men of might in his own sight All young children to slay."

Hamnet Sadler was the last to take his seat on the Yule log and the evening flew by as he played his lute and took requests from the guests to play "Make We Joy," "The Salutation Carol," "Good Christian Men, Rejoice," and many more. William had his arm around Anne's growing waist, and she put her head on his shoulder as they welcomed their first Christmas!

For William and Anne, it was a happy twelve days of Christmas with parties at the Shakespeare home on Henley Street, at the Hathaway cottage in Shottery, and at Judith and Hamnet's bakery. At the Shakespeare's, they enjoyed roast goose, hen, and dried apricots and apples. They played cards, marbles, and cribbage. Anne's younger siblings made Christmas at Shottery a joy. They played Hoodman Blind, Hot Cockles, and Handy Dandy all of which William joined with much enthusiasm. They laughed until they cried at Hamnet and Judith's house playing Cherry Pit and Dice.

Hamnet and William easily out spit Judith and Anne aiming their cherry pit missiles at the bucket across the room, but the women had the best luck at dice and conspired together that only the winners of the dice game got to eat the amazing holiday breads Judith had baked. Most of all, they enjoyed each other and dreamt of all the Christmases they would be together. They thought of the approaching new year and realized in wonder that in 1583, they would have a child with which to share the beautiful Christmas season.

William surprised Anne with a pair of warm rabbit gloves, and Anne gave William a new quill pen.

"William, you told me you were no good at making gloves. These are beautiful!" Anne gushed.

"I never had such a beautiful model to inspire me before! Besides, you always warm your cold hands on my back, so the gift is as much for me as for you," William laughed. "Where did you find this exquisite quill?"

"The butcher allowed me to trade him honey for the best goose feather he could find. Your father helped carve the nib."

"My father! Now that is a true Christmas miracle!" exclaimed William as he drew Anne into his arms for a thank you kiss.

Their first winter together, Anne and William proved how resourceful they each were. William continued to tutor and spent every other waking minute writing. Anne had nearly mastered the art of skeps and had a growing stockpile to take to the market in spring. Their baby continued to grow, and Anne found it difficult to rise from the stool by the fire, often needing assistance from William.

When April finally came and the birds began to chirp in the woods, Anne ventured forth from the cottage. She was too large with child to go into Stratford to the market, but

William and Richard took four of her skeps, and she went as far as the marsh to seek new grasses to weave.

In the evening when William returned, he found Anne fast asleep on the stool surrounded by coils of grass she had been weaving. Afraid she would topple to the floor and hurt herself or the baby, William gently lifted her. But Anne awoke in fright and flayed at him.

"Anne, Anne! It's me. Surely you won't beat the father of your unborn child?"

Through groggy eyes, Anne realized that it was indeed her dear William. "I am so sorry," Anne said in a sleepy voice. "I was having a bad dream. A green-eyed monster was chasing me."

"I'm glad I got here in time to save you!"

"You were in the dream, William, and I was mad at you. I can't imagine why I would ever be mad at you."

"It's a good thing you warned me you could be mad at me, so I better be totally honest about what happened at the market today," William said in a serious voice.

Anne was fully awake now and pushed herself away from William, still feeling the emotions of the nightmare. "What are you telling me Will?" Anne asked suspiciously.

In response, William pulled the leather pouch from within his sleeve and asked Anne to hold out her hand, palm up. She did so, and he tipped the contents of the bag into her soft pink palm. She could barely contain the coins and had to join her other hand to form a tray for the falling pence. "Your skeps sold, and I could have sold twice that number if I had only had more faith and taken all eight of your finished skeps to market today."

Tears glistened in Anne's eyes, "I see swaddling clothes, a cradle, and warm blankets for our baby."

William put his arms around Anne and said, "I see the most beautiful woman in the world. A woman with a mean right upper cut who I hope to never have mad at me!"

In mid-May, Anne started out toward the marshes to see if any good grasses were close enough for her to cut. She was large with child and had an awkward gait, but she was determined to complete as many skeps as she could before the baby was born. As she reached down to examine the closest grass, a wave of pain washed over her, and she clutched her stomach. She could barely breathe and didn't know what was happening to her. When she looked down at her skirt, she saw it was dark with wetness, yet she was not near the river's water. The pain subsided a little, and she turned to go toward the Spencer's home.

As she walked up the path, she had to stop several times and endure a pain she never thought was possible. Finally, she made it to the Spencer's door and knocked feebly while leaning against the threshold. Presently, Sarah Spencer opened the door.

"Anne! Are you all right?"

"I think I'm dying! My body is being torn apart."

Sarah put Anne's arm around her shoulder, "Lean on me, child, and we will get you inside."

"Richard!" yelled Sarah. "Hurry down the lane to Claire Bates and tell her we need her now! Don't stand there gawking at me! Go now!" Sarah supported Anne as another contraction roared through her tender body.

Richard did as he was bidden, and hurried to his neighbor's farm. Lyman Bates went to sea in 1578 and came home with a robust, Irish bride, Claire, now the best midwife in Warwickshire.

"What is happening to me?" Anne cried.

"Just breathe, Anne dear. You are in labor, and that beautiful child of yours is ready to join us in this world."

"Breathe! Breathe! I can't breathe. I'm dying," screamed Anne.

"Calm down and look at me, child. Come on, look me in the eyes," Sarah encouraged.

After the ravage of yet another pain, Anne looked up at Sarah Spencer. Sarah said, "I want you to think about the beautiful swaddling clothes you have waiting in your cottage. Think of the tiny cradle lined with the multicolored quilt your mother, Joan, made for the baby. Can you see them in your mind? Picture the little gown and matching cap Mary Shakespeare made this little one."

"Yes," Anne responded weakly.

"Now picture your new baby wrapped in those swaddling clothes, tucked into that beautiful cradle. Picture your healthy baby warm on your breast. Think only good thoughts, Anne. The pain is horrible, but the pain is worth it. I am here. You will get through this."

Sarah's soothing words helped calm Anne, and though she felt each new pain was more than she could endure, she tried to breathe deeply, and she imagined her child in her arms.

Richard charged into the cottage with Claire Bates, the midwife, at his heels. "Is Anne all right?" Richard demanded.

"Yes, she is about to present us with a beautiful baby. You need to go to Henley Street and tell William that he is needed at home. Now go, Richard! We have woman's work to do, and you need to be gone!"

Anne's labor was extremely painful, but the great pain was doing its work. While some women took eight hours or more in hard labor, Anne had only been suffering for two hours, when Claire Bates declared that the baby was crowning. "Push me lady! Push! The path is open. Let your wee one out!"

Anne bore down as hard as she could and pushed with all her might. "Oh, you're a strong one, me lady. I have a fine shaped dark-haired head here. One more big push for the shoulders, dear."

Anne was exhausted, but she pushed again as hard as she could and closed her eyes and nearly passed out. A faint gurgling sound roused her and soon the gurgle turned louder and evolved into a high pitched cry. "Ah, your wee one has 'er mother's lungs! She is crying nearly as loud as you was a screamin'," Claire Bates declared as she placed Anne's newborn baby girl on her warm chest.

Anne shed fresh tears at the sight of her beautiful little girl. She was amazed at how completely in love she was with this new little stranger that had grown inside of her. Her heart was full, and her emotions over flowed. Just when she thought she had a grip on herself, William entered the room, and she started crying again.

"Oh, Anne, Anne. She is beautiful. I am so proud of you! We have a beautiful baby girl! *Though she be but little, she is fierce.* (Midsummer Night's Dream, 3.2). I could hear her first cries from within our cottage where Richard and I paced helplessly! I am so relieved that you are both alive!"

Chapter 11

Five days later on May 26, 1583, Susanna Shakespeare was baptized at Trinity Church in Stratford-upon-Avon. Anne and William's lives had changed forever. They were no longer living and working for themselves; they were a team working to make the best possible life they could for little Susanna.

Susanna was a strong child, and her shrill cries echoed through the small cottage at Wilmcote, but those screams delighted her parents who knew strong lungs bode well for babies in 16th Century England where smallpox, dysentery, scarlet fever, and pneumonia claimed 30% of newborns. Anne cherished the closeness she felt with Susanna as she gave her suckle and nourishment. With Susanna at her breast, all was right with the world. William thrilled at the sight of his wife and daughter, but Anne laughed at his unease at holding Susanna.

"She won't break, Will," Anne teased. "Just hold her tight and help her feel secure."

Despite Anne's encouragement, William was happiest watching Anne care for Susanna. He knew his darling child was in the best possible care with her mother. His job, he knew now more than ever before, was to earn a living to provide for the two women he loved more than anything else in the world.

He had been working on his first full length play, the saga of Henry VI who came to the throne at the tender age of nine months, though William altered history to make Henry older at the time of his father's death. William loved the freedom he had as a writer to alter history to bring drama to his play. The idea for the play had first come to him as he was trying to interest his young pupils in English history. He found the lads to be disinterested and bored with the facts of the past. William thought it was essential for his scholars to know the heroes of their country. Henry V had gained important territory from France, and it fell to his son to retain those gains. Henry VI was thrown into conflict with the Dauphin Charles of France. In addition to the wars in France, young Henry was plagued with the infighting of his own British noblemen York and Somerset.

William saw the potential for great theatre in the history of Henry VI but also, and perhaps more importantly, the lessons in values and ethics he could share with his students. What better way to teach his young boys the importance of working together selflessly for the betterment of the entire country? After all, the internal struggle of York and Somerset was the beginning of the War of the Roses which weakened the kingdom.

In contrast, the chivalrous Lord Talbot, refused to compromise on his principles, and always put his country's needs above his own. Simply telling his students about Lord Talbot's character did not impress the young lads, so he wrote a scene for his students to perform which brought the hero to life. William was amazed at the enthusiasm his students displayed while preparing for the performance of the scene. They volunteered for parts, memorized their lines, and had their parents help them prepare simple costumes and props. They took their rehearsal time seriously and listened to Master Shakespeare's suggestions for improvement. When they were ready to present the scene for William, they surprised him further by saying they wanted to perform for an audience.

William chuckled at his young charges and said, "Let's see how you do for me first, okay?"

The young actors clambered up a small hill which served as their stage. William settled on the grass, clapped his hands, and said, "Let the play begin."

The students performed their roles with a seriousness beyond their years. No one laughed, joked, or chided their fellow actors. They spoke their lines with sincerity and a depth of feeling William thought them incapable of achieving.

When they finished the scene, William Shakespeare sat perfectly still and silent. The boys stood uncomfortably in front of him afraid they had disappointed their school master. But William was anything but disappointed. He was reeling from the powerful emotion of seeing his young acting troupe bring his words to life. It was the realization of the dream of his life, to be a playwright.

William Shakespeare started to clap his hands slowly at first and increasing in speed as his young actors relaxed and realized they had not disappointed him. He stood and walked to the boys, shaking their hands, and clapping them on the back with praise.

"Boys, you are correct! You need to perform in front of an audience! What do you think?" William asked his enthusiastic troupe of actors.

"Let's invite our parents," shouted John.

"Parents have to be polite," Matthew pointed out. "We need an audience of strangers to show that we really are actors!"

"You make a good argument, Matthew," William said thoughtfully. "Let me think about this for a bit. I am so proud of you for your performance; you can all go home early today."

William hurried home to Wilmcote to share his wonderful news with Anne and Susanna. When he entered the cottage,

Anne was surprised and happy to see him home so early, and Susanna cooed and blew bubbles at her proud daddy.

"What has happened, William?" Anne asked.

"I just experienced my scribblings performed by a very professional company of actors, and I am overjoyed!"

"Professional actors?" Anne quizzed.

"Yes! You would not have recognized my students. They were not themselves; they became the characters I had put on paper. It was amazing, and they were so proud of their accomplishment! They want an audience, Anne, a real audience that will acknowledge all their hard work. I'm just not sure how to arrange it."

"Oh, William, that is wonderful! Could you plan something for market day? High Street is always full of people, and often venders are juggling or singing loudly to attract customers to their wares. When the traveling players come from Oxford or London, they have a cryer who goes through the streets letting people know about their performance and people gather. Do you think people would stop and watch the boys?"

"I thought about that, but I don't want the boys to be disappointed if folks just go about their business and don't pay them any heed. It would dampen their spirits to have their hard work ignored."

"You just need to start with a crowd of their parents around them, and then other folks will be curious about what is happening, and they won't want to be left out. You need your own cryer with a loud voice to announce a performance is about to begin. That might quiet the crowd," Anne suggested.

"Good idea, and I know just the chap for the job. Matthew's father Kenneth Burton is the auctioneer for the sheep market and has the loudest voice in Stratford! When he speaks, people definitely listen!"

"Perfect! If the sheep have been sold for the day, your boys can perform on the platform at the top of High Street. It won't be as fancy as the stage the traveling players bring with them, but it is a good place to begin their acting careers!"

"It is a fitting place for me to begin my budding career as a playwright! If I can't get my own village of friends and family to watch and listen to my plays, I might just as well buy some sheep and help your brother on the farm!"

"I'm afraid you would make a dismal shepherd, Will. The sheep would wander away while you were contemplating just the right rhyme for your latest poem," laughed Anne.

"It's still early," said William. "Will you and Susanna be okay if I walk over to Kenneth's house and discuss our idea with him? I'm sure his son returned home with stories of his magnificent performance, and I want to use Matthew's enthusiasm to help convince his father of our plan for market day!"

"That's a fine idea, William. Susanna and I will have stew and fresh bread for you when you return." Anne kissed William good-bye and went to the hearth to check on the evening meal.

William was correct that Matthew had regaled his father with tales of his portrayal of the Duke of Bedford at King Henry V's funeral. Kenneth Burton greeted William with enthusiasm and thanked him for working with his son.

"The lad speaks with such surety now! He used to mumble and hardly speak two words, but he has been telling his mum and me about this production of yours ever since he arrived home. What can I do to help you?"

William told the Burtons about the boys' desire for an audience and the idea of having them perform at the Thursday market.

"Do you think people will listen?" William asked.

"Not listen to my boy? I'll knock their thick heads in if they don't!"

William laughed and shook his head, "Forcing people to listen with the threat of physical violence is not the way I want to start my career as a playwright, but I appreciate your willingness! A few of the regulars at the market could use a good thump up alongside their head! No, I was thinking of something a bit more subtle. First, would it be okay for us to use the auction block for their stage?"

"If your young charges are willing to help wash it down with some buckets of water first, it would be fine. I don't want them slipping around in sheep dung while they are trying to say their parts."

Matthew jumped into the conversation, "We could do that Dad. It wouldn't take us long at all."

"It's not as broad and fancy as the traveling troupe's platform," Kenneth continued.

"We understand that," said William. "My actors aren't grown men, and we can adjust our scenes to fit the space."

"Good. When I'm through selling the last of the sheep and the boys clean things up, your play can begin," Kenneth said.

"One other favor, Mr. Burton. Could you use your strong voice to walk amongst the villagers and announce that a play is about to begin? The other boys will have their parents in place around the platform, so those at the market will see a crowd is gathering. We want as many people in place as we can when the boys begin the scene," William explained.

"No, problem! If I can't knock heads, my next favorite thing is to tell people where to go!" Kenneth replied eagerly.

"Good," William hesitated. "Perhaps, we could work on a loud, but friendly invitation to join us at the platform for a short entertainment."

"I'm always friendly. Don't I sound friendly?"

"Dad," Matthew interjected, "you sound scary, not friendly."

William quickly said, "Your voice is just perfect for this job, Kenneth. All the villagers listen when you speak. That's why you are the first person I thought of for this important task!"

"Really?" Kenneth asked modestly.

"Yes! Will you do it?"

"Okay, but I guess you better coach me like you do the boys so I don't scare folks away," he said as he mussed Matthew's hair with his big rough hands.

"Thank you, Kenneth! You and your wife have raised a fine son. You won't even recognize him as Lord Bedford."

As William happily walked back to his little cottage, he started to think about the way he had written the scene the boys would create for the villagers. He realized that the responsibility to capture the audience's attention and interest couldn't be placed in Kenneth Burton's hands alone. He, as the playwright, had the duty to make the audience want to quiet down and listen. When the boys performed for him, he already knew what the scene was about and where it was set, so he had no confusion. The people at the market would have no idea what the boys were presenting unless he informed them in the opening lines.

He started rewriting the beginning of *Henry VI* as he walked. He determined that he would have the boys walk solemnly through the market in their costumes depicting mourning. As their procession made its way to the platform, the villagers' curiosity would be aroused. Then when they heard Kenneth Burton announcing that a play was about to begin, they would already know it was about someone's death. He would add two lines to Matthew's speech as the Duke of Bedford.

The play opened with Matthew saying, "*Hung be the heavens with black, yield day to night! Comets, importing change of times and states, Brandish your crystal tresses in the sky, and with them scourge the bad revolting stars that have consented onto Henry's death!* (Henry VI, 1 1)

Those lines, William now realized, let the audience know it was a time of mourning, but they didn't clarify which Henry was dead.

He would add, "*King Henry the Fifth, too famous to live long! England ne'er lost a King of such worth*" (Henry VI, 1.1).

The people would quiet down to listen to tributes to their beloved Henry the Fifth, and his young actors would have the audience they desired. William was quite pleased with himself as he entered his little cottage at Wilmcote and embraced Anne.

"It would seem that Kenneth Burton agreed to your plan!" Anne exclaimed.

"He improved upon my plan! He is going to box the ears of anyone who dares to continue buying onions while the boys are performing!"

"What?" Anne shrieked.

William just winked at her and said, "Suffice it to say, I am no longer worried about an audience for Thursday's performance, the premiere of *King Henry VI*!"

Matthew Burton was happy to learn the two additional lines given him by William at their next rehearsal. The boys had already counted their lines and compared their roles to see who had the bigger parts. Stephen was given the part of a messenger and was quite disappointed until he discovered that he had more lines than the Duke of Gloucester. Arthur, a slight lad with a pale complexion, refused to play the part of Joan of Arc until William explained that though he was playing a woman's part, he would have a sword fight which he would win!

Watching the rivalries of his young students gave William a preview of what his life would be like writing for professional actors with egos to stroke and temperaments to assuage. He also learned that his play was a fluid organism changing as staging and timing demanded. Unlike his poems that were fixed to the page, his play seemed to take on new life in the young actors' hands. Some of the changes, like those he made to the opening of *King Henry VI* were good, but others, caused by his students forgetting or changing lines pained William deeply. He would have to learn patience as a playwright!

The days before the performance passed quickly, and the young actors were as prepared as time would permit. William was more nervous than the boys about the success of the market day performance. He paced the cottage at Wilmcote in a frenzy of nerves until Anne chastised him, "You will curdle my milk and give poor Susanna the colic if you don't stop that incessant pacing! Your lads will be fine; your play will be a success. Why don't you go into town and visit Hamnet and Judith? You always return from visits with them in a better mood!"

"Good idea, Anne. That is a fine idea. I will ride Barbary into Stratford and talk to Hamnet. Is that a good idea?"

"Yes, you foolish man, be gone!" Anne said as she hugged him and moved him toward the door.

As William rode toward Stratford, he recited the lines of his play in his mind. He was happy with the rhythm and content he had created, but he was uncertain if the villagers would understand and relate to his words. His subject was royal, but his intent was to show the humanity of King Henry V and his heir King Henry VI. He wanted the audience to learn not just about history but about the passion and fallibility of man. He knew he was expecting too much of this first, simple production, but he couldn't stop himself from going over and over each scene in his mind.

He felt calmer when he reached the Sadler's bakery and felt even better when Hamnet clasped him in his arms and welcomed him. "To what do we owe this honor? Judith!" he shouted back towards the ovens. "We have a stranger in our midst. William has blessed us with a visit."

Judith came around the counter with flour on her face and wisps of her black hair sweated to her forehead. "Here's the worker of the house," Hamnet laughed.

"Will, I would give you a rib-smashing hug if it weren't for this lovely flour I'm wearing! How about a fresh biscuit instead?"

"Nothing can compare to your hugs, Judith, but I would accept one of your biscuits hot from the oven with just a smattering of honey as second best compensation." The three friends laughed together, and William felt his spirits rising. "*Why*," William thought, "*does Anne always know just what I need?*"

Judith brought William a large, golden brown biscuit dripping with honey and returned to work while Hamnet retrieved his lute from behind the door where he had placed it when William entered. "I was just working on a new tune by John Dowland. Since your mouth is full, you won't be able to talk for once, and I can sing my song in peace."

William nodded eagerly toward his friend and chewed his heavenly biscuit.

Hamnet sang:
"Flow, my tears, fall from your springs!
Exiled for ever, let me mourn;
Where night's black bird her sad infamy sings,
There let me live forlorn.
Down vain lights, shine you no more!
No nights are dark enough for those
That in despair their last fortunes deplore.
Light doth but shame disclose.
Never may my woes be relieved,
Since pity is fled;
And tears and sighs and groans my weary days, my weary days
Of all joys have deprived"
("Flow my Tears," John Dowland).

"What do you think?" Hamnet asked when he had finished.

"I think I'm glad you didn't sing that at our wedding! It is too sad and fit for a funeral." Suddenly, William leapt to his feet. "A funeral! It is like a funeral dirge! It is perfect for my funeral!"

"Have you lost your mind, Will? Are you planning on dying soon because if you are, this is not funny."

"No, no! Not me, Henry V! It's the perfect funeral song for Henry V!" William shouted.

"Just sit down my friend," Hamnet said calmly. "I don't want to alarm you, but Henry has been dead for some long time now." He patted William on the back and encouraged him to sit down on the stool. "Queen Elizabeth is on the throne now."

William finally looked at his friend and laughed, "I know where I am, Hamnet, and I know this is 1583, but I set my play in 1422 at the time of Henry's death." William quickly told Hamnet about his play and his young actors' performance. "It's one of the reasons I am here today. Anne sent me out of the house because my nervous energy was making her edgy."

"Anne makes you come to visit us now, huh?" responded Hamnet and made a show of putting his head down under the low table to study William.

"What are you doing, Hamnet?"

"I'm just looking to see if you are wearing Anne's petticoats because it's a sure thing that she wears the hose in the family!" laughed Hamnet.

Judith's voice rang out from back of the bakery, "The only reason you have breeches on today, Hamnet Sadler, is because your belly is too big for my skirts, so you watch yourself!" she teased.

After much laughter and teasing, William turned serious, "Hamnet, can you do me a favor tomorrow?"

"We are always really busy on market day, William, but if we can help you out, we would be glad to," over his shoulder, he added, "Is that okay wife dear? Is it okay for us to help William?" Laughter and a cloud of flour came from the table where Judith was furiously kneading dough. "What do you need?"

"I want to let the folks in the market know that my lads are going to present some scenes from my play. The boys are going to walk slowly from here--they will get their costumes on at my mother and father's house. They will be dressed in their darkest robes to depict mourning, and I want it to look like they are a funeral procession as they walk up Henley Street to High Street and onto the platform at the top of the street. We don't have a coffin, but if you could lead them singing your sad tune, it would do much to capture the attention of all the people on the street. Kenneth Burton is going to announce that a show is about to begin, but I want to set the right mood before he "commands" everyone to attend!"

"I'm glad you have that man on your side!" Hamnet chuckled. "You know that I am always looking for a place to share my music. I will be glad to lead your sad little actors to the stage. Will I Judith?"

"Absolutely, you burnt crust old fool!"

William said, "Oh, oh, Hamnet. I'm afraid Anne has rubbed off on your dear, meek wife."

"What? Where is a dear, meek wife? I can only see Judith through that haze of flour dust, and why do I get the impression that when she is pounding on that dough, she is thinking of me?"

William's spirits were always improved after a visit with the Sadlers, and when he presented Anne with a package containing two of Judith's famous hot cross buns, Anne joined his happy mood. "Now I see the man I fell in love with, and the crazy, pacing playwright has been drowned by laughter and honey!"

Chapter 12
August 1583

Market day dawned sunny and bright as though all of nature was championing William's success. The birds sang cheerfully, and the flowers nodded their heads at William Shakespeare as he rode Barbary quietly to Stratford. To add to his joy, Anne planned to bring three-month-old Susanna on her first outing to see her father's premiere public performance. They would be leaving Wilmcote soon accompanied by the Spencers for a leisurely walk to the village, but William needed the steady support of Barbary beneath him on this special day in his life. He must calm his young students' nerves while keeping his own excitement and fear in check.

He stabled Barbary at the Shakespeare home in Henley Street and quickly crossed over to the bakery. Before he reached the door, he could hear Hamnet's deep, mellifluous voice singing the funeral dirge planned for the play. He entered and was dismayed to see Judith sitting on a stool in front of Hamnet with tears streaming down her checks.

He strode to her and gently put his hand on her shoulder, "What is it, Judith? What has happened?"

Judith shook her head gently, "It is nothing, Will. I just can't listen to this sad song anymore. Hamnet usually keeps me laughing in the mornings while I bake. He plays happy songs and flips flour at me, but now all he plays over and over again is that mournful song which is about to put me in my grave."

William squeezed Judith to him, "I am so sorry, my dear. It will be over in a matter of hours, and I promise I will only ask Hamnet to play happy songs in the future." Then turning to Hamnet he said, "Your song will have the whole market place in tears by the time my young actors reach the top of High Street! Excellent work, my friend!"

William told Hamnet he would remain at the platform to prepare the "stage" for his actors, but he would send one of the younger boys to alert Hamnet it was time to put on his black robe, grab his lute, and meet the acting troupe in the street. William left the Sadlers without even taking the fresh, hot bun Judith offered him.

After he left, Hamnet looked at Judith and said, "He is far gone. He didn't even notice that bun you offered him. Let's hope this show is a success, or we are going to have one sad friend."

William knocked lightly and entered his former home. His mother turned from the hearth where she was stirring the fire and went quickly to him for a light embrace. "William, you look horrible. You are pale. What ever is wrong?"

"I'm fine, mother. It's just the play. Today is the first public appearance of my play."

"Oh that. You must not bother yourself about that. They are just boys, and boys will be boys. The play is bound to be marred by all kinds of mistakes. Why fuss about it?"

"Mother, it is my words that I am worried about! What if the audience is not interested in my words?"

"Don't be silly, William. You say the most absurd things. No one understands you and because of that, they will be hanging on every word to prove to themselves and their neighbors that they **do** understand you! Your play will be....how do you say it? It will be a smash up!"

William didn't know whether to feel better or worse after his mother's "comforting" words, but he did calm himself enough to take a seat by the fire and accept the cake she offered him. "Could I have some honey for my cake, mother?"

"Humph! You've been living around those Spencers too long. Sarah even brought me a crock of honey the last time she visited. All that sweetness just destroys the flavor of my rich cakes."

Mary Shakespeare retrieved some honey from the shelf for her son and then sat next to him by the fire. "John and I have decided to help out with your little street procession this morning," Mary declared.

William nearly choked on his dry cake but managed to sputter, "How?"

"I already agreed to help the little urchins get their mourning costumes on, but when your father and I heard your corpulent friend, Hamnet Sadler, was to lead the procession, we decided we needed to add some dignity to the parade. Your father has dusted off his high bailiff robes and gathered his ceremonial ribbons. I will be attired in my formal black gown, and we will follow the boys keeping them in order and giving some sense of the serious nature of this funeral procession. A procession for King Henry the Fifth lead by a comic baker and followed by young boys is unacceptable."

William tried to interrupt his mother several times during her tirade, but he was unable to do so.

Mary wagged her finger at him, "No, don't thank us William. We are just pleased to be able to help out. Your father cuts quite a figure in his official garb. When I saw him this morning it took me right back to happier days," Mary sighed heavily.

William just stared at his mother and for a moment, he thought he saw tears in her eyes. *It couldn't possibly hurt to have them follow the boys, could it?* William pondered. "Mother, thank you so much for your support. I was just hoping you and father would come to the play but to have you participate is just...just," William struggled to find the right word.

"Necessary!" his mother declared. "It is absolutely necessary to have people of stature in a King's funeral procession."

That settled it. For a few minutes William sat contemplating the fire on the hearth and wondering whether the boys could have put their costumes on at the bakery, but he knew having flour all over their black robes would be worse than having his parents join the funeral procession, so he just finished his cake, dousing it with honey as he ate.

William kissed his mother good-bye and told her Hamnet would come fetch the boys and them when it was time for the march up Henley Street to begin. Then he walked up Henley to the corner of High and Sheep Street where Kenneth Burton's booming voice was encouraging higher bids on a handsome Cotswold sheep. Because the weather was so fine, a large number of people were crowded around the market stalls on either side of the auctioneer's platform. Women were choosing fresh vegetables and eggs, placing them in the sturdy wicker baskets on their arms. Men were standing in clusters talking about their crops and the good harvest they were anticipating.

William began to pace as he worried about every facet of the simple production. He finally stopped and started laughing at himself. "If I am this tense about a couple of scenes performed by young boys, what will I be like when my plays are performed by professional actors in front of London audiences. I need to settle down." Just then, he saw Anne with Susanna in her arms coming towards him. The Spencers were close behind, but Anne strode forward anxious to embrace William.

"Don't be nervous, Will! This is a wonderful opportunity!" She kissed him and placed Susanna in his arms.

His daughter in his arms was the healing balm he needed. What were a few scribbled words on paper compared to her? She was his best creation, and he knew no play would take her place in his heart. He greeted the Spencers and thanked them for coming.

"I see your young actors arriving, Will," Anne said and pointed toward Bridge Street where an enthusiastic young group of boys pranced towards them.

"We've been rehearsing!" Matthew Burton shouted as the boys drew closer to the Shakepeares and Spencers.

"Without me?" William asked, "You don't need my direction any more?"

The boys laughed and Stephen said, "We just want to please you, Master Shakespeare."

Arthur timidly added, "We want it to be perfect for you."

William felt guilty. He was so concerned about himself and whether his writing would be successful, he hadn't really considered the boys' feelings. "You have already pleased me beyond measure, boys! Now, those of you who are part of the funeral procession, hurry down to Henley Street to get ready. My parents are expecting you, and they will walk with you back here to the platform. The rest of you boys come with me. We have a platform to prepare."

"Your parents are accompanying the boys?" Anne asked nervously.

William laughed and passed Susanna to her. "Don't ask, Anne, just watch what you see coming up the street!"

Kenneth Burton finished selling the last sheep of the day and used a pitchfork to clean the dirty straw from the platform. "I added extra straw today lads, so you won't have much muck to worry about. Just run and fill those two wooden buckets with water from the river, and we'll have your stage ready in no time."

Soon the boys returned from the river, and Kenneth showed them where to slosh the water while the other boys used coarse brushes and rags to remove the remaining, sticky manure.

When they had the platform cleansed and the sun had dried the rough boards, William placed an English banner on a tall pole at the right corner of the stage. For scene two which took place in France, he would remove St. George's red cross and replace it with France's deep blue fleur-de-lis. This was all the scenery necessary for the simple production which relied primarily on Shakespeare's words.

Soon it was time to send the youngest student down the hill to the bakery to tell Hamnet it was time to begin. With the students for the second scene off to the side of the platform in the imaginary wings of the theatre, it was time for William to take his place with Anne and Susanna in the audience. He had been so intent on preparing the platform he hadn't noticed how many parents of his scholars were already gathered waiting for their sons to perform for them. They had a good sized audience already!

Hamnet's plaintive voice could be heard at the top of High Street, and its effect on the villagers in the market was palpable. His beautiful, rich voice tore at their heart strings, and the crowd naturally moved along the street following him and wondering what the boys in dark clothing signified. They were even more surprised to see John and Mary Shakespeare adorned in their finest bringing up the rear of the solemn procession.

When Hamnet reached the base of the platform, he finished the last chord of "Flow My Tears," and nodded to

Kenneth Burton who climbed on the platform, cleared his throat and declared, "A powerful production by our own William Shakespeare, featuring my son, Matthew, is about to begin. Your attention is deman. . . 'er requested!'"

William rolled his eyes at Anne, and she smiled back in merriment. "Are your parents in the play?"

William shrugged and said, "Nothing would surprise me today!"

The boys filed up the steps to the platform and to William's relief, his parents stayed at the side with the boys for Scene Two. Matthew Burton stepped forward and spoke his lines loudly but with real feeling. William looked around the crowd and saw they were intently watching, and he heard a few murmurings of "its King Henry whats dead" and "oh, poor Henry."

The Duke of Gloucester came in right on his cue as did the Duke of Exeter, but the Bishop of Winchester had to be pushed forward by the other boys and looked as though he would pass out. Fortunately, Matthew knew Stephen's first line and got him going after which the Bishop of Winchester was in fine form. All went smoothly until it was time for the 3rd messenger to enter with an important missive from France. The actors stood frozen on the stage until Matthew said in his loudest voice, "The messenger from France must have a very slow horse." The crowd laughed, the tension was broken, and the young lad playing the 3rd messenger part stomped quickly up the steps to deliver his important lines.

The boys all bowed at the end of Scene One and much to their amazement, they were greeted with cheers and clapping. William quietly left Anne's side and removed the British banner, replacing it with its French equivalent. As he quickly returned to his place in the audience, he heard whispers of, "they are in France now," coming from the crowd. The simple props were working!

Scene Two was moving along quite nicely until Arthur stepped forward as Joan of Arc and said, *"Reignier, is 't thou that thinkest to beguile me?"* (<u>Henry VI</u>, 1.2).

From the audience came, "Speak up me boy. I can't hear you."

William looked around nervously to see if Kenneth Burton was about to bash the poor old man's brains in, but he heard Arthur say in a loud, clear voice, "I'm sorry Grandfather. I will begin again." And he did.

William made a note to himself to talk to his young actors about the imaginary fourth wall between them and their audience that they must not break, but there was plenty of time for that. His young actors had made him proud, and the applause they received at the end of the second scene was even louder than the first. All the boys grinned from ear to ear and couldn't stop bowing. Many people in the crowd shook William's hand and congratulated him on a wonderful production. He was a real playwright with the first two scenes of his historical play successfully performed. He could breathe and hug Anne and enjoy the moment.

Chapter 13

William and Anne's life settled into a comfortable routine. They celebrated each milestone in Susanna's life: her first smile, her first full belly laugh, the day she astonished them both by rolling over, and her sweet babbling they interpreted as her very own language. As Susanna grew, William's manuscript grew as well. He completed five full acts for *Henry VI* and still had more to write about the history of the King's reign, so he started a second play to follow the first.

His students spurred him forward in his writing with more demands for scenes which they could perform. They wanted action and would have been pleased if William included sword fights in every scene, but they also grew to appreciate the pathos their school master developed among the characters in the scenes. They had fallen comfortably into the routine of learning two scenes a month in addition to their Latin lessons. The first Thursday market of each month, the boys performed the new scenes they had learned.

Though not all scenes required a funeral procession, William stayed with the strategy of having his actors walk up the streets, through the market place to alert the villagers another play was about to be presented. Hamnet was pleased to play his lute and set the tone for the scenes of the day. Sometimes he played a cacophonous, jarring tune denoting war; other Thursdays, his song was a melodious harmony befitting a time of accord. Mary and John Shakespeare no longer joined the formal procession to the sheep platform, but they did attend every performance their son directed.

As fall turned to winter, Anne gathered the last honey of the season from the three skeps she and Richard Spencer had mounted at the edge of the forest behind their cottage. They no longer had to traipse through the woods to find the bees which was a double blessing. Not only was Richard slowing down in his old age, but it was nearly impossible for Anne to contain active Susanna on extended walks. Having skeps of honey close to home was something the villagers in Stratford and surrounding Warwickshire embraced whole-heartedly, and Anne was able to sell every skep she made. However, she discovered that watching an increasingly mobile child limited her ability to sit quietly and weave grasses!

Susanna loved her new mobility! She started by scooting herself on her bottom from one place to another until she discovered that she could move faster on her tummy and even faster when she propped her bottom up with her knees tucked under her, and she rested on her elbows, giving her a new outlook on her magical world. William and Anne smiled in amusement when Susanna stuck her hind end up like the ducks on the Avon. Next, she learned to move from her elbows to her hands and rock back and forth on her hands and knees as though she was building up steam to move forward. Soon there was no hesitation, and she was crawling full speed everywhere. The hearth, the heart of their little cottage, became a dangerous place as Susanna did not understand the danger of fire. William tied a cord to the bed post and stretched it to within a foot of the hearth, then he created a soft harness of rags which he placed around Susanna's shoulders and tummy. Now Susanna could crawl anywhere she wanted but not into the fire!

By nine months, Susanna was pulling herself up on stools, her cradle, the butter churn; anything she could reach acted as a platform for her to stand on her own two feet. One day when William was holding her hands and helping her walk towards him, Anne came through the door, and Susanna turned to look at her, let go of William's hands, and stood on her own with no support. Of course, once she noticed that

William was no longer holding her, she promptly sat down on the floor. William and Anne both clapped their hands in delight, and Susanna eagerly clapped her little hands together as well.

Though Anne was delighted to see Susanna growing stronger and more independent every day, it also saddened her. She no longer had the comfort of holding Susanna to her breasts and nursing her. Just as Susanna needed more nutrients to sustain her growth and mobility, Anne's milk diminished and dried up. Anne and William's baby girl was no longer a baby, she had grown into a toddler. She could stand on her own, and she ate the same food from the hearth that William and Anne enjoyed. At first Anne mashed little Susanna's carrots and peas, but soon Susanna was demanding to feed herself, and her little fingers grasped the peas and plopped them into her mouth, all on her own like a big girl!

On May 26, 1584, Anne and William gave Susanna her first birthday celebration. It was a warm day and the extended family enjoyed an afternoon of good food and entertaining games. The proud grandparents marveled at Susanna's accomplishments as she toddled about the yard chasing her aunts and uncles. Hamnet played his lute, and they all sang happy songs.

The Thursday after Susanna's first birthday, William's lads performed the final two scenes of *Henry VI* at the market, and unbeknownst to William, Lord Strange's Men, a traveling troupe from London, arrived in Stratford and watched the performance. After William had congratulated his students on their fine acting and sent them home, Russell Northcutt stepped forward and introduced himself.

"We've heard about you and your young players," Russell began. "Most folks have told us about the enthusiasm of the boys, but no one told us just how good a writer you are."

William was taken back and before he could say anything, Russell Northcutt continued, "We are always short of plays. Do you think you could write for us?"

"I would be honored, but I'm not sure," William hesitated with embarrassment, "I change scenes as I see the boys rehearse, and my pages are covered with writing across the page, in the margins, diagonally across my first draft, and they are marred by blots of ink. I always have to help my young students interpret my meaning!"

"All of our scripts are like that," laughed Russell. "The two scenes I just witnessed are the final two scenes of a full length play, is that correct?"

"Yes. *Henry VI* is a five act play that I just completed. I have already started on *Henry VI Part II.*"

"For a price, would you allow us to perform *Henry VI* on our next circuit? We could arrange to have our first performance here in Stratford, so you could watch, and we could collaborate on things you want altered."

William stopped breathing after the words, "for a price," and he could barely concentrate on the words coming from Russell Northcutt's mouth. "You don't look pleased," Russell said sadly. "Are you unwilling to place your play in strangers' hands? I assure you we are a very professional company."

William recovered himself enough to say, "Oh yes. I have attended all of your performances here in Stratford, and your men do an accomplished job. I have often imagined my words being brought to life by your company."

"Well then, let's do this. We can pay you one schilling for each performance, and you will retain ownership of the play for any future use you want to make of it. We only ask that

you don't allow any of the competing touring groups to perform the play next season."

"A schilling for each performance," William echoed.

"I know it's not much, but that is what we can afford. We
are planning on our usual fifteen village tour starting in the
spring of 1585. You could earn a pound sterling and six
schillings by allowing us to take your manuscript with us
now. Our writers in London earn more, but they give us more
plays, and they help us with staging before we take the production out on tour."

The money sounded like a windfall to William, but
nervousness unsettled his stomach as he thought of allowing
his precious manuscript to leave his hands. Russell Northcutt
could sense his misgivings, and he placed his hand on
William's back to reassure him. "We will be in Stratford all
week, William. You think about our offer, and we will talk
again before we leave."

"Thank you, Mr. Northcutt. I am very grateful for your
offer. I just haven't had a chance to think about my plays being under someone else's control, and it is a very strange
feeling."

William covered the distance to Wilmcote as if in a
dream. He could be a paid writer, a professional playwright.
It was the dream of his life, but he was hesitating. Why
hadn't he told Russell Northcutt "Yes! A million times yes!"
when he asked? William did not think of himself as a man
who had to be in control of situations around him, but he realized that he wanted absolute control of his writing. He
loved having his young students act out his words because
they listened to him, and when he changed lines or re-
arranged scenes, his young students did as he asked without
challenging him. Of course, they didn't always say their lines
perfectly, but their intention was to do just as their school

master instructed. Lord Strange's Men were professional actors; they had strong opinions about what worked on stage and what didn't. They had powerful egos that needed stroking. What would become of his play in their hands without him to guide them in the direction he wanted the manuscript to go? These unsettling thoughts charged through William's mind as he reached Wilmcote and his precious Anne and Susanna.

"How did the lads do today, Will?" Anne greeted William as he came through the door.

"They were fine," William said quietly.

"Fine?" Anne questioned.

"They performed just as I directed them," William said rather sadly.

"Will, what is wrong?"

"I met a fellow from Lord Strange's Men today, Russell Northcutt. He and the rest of the troupe arrived in Stratford in time to watch the boys perform."

"Why that is wonderful!" Anne said with enthusiasm. "What did he say?"

"He wants to perform *Henry VI*."

"What?" Anne said as she rushed to William's side. "He wants to perform the entire play? He wants to perform the entire play by himself?" Anne asked in confusion.

William smiled at Anne's puzzled expression. "He wants Lord Strange's Men to perform the entire play. They travel out of London every spring, to fifteen different locations, staying a week, and then moving. They have five different plays in their repertoire, so they can attract an audience each night. Five fresh plays are hard to come by, and he wants one of their plays for next season to be my *Henry VI*."

"That is wonderful, Will," Anne gave William a warm hug. "It is the answer to your dreams! You are a playwright for professional actors! Hundreds of people, perhaps thousands will see your play!" Anne drew herself from William's arms and studied his face. "Why are you troubled by this good news?"

"It is the strangest sensation, Anne. My ambition has always been the theatre, to see my words come to life on stage, but now that the opportunity is placed in my hand, I feel fear and dread."

Anne grasped William's arm and said, "Susanna is sound asleep. Let's sit by the fire so you can explain what you are thinking. I don't understand."

"I don't know if I can explain it, Anne. It's as though my plays only exist when I am a part of them. To give my words on paper to complete strangers and let them do with them as they will frightens me. I have the staging of the entire play in my head. I know where the actors should enter, where they should pause, how slowly or rapidly they should speak the lines. All of that information is in my head, and I communicate it to the boys as they rehearse for each scene. Sometimes what I have envisioned doesn't work, but because I am there, I can make adjustments. Does any of this make sense to you?"

Anne slowly nodded her head, "Yes, I guess I hadn't thought of it this way. If you give Lord Strange's Men the parts you have written, they can take your words and perform them in a very different way than you intended. Would that be an awful thing? I mean they are really wonderful actors."

"I know they are! That is what has me so confused. I should be floating on air with excitement, but I can't shake the feeling of dread that has come over me. And they offered to pay me! Not a huge amount but enough to help our household budget tremendously. They will pay me a schilling a performance."

"Will! Think how that money could help us with the expenses of a growing child! Susanna's appetite grows every day, and she outgrows her gowns faster than I can make them."

"I know that Anne," William's voice began to rise even though he tried to remain calm. "Don't you think I know that! I spend every minute that I am not tutoring figuring out how I can make more money. I can barely focus on my writing."

"I'm sorry, Will. I didn't mean to upset you. It's just that I am here every day trying to stretch our food budget so we have at least one good meal, and sometimes, it's as though you don't even notice."

"I do notice, Anne," William said forcefully. "It makes me feel like a failure as a husband and father when I see how hard you are working."

Anne stood and walked behind the stool where William was sitting with his head in his hands. She put her arms around him and eased his back to her chest, rocking him as she would Susanna. "You are the best possible husband and father. Don't you ever doubt that. We will work this out. The three of us don't eat that much!" she laughed trying to lighten the mood.

That night they held each other tight, but neither of them slept. Anne was so confused by Will's reaction to the generous offer by Lord Strange's Men. She thought Will's dream was to sell his plays and make a living as a playwright. He had promised her that he would not take her away from Stratford and her family. If he refused to sell his plays without going with them, how could they stay in Stratford?

William tried to convince himself that selling his play to Lord Strange's Men was the only sensible thing he could do. Why was he spending so much time and effort writing if he wasn't willing to sell his manuscript? What good did it do for him to direct his students' productions of his plays if he wasn't polishing them for a bigger stage and professional actors? He couldn't travel with Lord Strange's Men and oversee each production. He would lose the money he made tutoring and a schilling a performance would do nothing to keep Susanna fed and clothed.

When the first light of dawn crossed the sky, William Shakespeare arose from his wedding bed, left the cottage, and faced the uncertainty of his future. As he walked in the forest and listened to the morning birds sing their songs, he faced the reality that he not only wanted to be a playwright, he wanted to be an integral part of each production of his plays. He wanted to be on the stage and a part of the action. He knew also that he would never abandon Anne and Susanna. He did not know, however, how he was going to achieve both of these goals.

Anne managed to fall asleep in the wee hours of the morning, but before she let herself drift into sleep, she resolved that she would support William in whatever decision he made. After all, they were happy with their tiny cottage and meagre furnishings. They did not need the extra money to survive. The three of them would be just fine.

Anne awoke screaming and reached for William, but he was not in the bed. She pulled her knees up to her chest and hugged herself, trying to stop shivering. It was the same dream, the horrible nightmare with the green-eyed monster, and this time the monster caught her and was clutching her to his mouth when she awoke petrified. Where was William? She had awakened Susanna with her screams, and she quickly lifted her baby from the cradle and pressed Susanna's sweet face to her chest. She murmured, "It's okay. Everything is okay," to calm both Susanna and herself.

Anne could not convince herself that everything was okay. She quickly dressed herself and Susanna. She rushed to the Spencer's cottage and knocked on the door.

Sarah greeted Anne and Susanna with a warm smile. "Anne, it is so good to see you. Richard and I are about to have some porridge for breakfast. Won't you join us?"

Sarah's kind words and smile caused tears to form in Anne's eyes, and she couldn't hold them back. "Oh, Sarah. I've lost him. Will is gone," she sobbed.

Richard jumped from his stool by the hearth, "What?" he shouted.

Anne sniffled, "I awoke this morning from a horrible dream, and Will was gone. He has left Susanna and me."

Sarah said in a calm voice, "Why in the world would William leave you and Susanna?"

"Because he wants to be a writer, and we are in his way," Anne sobbed.

Richard raised his eyebrows and looked at Sarah. She nodded her head toward the door, and Richard was glad to escape from the emotional scene. "I'll go fetch him," he said as he grabbed his hat and hurried out of the house.

"Start at the beginning, Anne," Sarah encouraged.

Anne wiped her nose and told Sarah about the offer Lord Strange's Men had made William and how she thought he would be pleased, but he was not pleased, and she was confused and that was why William had left her.

Sarah said, "So William has run away with Lord Strange's Men?"

For the first time, Anne calmed down enough to rethink the things she had been ranting about, and she stared at Sarah. "That doesn't make much sense, does it?"

"No, dear," Sarah said gently, "but I know something that makes perfect sense."

"What?"

"Susanna is a toddler now, and you are no longer nursing her, correct?"

"Yes, but Will wouldn't leave me because of that. He promised me that I had given Susanna such a healthy start that she would be fine. Do you think he is mad at me?"

Sarah gently caressed Anne's hand and said, "No! I do not think William is mad at you, and if what I suspect is true, he now has reason to love you more than ever before."

"I don't understand."

"You were so young when your mother passed away that she didn't have a chance to explain the mysteries of the female body. While you were nursing Susanna, you didn't have your menses. It's God's gift to women to help them heal from the rigor of pregnancy and childbirth before they bring another child into the world. Susanna is now over a year old, and your menses have returned haven't they?" Sarah asked.

Anne looked at Sarah in awe. "How do you know so much about life? You are correct. I noticed spotting in March, and then in April things were back the way they were before I conceived Susanna. Then in May and so far this month, I have had nothing. But I don't think I can be pregnant because I haven't been sick at all. I wake up feeling good in the morning, and I can eat anything I want. Susanna made me so sick those first months."

Sarah laughed, "That's the way children are, Anne. When you think you have things figured out, they mix things up. Though you haven't had stomach issues, you are having a bit of an emotional breakdown this morning. Do you agree that you just aren't yourself?"

"I am just so sad that Will has left me," Anne said uncertainly.

"Do you really think that William Shakespeare would just walk out on you without saying good-bye?"

Anne burst into tears again, but she shook her head and managed to gasp, "He would never do that to me."

"Some babies crowd their mother's stomachs right from the beginning and make them nauseous. Other babies don't care about their mother's eating habits, they start messing with their mother's emotions. You can be happy one moment and sobbing the next, but it is all perfectly normal, Anne. I think it is time for celebration. Your father-in-law is about to have his second grandchild, and he thought you were too old! How absurd!"

William and Richard walked through the door just as Sarah said, "Your father-in-law is about to have his second grandchild," and they both froze in mid step.

"Anne!" William rushed to her side, "Why didn't you tell me?"

Anne fell into William's arms sobbing uncontrollably.

"Sarah, what is wrong? Why is she crying? Anne, don't you want another child?"

Anne responded by crying even harder. William held her close and let her tears soak his tunic. "What have I done wrong, Sarah?"

"You ran away with Lord Strange's Men! You horrible man!" Sarah laughed.

After much explanation by Sarah and after Anne had dried her tears, the four friends had honey cakes and cider and enjoyed a good laugh about the confusion of the morning. William was thrilled to imagine his second child and a bit ashamed of himself that he hoped for a son. He loved Susanna with all of his heart, and he knew that a second daughter would make him just as happy, but a son. . . a son would carry his name into posterity and be his heir.

Chapter 14

Anne's pregnancy, though welcomed by both Anne and William, complicated William's already stressful decision about *King Henry VI*. Lord Strange's Men were leaving Stratford in two days, and William had yet to speak to Russell Northcutt. Anne told him that she would support him in whatever decision he made, but William understood "whatever decision he made," did not include leaving her alone in Wilmcote pregnant and with a one year old to care for on her own. They were struggling financially with only three in the family. What would they do with another child to feed and clothe?

Though William had still not made a final decision on what to tell Russell Northcutt, he could no longer put off speaking with the man. He decided he would simply tell the man the truth and remain true to himself. He kissed Anne and Susanna farewell, promising them to return in a few hours. "I will not, under any circumstances, run away with Master Northcutt and his actors," William teased Anne.

William found the acting troupe at the Royal Arms on High Street, and he asked Russell to walk with him to Hamnet's bakery so they could speak privately. Russell was glad for a break from his boisterous company, and the two men ambled down High Street past Bridge Street to Henley talking inanely about the weather and the citizenry of Stratford.

Judith and Hamnet welcomed their good friend, and William introduced them to Russell Northcut. "Master Northcutt is a member of Lord Strange's Men," William said proudly.

"This is a pleasure," gushed Judith. "I will fetch both of you a fresh bun and some cool cider." She nudged Hamnet to join her in her errand as he was standing stock still staring at Russell Northcutt.

"Don't get any ideas about stealing this fine man from us, Northcutt. William is a Stratford boy, born and bred, and he is our playwright." Hamnet sneered.

"Hamnet! What has gotten into you? William has brought this man here as a friend, and you act like he is a French interloper. Where are your manners?" Judith scolded. To Russell Northcutt Judith added, "He's a strange man, my Hamnet, but he is a fierce friend. Just relax and enjoy your talk with William. I will be right back with the best buns in the shire."

After Judith and Hamnet had retreated to the back of the bakery, William began to tell Russell Northcutt the indecision he felt about allowing Lord Strange's Men to perform *Henry VI*. "I am deeply flattered that you are interested in my play, and it is my dream to see it performed by a company of your fine reputation, but I am not yet ready to let it go. If I could come to London and help prepare the company for the spring tour, I would do so, but my wife is pregnant, and I have a year-old daughter to consider. I'm afraid the timing is not right, but I hope you won't forget me."

Russell smiled at William and said, "I won't forget you. I doubt that anyone who has heard your words on stage can forget you. We will be here next year, and the offer will still be in place."

William was astounded by Russell Northcutt's kind words. "Do you really think my writing has promise?"

"I do indeed, and I have been in theatre for ten years. Your plays will leave a mark on our profession, believe me. Do you write anything besides plays?"

"I have several sonnets which please me, and I am working on a long poem, "Venus and Adonis," but it needs much refinement. I spend most of my free time working on *Henry VI Part II*."

"If you are not ready to let your plays fall into the hands of other playwrights and stage managers, might I suggest that you focus on your poetry for now? London publishes poetry, and you could read the proofs before the printing, so you could be assured every word was the way you wanted it to be. Also, wealthy noble men sometimes offer patronage to poets."

"What is patronage?" William questioned.

"Patrons pay the price of publication and often give artists a monetary amount so talented writers can afford to live and spend all of their time on their craft. Now you must spend many hours of the day tutoring your students so you can put food on your family's table. A patron makes it possible for artists to be artists, not tutors or clerks. Lord Strange's Men exists because of the patronage of Ferdinando Stanley, the Fifth Earl of Derby. The Derbys are a powerful and wealthy family in Lancashire who support the arts."

"Do you think I could find a patron?" William asked eagerly.

Russell Northcutt laughed, "Not in Stratford-upon-Avon, but if your poetry is as good as I suspect it is, you could find a patron in London."

Judith delivered warm buns dripping with butter and honey to the two men. "I made Hamnet stay in the back, so he wouldn't make a fool of himself again," Judith confided.

William yelled, "Hamnet, come out here. It is safe. Master Northcutt has agreed not to kidnap me and take me to London. All teasing aside, William had to admit to himself that going to London and having a patron pay all his bills seemed very appealing.

Chapter 15

William, encouraged by Russell Northcutt's praise and advice, attacked his writing with renewed vigor. He spent hours developing "Venus and Adonis." He felt it had promise, but his heart was in his plays. When he was exhausted and could no longer work on the long poem, he would turn to *King Henry VI Part II* and his energy would return. William chastised himself, "I could sell 'Venus and Adonis' and increase our budget, but I spend more time on a play that I am not willing to sell. What is wrong with me?"

Fortunately, the little family of three was getting along just fine. The bees in Anne's skeps produced record honey that summer, and Anne and Sarah prepared large crocks of the sweet concoction which William sold by the ladle at the market. Sarah and Anne also made beeswax candles which not only kept William writing well into darkness, but also allowed them to market the extras. Stratford was a village where everyone was suffering from the same economic condition, so a system of bartering and exchange helped everyone survive. Sometimes William's tutoring fees were payed in linen and fresh produce. Anne, with her stepmother Joan's help, enjoyed turning the linen into clothes and bonnets for Susanna.

William and Anne were very grateful to have family and friends close to them. The security of having those who loved them near gave them both peace of mind. Though William continued to dream of staging his plays in London, the thought of being alone in the big city with everyone he loved a hundred miles away was frightening. He knew it would happen one day, but he couldn't fathom how he would accomplish this massive feat.

Early in September, Anne and William walked into Stratford with little Susanna ambling along between them. Susanna's little legs soon wore out, and William scooped her up on his shoulders for a ride the rest of the way to the village. They had promised John and Mary Shakespeare some time with their granddaughter. Once they greeted the Shakespeares and Grandmother Mary gathered Susanna to her for a hug, William and Anne crossed the street to their good friends, the Sadlers.

Judith let out a squeal when Anne and William walked through the door to the bakery. "Anne, you didn't tell me you were with child!" she scolded.

Anne laughed and hugged her friend, "I'm glad to see you too, Judith."

"Judith is a little ditzy these days," Hamnet said with a wink.

Anne stepped back from Judith and gave her an appraising look, "Are you going to have a baby?"

Judith just smiled shyly, but Hamnet said proudly, "We have a bun in the oven!"

The three friends groaned at Hamnet's pun and then exchanged hugs all around.

"Will your little one be here by Christmas, Anne?" Judith asked.

Anne laughed, "I look big enough to have a baby in four months, but this child shouldn't arrive until the end of February. When will your little darling appear?"

"I'm due around that time as well, but I am not even showing yet. Are you sure you have the date correct?"

"I'm not sure of anything," Anne confessed, "but Sarah Spencer is very wise, and she calculated the end of February."

"How wonderful! Our children can be best friends just like we are!" Judith gushed.

"Let's make a pact," Hamnet said slyly.

"What?" William asked skeptically. "If you want to trade children at their birth because your child comes out looking too much like you and not enough like Judith, no deal!"

Hamnet laughed and said, "No, no. I have nothing that drastic in mind. Let's agree that you will name your baby either Hamnet or Judith depending on whether you have a boy or a girl, and we will name our baby either William or Anne."

Anne clapped her hands and said, "What a wonderful idea! We worried so much about Susanna's name. We have too much family and too many family names to honor, so we chose a name that no one on either side of our families had used for two generations. We love both you and your names! What do you think, William?"

"Hamnet Shakespeare. It has a good ring to it," William declared.

"William Sadler!" declared Hamnet. "I like it."

"You men are both ridiculous," said Judith, "because I am carrying Anne Sadler, and I can tell by looking at Anne that she is going to have a very healthy Judith Shakespeare!"

The friends enjoyed each other's company and Hamnet's sweet music before crossing the street to William's childhood home. They were delighted to see John Shakespeare watching Susanna chase William's little brothers, four-year-old Edmund and ten-year-old Richard around the rose garden behind the stately house. Mary Shakespeare was busying herself preparing a simple meal. When Anne asked if she could help, she was shocked to see tears in her normally unemotional mother-in-law's eyes.

"What's the matter, Mary? What has happened?" Anne asked with concern.

113

"It's nothing, Anne. Just the memories. I have such memories of the three daughters I lost. A mother never really recovers from losing a child, Anne. I'm just happy that Susanna is healthy! Look at you. It looks like you are carrying another very healthy baby!"

Anne gave Mary a warm hug as Mary quickly recovered her emotions, "Set the pewter out Anne and for goodness sake, get out of my way so I can finish this meal."

William rarely talked about his siblings. Anne knew that Mary and John Shakespeare had lost two daughters to the plague before William was born. William was their first child to live past two years of age. His eight-year-old sister, Anne, died when William was fifteen. Anne only knew about William's deceased sisters when he confided that he was worried about Susanna. He simply said, "Little girls struggle to live in this world, Anne."

Anne knew how blessed they were to have such a healthy little girl, and she said a silent prayer for the child within her. "Grow strong, little stranger. I can't bear to lose you."

William did have one living sister, Joan, who was five years younger than he. Joan was a serious young woman who Mary Shakespeare was grooming to be a successful businessman's wife. Joan was now fifteen and was being courted by William Hart, a local haberdasher. William and Anne rarely saw her.

William had three younger brothers, but he was not close to any of them. Gilbert was only two years younger than William, but he was aloof and hard to know. Anne had tried to start conversations with the young man, but Gilbert always seemed bored and eventually just walked away from her. Richard was ten years old, and little Edmund, the youngest Shakespeare boy, was only four. To William, the little boys were simply noisy distractions when he was living in Henley Street trying to write!

When they first started dating, Anne was concerned about William's detachment from his family. She couldn't understand how William could be so warm and interested in her half siblings and so disinterested in his own brothers. As Anne got to know her in-laws, she began to understand William's family dynamics. Though Mary Shakespeare clearly loved her children, she was not a demonstrative woman, and she did not encourage emotional attachments within the family. The loss of her three daughters left a scar not only on her, but on the entire Shakespeare family. Anne gained new respect for her stepmother Joan and the warm environment she created at Shottery. A mother had a profound influence in the home, and Anne was determined to provide a secure, loving place that her children and husband would never forsake.

Chapter 16

As winter came to Warwickshire, the Shakespeare family enjoyed quiet times by the fireside. William read from his latest manuscript, and Anne gave him honest critical comments. She had to admit that she liked *Henry VI* much better than "Venus and Adonis."

"Is it because you recognize yourself in Venus, my temptress?" William teased Anne.

"Me the temptress!" Anne responded. "Was I the one that chased you all over Stratford trying to capture your attention? Is that what you remember of our courtship?"

"Though I may have pursued you, Anne dear, you tempted me with your charm and put me under a spell from which I could not escape. I must admit that "Venus and Adonis" may have some echoes of our great love, but I have been inspired more by Ovid's *Metamorphoses.*"

"I think our love story would make a delightful play, Will. Why must everything you write be about history or Ovid?"

"I promise when I have finished *Henry VI* and "Venus and Adonis," I will write a play about us. I even have the perfect title," William said with a smile.

"What?" Anne asked.

"*The Taming of the Shrew!*"

William ducked as Anne threw her mending at him. "You artless beef-witted dewberry! *The Catching of an Angel* is a more appropriate title."

Susanna laughed to see her parents playing and threw her doll at both of them as they embraced.

"My your belly is tight, Anne!" William said as he backed from their embrace and placed his hand on Anne's expanding stomach. It's not yet Christmas, and you seem almost as big as you were with Susanna when you had her."

"Thank you very much, dear husband! Every wife wants to hear how big her stomach has grown."

"Anne, you know what I mean. I just worry about you. Are you sure the baby is not due until the end of February?"

"This baby is much different from Susanna. I think I am carrying an over-active little boy. He kicks me in three places at once and seems to be doing cartwheels inside of me. Sarah thinks I am bigger than last time because my muscles were still stretched from Susanna when I became pregnant again."

By the time Christmas arrived, everyone was noticing how large Anne was. She was extremely uncomfortable and could barely get out of the bed in the morning without William's help. She couldn't bend over to pick up Susanna and had a hard time walking farther than the Spencers' cottage. Thus, they had a much quieter Christmas in 1585 than they had the year before. William picked the Yule log by himself, and Susanna and Anne decorated it. They had their families at the little cottage, but Anne did not venture to Stratford or Shottery for any holiday parties. Thankfully, Judith Sadler was still quite mobile despite her pregnancy, and she and Hamnet came several times during the twelve days of Christmas to celebrate with them.

Anne's sister Jo, a grown up nineteen-year-old young woman made a special trip to visit William and Anne and announce her happy news. "I will be marrying Angus Macleod in January, and we will leave immediately for Edinburgh. I'm so sorry I won't see the baby before I go, but I can come back to Stratford when Angus makes his sales trips here. We will live in his house above the mercer's shop on High Street in Edinburgh. I am very happy!"

"What wonderful news, Jo! You will have all the pretty dresses you want," Anne laughed. "But I am too far along with this baby to come to your wedding. I'm so sorry."

"It is all right Anne. We want a very small service with Mother and Bartholomew as our witnesses. We love each other; I have found love and beautiful dresses!" Jo laughed and embraced her older sister.

January was a miserable month. It was frigidly cold, windy, and snowy. Anne, William, and Susanna stayed inside by the hearth. William continued to work on *Henry VI Part Two* with *Henry VI Part Three* already percolating in his head which Anne said was not fair as he had promised to start their love story next.

One day towards the middle of the month, they heard a timid knock on the door, and when William opened it, Beatrice Larrington Cole stood outside the door shaking and nearly frozen with cold. "Beatrice, quickly come in by the fire," William said as he put his arm around the young woman's waist and guided her to the hearth. Anne was shocked to see her friend. She had not heard from Beatrice since her wedding day when Anne had waved goodbye. Beatrice could not read or write, so no letters had passed between the friends.

Anne removed Beatrice's wet scarf, shawl, and mittens and began rubbing her friend's hands, gently at first and then with increasing speed to get the blood flowing. She encouraged Beatrice to sit on a low stool by the fire while she removed her soaked boots and soppy socks and started rubbing her feet the way she had her hands. Finally, Beatrice was warm enough to find her voice, "Thank you, Anne. I just needed someone to talk to, and I didn't remember your cottage being so far. I guess it was too far to walk in the cold."

"No, no, Beatrice we are glad you are here. Can you feel your fingers and toes now?"

"Yes," Beatrice cringed, "I feel like someone is sticking me with pins and needles. I was better off not feeling them."

Anne laughed in relief, "It is much better that you can feel them, Beatrice! Tell me what you are doing back in Warwickshire. Is Mr. Cole here as well?"

"Mr. Cole is dead," Beatrice said with no feeling.

William and Anne were shocked and William blurted, "Did you kill him?"

"Will!" Anne scolded.

However, William's outlandish accusation drew a big smile from Beatrice.

"No," she sighed. "He had the good sense to walk out in front of a heavy wagon pulled by runaway horses. They say he didn't suffer which was a blessing. I tried to be sad when he died, but I think I just felt relief. I could have had a worse marriage. He didn't beat me; he just ignored me until he was hungry for food or pleasure. It would have been nice to have someone to talk to."

"Oh, Beatrice," Anne held her friend, "I am so sorry."

"It's okay, Anne. I'm just not sure what to do now. Mr. Cole's parents asked me to leave after the funeral. I was confused at first. I thought they just meant leave the church, but they told me to pack anything I had brought with me to Cambridge and leave everything else in our house on Windsor Street. They had arranged transport for me the next day back to my farm. I got here yesterday, and my mother and brothers and sisters were happy to see me, but my father was angry.

Father said, 'If you were any kind of woman, you would have had Mr. Cole's baby by now, and the family would have had to keep you. What am I to do with you now? You are damaged goods, and I won't find anyone to marry you.'"

William and Anne embraced Beatrice and let her cry the tears she had been holding inside since her return to Warwickshire. When she had recovered enough, Anne offered Beatrice warm cider and said, "Well, William and I are delighted to see you, and Susanna has given you her stamp of approval!"

Susanna had crawled up on Beatrice's lap after William and Anne broke from their embrace with her. Susanna snuggled her check into Beatrice's chest and put her little arms around her. The heat from the toddler warmed Beatrice physically, and the unconditional love she felt from Susanna warmed her emotionally. She was glad she had endured the cold to be where she was loved.

Beatrice enjoyed talking with the Shakespeares and was delighted to see that Anne was with child. She wanted to hear about everything she had missed while in Cambridge. "The biggest news is that a London theatre company wants to buy Will's play," Anne declared proudly.

Beatrice said, "Oh my goodness. That is wonderful news."

"He decided not to sell it yet," Anne continued. "He has bigger things planned."

"Oh, good," Beatrice said rather confused. She looked at William and said, "Have you decided to be a full-time teacher? You are so good with the boys. My brothers' friends all want to learn from you."

William turned red and said, "Thank you for the compliment Beatrice. I am not going to be a full-time teacher. Anne is just teasing me because she doesn't think I know what I want!"

"That's not true," Anne quickly interjected, but she knew she shouldn't have said what she did to Beatrice.

The Shakespeares asked Beatrice to stay the night as the sun had gone down, and it was even colder outside than when Beatrice had arrived. Susanna clapped her hands and led

Beatrice to the little trundle bed which was nestled under William and Anne's bed. "Sleep with Susanna," she invited Beatrice.

"We can make a bed for you by the hearth if you would rather," Anne quickly said.

"No, I would much rather cuddle with Susanna tonight if that is okay with you!"

William pulled the trundle from under the bed and soon the four friends settled down for the night. In the morning, William walked with Beatrice to the Larrington farm and then on to Shottery to visit the Hathaways and let them know that the family was doing fine. Joan insisted on giving William a large hamper of food which he tried to refuse but was very happy to take back to Anne and Susanna.

Anne thanked William for his kindness to Beatrice, "I don't know what I would do if I couldn't talk to you Will. I am so grateful to have you as my very own, and I love you very much."

William knew that Anne was afraid he was mad at her for her comment to Beatrice about not selling *Henry VI*, but he didn't want to discuss his decision, a decision he had struggled so mightily to make which well could have been the wrong decision. He simply hugged Anne and said, "I love you too, my beautiful shrew!"

Anne playfully hit William on the shoulder and said, "Did I hear you say, 'my beautiful angel?' Or are you a villainous milk-livered pigeon-egg?"

Chapter 17

On the morning of January 23rd, Anne awoke with excruciating pain coursing through her body. She screamed, and William was instantly awake and holding her. "What is it Anne?" William asked fearfully.

"I think the baby is coming, but it isn't time. It's too soon Will!"

"Try to breathe, Anne. Sarah says only babies know when it is time for them to come."

Anne tried to relax, but it was no use. She recognized labor this time, and she knew her baby was coming whether it was time or not. "Go and tell Sarah," she moaned.

William hurriedly dressed and rushed out in the snow to the Spencer's cottage. Fortunately, the Spencers were early risers, and they were both sitting by the hearth when William rushed in without knocking. They jumped to their feet when they saw the expression on William's face.

"What is it, William?" Richard asked.

"It's Anne. She thinks the baby is coming. She needs Sarah."

Sarah was already putting her heavy shawl around her shoulders before William could finish. "Stay here Richard," she said as she ushered William ahead of her out the door.

Anne's water had burst, and she was in full labor by the time William and Sarah got to her. Susanna was holding her mother's hand and crying, "Mommy, mommy."

"Bundle Susanna up and take her to Richard," Sarah ordered, "then ride Barbery to the Bates's house. Hurry, William."

After William had left the cottage with Susanna, Sarah asked Anne, "Are you feeling the need to push, dear?"

"Not yet," Anne gasped, "but it is so much faster than with Susanna, and it's too soon. What has gone wrong, Sarah?"

"We don't know that anything is wrong, child. We all noticed how big you were. Maybe we just miscalculated," Sarah soothed, but she knew that something was wrong indeed. The sheets under Anne were soaked with blood.

Sarah wiped Anne's brow, encouraged her to breathe, boiled water, and gathered the clean linen Anne had ready for the new baby. William had not yet returned with Claire Bates when Anne started pushing, and Sarah knew she was going to have to deliver Anne's baby by herself without the help of the midwife.

"That's it, Anne. You are doing fine. Keep pushing. I see a fine head of hair."

Anne pushed with all her might and delivered a tiny baby boy into Sarah's waiting hands. He started to scream immediately as Sarah wrapped him tightly and prepared to cut the umbilical cord. "You have a beautiful baby boy, Anne."

Anne could not understand what was happening to her. She saw the tiny baby in Sarah's arms, but she was still wracked with pain and felt she had not yet given birth. Claire Bates ran into the room, washed her hands in the water Sarah had prepared, and hurried to Anne's side.

"You've done me work, Sarah. William Shakespeare nearly killt me on that wild horseback ride and bless my soul if you even need me. Has the afterbirth come yet?" Claire asked as she placed her hand on Anne's stomach.

"No," Sarah answered, "and Anne seems to be in distress. I don't know what is wrong."

"We best check," said Claire as she pressed harder on Anne's stomach, manipulating her fingers across Anne's body. "Dearie, is you a feelin' contractions?"

"Yes," Anne whimpered.

Claire looked at Sarah and winked, "I didn't risk me life for nothin'. We have yet another baby to deliver, and we best hurry. Put that wee one in the bed next to Anne for warmth and come rub Anne's stomach like I was a doin'. Can you feel that mass? Work the stubborn child down with your hands while I reach inside."

The pain was so intense, Anne barely remained conscious when Claire reached up inside of her to help her second baby enter this world. The tiny baby was trapped in Anne's uterus which had turned inside out and been delivered with the baby. Claire quickly freed the baby by turning the uterus right side out and then she attempted to replace the womb in Anne. There was too much blood and replacing the uterus did not stop its flow. "Sop the linen in boiling water, wring it as best you can and bring it to me now, Sarah."

Sarah did as she was told, and Claire handed her the tiny baby in exchange for the hot compacted linen. She pressed it between Anne's legs and applied pressure. She used the sharp knife she had used to cut the umbilical cords to cut the now useless uterus from Anne's body.

"Bless me, you've a girl to join that wee lad in your arms," Claire said shakily to prevent Anne from becoming further alarmed at what was happening to her.

Anne held her baby boy to her chest and muttered a silent prayer that all would be well before she passed out.

Claire and Sarah worked furiously to warm the tiny baby girl and clear her lungs. Finally, their work was rewarded by a tiny squeak from the little blue creature. They continued to rub and clean her until she turned pink and gave a healthy cry.

Sarah was alarmed that Anne was not responsive and had lost a tremendous amount of blood, but Claire checked for a pulse and said, "Anne'll do. It's best she can't see what we have to clean up here, Sarah. The poor girl has two fine babes, but I'm afraid they're the last she'll e'er have. The uterus came with the wee girl, and I couldn't save it."

Sarah was shocked at Claire's revelation and had no idea how she would tell William and Anne the sad news. She busied herself washing the twins in warm water and dressing them in fresh linen gowns, so she could present them both to their mother. Anne soon stirred, and Sarah went directly to her side, placing a baby in each of her arms, and congratulating Anne on her wonderful blessing.

Anne was still groggy as she looked in amazement from one baby to the next. "Oh my. Oh my goodness. Look how handsome Hamnet is and how beautiful Judith is."

"You have names already, dear?" Sarah asked.

"Yes! We promised the Sadlers and now Judith has to have William and Anne. Where's Will?"

"He will be right here Anne. You want to be beautiful when you show him your twins. Let me help you, won't you."

Claire had been applying warm compresses to Anne to stop the bleeding and to her relief, she had eased the flow so Anne was out of danger of further hemorrhaging. It was safe for Anne to scoot up in the bed, so they could remove the linen. They didn't want William to faint from the sight of the blood that Anne had lost. Anne was so enchanted by her two new little charges that she noticed nothing else in the room. Sarah held the babies, and Claire helped Anne sit upright in bed. Claire gave Anne a pewter mug of milk and encouraged her to drink it all. "You need some nourishment after all your hard work," Claire declared and she watched carefully that Anne drank the full mug.

Helen E. Burton

Once the bed was clean with fresh linen, Claire and Sarah gave Anne a soothing sponge bath and placed a clean linen gown on her. Sarah brushed Anne's lovely auburn hair while Claire prepared the twins to meet their father. Once Anne was arranged in bed with a child in each arm, Claire went to the Spencer's to tell William and Richard it was okay for them to come to the cottage.

William nearly knocked Claire over as he rushed out the door and ran to his little cottage. He was panicked because it had been hours since he had gone to get Claire Bates, and unlike when Susanna was born and he heard her cry right way, he had heard nothing but Anne's screams for the first few hours and then nothing but silence for what seemed like additional hours. Was Anne okay?

He was astonished when he walked from the ice and snow of the wintery outside into the warmth of his tidy little cottage and saw his beautiful Anne sitting up in bed with not one baby, but two babies in her arms.

He rushed to her side, "Anne, sweet, sweet Anne. What have you done?"

"Meet Hamnet," Anne said as she nodded to her right arm. "And this sweet little girl is Judith," she said as she nodded to her left arm.

"They are so tiny! Claire, will they be okay? Is Anne okay?" William asked in fright.

"Everything is fine, William," Sarah lied. She knew there would be a better time to tell the young couple that these were the last babies they would ever have.

Richard entered the cottage with Susanna in his arms, and he was as shocked as William had been to see not one, but two babies in Anne's arms. "Susanna, it looks like you have two new strangers to play with!"

Susanna clapped her hands and ran to her mother's side, "Pretty babies! One for Susanna! One for mommy."

Everyone laughed and Anne assured Susanna that they would all share both babies. Sarah asked William to take Claire home, but Claire quickly said, "I'll be a goin' on me own two feet. Thank you. I will ne'r get on a horse with crazy William again."

The Spencers and Shakespeares laughed and thanked Claire Bates before she bundled up and headed out into the cold. Anne could barely keep her eyes open after the trauma of the birth, and Sarah was still worried about the amount of blood she had lost, so Sarah said, "William and Richard, could you take little Susanna back to our cottage. Anne and I have to get these babies used to nursing before Anne goes fast asleep."

The men knew better than to argue with Sarah, and William scooped Susanna into his arms, wrapped her in a blanket, pulled his own heavy coat tightly around him and followed Richard out of his cottage with a sense of both wonder and dread in his heart. How would he provide for a family of five?

With much encouragement from Sarah, Anne was able to manipulate the tiny babies at her breasts and soon, both babies were contentedly sucking their first important nourishment from their adoring mother. Sarah looked around the tiny cottage at the roaring fire on the hearth with a boiling pot of soiled linen hanging from the hearthside hook. A rope extending the width of the room in front of the hearth and acting as a clothesline was already sagging from the weight of the linen Sarah and Claire had washed. Sarah sighed and wondered how Anne would be able to keep two babies clean and dry. She would be washing and drying linen day and night.

When Anne could no longer stay awake and the babies were content, Sarah tucked them into the waiting cradle, kissed Anne on the forehead, and went to fetch William and Susanna.

"William, these two little ones are going to be more than Anne can handle on her own. Are you willing to change and wash nappies?"

William was taken back, but he knew that keeping Susanna cleansed and fed had taken all of Anne's attention the first month or two. "I will have to learn," William said hesitantly.

When William and Susanna entered the warm little cottage, all was quiet. Anne, Hamnet, and Judith were sound asleep. The peaceful setting gave William a false sense of confidence, and he thought, "I can do this."

Susanna went straight to the cradle holding the twins and began to rock it roughly. Hamnet stayed asleep, but Judith woke and started screaming. Her screaming awakened Hamnet, and he joined her in screaming at the top of his little lungs. William gently scolded Susanna for disturbing the babies, and she began to wail. The chorus of cries woke Anne who felt like she had just fallen asleep. "What happened?" she asked groggily.

William picked Judith up carefully and placed her in Anne's arms. Then he returned to the cradle and gathered his son in his arms and began gently talking to him. He hugged Susanna close and said, "You have to be gentle with your brother and sister, Susanna. They are so little and new, they are frightened when the cradle rocks so fast. You can't remember when you were their size, but you were the same way. You loved it when I rocked the cradle very gently. You only started liking me to rock the cradle fast when you got older and were a big girl.

William's quiet voice calmed Susanna, and she stopped sobbing and admired her little brother in her father's arms. She caressed Hamnet's cheek gently and said, "Sorry b'other. Love you."

When William turned to Anne to see if she had heard Susanna's sweet words, Anne and Judith were both sleeping soundly. William rocked Hamnet gently in his arms until he closed his little eyes, and William thought it was safe to place him back in the cradle. He continued to talk to Susanna and explained that she could help with Hamnet if she just barely rocked the cradle, and Susanna did just as he asked. "You are such a good big sister, Susanna. I think you have rocked Hamnet back to sleep."

Susanna grinned at her father and said, "I'm hungry."

William looked to the hearth where Anne nearly always had porridge or stew steaming, but all he saw was boiling linen and hanging nappies. Obviously, Anne had not done her usual morning baking. William went to the larder and found a leftover corn muffin which he drenched in honey for Susanna. He wondered if Anne would feel well enough to cook in the morning.

William soon realized that *time was out of joint* in his household. There was no real morning, afternoon, or night. There was only crying hungry babies and crying wet babies constantly. The twins wanted to eat and sleep at different times, so Anne was always nursing one or the other. She was so sleep deprived that William was worried he would lose her.

Thankfully, Anne's stepmother Joan and little sister, Margaret came by the first afternoon with a basket of food, and Joan spooned broth into Anne and encouraged her to drink as much milk as she could. When Joan returned home, twelve-year-old Margaret stayed to help with the babies. She was wonderful at playing with Susanna and rocking the twins, but she was almost as bad at cooking and washing as William was.

When the twins were two days old, Sarah Spencer brought the family dinner and checked to see that they were doing okay. William, Margaret, and Susanna sat down and began to devour Sarah's wonderful cooking. Sarah laughed, "Are we short a cook in this household?"

"Yes!" everyone including Anne answered with laughter.

Sarah examined the nappies William had washed and hung in front of the fire to dry. "Did you wash these, William?"

"Yes," William answered proudly.

"I don't wish to insult you, William, but these nappies look freshly soiled, not freshly washed. How exactly are you washing them?"

"I put them in the large pot, add some lye soap, and pour boiling water on them. I stir them around a bit with the long handled wooden spoon and pull them out, wring them, and hang them on the line to dry."

"William, sad to say, the handle of the wooden spoon is not doing the job your two hands must do. First, you must remove as much of the solid waste as you can from the nappy. Just scrape it into the chamber pot. Then you must put your hands into the hot water, rub the nappies with the soap, and rub the material together to remove any remaining soil. After you have cleaned them as much as you can, you must then rinse them with clear water to remove any trace of the harsh soap which can give the twins a bad rash."

William listened incredulously to Sarah's detailed instructions. How could the simple act of washing out a nappy be so nasty and time-consuming? "I will spend my entire day washing nappies. All the twins do all day is mess them."

Sarah laughed, "It's true. That and eating is their only job for now."

William was a fantastic father, a loving, supportive husband, and a halfway decent laundry man, but he was a dismal failure at cooking. He burned the porridge, made biscuits as hard as rocks, and had no idea what even went into a stew. Thankfully, his parents came to visit when the twins were four days old and just as Joan had, they brought a basket of food. They raved about how beautiful the twins were, suggested that John and Mary were much more suitable names, and urged them to have the twins christened the following Sunday on February 2, 1585.

Judith and Hamnet Sadler's visit when the twins were a week old was the most pleasant visit of all. Not only did they bring fresh bread and buns and a crock of Judith's rabbit stew, but they also brought fun conversation and songs to the little cottage. Hamnet thought his little namesake was the spitting image of him, which thankfully was not true. The twins both favored their father as much as Susanna favored her mother. They had dark hair and eyes and fair complexions. Thus Judith did look like her namesake which pleased the baker's wife very much.

"Now Judith," William declared, "we are counting on you to have twins so do not disappoint us."

Judith looked around the tiny cottage at the hanging linen and boiling pots of soiled nappies and said, "I think I will take them one at a time, thank you!"

When the twins were eleven days old, on February 2nd, John Shakespeare drove a borrowed team of Morgan horses and a large sleigh to Wilmcote. Anne, William, Margaret, and the children cuddled under quilts and rugs for the ride to Trinity Church for the christening. There the little Shakespeare twins officially became Hamnet and Judith Shakespeare much to their paternal grandparents disappointment. Fortunately, the twins were so beautiful, and Susanna was so loving to her grandparents that they soon forgot to be mad and enjoyed the christening party after the service. The Hathaways, Spencers, Sadlers, and Beatrice Cole all convened at the Shakespeare home on Henley Street for food and story telling. Anne was presented with the gift of extra nappies from her stepmother (a gift for which William cheered), matching quilts from the Shakespeares, delicate rattles from the Sadlers, and two silver spoons from the Spencers. Unbeknownst to Anne, Beatrice's gift--the best gift possible-- would come later.

Soon it was time for the little family to return to Wilmcote, and John Shakespeare insisted that it was too cold for Richard and Sarah Spencer to walk back to Wilmcote, and they should join them in the sled. Of course, that was the right thing to do, but William had not told his father about the surprise he had arranged for Anne. Margaret Hathaway had done her best to help her sister Anne with the babies, but the work of cooking and cleaning was too much to expect from such a young girl. She was going home to Shottery with her mother, Joan, and Beatrice Cole was coming home with William and Anne.

When Beatrice came out of the Shakespeare house with a small valise, she had to sit on Richard Spencer's lap, but they all fit! Anne was surprised but happy to see that Beatrice was joining them.

William said, "Tell Anne what your christening gift is, Beatrice."

Beatrice took Anne's hand and said, "If you will have me, I would like to come and stay with you to cook and clean and help with the babies."

Anne hugged Beatrice and exclaimed, "Beatrice, you have saved my life!"

"Has it really been that hard caring for the twins?" Beatrice asked with concern.

"No, it is exhausting keeping these two fed," Anne gestured to the babies in her arms, "but it is also a delight. No, it is Will's cooking that might kill me," she laughed, and the whole sleigh full of friends joined in her merriment.

Beatrice was the perfect addition to the young Shakespeare family. She was a wonderful cook, anticipated Anne's needs, and most importantly to William, she could scrub and wash nappies twice as clean in half the time as he could! William wasn't sure how they had survived the first eleven days of the twins existence without her. He felt guilty that they had no money to pay Beatrice, but she said she was just happy to be living where she was loved and needed.

The entire family did love and need Beatrice, but she was one more person for William to feed. Having her at the cottage meant that he could resume his tutoring and even do some writing, though the twins usually interrupted any lucid thought he managed to form. William felt more love and happiness in his life that winter than he ever had before, but he also felt more pressure and stress. He was only twenty years old, and he was responsible to feed, clothe, and house six people.

Chapter 18

On April 19 just four days before William Shakespeare's twenty-first birthday, Judith Sadler had a baby boy, and true to their word, Hamnet and Judith named him William. He had dark hair which stuck out in all directions, plump cheeks, and his father's mighty lungs. His screams could be heard at the top of Henley Street! Though Anne was confined to Wilmcote with the twins and would have to wait to meet baby William, she asked Will to tell Judith that she forgave her for not having twins.

"Anne said to tell you she is glad to wait two years for you to have baby Anne. Having one baby at a time is the best way to keep a mother sane."

April not only brought a new baby boy for the Sadlers but also melted the snow and ushered in spring. The first day that Anne was able to leave the cottage and go for a short walk in her beloved woods seemed like a rebirth to her. The twins were completely dependent upon her, and she could never be far from them. Though she loved them with all of her might, she needed some space for herself. Fortunately, both William and Beatrice understood this, and they encouraged her to take advantage of the sun and the sleeping twins to leave the cottage.

As Anne walked, she allowed herself to think about her precious family. She had felt prepared to have a second baby. She had learned so much from Susanna, both what to do and what not to do. However, she wasn't prepared to have two new babies at once. She had to admit that she was struggling to keep up. She was always tired. She was worried that her milk would dry up. If her milk dried up, she would have yet another baby, and then she would go completely crazy. Then she thought she wouldn't have another baby because with

Beatrice and Susanna in the trundle bed right next to her and Will, they would never be intimate again and so she would never have another baby which was what she wanted but not really what she wanted. The more she walked, the more confusing her inner monologue became until Anne feared she had already gone crazy and couldn't recognize it. That made perfect sense to her. Crazy people probably never know they are crazy.

Crazy or not, she loved the fresh air in the woods. The song birds greeted her, and the squirrels dashed up the trees ahead of her. The first wild flowers of spring were beginning to bloom, and she stooped and picked a purple pasque. Soon her thoughts were quieted. She breathed the crisp air and hugged herself. She was so happy to be alive, to have three healthy children, to be married to William Shakespeare. Yes, she probably was crazy, but craziness made her very happy.

When she returned from her walk, it was back to the routine of nursing the babies, helping Beatrice with the laundry, and playing with Susanna. William helped as much as he could, but Anne and Beatrice both knew it was better for him to be earning money than trying to cook and clean. Fortunately, he was a wonderful father, and he occupied Susanna, so the women could get their work done.

Not long after Anne returned from her walk, Sarah Spencer knocked lightly on the door, and William opened the door wide, inviting her in. "I saw Anne out walking, and it made me happy to see her up and around. I thought I would come and visit for a spell. I wonder, Beatrice, could you take Susanna for a little walk while we talk?"

"Sure," Beatrice answered eagerly, "Susanna and I love to listen to the birdies, right Susanna?"

"Birds," said Susanna pointing to the door.

When Beatrice and Susanna were gone, William turned to Sarah, "What's wrong, Sarah? Is it Richard? Is he ill? Why do you need to speak to us alone?"

"It's not Richard, dear. I'm afraid it's sad news for you that I have to share. I should have told you right away, but Anne was so fragile, and the babies were so tiny and well, I just didn't know how to tell you, so I didn't."

"You didn't tell us what?" Anne asked.

"Dear," Sarah said gently, "you are not going to have any more babies.

"Sure I am. I mean I am really tired now, and the twins have made me a little crazy, and we have no privacy here, but Will and I will have more children."

"No," Sarah shook her head sadly. "You are unable to have children because Judith was not moving down the birth canal properly, and you were too exhausted from birthing Hamnet to push. To save Judith, Claire Bates had to take her quickly, and your womb came with her. Claire worked furiously to clean Judith's lungs, so she could live, and we rubbed her pink. Then Claire had to stench your bleeding, or we would have lost you. Your uterus is gone, Anne."

William and Anne listened in disbelief to Sarah, and when she finished, they both remained silent.

"I'm so sorry. I didn't want to tell you, but I knew I had to. Please believe me that Claire Bates and I did everything we could, but it was a very difficult delivery. Please say something. I feel horrible about this."

Anne fell into William's arms and sobbed. "Sarah," William finally said. "Anne and I need some time to absorb this news."

"I understand," Sarah said and she quickly left the cottage.

William held Anne, stroked her hair, and whispered, "It's all right, Anne. We are fine. We have two beautiful daughters and a handsome son. Our family is complete."

"This is all my fault," Anne gasped. "When I was walking in the woods, I was thinking about how I couldn't maintain my wits with the twins, and God heard me and now we can't have anymore sweet babies."

"That makes no sense Anne. You didn't cause anything, *there's a Divinity that shapes our ends, Rough-hew them how we will* (Hamlet, 5.2). If our thoughts could command the fates, I could well have brought this upon us as I have been struggling with the responsibility of caring for our family. I don't know whether I can earn enough to care for the five of us. Any more children might force us to move in with my parents on Henley Street."

Anne quickly inhaled her breath, "Don't even think such things, Will. I mean, I love your parents . . ."

William patted Anne's back and said, "I love my parents too, and I couldn't wait to move out and be here with you."

The couple held each other close until they both determined their fate must be accepted. "We can move forward from this tragedy, Anne, or we can let it define us. What do you want for the future?"

"I want to raise Susanna, Hamnet, and Judith in a healthy home with parents who love each other."

"That is my wish as well," William said. "Now, someone who loves us very much is feeling responsible for something for which she had no control. We need to ease Sarah's mind."

Sweet Hamnet and Judith slept through their parents' emotional loss, but as if on cue, they both awakened and demanded their parents' attention. William scooped up Judith and started to change her nappy while Anne did the same with Hamnet. Though William was not good at washing nappies, he was excellent at fastening fresh ones on his wiggling little girl.

With the babies in their arms, William and Anne walked to the Spencers' cottage and knocked. Sarah answered the knock, her eyes red from crying. The couple embraced her and William told her, "We love you so, and we are sorry that it fell to you to deliver our sad news. Anne and I will continue to mourn the loss of our unborn children and wonder what might have been, but we choose to focus on those in our lives who we love: the babies in our arms, sweet Susanna, you and Richard, and our families. We have been blessed a thousand fold. Please don't cry, Sarah. If not for you, we would not be together."

After many tears and embraces, Anne and William left the Spencers and called toward the woods for Beatrice and Susanna. "Come home, come home! It's time for cider and honey cakes!" The secret to immediate obedience from their toddler was the mention of honey cakes.

Anne and William knew there would be days ahead when they would feel great sorrow for the children they would never have. They knew it was okay to be sad, and they also knew that it was all right to be a little relieved they didn't have to worry about having more mouths to feed. When William thought about his mother and the three children she had lost to illness, he knew there was something worse than not having more children. Mary Shakespeare had five living children, but William wondered if she enjoyed any of them. Losing his sisters, Joan, Margaret, and Anne, blanketed Mary Shakespeare with a profound sadness which manifest itself as coldness.

Anne focused on her three children, and she rejoiced each time she lifted the twins and felt them getting heavier. Hamnet was still bigger than Judith, but she was gaining weight quickly, and William thought she might weigh as much an Hamnet soon. Susanna was the best big sister the twins could have. She brought clean nappies when they needed changing, rocked the cradle gently when they needed to nap, and tick- led their toes and played peek-a-boo with them when they needed attention. Susanna decided before her second birthday that nappies were for babies and chamber pots were for grown up girls. Anne and Beatrice rejoiced in having less linen to scrub and fewer nappies to change. Life was good.

Part Two

Chapter 19
Five years later, 1590

When Anne and William were struggling to keep their wits about them as they cared for two infants who never slept, they had many well-meaning friends tell them, "Enjoy them while they are young. Those days go by so rapidly." They rolled their eyes at each other and laughed because that was all they had energy to do!

Now they realized that those friends had been correct. Susanna was now seven years old, the picture of her mother with long, wavy auburn hair and sparkling green eyes. She was a little mother to the five-year-old twins and spent hours entertaining them. Hamnet was strikingly like his father with raven black hair and deep brown eyes that flashed with mischief. Judith was a petite brunette with a pleasing personality. She was happy to have Susanna and Hamnet plan the activities of the day, and she played whatever part assigned to her in their make-believe world. All three children were extremely creative, and William and Anne loved listening to their schemes and watching the little plays they acted out.

Hamnet and Judith Sadler's five-year-old William had been joined by a sister, Anne, now three, and a baby brother, Henry, who was just three months old. When the Sadlers and Shakespeares got together with their six children it was indeed a riotous experience!

The five years between 1585 and 1590 were full of growth for the Shakespeare family and their friends, but the years were also marked by loss. In the spring of 1588, Richard Spencer died of consumption leaving Sarah alone in the cottage. Her daughter, Betsy, in Oxford wanted Sarah to come and live with her, but Sarah loved Wilmcote, and the Shakespeare children were like her own dear grandchildren, so she stayed. The Shakespeare's also lost Beatrice, but this was a happy loss as Beatrice remarried in June of 1589. This marriage was not arranged but rather a marriage of mutual love and attraction. Beatrice's new husband, Howard Martin, was a former student of William's who she met through the Shakespeares. Beatrice came to realize after living with Anne and William and witnessing the love and respect they showed each other, that good marriages existed, and when she met Howard, they clicked immediately. To her delight, she was expecting her first child. Evidently, it was Mr. Cole that could not produce children, not Beatrice.

The Shakespeare children had grown considerably; however, the little cottage had not. Two five year olds and a seven year old took up every inch of space, so though the family felt great sorrow when Beatrice moved into Stratford with Howard, they also gained a bit of living space. Beatrice must have been in heaven to no longer share her bed with three wiggling children. She had never complained to Anne or William about her cramped condition and loved the children unconditionally.

As the children grew more independent, Anne was again able to weave skeps for the market to help with expenses. William was a hands-on father and helpmate to Anne in caring for the children, but he continued his tutoring and had as many students as he had hours in the day. He had finished *Henry VI Part Two* and had fallen into the routine of having the boys present two scenes a month at the Thursday market. Staging and directing the scenes helped him make improvements to the script, and he felt he was writing more efficiently with each effort. He didn't want to anger Anne, but he was working on *Henry VI Part Three* instead of their love story, and he was making great progress.

The first week of June, Lord Strange's Men arrived in Stratford for their week of performances. It had been five years since Russell Northcutt first asked William if he would allow the company to perform *Henry VI*, and he had asked him every year since, but this year circumstances were different. Russell heard that William was at the Sadlers' bakery, and he hurried there to meet him. Russell started to shout to William, but he saw that he was gently rocking a baby in his arms, and the fat baker was singing a sweet lullaby. The expressions on the men's faces let Russell know that if he woke the baby there would be hell to pay. He was an actor, however, and he knew how to deliver his lines in a lilting, soothing manner which wouldn't wake the child. When the baker reached the end of his refrain, Russell Northcutt took up the melody thus, "Two of our actors got into a skirmish in Kenilworth, and one of them killed the other. Now we are looking for a quick study to take his place for the rest of the tour. We can pay you 30 pounds for acting, and we will increase the payment for the use of your plays to two schillings a performance."

Hamnet stopped strumming and stared at Northcutt. William was so jolted by this news that he nearly dropped baby Henry. Judith came from the back of the bakery with a look of astonishment on her face and took the baby from William.

"It's your line, Shakespeare," Northcutt exclaimed. "Say something."

"I accept," William said tentatively looking across the table at his friend Hamnet.

"I know I told you before that you couldn't leave Stratford, William, but Stratford is too small to contain your ideas and your words. You have too many children to feed to turn down the fortune this crazy man is offering you," Hamnet said softly.

Strange but true, William Shakespeare's career on the stage began because of a tavern brawl. If Henry Adams hadn't drunk too much ale and insulted George Reynolds' afternoon performance at Kenilworth Castle, and if George Reynolds hadn't overreacted by pulling a knife on Henry Adams, and if Henry Adams hadn't been the best swordsman in the company and easily turned the knife on George Reynolds and unintentionally stabbed his friend and fellow actor to death, William Shakespeare would not have joined Lord Strange's Men in June 1590.

Now William had to explain and justify his acceptance to his dear wife, Anne. He hoped he wouldn't be stabbed in the process. The money would be his main argument because it was the money that made William decide he could not turn down Russell Northcutt's offer. The actor had made the deal even sweeter by saying William could have ten pounds up front to help provide for his family while he was gone. Hamnet told William that a fine house on Chapel Street was for lease and with ten pounds, William could pay for six months rent and have plenty of money left for the family's expenses.

William practiced his speech to Anne as he walked toward Wilmcote. "Think how fine it will be for you to live in Stratford. You can go to the market whenever you want. You can even bring the children; it is such a short and pleasant walk. You are isolated at Wilmcote. You have Sarah, but you can't go anywhere because of the children. In Stratford, you will be close to the Sadlers, and you and Judith can see each other every day if you want. You will also be close to my parents if you need help with anything. It would also be a shorter walk to Hewlands farm to visit your family," William felt good about his speech so far.

"The house is beautiful and has three rooms. We will have our own room and privacy when I am home from the tour. The children will share a room, and we will have enough money to buy a table large enough to seat all of us." William realized the reason his argument was going so well was because he was engaged in a great monologue. Once Anne added her lines, things would not go nearly as smoothly. As he contemplated her opposition, he grew agitated and shouted to the roadway and the birds in the trees, "I am your husband, and you will do as I say!" This rant was barely out of his mouth, when he looked around guiltily and hoped no one had heard him. He knew this was not the tactic to take with independent Anne.

In the end, Anne was not impressed by the money or the house, but she was impressed with her husband's passionate plea. "Will, it would be wrong for me to deny you this opportunity. My focus is one hundred percent on the children right now and though it is exhausting and some days I don't think I can go on, I love what I am doing. I know that all the hours I put into our children will come back to me twelve fold as I watch them grow into independent, happy adults. They are my passion right now, and I have been feeling guilty that my role as mother has overshadowed my role as wife. You have been here for me through the twins difficult early years, and you sacrificed your writing. You have been a patient and loving husband, and you don't seem to resent me or the children. You are the best father any child could ask for. But if I deny you the opportunity to follow your passion in life, your writing and the theatre, you will soon resent me and the children. That can't happen, so how do we make your career on the stage and our marriage both work?"

That was it. From that moment forward, they worked as a team to decide how they would care for their relationship though they would be far apart geographically. The physical move from Wilmcote to Stratford was easily accomplished with the help of Bartholomew Hathaway and a heavy team and wagon. The Shakespeares had very few material goods, their wedding bed which had been the Hathaways, the trundle, the cradle, three stools, a chair, and a rough hewn table. Anne packed their few household goods, the linen, cooking pots, mugs, and clothes which joined her and the children in the second wagon load to Stratford. With sad hugs and many thanks to Sarah, the Shakespeare's left the little cottage where they had spent the first seven happy years of their lives together.

Though Anne had shown little interest in the house in Stratford when William described it to her, she couldn't help but be impressed when Bartholomew brought the wagon to a stop at the front door. It was a one story plaster and beam house with an arched front door and two large windows, one on each side of the door. Rose bushes in full bloom lined the stone walkway to the door. The main room was twice the size of the cottage in Wilmcote with room for a large table. The two bedrooms to the left of the main room were good sized and each had a small window to let in light. The garden was large and planted with flowers. The patch for a vegetable garden lay dormant and unplanted, and Anne could feel her hands itching to get into the soil and make things grow. She envisioned two skeps of honey bees at the rear of the yard under the apple trees.

Susanna, Hamnet, and Judith were running around the yard exploring with their uncles, Edmond and Richard Shakespeare, who had come to welcome Anne and William to Stratford. Anne saw what an advantage it would be for the children to have family nearby, something they did not have in Wilmcote.

Anne happily arranged the children's toys and clothes and found a place for William's ink and quills. She loved the large room which had a counter running across the back wall. There was room to store the family's cookware and linen. She would be able to watch the children play in the garden while she prepared meals.

Hamnet and Judith Sadler arrived with the children, and after hugs all around, Anne took Henry into her arms. "He is perfect! He is just beautiful," Anne said. "He is growing so quickly." Little Anne and William Sadler hurried out to the garden to join the other children. Anne turned to look at Judith and Hamnet, and she knew William was right; it would be wonderful to be in town with Judith and Hamnet close.

While Anne and the children were settling into their new home on Chapel Street, William was absorbed in learning lines and stage directions for Lord Strange's Men. Fortunately, the seven remaining players in the company doubled on George Reynold's major parts, and they assigned William minor parts, so he could start out slowly. Russell Northcutt wanted William to help the company put up *Henry VI* immediately, and William would have large roles in that production as he clearly knew all the lines. Within the first few days with the company, William Shakespeare had a positive feeling about his abilities as both an actor and a playwright. Though he had allowed his students to play all roles in the productions in Stratford, William had often modeled the roles for the young boys, so they could see what the character's body language and inflection should be as the lines were delivered. This experience made it easy for William to transition to the stage. The difficult part about performing the parts he was assigned was not in his inability to create the character but rather in the poor quality of the writing. William had been amazed at Russell Northcutt's desire to produce *Henry VI* when he had only seen school boys perform the scenes, but now that William was working directly with the scripts from other playwrights, he realized his writing was good, very good. The rhythm he created with his iambic pentameter lines was easy to memorize and flowed from an actor's lips smoothly. The lines he had to memorize for the other plays the company was performing were choppy, inconsistent, and often nonsensical.

As a repertory company, Lord Strange's Men were accustomed to keeping five plays in their heads as they performed a different play each afternoon on five consecutive days in each village. William found memorizing the lines from five different plays, written in varying styles very difficult. Perhaps it was because he had so many of his own lines floating in his head. Despite his discomfort, William did a tolerable job in his first performances with Lord Strange's Men. His biggest challenge would be Tuesday afternoon.

William Shakespeare paced by the platform as a large crowd gathered to watch *Henry VI*. His stomach rumbled and his nerves twitched as he anticipated the first professional performance of his play. He took deep breaths to calm himself. The rehearsals had gone well. Lord Strange's Men were pleased with the scripts he had presented them, and they took his stage directions well. Some of the actors had suggestions for changes, and William listened patiently to each revision, accepting some and rejecting others. Overall, the players praised William for his writing style, and their respect for him as an actor and playwright was exhibited in the serious manner in which they prepared for the performance.

William caught a glimpse of Anne standing with Beatrice and Howard Martin. Judith Sadler had offered to stay with the children on Chapel Street, so Anne could watch the play with no distractions. He also saw his parents and brother Richard standing proudly near the platform. Hamnet was just finishing the last strains of his entree music and the play was about to begin.

The next two hours flew by and soon the players were in Act five, Scene five, and William Shakespeare in the role of the Earl of Suffolk was heaping praise upon young King Henry's marriage to fair Margaret:

> *A dower, my lords! disgrace not so your king,*
> *That he should be so abject, base, and poor,*
> *To choose for wealth and not for perfect love,*
> *Henry is able to enrich his queen,*
> *And not to seek a queen to make him rich:*
> *So worthless peasants bargain for their wives,*
> *As market-men for oxen, sheep, or horse.*
> *Marriage is a matter of more worth*
> *Than to be dealt in by attorneyship:*
> *Not whom we will, but whom his Grace affects,*
> *Must be companion of his nuptial bed;*
> *And therefore, lords, since he affects her most*
> *It most of all these reasons bindeth us,*
> *In our opinions she should be preferr'd.*
> *For what is wedlock forced, but a hell,*
> *An age of discord and continual strife?*
> *Whereas the contrary bringeth bliss,*
> *And is a pattern of celestial peace* (Henry VI, 5.5).

Anne glanced at Beatrice as William delivered these lines, and she saw tears flowing down the young woman's face. Anne choked back her own tears as she thought about her love for William. As she looked around the crowded street, she saw all eyes on William, in rapt attention. They had been standing in the sun for two hours, and yet, William's words mesmerized them.

Suffolk's last speech, the final speech of the play was both masterful in revealing Suffolk's duplicity and skillful in making the audience want more:

> *Thus Suffolk hath prevail'd; and thus he goes,*
> *'As did the youthful Paris once to Greece;*
> *With hope to find the like event in love,*
> *But prosper better than the Trojan did.*
> *Margaret shall now be queen, and rule the king'*
> *But I will rule both her, the king, and realm*
> (Henry VI,5.5).

Anne understood why William had started writing *Henry VI Part Two* so soon after completing *Henry VI.* So much was left to be said about young King Henry. Would Suffolk succeed in his plots against the King? Would his marriage with Margaret be good for Henry and the country? William had brought the King to life on stage. The audience was allowed inside their former King's heart and mind, and they longed to hear more. Though the crowd remained silent after William Shakespeare concluded his first performance, they soon erupted in shouts of "huzzah," and thunderous applause. William Shakespeare would not be viewed in the same way ever again in Stratford-upon-Avon. Even his home town skeptics could sense Shakespeare's great talent.

The beauty of William beginning his official career in Stratford-upon-Avon was that each evening after morning rehearsals and afternoon productions, William returned to his new little home on Chapel Street and was surrounded by the simple life he loved. He played with the twins and Susanna in the garden, and he tucked them into bed and told them stories until they drifted to sleep. Best of all, he joined Anne in their wedding bed, in their own room, with no trundle bed next to them. They whispered sweet nothings into each other's ears, cuddled together, and enjoyed the pleasures of their love for one another.

Though the production of *Henry VI,* marked the beginning of William Shakespeare's career, it also marked the end of the company's stay in Stratford. Lord Strange's Men had productions scheduled in Worcester the following week and from there, they would work their way to Birmingham, Coventry, Leicester, Peterborough, Cambridge, Northampton, Bedford, and Oxford edging their way back toward London.

William had to say goodbye to the only place he had ever known and a hundred times worse, he had to say goodbye to his beloved Anne, Susanna, Hamnet, and Judith. One at a time, William held each of his children on his lap and talked to them. "Susanna, I will be home soon to read to you and play hide and seek. Can you be your mother's helper and look after Hamnet and Judith while I am gone? Will you listen to your mother and practice your alphabet letters, so you can read to me when I return?"

"Yes, father. I will be good, but I will miss you terribly. If you write me letters, I will learn to read them. Will you?" Susanna implored.

"Oh my little sweetheart. You are so like your mother. Yes, I will write you letters, and your mother will help you read them! I love you more than my words can say." William said as he pressed his sweet daughter's head to his breast.

Judith was next to crawl on her father's lap, and she was already crying. "I can't bear to have you gone, father."

William hugged her to him and said, "Judith, my darling girl. You have an important assignment while I am away. You must help Hamnet stay out of mischief. Can you do that?"

Judith looked at her father and said very seriously, "That is a big job for a little girl, father. Can Susanna help?"

William laughed and said, "Yes, your big sister will help you with everything that you need. Just remember how much I love you!" He squeezed Judith tightly to him and inhaled the sweet scent of his precious baby girl.

William had to go to the garden to find his son Hamnet who was idly tossing stones at one of the apple trees. William gathered pebbles in his hand and joined his son. "What are we aiming at?" he asked.

"The dried up apple way towards the top of the tree," Hamnet responded.

"Have you hit it yet?"

"No, father."

William hurled one of his pebbles toward the apple, but he was wide to the right. "Your turn, Hamnet."

Five-year-old Hamnet threw with all his strength, but his stone fell well beneath the target.

After several attempts by both of the Shakespeares to hit the apple, William crouched by Hamnet, placing his hands on the boy's shoulders and turning him toward him. "Hamnet, let's make a plan," William said gently. When he saw that he had the boy's attention, he continued, "While I am gone, I want you to continue practicing your throwing, and I will do the same while I am traveling between the villages where I have to perform. When I get home, we will see if we are any better at hitting our mark. Is that okay?"

Hamnet just nodded his head and didn't look at his father. "I am going to miss you just as much as you will miss me, Hamnet." He took his only son into his arms and let the tears that had been building in his eyes flow down his cheeks. Hamnet, who had been crying, realized that he didn't have to pretend to be strong. He knew he was safe in his father's arms.

Anne and William had spent most of the evening before his departure talking about the logistics of their separation. They rejoiced in the knowledge that the Royal Mail system would link them. The post riders used fresh horses every ten miles and could cover the distance from London in two days. Most of William's letters would come from locations closer to Stratford, and Anne and William could communicate almost daily while he was on tour. Lord Strange's Men would be on the road until the end of August and then William would return to Stratford for a month before rehearsals for the next season started in October in London.

Their last night together before William left was filled with passion, tears, and laughter. Though it was breaking their hearts to be apart, they knew it was the best decision for the health of the family. They both understood the paradox that William needed to leave the family to preserve the family; he needed to follow his dream and become an actor and playwright or he would never be able to be the father and husband he wanted to be. They were confident that the love they had for each other would carry them through the challenges that lay ahead.

Chapter 20

Anne and the children watched as long as they could to see William riding along with Lord Strange's Men, their wagon loaded down with costumes, props, and the portable platform. The departing players created quite a sight in Stratford, and young boys and their dogs ran along beside them as they left the town. Anne sighed heavily and turned back to the little house on Chapel Street to face her new life without William. She controlled her emotions, so she wouldn't break down in tears and frighten the children. She gained strength from the thought that she had the easier task to face; she was in familiar surroundings with her children and friends near her. William was entering a completely new environment with no friends or family to support him. She must be strong for him.

William looked back frequently and waved to his little family as he rode out of Stratford toward the biggest adventure of his life. Fear tempted him to turn Barbary around and gallop back to the security of all he knew and loved, but hope and ambition drove him forward and helped him leave Stratford behind. Most of the actors he rode with lived much different lives than he. Russell Northcutt, Henry Adams, and Richard Clark did not have wives and appeared to be married to their craft. Simon Morris, Robert Andrews, and David Thomas attested to being married, but they did not seem like married men in the evenings after rehearsal, and William did not like the way the men looked at Anne when he introduced her to them. William knew the final member of the company only as Rat. He had never heard him called anything else, and though he did move a bit like a rodent, he seemed pleasant enough. As interesting as Lord Strange's Men were, they could never replace his sweet family, and William knew that the three months before his return to Stratford would be long indeed.

On the ride to Worcester, William's mind darted from enjoying the countryside, to pondering what Anne and the children were doing, to reciting his lines for the five plays they would perform. He couldn't contain the excitement he felt about his new life. When doubts crept in, he replayed Stratford's applause at the end of *Henry VI*.

In the late afternoon, just outside Worcester, Russell Northcutt rode up next to William and said, "I've decided we will open with *Henry VI* this week. If I am correct in my judgment, it will help draw large crowds for the rest of our performances."

"Are you sure? No one knows anything about the play or the playwright," William said with some embarrassment. He was worried that *Henry VI*'s success in Stratford was due more to it playing in his home town rather than to it being an entertaining production.

"I've invested £30 in you, young man. It is time for me to find out if I am a fool." Russell Northcutt spurred his horse forward and joined Henry Adams at the front of the procession of players.

William broke out in a cold sweat. What would he tell Anne if he was sent home after the first village on the tour? He spent the rest of the ride into Worcester staging and re-staging *Henry VI* in his mind's eye. He did not discover any flaws that he had not already corrected with his young lads and with Lord Strange's Men in Stratford. He just needed to have faith the play would speak for itself.

The players reached Worcester in early evening and stabled their horses at the Boar's Head. For an extra schilling, the stable boy said he would watch the wagon, so they didn't have to unload the platform, props, and costumes until morning. William was exhausted as he was not used to riding Barbary such a long distance. The twenty-five miles Lord Strange's Men had traveled to Worcester though taken at a leisurely pace had worn him out. His legs felt like jelly when he climbed off Barbary, and he was happy to give both Barbary and himself a rest from riding for the next five days.

The Boar's Head was a popular pub in Worcester with lodging up narrow stairs above the bar. The actors would be crowded four to a room, but it was better than camping out under the stars. William was used to sleeping in crowded conditions, but he had never done so with relative strangers. Everything about being a part of a touring company of actors was new to him, exciting and frightening at the same time.

After the actors had groomed their horses and washed up using a bucket of water provided by the stable boy, they sat at a long, broad-board table and drank ale. The cool liquid soothed William's throat and washed down much of the dust he had swallowed on the long ride.

A plump maid with rosy cheeks and blonde wiry hair brought a tray of cheese and bread which the hungry men soon devoured. The maid then delivered a tray of meats and fruit which was set upon by the actors as though it would sprout legs and run off if they didn't grab it immediately. William was slow to react and by the time he reached the tray, a brown apple and the butt end of a sausage were all that was left. Rat laughed and said, "You best be quicker than that Shakespeare or your first tour will be your last! You'll be mere bones by the time we reach Oxford."

William hoped Rat's words weren't prophetic. Not that he thought he would starve. He had learned his lesson and would fall on the meat much sooner the next evening. William was worried that this would be his last tour because

Northcutt was counting on *Henry VI* to draw a crowd. What if it didn't?

William slept fitfully, tossing, turning, and trying to block out the loud snoring coming from his fellow actors who had consumed three times the ale he had. He arose early and went down to the darkened pub, lit a candle, and wrote his first letter to Susanna.

Dear Susanna,
When daisies pied and violets blue,
And lady-smocks all silver-white
And cuckoo-buds of yellow hue
Do paint the meadows with delight,
The cuckoo then, on every tree,
Sings "Cuckoo! cuckoo!"
(Love's Labour's Lost, 5.2).

William knew it was a silly rhyme, but he knew Susanna could sound out the words, and Anne could help her learn the ones she didn't yet know. Besides, it briefly took his mind off the afternoon performance of *Henry VI.*

Lord Strange's Men were an established, successful acting company, and they moved like a well-oiled machine to prepare for their productions in Worcester. Northcutt, Adams, Clark, and Shakespeare constructed the platform. Thomas and Morris arranged the costumes and props. Rat and Andrews canvased the entire town with flyers while shouting, "Join us at two o'clock for the amazing theatrical perfor-mance of *King Henry VI.*"

The men were ready for their performance by noon and returned to the Boar's Head for a lunch of cheese, pickles, and bread. The actors were in high spirits as they always were before the opening of a play, and there was much laugh-ter and teasing. William sat quietly as though he was deaf to the cacophony surrounding him. Russell Northcutt stood with his pewter mug in hand and said, "A toast. A toast to William Shakespeare, the newest member of Lord Strange's Men. May his time with us be long and prosperous."

"Here, here!" the men shouted and raised their mugs.

William tentatively raised his mug, nodded to his fellow players, and clinked his mug against each of theirs, looking into each man's eyes and hoping it wouldn't be the last time they toasted him.

Chapter 21

The post rider delivered William's first letter to Chapel Street three days after William's departure from Stratford. By then, Anne was sick with worry as she thought she would hear from him sooner. She kept telling herself that he had a full day of travel to Worcester, and he would be busy setting up for the performances the next day, so really she wouldn't hear from him until today, but she couldn't stop herself from watching for a rider to stop at her door.

When the letter arrived, she was in the garden tending to the poppies she had planted to attract bees for her skeps. She heard a shout and hurried to the street with the three children trailing after her.

"It's from your father!" Anne said with excitement in her voice.

"That's for me!" Susanna shouted. "Father promised he would write me."

"I think it is for all of us, Susanna. Let's go back to the garden and sit in the shade of the apple tree to read it."

Once the children were comfortably seated around Anne, she let Hamnet carefully break the seal, and Judith gently unfolded the seven by nine inch parchment paper. To Susanna's delight, a small carefully folded paper with her name on it fell from the bigger letter.

"I told you father wrote me," Susanna said as she carefully unfolded the note which was shaped like its own envelope. She started to sound out the words she knew, "Father knows I can read my name, 'Susanna,' and the names of the colors 'blue,' 'white,' and 'yellow.' "

"Very good, sweetheart," Anne hugged Susanna close and read the entire verse to her, helping Susanna with the new words it contained. After only three readings, Susanna could read the verse to Hamnet and Judith! Anne wasn't sure whether Susanna was reading or whether she had memorized the easy verse, but either way pleased her greatly.

"Susanna, why don't you get the slates, and you children can draw a picture of the cuckoo. When you have each decided on your best picture, I will give you a piece of brown paper so you can draw your pictures on it, and we will send it to your father."

The children were delighted by their mother's suggestion and scurried to the house to get their slates and chalk. Anne turned to William's letter:

To the celestial and my soul's idol, Anne *the most beautified* (Hamlet, 2.2). When I awaken in the morning, I reach for you. But alas, I am alone in a narrow cot with three snoring men for company rather than my sweet Anne. I think of you constantly and miss you each moment of the day. When I sit at the table to break bread, I have to fight my fellow actors for each crumb. I think of your sweet honey cakes made just for me. . . and Susanna, Hamnet, and Judith, but I can fight them off easier than I can Northcutt, Adams, and Rat.

As I fall to sleep at night, I try to picture you tucking the children into their little trundle bed and reading to them from Aesop's Fables. Perhaps you could read them this letter tonight. I hope Susanna liked her verse and will share it with Hamnet and Judith.

My heart aches so to be there with you and the children, Anne, but today an amazing thing happened. Russell Northcutt decided that we would alter the order of our performances and present *Henry VI* first. I was taken back and thought my time with the company might be over if it was not successful, but Anne dear, the crowds cheered and cheered. We returned to the stage and presented Act 5, Scene 5 again and yet they still cheered. After the crowd had dispersed, several men of the company came to me and congratulated me and slapped me on the back. Then Russell Northcutt said, "Get the scripts ready for *King Henry VI Part Two.* We will rehearse in Birmingham and add it to the tour in Coventry to replace Lyly's *Mother Bombie.* I guess you are worth more than thirty pounds. You'll get your two schillings for each performance of *Part Two* at the end of the season."

He shook my hand and walked away. Anne, I couldn't contain my joy, and as soon as I could break away from the company, I found a quiet table at the back of the Boar's Head where I am now, writing you this wonderful news! You are the only person I want to be with right now.

Doubt thou the stars are fire,/ Doubt that the sun doth move,/Doubt truth to be a liar,/But never doubt I love (Hamlet, 2.2).

Forever yours, William

Anne wiped the tears from her eyes and reread William's letter. The suffering of being apart was worth it. William's plays were a success! She was so proud of him, her heart was bursting. She left the garden and went to the house in search of the children. They were happily creating their Cuckoo bird pictures, and she decided she would save William's letter to read to them at bedtime.

Reading William's letters as a bedtime treat became a ritual in the little house on Chapel Street. The children loved feeling close to their father before they fell asleep, and though they missed him horribly, even at their young ages, they seemed to grasp how important their father's work was to him and to them. Anne kept every letter from William in a carved wooden box her father had given her when she was just a young girl. Anne found Susanna a similar box at the market, and Susanna loved putting her father's verses and stories into it for safe keeping.

William treasured the drawings he received from his three children, and they motivated him to create verses with vivid images to give the children ideas for their drawings. Though he loved all the children's artwork, it was clear that Judith was the artist in the family. Her animals were captured perfectly, and William realized his quiet daughter was busy observing the world around her.

William spent as much time as he could away from the commotion of Lord Strange's Men. He retired early to his room in the inn while the others remained in the pub drinking and carousing late into the night. He spent his solitary time writing, but he also spent hours thinking about his family. The twins fascinated him. Hamnet and Judith had totally unique personalities, but their physical features and move-ments were nearly identical. They walked the same, gestured the same, and sat cross legged the same. When Hamnet's and Judith's black hair grew longer and fell to their shoulders, William and Anne realized that walking behind their twins, they could not tell them apart. Anne joked, "We are going to have to put Hamnet in britches early or those two will be trading places with each other and tricking us! That would be more fun in one of your plays than it would be in our own household."

Susanna had none of the same physicality as the twins; she had a distinct walk that resembled Anne's but was defi-nitely her own. The twins had connections beyond their physical sameness. One day Judith was sitting at the table drawing, and she jumped up and ran toward the garden shouting, "Hamnet needs us." Neither Anne nor William had heard a peep from the backyard, but they followed Judith out of the cottage only to see Hamnet sprawled beneath the apple tree. He had taken a bad fall, but once they brushed him off and examined him, they were happy to discover he had not broken any bones. His bruises, however, would be large and painful for a few days.

"Thanks for coming and finding me, Judith," Hamnet said seriously after his parents had assured him he would be okay.

Judith just nodded shyly and took Hamnet's hand as they walked towards the house.

"Judith," Anne asked, "did you hear Hamnet fall from the tree?"

"No, I just heard him calling me," Judith answered.

Anne and William looked at each other. They had been as close to the garden door as Judith had been, but they had not heard anything.

"Hamnet called to you?" William asked.

"Yes, I heard him in my head," Judith answered nonchalantly.

After that day, William and Anne began to take note of the twins ability to anticipate each other's needs. Hamnet would pass the chalk to Judith without her asking for it. Judith would get both children's sweaters while Hamnet went to fetch the little bow and arrows William had given them. It was not unusual for children to do things for each other, but the twins never had to say, "Let's go outside and shoot arrows." They just knew instinctively what they were going to do.

Though William missed his family desperately and day-dreamed about them, he also used his longing for family in his writing. He was making great progress on the comedy, *Taming of the Shrew* which he hoped Anne would find as humorous as he did. Russell Northcutt was pushing William to produce a comedy of the same quality as his historical plays about Henry, and William thought *Taming of the Shrew* would fit very nicely into their repertoire.

Birmingham, the second stop on William's acting debut, was a larger town, and Lord Strange's Men were given four rooms at the Fox and Hare. They were still small rooms at the top of the Inn with low ceilings, but William only had to share with Rat who stayed out most of the night anyway, so William completed the scripts for *King Henry VI Part Two* very quickly.

The company spent two to three hours each morning staging and rehearsing *Henry VI Part Two,* and William was pleased with its progression. Suggestions from Lord Strange's Men strengthened the flow of the play, and William was happy his fellow players recognized its strengths and weaknesses. The respect the professional players showed him helped boost his confidence. At times, William feared that having only his Stratford schooling left him at a disadvantage to the university trained playwrights of the time. However, after only three weeks on the road with Lord Strange's Men, William realized he had chosen the perfect venue for his higher education. Working and living with a professional company of actors and being on the stage daily as an actor himself was the best education a playwright could have.

The crowds in Birmingham were large, and they cheered Lord Strange's afternoon performances. William was becoming more comfortable in his roles and was now enjoying being on the stage almost as much as he enjoyed being behind the scenes as the writer. It did seem to William that the crowds responded more boisterously to *King Henry VI* than to the other four plays the company presented, but it could have been his imagination. Also, he had noticed that the first performance in any town attracted the biggest audience, so he was very appreciative Russell Northcutt had given his play the honor of opening the week.

Soon it was time to move on to Coventry, and William's anxiety grew as he thought about *Henry VI Part Two* being performed for the first time in front of a paying audience. He was impressed by the approach to Coventry through the old stone gates of the city and even more impressed by how large the city was. His play would premier in front of a large audience.

When the company reached their lodgings at the Greyhound Inn, the innkeeper had a letter for William from Anne and the children. William tucked the letter into his sleeve and the knowledge that he would be able to spend a few quiet moments reading the letter and thinking about Stratford helped to calm his nerves. Caring for the horses and settling into their rooms at the back of the Greyhound seemed to take longer than usual, but finally, Lord Strange's Men finished their evening meal of pickled eggs and cheese, and William was able to sit at a quiet table in the pub and open Anne's letter. The children had sent pictures of Hoot Owl the latest character he had created for them. They made him smile. He set them aside and turned to Anne's letter.

My Dearest Will,

We miss you every day and every night and look for your letters to keep us close to you. I hope this letter finds you well in Coventry. You must not worry about *King Henry VI Part Two*. The audience will love it almost as much as I love you.

The children seem to grow taller every day, and
Hamnet is getting better at throwing stones, so you
need to be practicing your own throwing. Your verses
are increasing Susanna's reading vocabulary, and she
is sharing everything she learns with Judith and Hamnet. I think we should enroll Hamnet in the Stratford
Grammar School when you return to Stratford. He
needs discipline to focus on his studies and doesn't
enjoy it like Susanna and Judith. I had hoped the
school would be open to the girls by this time, but I
don't mind teaching them at home.

Sarah Spencer has moved to Oxford to live with
her daughter, and the family is leasing the farm at
Wilmcote to the neighbors, John and Norma Stone.
Sarah came to the cottage for cider and honey cakes
before she left, and it was very difficult to say goodbye. The children all cried, and Sarah and I joined
them. She is the sweetest woman, and I love her. Perhaps you can see her when you reach Oxford.

This seems like a long letter, so I should close. I
dreamt of you last night and when I awoke, I expected to find you next to me. I live for that day in September when you return to me.

With all my love, Anne

William read the letter twice and savored every word.
Just as he finished, Russell Northcutt pulled up a stool and
sat down at William's table. "I didn't mention something to
you before. Coventry has a large Guild Hall and the Council
decrees that all plays be performed in it rather than the open
air of the market place."

William couldn't believe what he was hearing. "But I've
never performed inside," he said in a panic.

"Don't worry about it, William. You will like it once you get used to it. You don't have to speak quite as loudly to be heard. The best thing about being inside is we can charge those who sit two pence, and we can still charge a penny each for the groundlings."

The calm that William had felt after reading Anne's letter and admiring the children's artwork was gone. Russell told William, "The Guild Hall is not far away. Let's walk over there. It looks as if you could use some fresh air."

They left the Greyhound and followed the cobble streets along the river until they rounded a bend, and William saw a large stone building ahead on the right. The building was massive and seeing it did nothing to calm his nerves.

Russell put his hand on William's shoulder and said, "William, I'm not going to say this again, so listen carefully. You're the best playwright I have ever had the pleasure to work with, and your acting is growing stronger with every performance. You need to relax and enjoy this moment. This is your time to shine."

William was stunned into silence. He respected Russell Northcutt more than any man he had ever worked with, and he looked to him as an example of what good actors could achieve. He was embarrassed as he realized Russell was so concerned about his new actor's nerves, he had been forced to say things he would not normally say. William knew he could not let Russell Northcutt or himself down. "Thank you, Russell. I understand, and you can count on me tomorrow."

****

The inside of the Guild Hall was even more imposing than the outside had been, and William had a hard time focusing on preparing the platform as he looked around at the elaborate carvings and inlaid wood. Beautiful tapestries hung on the walls and imposing six foot candlesticks stood at each side of the grand entrance.

While Lord Strange's Men were still putting the last touches on their costumes and make up, patrons began to enter the Guild Hall and take their seats. William learned that those who paid two pence not only got to sit, they were also allowed in before those who would be standing, so they didn't have to make their way through the crowd. By two o'clock, the entire hall was packed. William wasn't sure whether it was the biggest crowd he had ever seen or whether it was just that they were crammed close together rather than being spread out in the streets. The audience also seemed to be right on top of the platform, and William was afraid some of the rowdy ones in the front row might decide to join the actors on stage.

Before his entrance, he breathed deeply, thought of Anne and the children, remembered that Russell and the entire company were counting on him and delivered his opening line so loudly it echoed back to him and scared him. Thankfully, the other actors on stage carried on as though nothing unusual had happened, and William's next line was on time and at the correct volume. He soon found himself enjoying the performance and enjoying the fact that he could clearly see the audience's rapt attention.

When William delivered the final lines of *Henry VI*, no one applauded and a restless murmur went through the crowd. Russell Northcutt quickly stepped forward and said, "Thus ends *King Henry VI, Part One*. Tomorrow at two o'clock, Lord Strange's Men will present *King Henry VI, Part Two* by our own player and playwright, William Shakespeare." Russell motioned for William to step forward, and when he did, the audience erupted into applause. Those who were seated, stood; those who were standing shouted "Huzzah!"

William's exuberance could not be contained, and he could not stop talking as he and the rest of Lord Strange's Men walked back to the Greyhound Inn that night. The players were entertained by the usually quiet member of their troupe and joined with William in congratulating themselves on a very successful performance. Many toasts were made and much ale was consumed in the pub that night, and William stayed with the company longer than he had any other night of the tour. He did not attempt to keep up with the other men in the number of ales consumed, but he did participate in the witty conversations and barbs. He was able to laugh heartily when Rat said, "Mercy, Will, I thought you would blow the roof right off the Guild Hall with your excellent elocution in Act One!"

When William left for his room, he felt like a full member of Lord Strange's Company. Until now, he had felt like a temporary replacement. His journey with the acting company seemed ephemeral, like it could disappear in an instant. He finally felt like he was among friends and equals. He was an actor, an actor who wrote very good plays.

William slept well that night with no fears for the premiere of *Henry VI, Part Two.* He could hear his mother's voice in his head, "Of course it won't be perfect," and it didn't make him squirm, it made him smile. This was the opening of the play. He knew problems would arise, lines would be dropped, entrances would be missed, but he now knew he had seven men on stage with him who believed in him and his play. They would cover for each other. They would entertain the audience like the professionals they were.

Chapter 22

The first week in July of 1590 in Coventry changed William Shakespeare's life dramatically. *King Henry VI Part Two* was not presented flawlessly. William wasn't sure how to react when his character Suffolk sent assassins to kill Gloucester and the audience hissed and booed at him. Never had a play brought out such strong reactions from the crowd. The patrons cheered when Lord Clifford put down Cade's rebellion, and hissed when Margaret entered a scene. The actors had to wait several beats before delivering their lines to be heard.

King Henry VI Part Two had so many characters that each actor was playing four roles, and chaos ensued off stage as they hurried to drop swords and don the robes of their next character. The audience waited patiently for the next scene to begin and their boos were reserved for the action of the play, not for the actors themselves. At times, William felt discomfort as members of the audience seemed to be staring at him even when he wasn't delivering lines. At first, he backed upstage as he thought he was unintentionally taking the focus from the actor speaking, but that seemed to make no difference.

The audience roared their approval at the end of the play, and William silently thanked his young students for loving battles and encouraging him to include as many fight scenes as he could in his next play. Evidently, his students weren't the only ones who enjoyed clashes on stage! Lord Strange's Men were physically exhausted after the performance, but they were energized by the audience's response to their hard work.

The men gathered at the Greyhound for mugs of ale, and stories of the ups and downs of their first production of *King*

Henry VI, Part Two. Rat soon singled out William and said, "You young stallion."

"What?" William asked having no idea what Rat was implying.

"You saw those women staring at you. You couldn't miss it. I practically fell off the stage trying to get their attention when I was delivering my speech as Cade and still their eyes stayed on you, a soldier standing in the background."

William felt himself blush, and he started to deny what Rat had said, but Robert Andrews added, "You can have as many of those women as you want, William. You better get used to it."

"You are crazy!" William declared. "Those women don't even know me!"

"Ah but they think they do," David Thomas joined the conversation. "It is better they don't know you. They swoon for the man they think you are. It works every time!"

"A handsome fellow like you doesn't ever have to feel lonely on tour," Simon Morris quipped.

William had heard enough. "I am happily married. I love Anne!" William shouted.

Robert Andrews laughed, *"The man protests too much, me thinks!"* (Hamlet, 2.3).

The actors all burst into laughter, and William excused himself and left the table. He felt hot inside and out and left for a walk in the evening air. He tried to calm down. He wanted to be honest with himself, and honestly, it felt good to be admired. He was a healthy, twenty-six year old male. He had observed the cavalier attitude of the members of his company who entertained a different woman every night of the tour. He did not admire their behavior. He knew himself and he silently schooled himself, *"This above all: to thine*

own self be true, and it must follow, as the night the day,
Thou canst then be false to any man." (Hamlet, 1.3).

William Shakespeare vowed that night to never be false
to his dear Anne. She was home in Stratford devoting her entire life to their children. He could not live with himself if he
violated her trust. He now knew the enemy, and he would be
on guard.

William enjoyed the week in Coventry and had free time
some mornings to explore the city. He followed the founda-
tions of the old city walls to several of the city gates, each
with a unique design. He admired the Cathedral and walked
among the book stalls choosing an illustrated copy of Aesop's fable "The Lion and the Mouse" for the children. Often
on his ramblings, he would be recognized. "Aren't you the
famous actor?" a woman selling leeks shouted at him.
William just nodded and continued to walk. Being on the
stage was a very different life than he had envisioned, but he
was beginning to like it very much.

The two weeks in Leicester and Peterborough went by in
a flash, and Lord Strange's Men arrived in Cambridge.
William's senses were alive when he entered the city he
would have chosen for his higher education had the opportunity afforded itself. Cambridge was a hundred miles from
Stratford-upon-Avon and was the city William dreamt most
of visiting. The schoolmasters at William's Stratford school
had been educated at Oxford, and perhaps that is why
William dismissed Oxford and preferred Cambridge. However, William had another reason for admiring Cambridge:
Christopher Marlowe had graduated from the University of
Cambridge three years prior in 1587.

William knew when Russell Northcutt gave him high
praise in Coventry, Northcutt was careful to say, "You are the
best playwright I have ever worked with." Russell Northcutt

had never had the pleasure of working with Christopher Marlowe. William had seen Marlowe's *Dido, Queen of Carthage* and *Tamburlaine the Great* performed in Stratford, and thenceforth, Marlowe was his role model as a playwright. He was not, however, a role model for the life William wanted. Marlowe was reputed to be a drunkard, a liar, and a blasphemer.

Lord Strange's Men crossed the River Cam on the Clare Bridge and entered the city of Cambridge which contained one amazing building after another, many of which represented the different colleges of the University. The players were housed at The Eagle, a bustling inn and pub at the city center. As in Coventry, their plays would be performed inside in Cambridge. The Guild or Corn Market in Cambridge was larger than the Guild Hall of Coventry, and Russell Northcutt anticipated their largest crowd thus far on the tour. "Playing for these University folks will give us a better idea of how well your Henry plays will do in Oxford and London, Will," Russell said. "Don't worry, I expect we will be just fine. The play we cut from our repertoire was written by John Lyly, an Oxford man. I expect our Cambridge audience will prefer *Henry VI, Part Two* over his comedy."

The crowds were huge and the audience more sophisticated in Cambridge though the actors were still interrupted by boos and hisses for Margaret and Suffolk and cheers for Gloucester and Lord Clifford. The audience did not hesitate to applaud and cheer at the end of *Henry VI* as they knew from the criers and posters in the town that *Henry VI Part Two* would be performed the following night. It too was received with loud shouts and applause. William felt vindicated; his Stratford education had served him well in the famous university town!

William spent his free time in Cambridge wandering from one college to another. He was drawn to Christopher Marlowe's alma mater Corpus Christi College with St Benet's Church and its magnificent tower. As he stared at the Old Court, William could imagine Marlowe sitting at a table writing his verse. On another morning walk, William admired the Gothic arches in Christ's College. He was delighted that several young men, some who recognized him from the play the night before, stopped him in his wanderings and encouraged him to come to Cambridge to study. "I have found my college but thank you for your interest." Most of the young men took him at his word and hurried on about their way, but a grey haired man in the robes of a professor challenged him further, "What college is that young man?"

"I'm attending Lord Strange's College of Acting full time and writing at Low Ceiling University part time," William responded with a smirk on his face.

William and Anne continued to exchange letters, and Anne's newsy letters from Stratford kept him abreast of all the gossip in the town. Judith and Hamnet Sadler and their family spent a great deal of time with Anne and the children to help assuage her loneliness. Anne had even developed a closer understanding and friendship with Mary Shakespeare in William's absence. The children loved the book he had sent them from Coventry, but they all agreed that their father's stories were the best. Anne asked how "Capturing an Angel" was coming, and William responded that the shrew was almost tamed!

William sent detailed descriptions of all the places he visited and made special note of the sights he would show the children and Anne someday. Overall, William was enjoying every day of his new experience, but he knew he would never adjust to sleeping in crowded inns with snoring actors. He would chose Anne and all three children in the same bed with him in Stratford over the nicest inn in England!

The Company's stay in Northampton and Bedford were both successful and uneventful, and William had time to complete *Taming of the Shrew.* He found it comforting to write about Warwickshire and think about Anne as he had been away from his family now for over two months. *Taming of the Shrew* was markedly different from his historical plays, and when Russell Northcutt read it, he was delighted. "Your comedy is even better than your historical plays," he declared. "We will open this in London in the fall."

Oxford was the last city on the circuit and from there William would return to Stratford while the rest of the Company continued to London to their families and homes. William held Cambridge is such high esteem that he was amazed at how impressed he was with Oxford. Though Oxford was only fifty-two miles from Stratford, William had never had the opportunity to visit the city. The farthest he had traveled from Stratford before the tour was Kenilworth where his family had gone to see the pageantry of Queen Elizabeth's visit to Kenilworth Castle when William was only a boy of eleven. The castle seemed the most magnificent structure ever built to young William, and it still was at the top of his list. Now having seen the architecture of Coventry, Cambridge, and Oxford, he realized *there were more things in heaven and earth than he dreamt of in his philosophy* (Hamlet, 5.5).

Oxford was grand. The company stayed at the Bear Inn and once the minutia of stabling the horses and acquiring the rooms was accomplished, the men met in the pub for a hearty meal of bread, cheese, sausage, pickles, eggs, and ale. It was time for celebration! Lord Strange's tour had been extremely successful, and they had only five more performances before they would part company for a month.

A letter from Anne was waiting for William, and she reminded him that Sarah Spencer was now living in Oxford with her daughter, Betsy. The innkeeper at the Bear Inn gave William the best directions he could to the address Anne had sent, and William took an early morning walk to explore Oxford and find Sarah. He started down Carfax Street keeping his eye on the towers of Christ Church. He turned onto Cornmarket Street and then onto Broad Street which brought him to the Bodleian Library. It was closed, so he peered in the windows at the magnificent hall and the shelves of books. He would return another day to browse the books. He continued on and after asking for additional directions, he arrived at a pleasant Tudor style home and knocked.

A striking young woman with long brown hair and dark eyes opened the door. She gasped and said, "Mother! Mother! It's William Shakespeare." She grabbed William by the wrist and hurried him into the house, and Sarah Spencer clasped William in a warm embrace.

"William! Let me look at you! You are too thin, way too thin. Betsy, get some cakes and honey for William. He has been traipsing about the country for weeks without his wife, Anne, to care for him, and he looks horrible."

"Why thank you, Sarah," William laughed. "Fortunately, you look as lovely as ever!"

"Oh, William! You know I love you! I have just been worrying about you. Come and sit and tell me everything."

"I am glad that you are living in Oxford now. Anne was so sad to see you leave Wilmcote, but both of us worried about you living alone."

"You think you worried," joked Betsy from the buttery where she was preparing a tray of honey cakes and cold cider. "Andrew and I thought mother would never agree to come and live with us."

"William, you know how stubborn I am. I just couldn't bear to leave after Richard died. I saw so much of him in that house. I couldn't give him up yet, but once you and Anne and the children moved into Stratford, well, it just didn't make sense for me to stay there when Betsy and her husband Andrew are so good to me here. I have five grandsons here! They are all off to school this morning."

"I am very grateful to have a dear friend living in Oxford. I have seen nothing but inn after pub after inn, all of them much the same: dark, dingy, and depressing. Betsy, your home is so airy and bright. To sit and have a conversation with two ladies is a gift beyond measure. I have been surrounded by nothing but belching, bragging, bawdy men for weeks," William laughed.

Sarah spoke in a serious tone, "Don't you become one of those men, William. I worked hard to put you and Anne together, and if you ever do anything to harm that girl, I will come back and haunt you. I'll send Richard to haunt you. He loved Anne so much."

William smiled at his dear Sarah and said, "The last thing I want in this world is to be haunted by the ghost of Richard Spenser, but I am more afraid of what Anne would do to me than what any ghost could do to me! The player's bad behaviors are the only warning I need. The married men who turn their backs on their vows and settle for one night of pleasure suffer such guilt of conscience the next day that I watch them, grown men, sob into their ale. Then two nights later they are back to their debauchery; they never learn, but they have taught me well."

"Keep that lesson in your heart, William. It is your ability to see the souls of those around you that makes you such a good writer. In this chaotic world, you give people a sense of order in your plays. Never change!"

Sarah's words echoed in William's mind as he took his leave from Betsy's home and started back toward the Bear Inn. He realized that wise Sarah had put into words what his true gift was. Just as his darling baby girl, Judith, observed the world around her and drew what she saw, William observed the people around him and depicted human nature in his plays. He knew his historical plays were much less about history and much more about the human characteristics of greed, ambition, honor, and love.

The plays were met with great applause in Oxford, and no shouts of, "We want Lyly" were heard. Russell Northcutt was pleased that opening with the two Henry plays had successfully drawn crowds to their performances. "We will start our London run with the five plays we have done on tour, but after the holiday, in 1591, I want to adjust the plays to *Henry VI, Part Two* and *Henry VI, Part Three*. Will your comedy be ready to perform by then?"

"Yes, I think so. It includes a very strong female lead. I'm not sure Simon Morris fits the part though he did an admirable job as Margaret. His beard is getting darker and thicker."

"Some changes will be made once we are back in London, William. All you need to worry about is going home and resting for a month. Not too much resting. Make sure *Part Three* and the comedy are up to standard. I will contact you the end of September to let you know where you should meet me in London. If you think Cambridge and Oxford are amazing cities, wait until you first view London!"

William said his goodbyes to the company, packed Barbary with his few possessions, and rode briskly out of Oxford toward Stratford, toward home and Anne and Susanna and Judith and Hamnet. He had a handful of stones to practice his throwing along the way.

Chapter 23

William's excitement grew the closer he got to Stratford, and Barbary sensing a long deserved rest in the stable increased his speed. Each familiar landmark made William's heart soar, and he reflected that though he had seen many wonders on his tour of the Midlands, home was the greatest sight of all.

William thought he could enter the little house on Chapel Street and catch the family by total surprise, but he underestimated his children. When Anne told them their father was on his way home, they began calculating how long it would take him to ride the fifty-two miles from Oxford. Sarah Spencer had told the children that her daughter, Betsy and son-in-law Andrew broke the trip from Oxford into two equal days, so they did not tire the horses and themselves.

The children knew their father loved Barbary and would not overwork him, but they decided that he would travel thirty-two miles the first day, and he would only have to come twenty more the second day. Anne was quite impressed with Susanna's math skills as she was, as usual, the leader of the let's-meet-father-at-the-gate plan. With their calculations complete, the children devised a sentinel schedule. They would take turns at hour intervals watching for their father at the front gate on Chapel Street.

It happened that Judith was on sentinel duty in the early afternoon when she first saw puffs of dust blowing from the south where the street dipped toward the river, then a rider came into view, and she knew it was her father. She banged the rusty bread pan that Anne had contributed as the signal for the children's plan. In an instant, all four Shakespeares were at the gate, and William could not believe his eyes.

As he reined Barbary to a halt, he said, "Have you lovelies been standing here at the gate for the last three months waiting for me?" He dismounted and went to them with his arms spread wide. "I love you all so very much," he said as he embraced his family.

The children all talked at once and wanted to show their father everything they had done while he was gone. "Children, your father is going to be here a full month," Anne said, smiling at the enthusiasm of the children. "You don't have to tell him everything at once. Let's unpack Barbary, and you can all walk to the stable with your father while I get some food ready for our welcome home party."

After caring for Barbary, the children walked hand-in-hand with their father back up the street. They led him to the garden, and William was amazed at the transformation that had taken place in his absence. The once fallow garden space was overflowing with vegetables; squash and pumpkin vines wove their tendrils through rows of corn.

"You missed the peas," Susanna said. "They were so sweet we ate them right here in the garden before mother could even cook them! We just threw the pods in the air and at each other."

The children all giggled at the memory. William was stunned. He had spent his time creating plays and entertaining audiences while Anne had spent her time growing food for the family!

"We have chores, father," Hamnet explained. "We have to weed the garden and feed the chickens."

"Chickens!" William exclaimed, and then he noticed a rough timber lean-to in the far corner of the yard.

"We have five hens," Hamnet continued. "Mother says we don't need a rooster, but I want one because I like the noise they make."

William tipped his head back in a big laugh as he put his arm around Anne, "Roosters are usually just good for making noise."

Once William had been properly introduced to the hens and shown the skeps full of honey bees, Anne spread a quilt under the apple tree, and the family all sat down to fresh apple slices, boiled eggs, and William's favorite: honey cakes!

William was as impressed with the inside of the house as he had been by the garden. When he left Stratford, the family had just moved in, but now the house felt like a home. Lacy curtains hung at the windows, a bright cloth and flowers adorned the table, and the children's art work decorated the plaster walls.

William had brought each of the children a new book. Judith received Aesop's "The Ant and the Fly" and Hamnet got "The Crow With Borrowed Feathers." Susanna's book was each of the verses William had written for her with her illustrations on the facing pages. She was astonished and couldn't stop hugging her father.

"How did you manage such a perfect gift, William?" Anne asked in admiration.

"I met a book maker in Oxford, and he made it for us! It's our first published book, Susanna! I'm afraid it will only sell one copy though," William laughed.

Anne sent the children out to the garden to enjoy their books, and she and William enjoyed their first true kiss since his return. They did not want to release each other and though William was moving Anne gently towards the bedroom, they both knew they must wait until the children were asleep to enjoy a proper homecoming.

"You have accomplished wonderful things while I have been away, Anne. Thank you. Thank you for caring for the children and the house and the garden. It has to have been hard to do everything by yourself," William felt tears coming in his eyes.

Anne quickly kissed them away and said, "I love teaching the children how to work and watching them grow as the garden grows. Don't you once make it sound like a burden! I love you so much."

Soon it was as though William had never been away. The family integrated him into all of their activities. Hamnet warned William, "Watch out, father, or mother will give you chores, too!"

Despite his son's advice, William could not avoid the chores around the house and soon he was improving the rough chicken coop that Bartholomew had given his sister, Anne. He climbed the tree to get the highest apples, but not before allowing Hamnet to beat him in their throwing contest. Hamnet's accuracy had improved tremendously; the same could not be said for William.

William cherished his activities with the children, but he sometimes longed for the days when he had Anne all to himself. They had to steal moments to enjoy each other when the children were occupied. Neither of them could hold each other tight enough or kiss each other long enough to make up for the time they had been apart.

The month William had in Stratford went by entirely too fast. They had many happy days with Judith and Hamnet Sadler and their children. William asked for Hamnet's advice on the verses he had written for Susanna. Could Hamnet help him set them to music? He said he would be happy to try if Susanna was willing to let him borrow the book. Susanna told Hamnet in a very serious tone, "I can't let you borrow it yet, but I will let you know."

William got to meet Beatrice's new baby girl, Elizabeth Anne Martin, and he was pleased to see that Howard was an excellent husband and father. Beatrice deserved a love match after her miserable experience with Mr. Cole. The Martin family lived only two blocks from Chapel Street, so Anne and Beatrice spent many hours together. Howard could be counted on to help Anne with anything she needed around the house while William was gone.

William teased Howard, "You've got to watch out for this one, Howard. You know what happened to her first husband!"

"William!" Anne scolded. "What happened to Mr. Cole was just good luck! Beatrice had nothing to do with it."

William spent time with his parents and was shocked to see how much they had aged in just the short time he had been away. His younger brothers, Richard, sixteen, and Edmund, ten, were still living on Henley Street, so the Shakespeare's had two young men to care for them if they needed any assistance, but it was hard to think of his parents no longer being strong authoritative figures.

William dreaded having to again say goodbye to Stratford and his family and friends, but he was anticipating seeing London for the first time. He had an image in his mind of the great buildings of Cambridge, Coventry, and Oxford all combined in one city. Lord Strange's Men had told him countless stories of the ships on the Thames, the theatres on the South-bank, and the endless hordes of people all crowded together. They spoke of the bridge across the Thames and described it as full of pubs and shops with people living above the businesses. William could not imagine a bridge big enough to contain all of that, and he suspected that the players were just teasing him.

William's second departure was not as traumatic for the children because they had experienced three months without their father and the joy of him returning. This time they had a better idea of just how long three months was, and they were assured he would return. Anne had the comfort in knowing that she would receive letters from William. Not every other day as they had first planned, but a week would not pass without them communicating with each other. She could bear that.

William and Anne talked about moving the family to London. "Think of the opportunities for the children. We would have our choice of schools for them. We could be together as a family in the winter months, and you and the children could come back to Stratford for the months I am on tour with the company. Wouldn't you like to live on a bridge?"

"William you have spent too much time with men who have over-active imaginations. I suppose my apple trees will have their roots beneath the Thames and the boats will have to dodge around their trunks!"

"I'm not sure you could have a garden on London Bridge, Anne, but I will look and see!"

Chapter 24

William smelled London long before he rode through the gates of the city. He had never inhaled such a disgusting amalgam of sweat, excrement, and rot in his life. The noise emanating from the city was almost as jarring as the smell. Barkers along the road shouted out claims about their wares; sheep bleated as they were driven down the road; the click clack of carriage wheels echoed off the cobblestones as they rolled along. Urchins in rags ran in the streets and grabbed at William's stirrups begging for food or coins.

Russell Northcutt had instructed William to meet him at the Tower Pub next to the Tower of London because he knew even a country bumpkin could find that imposing structure in the crush that was London. He stayed with the main flow of human masses and reined in Barbary. Barbary was even more alarmed by the chaos around him than his master was. His ears stood at attention, and he high stepped trying to avoid the rough stones under his hooves. He was startled by each carriage that passed and tossed his head as children rushed towards him.

William knew that the Tower of London stood along the Thames, and he sensed he was nearing the waterway as he passed more carts full of wares coming his direction, and as the smell of sea water and fish accosted him. As the road started to descend, William could see the spires of St Paul's Cathedral to his right and the square-sided Tower of London to his left.

He dismounted Barbary and led him carefully, keeping the reins tightly grasped, so the horse would not bolt as he was jostled by the crowds of people in the street. William looked for the wooden board identifying The Tower Pub and finally found his destination.

He remembered Russell Northcutt's detailed instructions, "Shout for Tom Knox when you arrive. Don't leave your horse with anyone else. If a boy approaches you, ask him the name of his dog. If he doesn't say Russell, wait. Tom will get there as fast as he can. Don't trust anyone else."

William had thought these instructions bizarre when he first read them, but now they made sense. Young boys surrounded him shouting, "Care for your horse, sir!"

"I'm the stable boy here, give me your reins!"

"He's a liar. I'm the head boy here."

William held tightly to Barbary and shouted, "Tom Knox!" as loudly as he could.

"I'm Tom Knox," the ragamuffin boy who claimed to be the head boy at The Tower Pub declared.

"What's your dog's name, lad?" William asked.

The boy looked puzzled and said, "Bowser."

"Tom Knox!" William bellowed as his eyes searched the street around the pub. He noticed a commotion to his left and saw a young man with a mass of unkempt blond hair pushing his way through the crowd. "Tom Knox!" William yelled.

"I'm Tom Knox," the blond headed boy panted.

"What's your dog's name?" William asked with some trepidation.

"Why it's Russell, sir." Tom responded. "I will tend to your horse while my little brother runs to fetch Master Northcutt."

Relieved and exhausted, William patted Barbary on his neck and removed his saddle bags which contained among other things, the manuscripts for *King Henry VI, Part Three* and *The Taming of the Shrew.* He handed Barbary's reins to Tom and said, "I'll be in the pub."

The interior of the pub was dark and quieter than the street, but it was smoky and crowded with men. William finally found an unoccupied stool toward the back of the room. He was shocked by the contrast of what he had pictured London to be and the reality of what London was. Cambridge and Oxford had been bustling cities, but they had not prepared him for the onslaught of humanity that was London.

William was hungry and thirsty. He heard the men around him yelling, "Ale here," and "Bring some bread." He realized no one was going to come and ask him if he wanted anything, so he hollered, "cheese, bread, and ale" several times into the smoky room. To his surprise, a few minutes later a plump man with an apron tied around his waist set a platter of cheese, brown bread, pickles, and eggs down in front of him. Behind him, a young woman was holding a tray high above her head. She reached up, grabbed a tankard of ale, and slammed it down on the table in front of William. Then she was off to deliver the next drink on her tray.

William was on his second ale when he saw Russell Northcutt enter the tavern. With such a din and with so many people in the pub it was impossible for William to attract Russell, even by yelling and waving. Finally, William stood, put his fingers between his teeth and produced a horse whistle that caused many in the room to look his way, including his fellow player, Russell.

Russell held out his hand to William, and the two friends shook hands and then embraced. "Glad you made it safely, William," Russell said warmly. "What do you think of London so far?"

William didn't want to be negative about his friend's home town, so he tempered his response, "It's not exactly what I imagined."

"Oh, it's impossible to imagine London! You have to live in it, be a part of it, to understand the city," Russell said enthusiastically.

"It might take me a few days," William answered honestly.

"Let's get you out of here and over to Bankside. I've found lodging for you there. Don't worry about your horse. Tom has already taken him to a stable near the Rose where we will be rehearsing and performing."

William followed Russell out of the pub and into the vortex of London. The food and drink had helped revive him and having someone who knew the city guiding him eased William's fear somewhat. He still could not believe the number of people in the streets. Russell said over 100,000 people lived in London proper, and William felt that all of them were accompanying him toward London Bridge.

As the two men drew near the entrance to the bridge, William looked up and froze. The sea of people moved around him, and Russell Northcutt continued to walk assuming William was behind him, but William was stopped, stunned, for greeting him at London Bridge was not apple trees or roses, but rather human heads on stakes. William thought the ale had gone to his head or he was having some strange hallucination. The heads couldn't really be there because the people pushing past him didn't appear to see anything strange.

When Russell realized William was no longer behind him, he jumped up on a wall by the side of the bridge and searched the crowd for him. It wasn't difficult to locate him. He was the one standing dead still gawking up at the Bridge. Russell pushed his way through the crowd and made it to William. "Are you trying to get trampled to death?" he shouted and shook William. Russell followed William's gaze to the top of the gateway to the bridge and realized he was looking at the heads. He took William's arm, dragging him forward. "Don't worry, William. As long as you don't write anything bad about the Queen, your head won't end up there."

So they were real. William wasn't imagining them. He hardly saw the pubs and houses that lined the bridge because he couldn't erase the image of the macabre heads. This was the place where he had suggested Anne and the children live.

Once they crossed the great London Bridge and turned down a narrow lane along the Thames, the crowds thinned, and William could look back and see the houses and shops packed together along the bridge, smoke coming from their chimneys. The Thames was huge, but there were row boats the size of the one William had taken Anne out in when they were courting on the Avon in Stratford. The little boats were dwarfed by enormous merchant ships loaded with cargo and fishing vessels heavy with nets. William was amazed that the Thames River was almost as busy as the London streets.

Russell Northcutt was walking rapidly, and William could not look fast enough to take in the sights around him. His head was spinning as he looked toward the river and then toward the tall, narrow houses crammed together along the street. Northcutt seemed to be leading William to a riot as he could hear a din ahead. He hurried to walk beside Russell and asked, "Where are you taking me?"

"We will stop by your lodging first, so I can introduce you to Mistress Witherington. I've secured a room for you in her home."

"Is that horrible noise coming from where I will be living?" William asked with fear.

"What?" at first Russell wasn't sure what William meant, then he said, "Oh, you are just hearing the crowds at the bear-baiting. I'll show you."

Russell turned onto a narrow street leading closer to the river, and William could see a tall, circular fence ahead near the banks of the Thames. Loud shouts and horrible roars and yelps were coming from the structure. Russell yelled something in the young boy's ear at the gate and lead William inside the high fence for a view.

As William peered around the crowd by the entrance, he saw frantic spectators on bleachers which curved around inside the fence. Some were on their feet yelling at the action below. When William's gaze followed the screaming spectators, he saw a round dirt pit serving as a stage of sorts. He was astonished to see a large brown bear standing on its hind legs, roaring. The bear was attached to a large stake by a chain which gave the bear about five feet of movement. As William watched in horror, a brindle Mastiff charged towards the bear, barking and growling. The bear swiped his huge paws and claws at the dog, connected, and the dog flew across the arena as the crowd cheered. Though the dog was bleeding, he charged the bear again. William turned on his heel and walked back the way he and Russell Northcutt had come.

William couldn't breathe. He bent over with his hands on his knees and sucked the rancid air of London. Russell patted William on the back and said, "You've seen enough for today, William. Let's get you settled at Witherington's."

Mistress Witherington was a widow close to Mary Shakespeare's age. She had stooped shoulders, gray hair piled on top of her head, and a beguiling face that must have once been beautiful. William began to relax as she welcomed him to her home and explained that she had three boarders living with her. William would be her fourth. She led him up the stairs to a room at the top of the narrow three story structure. William expected to find a dark, low-ceilinged room, but was surprised to be able to walk into his room standing upright. The walls were shorter near the eaves of the house, but the room was wide enough that William had ample space to move about without crouching. A large window at one end of the room let in light and a fireplace on the left would provide heat. A simple table and chair stood by the window and Betty Witherington said, "Russell told me that you needed a good place to write, so I found that table for you. I hope it will do."

"Oh, yes, it will do nicely. Thank you. I will be quite comfortable here."

"Mr. Northcutt has paid me for your first month's rent which includes a morning and an evening meal. If you don't make it to the meals, there will be no refund. Once you taste my food, you won't miss many meals," Betty Witherington winked at William.

For the first time since his arrival in London, William was able to relax. Tom Knox had already placed William's few possessions on the low bed which stood opposite the fireplace. He would easily find a place to stow things in the large, comfortable room.

"Where is my horse stabled?" William asked.

"Mistress Witherington doesn't have a barn here, William. I will take you to your horse now if you are up for it," Russell said.

"I want to see that he is okay," William said. "Thank you, Mistress Witherington. I think I will be very content living here."

Betty Witherington handed William a large black key and said, "You may come and go as you please, and you are welcome to use the main sitting room downstairs anytime you wish. Your meals will be served in the dining area with my other guests. Please don't be loud and obnoxious, and we will get along just fine."

Russell Northcutt laughed and said, "This man is a writer and 'loud' and 'obnoxious' are not in his vocabulary."

It was only a five minute walk to the barn where Barbary was kept. Tom Knox jumped up from the pile of straw he had been sitting on when the two men entered. "He's settling in quite nicely, Master Russell."

William patted Barbary on the neck and rubbed his muzzle. He could see that the horse had been well groomed, and his stall, covered with fresh straw, was cleaner than the streets of London William had just come from.

"Thank you, Tom," William said and offered the young boy his hand. "You have done a fine job of caring for Barbary. Can you be my stable boy while I am in London?"

"Yes, sir!" Tom said with a big smile on his face.

"Come with me, William," Russell said. "I want to show you one more thing before you fall asleep on your feet."

A ten minute walk from Barbary's barn brought the two men to The Rose. William saw the tall, multi-sided structure from three blocks away, and even at that distance, it was an imposing building. The walls were of white plaster with intermittent wooden beams for support. William tipped his head back to see the roof which was thatched. Russell lead him inside, and William could see that the ceiling was open to the sky to allow in the sunlight. William stood in the middle of the structure and turned slowly around. The seats were similar to the rough bleachers he had seen at the bear baiting arena but they were sturdier and were separated into boxes or sections. Two tiers of seats circled the theatre and were interrupted by a magnificent platform that thrust out from the circle. The platform had two large columns in the front with a high gallery above the main performing space. William was already envisioning the scenes he could create for the upper space.

"The Rose can hold about 2,000 patrons. Those in the seats, both upper and lower galleries pay two pennies. Those who stand, our penny groundlings, get tightly packed together, but I've heard them say it keeps them from falling over during long productions. They have no room to fall over!" Russell laughed.

For the first time, William appreciated the appeal of London. This theatre was magnificent. The floor of the platform even had a trapdoor cut into it, so characters could "disappear" by slipping down into the area under the stage. He realized that Russell Northcutt could accept the hordes of people, London's nasty smell, and even the human heads on pikes to be able to perform in a theatre like The Rose before a crowd of thousands.

Russell and William walked back to Mistress Witherington's house, and Russell bid him good night. William went straight up the stairs, swept his things from the bed onto the floor, and collapsed with his clothes on for his first night's well-deserved sleep in London.

Chapter 25

William awoke to the smell of sausages and realized he was starving. He sat up and was surprised to find he was fully dressed. He looked around and realized where he was. Amazingly, he was in London, in a room in Mistress Witherington's home. He saw a large ceramic pitcher standing on a low counter. He poured water into his hands over a ceramic basin and splashed his face and patted his cheeks to remove the sleep that lingered. He knew he still looked as if he had ridden for two days with no grooming, but he didn't want to miss out on the sausages, so he hurried down the stairs.

Much to his dismay, he found the dining room empty, but the smell of sausages drew him to the back of the house where Betty Witherington was happily singing a tune and turning the sausages on a spit over the fire.

"Did I miss the morning meal?" William asked breathlessly.

"My boarders finished up an hour ago. I am just fixing myself something now," Betty answered with her back to William.

William sadly turned to return to his room and heard a loud infectious laugh behind him.

"Oh, son," Betty teased, "you've got to get used to my sense of humor."

"What?" William asked in confusion.

"The other boarders have eaten, but I knew how worn out you were. I didn't expect you to make it down early this morning. Come sit here at the little table, and we will have our sausage and eggs and fresh biscuits with honey together for your first morning in London!"

Russell Northcutt had found the perfect haven in London for young William. Mistress Witherington sat with William as they enjoyed her delicious food. "What do you think of London?"

William hesitated. He didn't want to offend his landlady as he already liked her very much. "It is bigger than I imagined, and it tests all of my senses."

Betty laughed, "You mean it stinks and is too loud!"

William was embarrassed that he had been so transparent in his failed attempt to be positive about London. "Do you ever get used to the noise and smell?"

"I hope you noticed a slight improvement here in Bankside. We are on the wrong side of the river according to the proper folks. We have the brothels, bear-baiting arenas, and theatres over here, but we also have fewer people crammed together because our big attractions take up building space that would otherwise be used for hovels for poor people. You will have a strong smell of fish and the sea here, but I prefer that to the odor of humans bunched up and exuding their stink on everything around them."

William had noticed a fishy smell when Russell was showing him around Bankside, but he agreed with Mistress Witherington that there were smells that were much worse.

"You haven't been out in this area in the morning yet, but you will find that before the patrons come over here from the city to be entertained, we have a nice, quiet neighborhood. Men stagger home from the brothels, of course, but they don't make noise. They just slither by like the snakes they are."

William continued to help himself to more sausages while Mistress Witherington continued to enjoy talking.

"My Lawrence, that's my dear departed husband Captain Lawrence Witherington, chose this house because it was close to the mooring of his ship the *Swiftsure*. We had twenty-six wonderful years together in this house before he was swept overboard to his death last winter. We had a good marriage. He was out at sea for most of it."

William wasn't sure how to respond to this information. "I'm sorry I didn't get to meet Captain Witherington."

"You didn't miss much. He wasn't a talker like I am. His mistress was the sea, and she finally took him. I expect he's happy where he is." Betty Witherington continued, "I imagine you will hear enough sea stories to fill ten volumes living here, My other three boarders are seamen, and they come and go, but when they are here, they like to romanticize their adventures."

"I don't know anything about the sea, but I would like to learn," William said, "Your boarder's stories will be interesting as are yours!"

Fortified with Mistress Wiltherington's stories and food, William washed, trimmed his beard, put on a clean shirt and went out into the streets of his new neighborhood. He found his way to Barbary's barn and checked in on his horse. Tom Knox was not around, but Barbary was content and had fresh hay in his manger.

William continued on to the Rose and with only a few wrong turns, he found the theatre. It was quiet and the double wooden doors were closed at the main entrance. William wandered around to the back and found a small door standing open. He entered and found himself underneath the stage. Actors could descend through the trapdoor on stage, exit through the back door, run around the theatre, and enter through the penny groundlings as a new character. William heard footsteps above him, and he looked around him in the dim light and found a set of stairs leading up to the side of the platform. He climbed the stairs and found his friend, Russell Northcutt pacing out distances on the stage.

"Good morning, William! You look much better this morning than you did when I left you last evening," Russell teased.

"I felt as bad as I looked last night," William retorted, "but I feel revitalized this morning! Mistress Witherington can cook!"

"I hope her cooking will make up for her nonstop talking," Russell laughed.

"I love her stories almost as much as her cooking," William responded.

Russell continued to pace and record numbers on a rough pad of papers. "We can do magnificent things with *King Henry VI, Part Two* on this stage. The fight scenes can have more action, and we will add bladders of sheep's blood inside the costumes, so the stabbings will be more realistic. As you saw from the bear-baiting arena, Londoners love the sight of blood, and we like to give them what they want."

"Maybe they won't like *Taming of the Shrew*," William said. "I didn't include any blood in it."

"Comedies are different, William. You need either laughter or blood. You don't have to have both. Laughter and blood are a good combination, but I know it is not always possible," Russell said seriously.

"What if an audience comes for blood and just gets laughter?" William asked.

"Our audiences are sophisticated, William. They can't read, but they can recognize the flags we fly at the top of the theatre: red is for blood; white is for comedy. We need a good mixture. You just keep writing whatever you are in the mood to write."

"Mistress Witherington has inspired me to write comedy this morning," William laughed.

"Good! I hope her incessant drivel doesn't move you to murder before your three month lease is over!"

Russell and William heard pounding on the theatre doors, and Russell jumped down from the stage. He walked to the large double doors, and lifted the beam which fit into two metal brackets locking the doors. Once the heavy beam was removed, the double doors swung back, and Henry Adams and two young men William had not seen before entered the theatre.

William jumped down from the stage and joined the men. He clapped Henry on the back and shook his hand. Henry said, "Good to see you, William. These lads are Roger and Solomon."

The young men nodded to William and shook his hand. "Could you scribble out some lines for them from *Taming of the Shrew.* We need to try them out to see which one will make the best apprentice for the season and play the female roles."

"Come with me, William," Russell said and lead William to the side of the platform where a small wooden table, complete with paper, ink, and quill sat inconspicuously in the corner. "Our playwrights are used to making changes during a production. Consider this your office while we are at the Rose."

William was not accustomed to being referred to as a playwright, but he liked it very much. He decided the scene where Petruchio forces Katerina to see the moon rather than the sun would be a good one for the young men to show their talents. He wrote the last words of Petruchio's speeches as their cues and then Kate's full lines on a piece of manuscript paper.

By the time William finished preparing the simple scripts, Richard Clark, David Thomas, Robert Andrews, and Rat had arrived at the Rose. The actors greeted William warmly, and Rat said, "I' m glad to see you again. I was afraid you wouldn't come to London."

The six members of Lord Strange's Company took seats in different parts of the theatre to listen to the young men audition for the part of Katherina.

"Solomon, you go first," Russell called. "William, begin when you are ready."

William and Solomon stood at the center of the stage, and William began,

Come on, a God's name; once more toward our father's.
God Lord, how bright and goodly shines the moon!
Solomon: *The moon? The sun! It is not moonlight now.*
William: *I say it is the moon that shines so bright.*
Solomon: *I know it is the sun that shines so bright.*
William: *Go on and fetch our horses back again,*
Evermore cross'd and cross'd; nothing but cross'd!
Solomon: *Forward, I pray, since we have come so far,*
And be it moon, or sun, or what you please;
And if you please to call it a rush-candle,
Henceforth I vow it shall be so for me.
(The Taming of the Shrew, 4.5).

The scene was then repeated with Roger as Katherina. When William and Roger had completed the scene, Russell said, "Thanks, boys. Wait outside and we will let you know our decision."

Lord Strange's Men convened in the middle of the theatre to discuss the two young actors' strengths and weaknesses. "I'll give you each a scrap of paper. Just mark S or R," Russell said.

"Don't waste your paper, Russell," Henry Adams declared. "It was no contest. On three, say the name of our new apprentice. One, two, three!"

"Roger!" all of the actors shouted.

"We have an unanimous choice for Roger Young! We have our Katherina!" Russell declared happily.

"And our Petruchio," Henry Adams clapped William on the back.

"Not so fast, Henry," Russell said, "we need William more for writing than acting right now."

"I was thinking you would be a good Petruchio, Henry," William lied. He had loved being on the large stage speaking his lines, but he knew Russell was right. He had plays to write.

Russell stepped outside and let Solomon know that he was free to go. He and Roger Young walked back into the theatre, and Russell introduced Roger to everyone. "Welcome to Lord Strange's Men, Roger!"

"Roger replaces Simon Morris. I know you men all liked Simon, but his beard has grown too thick and dark for him to continue in our female roles, and we don't have need for another man to fill the male roles. He has already acquired a position at The Red Lion."

Russell Northcutt continued, "Most of you know our procedure here at the Rose, but William and Roger are new to this theatre, so I will give you all our schedule. We have the stage here four days a week, that includes rehearsing in the morning and performing in the afternoon. You will have one day a week off, and the other two days we will be performing at various inns and courtyards of noble gentlemen in around London. These performances are very important to the company as a good review by influential men in the city is essential in helping us keep our patron happy and keeping good crowds flocking to see us here at the Rose."

"William, I know I told you we would perform *Taming of the Shrew* at the beginning of 1591, but I would like to have it ready for our private performances for the Lords and Ladies. The Henry plays don't lend themselves well to those spaces. We will perform the three Henry plays and Lyly's *Mother Bombie* here at the Rose," Russell concluded.

William was shocked. On only his second day in London, William learned that four of his plays, the only four he had completed, were to be performed by Lord Strange's Men.

Chapter 26

William sent Anne and the children a short letter telling them that he had arrived in London and where he was staying, but he shared very little about his first impressions of the city. With Russell Northcutt's announcement that all four of William's plays would be performed, William had something positive to share with his family! He regaled them with stories of Mistress Witherington and included a detailed description of the Rose. He hoped they wouldn't notice that he said little about the city of London itself. He asked the children to draw the Rose as he was interested to see their visualization of the most important place in his life, in London that is.

Life took on a routine for William. He awakened early and enjoyed his morning meal at Mistress Witherington's. Then he was off to the Rose for rehearsals and script writing. Roger Young, the new apprentice was eager to learn all aspects of theatre and was pleased to help William create the actors' scripts for *Henry VI Part Three* while William worked on *Taming of the Shrew.* One morning, near the middle of October, Russell Northcutt arrived late for rehearsal, out of breath and clearly agitated.

"What's wrong, Russell?" William asked, looking up from the table where he was scratching out Christopher Sly's lines for *Taming of the Shrew.*

"Do you have the scripts completed for *Shrew*?

"I'm just working on the minor characters. Why?"

"We have an unexpected engagement at Lord and Lady Montgomery's estate near Windsor. It's an opportunity we cannot afford to miss. We performed Lyly's *Mother Bombie* for them last season, and they enjoyed it. I think the *Shrew* would be perfect for them and their guests. Lord and Lady

Montgomery are good friends of our patron, the Fifth Earl of Derby, so we can't refuse this offer."

"I can finish the scripts by this afternoon. When do they want us to perform?"

"Three days from now," Russell sighed.

"Henry Adams has not even seen the script for Petruchio," William said. "I gave Roger his lines for Katherine yesterday."

"I worked on them all last evening," Roger said pausing in his copy work. "I think I can be ready in three days if you and William will help me."

"Good," Russell said. "William you will perform Petruchio for this performance, and Henry will play Lucentio. We will reverse the roles once we have completed this quick premiere."

William quickly scanned through his manuscript and found the servants parts. "Roger, stop working on *Henry,* and help me finish up the *Shrew*, so we can rehearse today."

Russell Northcutt gathered the actors at the front of the stage, and they did a read through of *Taming of the Shrew*. They discovered that some of the doubling of characters would not work as the characters were either on stage at the same time or were demanded on stage too soon for even simple costume changes. William was relieved to hear laughter from his fellow actors as they read through the play. If they could find humor in the play even under these stressful circumstances, it was a good omen.

They started walk throughs that afternoon, and with William and Russell both helping with blocking, they had a basic idea of how the play would flow by the time they lost their sunlight and broke up for the night. Fortunately, Russell knew the size of the Montgomery's grand hall, and the actors condensed the scenes into about half the space of the Rose's stage.

William returned to his lodging exhausted and exhilarated. His fellow lodgers were all out to sea, so William and Betty Witherington sat together for their evening meal. William devoured the braised beef and Yorkshire pudding Mistress Witherington placed before him, and he let her monologue wash over him.

"I had an actor lodge with me once before. That's how I met Russell Northcutt. Good looking man that Russell Northcutt, but try as I might, I can't turn his head."

William raised his eyebrows at that comment but kept eating.

"The actor that stayed here came to no good," Betty continued. "He was a sly one, or so he thought. He stole scripts from Northcutt's company and sold them to other companies, so their players could perform the play first and take Northcutt's audience. With five theatres trying to attract patrons, it gets as competitive as five dogs attacking a bear around here. I wouldn't trust anyone with your scripts if I were you."

William thought about the new apprentice, Roger Young, and wondered if he had been wrong to let the new man copy parts for him. He thought of himself as a good judge of character, but he would heed Betty Witherington's advice from now on.

The apprentice certainly didn't disappoint as an actor! He had Katherine's lines memorized, and he knew his cues when Lord Strange's Men met to rehearse the next morning. William relished playing Petruchio, and he longed to have his own Anne playing the role of Kate. However, William was glad that women were not allowed to perform on the London stages. He was totally comfortable flirting and cavorting with

Roger Young as he had no interest in young boys or men, but he wondered how he would react chasing a beautiful woman around the stage.

The only person who wasn't pleased with *Taming of the Shrew* was the costumer, Gilbert Bly, who Russell Northcutt had contracted for the season at the Rose. "Why are Katherine, Bianca, and the widow all brides at the end of this farce? Do you know how hard it is for me to find one wedding gown, let alone three. You cast Richard Clark as the widow. I will need a full bolt of material to cover his big belly. As if that isn't bad enough, I must make Katherine two identical gowns. One has to be pristine, and the other has to look as though the bride rolled in mud and muck," Bly shouted at Russell.

"Just find an older gown that resembles the beautiful gown enough that the audience will be fooled into thinking it is the same gown when it is muddied and torn. I need all the costumes in two days!" Russell delivered his last line as he quickly departed the theatre. The remaining members of the company had never imagined their usually mild-mannered tailor knew the words that exploded from his mouth. He ended his tirade with, "I quit! I refuse to be treated this way."

William didn't blame Bly for being upset, but he knew that no costumes meant no performance. "Did you notice that the play calls for a tailor?" William ventured.

"I'm not concerned about the costume for the tailor!" Gilbert Bly shouted in exasperation.

"Would you consider being the tailor? Your voice projects very well, and obviously, you fit the part."

The anger seemed to seep out of Gilbert Bly, and he quietly said, "Really? You think I could be in the play."

"Russell will have to approve, but if you can have all the costumes we need by Saturday, I think Russell will be happy to give you the part," William said, looking at his fellow actors for support.

"Sure," Henry Adams smiled. "Having a respected tailor such as yourself playing our tailor will add class to the performance." He winked at William, and the men knew they would have the costumes they needed by Saturday.

Rehearsals went well for *Taming of the Shrew.* Rat loved sashaying about the stage as Bianca, and Henry Adams was a believable Lucentio stricken with love at first sight. William and Roger exaggerated the love/hate relationship between Katherine and Petruchio to glean the most laughter from their scenes together. Russell Northcutt decided to cut the induction scene with Christopher Sly from the production at the Montgomery Estate, and the company would reinstate it when they performed in the Rose.

By Saturday, Lord Strange's men were prepared to present a credible performance of *Taming of the Shrew.* William was busy worrying about acting the part of Petruchio and didn't spend too much time worrying about the play itself. The first comedy he had ever written was to be presented to the world with only three days preparation. How quickly things had changed for him as a playwright. His historical plays had been perfected a scene at a time with the help of his student actors. Now William was relying on a team of professionals, including himself as the lead, and only three days rehearsal to make his play a success. As usual, Russell Northcutt told William, "Relax. They will love it."

Saturday was a perfect crisp October day with a cloudless blue sky. On the ride to Windsor, Barbary pranced and shook his head repeatedly. "Yes, Barbary, we are out of London! We can hear the birds singing, and I can hear my thoughts. We can breath the air and not choke. It is refreshing." William patted Barbary's neck affectionately.

Lord Strange's Men were all happy to be out of the city, and they felt the adrenaline of a new performance ahead of them. The Montgomery Manor House was a red brick edifice sitting atop a lush green hill. A sweeping drive lined with close cut hedges lead the players and their wagon of props and costumes to a tall arched gateway. Once through the gateway which was decorated with terra cotta tiles, the players reached an interior courtyard with fountains, gardens, and a maze consisting of the same type of hedges which lined the drive.

Servants greeted them and helped them load the costumes and platform into the great hall. William admired the mirrored walls, beautiful tapestries, and inlaid floors. The residence was as opulent as the Guild Halls of Oxford or Cambridge. William was suddenly painfully aware of his lack of education and worldly experience. He had nothing in common with the wealthy people who lived here. He had written *Taming of the Shrew* as entertainment for those of his station and situation in life. He had no idea if the Montgomerys would find humor in the play. The nerves which had faded into the background on his ride to Windsor returned with renewed vigor and made him feel ill.

Fortunately, Petruchio did not make his entrance until Act 1 scene ii, and William was able to peer from behind a temporary screen set at the side of the stage and watch the audience's reaction. The great hall was resplendent with fifty or sixty Lords and Ladies dressed in their finest clothing. They were laughing! They seemed to especially enjoy the fight between Bianca and Katherine. William's confidence returned, and he commanded the stage as the brash Petruchio.

Roger and William had worked extensively on their witty banter as Kate and Petruchio, and their scenes together brought raucous laughter from the crowd. The tender scenes with Lucentio courting Bianca seemed to satisfy the romantics in the audience, and though the play was not flawless, Lord Strange's Men did an admirable job overall.

The cast was called back to the platform twice for bows, and the crowd applauded warmly. Several men of the company congratulated William on the success of his comedy and said they had great fun playing their parts. William felt great relief as he helped pack the costumes and props for their departure from the manor house.

"William!" Russell Northcutt called from the courtyard

"Yes." William said as he placed Katherine's soiled wedding gown in a burlap bag. "I'm coming." He hurried out to see what Russell needed.

"This is Lord Montgomery and his wife, Lady Margaret." Russell said formally as he presented the fine looking couple to William.

William was instantly flustered but managed to say, "It is a great honor to meet you. It was an honor to perform for you."

"The honor was all ours," Lord Montgomery said stiffly. "My wife and I would like you and Mr. Northcutt to join us for our evening meal and spend the night with us before you return to London."

William tried to hide his amazement and looked to Russell for guidance. Russell gave a slight nod of his head, and William said, "We would be delighted. Thank you very much."

"Good. Once you have sent the rest of your company on their way, meet me in the drawing room." With that, the Montgomerys turned and walked toward the rose garden where many of their visitors were admiring the last blooms of the season.

Russell and William returned to the great hall and helped the rest of the company load things out to the wagon. "You didn't tell me we would be staying," William said to Russell.

"I had no idea. This has never happened before. I have played for many wealthy individuals, and I have always been treated as the servant that I am. Common players don't sit down to dine with aristocrats."

"Are we in trouble?" William asked fearfully.

"I think you may be," Russell answered with a sly grin on his face.

"Was it something in the play?"

"No. I think it was someone watching the play. Did you happen to notice the beautiful brunette in the pink gown on the front row?" Russell asked.

"Of course," William answered, "she is a real beauty. Who is she?"

"She just happens to be Lucy Montgomery, the daughter of Lord and Lady Montgomery who just asked us to dine with them. I don't suppose you noticed that Lucy could not keep her eyes off you the entire performance," Russell teased.

William thought he had been sick with nerves before the performance, but that was nothing compared to the nerves he now felt. Lord Strange's Men had left for London, and William and Russell went in search of the drawing room. With the help of the butler, they found themselves in a large, high-ceilinged room with heavy dark furniture and a huge fireplace with a roaring fire. Guests were sipping wine and talking amongst themselves. Some women were playing cards, and many men were enjoying their cigars. Though the entire audience from the *Shrew* did not seem to be present in the drawing room, the crowd was still large. The butler brought William and Russell each a glass of wine and said the Montgomerys would arrive presently.

William gulped his wine and instantly regretted it. His head now felt as bad as his stomach. He clung close to Russell like a five-year-old would to his mother. Several guests approached the two men and said flattering things about the play. William merely nodded and in embarrassment, Russell said, "Mr. Shakespeare is much more sociable when he has time to write his lines." Under his breath, he said to William, "Snap out of it boy. We don't want to be sent home before the first course is served."

Just then, they heard the tinkling of a bell, and the crowd quieted. The butler announced, "Lord and Lady Montgomery and Miss Lucy Montgomery."

The Montgomerys entered the drawing room, and the guests stood and applauded as a formal thank you to their hosts. "No need for that," Lord Montgomery said briskly. "We are pleased you could join us today. We have been most entertained by *Taming of the Shrew* and are grateful that Russell Northcutt, manager of the company and William Shakespeare, lead player and playwright have agreed to stay with us this evening." He gestured toward the two men, and the guests applauded for them. "Now, we need some music," Lord Montgomery continued. "Our daughter, Lucy, will play the harpsichord and sing for us before we eat." This announcement was also greeted with applause from the crowd.

William had not noticed the instrument at the far end of the drawing room, but all eyes followed Lucy Montgomery as she walked gracefully to the harpsichord and arranged herself on the bench. William was amazed that the young woman possessed musical talents which rivaled her beauty. Her hands flashed over the keyboard and coaxed out a magical melody. Then she slowed the tempo to a ballad and added her sweet voice to the song. William was entranced by her performance, and he could not take his eyes off her.

When she finished her song, she jumped up with a large smile on her face and said, "Finally, we can eat!"

The crowd protested that she should play on, but she kindly refused and gestured for everyone to move to the formal dining room. Russell elbowed William sharply in the side, and William realized he was still staring at Lucy. "William, just watch what the person across the table does and follow suit. This meal will not be like eating in the pub with the players."

William nodded and followed Russell to the dining room which contained a long wooden table covered in linen and set with sparkling pewter chargers, matching pewter goblets, and silver forks and knives. Sixteen place settings were on each side, with two at each end of the table. William thought he could sit next to Russell towards the end of the table and be inconspicuous, but Russell pointed to the formal white place cards above each plate and said, "You have to find your name and sit there."

Much jostling and laughter filled the room as guests found their seats and playfully called to those seated on either side of them. William stood frozen watching the elegant guests shuffle around him. Suddenly, he felt someone standing close to him, and Lucy Montgomery took his arm. "You are seated next to me. Let me escort you to your seat."

She smelled like lavender and though her hair and eyes were very dark, her skin was as fair and soft as a fresh white rose. Her pink gown rustled as she walked next to William, and he could not breathe. He knew he should say something, but he had no idea what to say.

Their places were in the center of table on the left-hand side. William was relieved to see Russell across from him and over one space. Russell was pulling out the chair for an older woman with a plentiful bust packed into a purple gown. William quickly helped Lucy into her seat and attempted to slide the chair forward without catching her gown. "Thank you, Mr. Shakespeare," Lucy said with a giggle.

William noticed that the men were still standing, so he waited and when Lord Montgomery sat down, all the men did. William's leg brushed Lucy's when he sat down as the place settings were quite close together. He moved away quickly as if he had been burned by a cinder.

Lucy giggled again, and he knew she was laughing at him, but he didn't care. She didn't seem to be laughing maliciously; she seemed joyful.

He finally found his voice, "You sing and play beautifully."

"Why thank you, Mr. Shakespeare. That is a very kind thing for such a talented man to say."

"I am not nearly as talented as you are," William said modestly.

"I thoroughly disagree with you, Mr. Shakespeare," Lucy giggled.

"You can call me William. Should I call you Miss Montgomery?" William asked.

"Just call me Lucy, please. Which do you like better, acting or writing?"

"I love them both, but I guess I am a playwright who likes to act. What about you? Do you like singing or playing better?"

Lucy did not respond to this question with a mere giggle; she laughed a delighted belly laugh. "I detest both. I like horseback riding, and I would love to be an actor. I may move to France to do just that because England is too provincial to allow women on stage."

William was so intrigued by the beautiful Lucy Montgomery that he forgot to watch the person across from him to see what he should be doing. When the serving man arrived with the first course, Lucy reached over and removed the napkin from William's plate and placed it in his lap. William thought her warm hand lingered a little too long on his lap, but his imagination seemed to be running away with him.

Roast pheasant was the first course, and William wasn't sure how to eat it, but he looked to Lucy, and she simply picked the meat up with her hands and pulled the flesh off with her teeth. He did the same and found the meat to be delicious. He was happy to be chewing and not conversing, but he realized that he was no longer tongue tied. Lucy was interesting and easy to talk with.

As each course was served, William's wine glass was refilled, and he soon became satiated with rich food and drink. His leg brushed Lucy's, and he didn't move it. Lucy leaned in to whisper something in his ear, and he laughed and wished she would do it again. He looked across the table once and saw Russell frowning at him, but he couldn't think what he had done wrong.

As William was peeling an orange for the last course, Lucy asked him, "Do you believe in love at first sight, like Lucentio in your play?"

"It depends on how beautiful the woman is," William answered flirtatiously.

"Love at first sight doesn't just happen to men, William," Lucy said looking William straight in the eyes.

William felt warm all over, and it wasn't the rich food or the wine, it was Lucy's dark eyes looking at him with admiration. He didn't know what to say to this beautiful young woman. He suddenly knew why Russell had been frowning at him. He had been flirting with the host's daughter. It was inappropriate on many levels, and his behavior was inexcusable. He didn't know how he could extricate himself from the situation without upsetting Lucy.

"I am afraid your parents fine food and wine has gone to my head, Lucy. I have forgotten my manners and my place. You are a wealthy single woman, and I am a poor married playwright. I have very much enjoyed our evening together, but I am sure we shall never see each other again."

Lucy focused her attention on her orange and didn't speak for some time. When she did, she said softly, "I have a way of getting what I want."

The guests were beginning to leave the table, and soon Russell was at William's elbow telling him that a servant would show them to their room for the night. "Good night, Miss Montgomery. Your parents have shown us a lovely evening, and I enjoyed your music very much," Russell said as he held Lucy's hand in his while William rose unstably from his seat.

"Good night, Lucy. Thank you for helping me eat like a gentleman," William joked trying to lighten the tension between them.

"Good night, William." Lucy stood and whispered in his ear, "Thank you for making me feel like a woman tonight."

Chapter 27

William awoke Sunday morning in a strange bed chamber with a pounding headache. Russell was already dressed and was seated on a chair by the small fireplace which provided heat for the room. "We should leave for London soon," Russell said in a clipped voice.

The prior evening came rushing back to William, and he sat on the edge of the bed with his head in his hands. "Did I make a total fool of myself?"

"It was not good. I thought you had more sense than that. You never paid the tarts we met on tour any heed. It was the blasted wine. You kept drinking that wine and lost yourself completely," Russell scolded.

"Nothing happened," William protested. "We just talked."

"I had a perfect view, and it was not just talking. I was talking to the battle ax next to me. You were flirting with Lucy Montgomery, a member of the aristocracy, a friend of our patron. Do you want to bring ruin to Lord Strange's Men?"

Russell had never addressed William with such venom in his words, and the venom hit its target.

"I'm sorry, Russell." William said shamefully. "I forgot myself. I guess I thought I was still Petruchio instead of William Shakespeare. I didn't think of the company. I didn't think of Anne. I made a mess of things."

"It's not irreparable. You will never see Lucy Montgomery again. Her parents were at the end of the table, and their view of your behavior was blocked by the many guests between you and them. I'm sure Lucy arranged the seating with that purpose in mind."

"She intimated that she was in love with me," William said morosely.

"Oh posh, women fall in love with the roles we play. She has no interest in a poor actor. She is in love with a wealthy Italian courtier named Petruchio. Believe it or not, I used to have women fawning over me when I played romantic leads."

"You have not lost your appeal, Russell," William said with his first smile of the morning. "I know a fine woman who would wrap you in her arms at the first opportunity."

"What are you talking about?"

"Just the other day, Mistress Witherington confided her abiding love for you."

"You scoundrel! Splash water on that arrogant face of yours and let's get out of here before Miss Montgomery knocks on our door with a morning kiss for you."

William was grateful that Russell did not stay angry with him for long. As the two men rode back to London, they talked about *Taming of the Shrew*, the casting, staging, and timing. They analyzed which lines produced the laughter they had hoped for and which scenes needed improvement. They both agreed that including the induction scene with Christopher Sly would add much laughter to the play. They did not speak of Lucy Montgomery or Mistress Witherington.

When William was safely alone in his room back in London, he wrote a long letter to Anne and the children. He described in great detail the Montgomery's manor house and grounds. He drew a maze similar to the one formed by the hedges on the grand estate. He challenged the children to find their way out and asked them to create a maze that he had to solve. He described the rich foods served and the grand dining room. He told them about the laughter *Taming of the Shrew* brought to the elegant audience of aristocrats. He failed to mention Lucy Montgomery.

As was his habit when he was upset about something, William turned to his sonnets. He had sheafs of them, written over the last ten years. Many of them had been written for his dear Anne, but he was looking for the sonnet that he wrote while in Coventry when he was disgusted with some of his fellow actors' inconstancy. He needed to listen to his own advice:

The' expense of spirit in a waste of shame
Is lust in action; and till action, lust
Is perjured, murd'rous, bloody, full of blame,
Savage, extreme, rude, cruel, not to trust;
Enjoyed no sooner but despised straight;
Past reason hunted, and no sooner had,
Past reason hated as a swallowed bait
On purpose laid to make the taker mad;
Mad in pursuit, and in possession so;
Had, having, and in quest to have, extreme;
A bliss in proof, and proved a very woe,
Before, a joy proposed; behind, a dream.
All this the world well knows, yet none knows well
To shun the heaven that leads men to this hell
(Sonnet 129).

He had fallen for Lucy's bait of flattery and beauty, and he enjoyed the hunt by flirting with her. Thankfully, reason or Russell, had intervened before his lust took action. Being away from Anne for such long periods of time was going to be William's biggest challenge. It made writing and performing plays seem an easy task.

William threw himself into his work at the Rose. The first week in November, Lord Strange's Men opened with *King Henry VI, Part One*, followed by *Mother Bombie, King Henry VI, Part Two, Taming of the Shrew*, and they finished their five day run with *King Henry VI, Part Three*. Philip

Henslowe, owner of the Rose, attended all five plays the first week they were performed. He stayed behind as the boisterous crowds left the theatre, and Russell Northcutt gathered the company together so the theatre owner could address them. "You men are making good use of my theatre. We should have large crowds this season despite the bold claims of the Theatre and Curtain that they will put me out of business. Keep up the good work, and I'll have a little extra for you at the end of the season. Shakespeare, you write good plays, keep writing."

Though William thought Henslowe had been brusk and brief, Russell and the other company members assured him that Henslowe's speech was effusive compared to his usual grunts of, "It will do."

The first performance of *King Henry VI, Part Three* was warmly received, and William marveled that having been in London only one month, he had four plays up and running. Everything moved quickly in the city and the stories William had been told about the rivalry and competitiveness between playwrights in London had not been exaggerated. On his day off, he often went to competing theatres to watch performances by other companies. Though he saw samples of several playwrights work, he was impressed by only two: Thomas Kyd and Christopher Marlowe. They were the gauge by which he would measure himself, and the bar was set very high. He always enjoyed a challenge, and he was driven to write more and increasingly better plays.

He enjoyed the quiet evenings in Bankside, and he worked on *The Comedy of Errors* a farce inspired by his twins, Hamnet and Judith. To increase humor and confusion in the play, he included two sets of twins who changed places with each other as easily as they changed clothes. He was also working on a historical play, *King Richard the II* and liked moving from comedy to history. It was like taking a rest from writing to switch to such disparate plots. William depicted Richard as an immature young man with a huge disconnect from the people of his kingdom. He banished Bolingbroke, a pragmatic, mature nobleman, and this act eventually lead to Richard's downfall. Having learned much from the *Henry VI* plays, William tried to limit the number of large battle scenes in *Richard II* but satisfy the audience's desire for blood through individual beheadings.

Knowing the acting strengths and weaknesses of Lord Strange's Men made William's task as a playwright easier. He was able to people his plays with characters that fit the actors who would perform the parts. When he wrote the *Henry VI* plays, he had no vision of who would be acting the parts, and he had little sense of the number of characters the average acting company could perform. His time with Lord Strange's Men had taught him volumes about utilizing the strengths of the men he worked with each day. When he wrote a strong part for a fellow actor, it strengthened both the play and William's place in the company. Alternatively, when he failed to include a good role for one of the main actors of the company, he reduced his value as a playwright in that actor's mind. Being a playwright in 1590 London was a delicate balance of appealing to the audience and satisfying the company of actors. William Shakespeare was well on his way to accomplishing both purposes.

Chapter 28

In the fall of 1590, Anne Shakespeare was finding great satisfaction in her role as mother and head of the household for three active children. She was also discovering that life with William away in London was much more difficult than during his first absence when he had been on tour in the Midlands. This was partly because their first separation seemed adventurous and partly because Cambridge and Coventry and the other cities on the tour hadn't seemed that far away, but London was very far away and there was no adventure for Anne in sleeping alone every night. She missed William.

She looked forward to his letters and read them again and again. She tried to picture what Mistress Witherington's house was like and was a bit jealous when William described the wonderful things his landlady cooked for him. Anne was surprised William didn't describe London more in his letters and wondered why he had not mentioned moving her and the children to London Bridge. She thought about coming to London to surprise him. She imagined sitting in Mistress Witherington's drawing room and having William come home from the Rose to find her there waiting for him.

Many people traveled between Stratford and London and when Anne went to the market, strangers would approach her and say, "I saw your husband perform at the Rose while I was up in the city. He is making quite a name for himself."

The wool dealer said, "I asked about your husband in the first pub I stopped at in the city, and they knew him! Can you imagine that? A city the size of London and the inn keeper knew William Shakespeare by name."

Unfortunately, some of the comments Anne received were negative. The woman selling leeks and turnips clicked her tongue at Anne, shook her head, and said, "It's a sad thing that your husband has gone off and left you with those children to raise on your own." When Anne tried to explain that William had not left her, that his absence was temporary, the woman just shook her head and turned back to her vegetables.

Anne was not deterred by gossip. She had endured being labeled a head-strong spinster by the women in Stratford. She could ignore people who knew absolutely nothing about her relationship with her husband. Anne was grateful every day to be surrounded by those who loved her. Hamnet and Judith, Howard and Beatrice, Mary and John Shakespeare, and her own family at Shottery all knew that Anne and William had a solid marriage. Despite the support she had around her, she still longed for the day William would be home in her arms.

"What do you hear from the famous playwright?" Hamnet greeted Anne as she swept into the bakery towing the children behind her.

"He spent the night at an elegant estate in Windsor," Anne replied after giving Hamnet and Judith each a warm hug.

"Father drew us a picture of the maze from the garden at the big house he visited, and I found my way out the very first try," Susanna said excitedly.

"I drew Father a better maze than the one he saw," little Hamnet said.

"I couldn't find my way out of Father's maze or Hamnet's maze," Judith said quietly. "I think mazes are scary things, and trees should be planted in straight rows, so you know where you are going."

"I agree with you my little namesake," Judith said while hugging the twin. "Can you help me get some cider and bread ready, and we will have a treat?"

The Shakespeare children joined Judith as she walked toward the back of the bakery knowing the Sadler children, William, Anne, and Henry would be glad to see them.

"Why did William have to stay the night in Windsor? It isn't that far from London," Hamnet asked.

"I'm not sure," Anne said. "I know only Russell Northcutt and William were invited to stay. They were served a banquet at a table that seated thirty-six people. Can you imagine that?"

Hamnet shook his head in wonder. "Maybe I should apply to be their baker! I'd like making special orders for that many fancy folks."

"They had seven courses and wine with every course."

"William must have passed out at the table drinking that much wine," Hamnet laughed. "That man gets tipsy on cider."

"Do you think William is forgetting himself in London?" Anne asked fearfully.

"No, Anne," Hamnet said quickly, "I am an idiot. I don't know why stupid things come out of my mouth. Judith says it is my best talent."

Just then young William Sadler, chased by Hamnet Shakespeare, ran to his father and put his arms around him.

"Save me, Father," William begged. "Hamnet is going to kill me."

Hamnet Sadler was so relieved to have Anne distracted from his intimations that William was getting drunk in London that he was glad to see his son being bullied.

"Hamnet!" Anne said sharply. "What is wrong with you?"

"He said Father left us and doesn't love us any more." Hamnet screeched trying to hit William.

"William, why would you say such a mean thing?" Hamnet asked his son, but he thought to himself, the apple doesn't fall far from the tree. My son is already saying dumb things.

"It's what Tommy told me when his mother was buying bread yesterday," William sobbed.

"Tommy's mother is the biggest gossip in town and will get our burnt loaves from now on. Has William Shakespeare, your own namesake, ever been mean to you?"

"No," William gulped.

"Of course not." Hamnet looked his son in the eye, "Think for yourself, William. Don't repeat things you hear or you will have meaner boys than Hamnet chasing you, and I won't always be there to protect you. Now apologize to Hamnet."

"I'm sorry, Hamnet," the little boy said.

Hamnet took William's hand, and they were off to find the other children to continue playing.

"I'm sorry Anne. The people in this town are just jealous that William is successful in London. When he comes home next, you two will have to stand in the town square and kiss passionately to dispel the rumors."

Anne laughed, "With my luck, the people won't recognize William, and they will accuse me of having an affair!"

Anne knew she shouldn't let what other people thought have a negative influence on her, but she had a difficult time getting to sleep that night. She kept wondering if there was something William had not told her about his stay in Windsor.

****

Anne and the children spent many happy hours with Beatrice and baby Elizabeth. Susanna loved holding the baby and pretending she was her own doll. "I want another baby at our house, Mother," Susanna said seriously.

Anne started to tear up, and Beatrice quickly said, "Susanna, you are like a big sister to Elizabeth. You are welcome to come and play with her anytime your mother says it is okay."

"Susanna," Anne gathered her emotions, "you remember your father and I told you that our family was complete with the twins. I'm sorry, but you are not going to have any more little brothers or sisters."

Susanna, sensing that she had made her mother sad, said, "I am going to adopt Elizabeth as my own baby sister. It's okay Mother."

Rationally, Anne knew that God had been kind in allowing both her twins to live, but she still had moments when she mourned the loss of more children. She knew that William would never have left her alone during a pregnancy, so he would not have pursued his dream in London if she had remained fertile. She scolded herself because sometimes she wished she had that excuse, so William would be home in Stratford with her forever.

John and Mary Shakespeare were very supportive of Anne and their grandchildren. John regretted that he had ever doubted Anne's ability as a mother. He saw that she was thoroughly committed to raising the children as bright, polite young people. Grandfather Shakespeare could often be seen walking by the Avon with his three grandchildren in tow. He taught them the names of the ducks and water birds on the river. He pointed out the weeping willows and the shadows the trees cast on the river. "That's the best place to catch fish. They love staying in the cool water caused by the shade of the tree."

John Shakespeare, the former mayor of Stratford, still associated with the town's business men, and he listened with great interest to the stories of those who had dealings in London. He took enormous pride in the fact that his son was making a name for himself in the capital city. He didn't entirely understand his son's passion for the theatre, but he could appreciate that he was very good at his craft.

Chapter 29

Lord Strange's Men continued to fill the Rose with their productions which pleased both Philip Henslowe, the owner, and Russell Northcutt, manager. One afternoon as *King Henry VI, Part One* was about to begin, Russell heard murmuring coming from the crowd. It was not the usual rowdy noise, but rather like a mass intake of breath. He peered at the crowd from his position down stage left, and to his amazement, he saw five well-dressed individuals entering the first tier boxes. They were definitely members of the upper class with a servant following them carrying cushions for their seats. They seemed familiar, and then like a bolt of lightening, Russell recognized Lord and Lady Montgomery and their daughter, Lucy.

I must warn William, Russell thought. Then he paused and thought again. *Knowing Lucy is in the audience will make William nervous and mar his performance*. Russell quickly went around the back of the stage, found William preparing for his entrance, and assured himself that William had not seen the Montgomerys enter the theatre. Russell clapped William on the back and said, "Have a good show today!"

William did have a good performance that afternoon. He always enjoyed acting in *Henry VI, Part One* as it was his very first play and thus his sentimental favorite. He liked playing the double-dealing Suffolk because the character's values were the antithesis of his own. The crowd roared at the ending, and William felt satisfied that they would be back at the Rose for *Parts Two and Three*.

As William was removing his costume, Rat slapped him on the back and said, "Well played, William!"

"Thanks, Rat. You did a fine job as well."

"Oh, I'm not talking about the play. Didn't you notice your girlfriend in the audience today?" Rat laughed.

"Girlfriend! What are you talking about you crazy man?"

"The lovely Lucy Montgomery has come all the way from Windsor to see her sweetheart perform on the big stage," Rat teased.

William Shakespeare blanched. Russell had assured him he would never see Lucy again. He quickly dressed in his street clothes and prepared to exit the theatre through the back door.

Rat continued to laugh which drew the other actors' attention, and they all began to tease their conservative play-wright. "Don't run from fun, William. Embrace your opportunities while you can."

Russell walked as slowly as he could to where he heard his actors' laughter, but it was not slowly enough. William had not made his escape from the theatre in time. "Lord Montgomery would like to congratulate you on your fine performance, William."

Rat said, "Lord Montgomery! Oh, yes, Lord Montgomery finds William irresistible!"

"Rat!" Russell barked, and the company dispersed.

"What should I do?" William asked meekly.

"Her parents are with her for pity sakes. Nothing is going to happen to you. They are waiting in their box. Go quickly. Have you had anything to drink today?"

"No!" William said annoyed at Russell and himself.

William bowed slightly to the Montgomery family and took Lord Montgomery's outstretched hand. "Very different production from *Taming of the Shrew,* Mr. Shakespeare. Quite enjoyable. Nicely done."

"Thank you very much, sir," William replied modestly.

"Our daughter convinced us we must see your play on the big stage," Lady Montgomery said formally. "The large rowdy crowd was upsetting, but once the play started, I enjoyed myself very much."

"Our daughter has determined that she wants to be an actor. She wants to leave us and go to France," Lord Montgomery said sadly.

"I am sorry to hear that," William said looking at Lucy's parents but never at her.

"Father, don't talk about me as if I'm not here. I can speak for myself. Please wait for me in the carriage. The two of you are so tedious. My handmaid, Heather, will be here to protect me from Mr Shakespeare." Lucy said snottily.

William was appalled. He had never heard anyone speak so rudely to their parents. He was further amazed when Lord and Lady Montgomery and their servants rose from their seats and bid him good day. He was left alone with Lucy and her servant.

Once her parents had left the theatre, Lucy said, "Heather, go sit over there." She pointed to the far side of the theatre. The handmaid did not argue; she simply stood and did as her young mistress bade.

William felt the sweat dripping down his back, and he looked around the theatre to see if Russell was watching and would rescue him.

"I have missed you, William," Lucy said.

"You don't know me well enough to miss me," William countered.

"You mean to say you haven't been thinking about me," Lucy flirted.

"I have only thought what a fool I was." William said.

Lucy laughed. "A fool. To drink good wine and share good conversation with a beautiful woman. You call that acting foolish."

"I do." William answered soberly.

"You are a strange man, William Shakespeare. I did not like the character you played today. You were much more attractive as Petruchio."

"Was there something you needed? I really must be going," William said, risking offending the young woman.

"You don't want to make love to me?" Lucy asked coyly.

"No!" William said adamantly stepping back from the audacious woman.

Lucy laughed and said, "Why, William, I believe you are afraid of me."

"No," William said confidently. "I am afraid **for** you."

Lucy rolled her eyes, "Not another gentlemen who wants to save my reputation and purity."

"No, I am worried about your health," William said boldly.

"Are you infected?" Lucy drew back in her seat.

"No."

"Then what could possibly happen to my health?" Lucy asked perplexed.

"You remember the character, Katherine, from *Taming of the Shrew*?"

"Of course."

"Do you remember how she beat her sister Bianca and pulled her hair? Remember her anger when she threw pots at Petruchio's head? That character is modeled after my wife, Anne. The biggest piece of fiction in that play is that her husband, Petruchio, tamed her. She is as head strong as ever, and if she were to see the two of us together? Well," William shook his head, "like I said. I would worry for your health."

229

Lucy laughed loudly when William had finished his long speech. "She is someone I would love to meet!"

"You do not want to meet her if you think that you and I can have any type of relationship."

"Not even a friendship?" Lucy asked.

"I don't see that as a possibility," William answered firmly.

"Would you be my mentor?"

"What?"

"Would you teach me about acting?" Lucy asked intently. "My father would pay you. Walk me to the carriage, and we will discuss the details there."

It was arranged that Lucy Montgomery would come to Mistress Witherington's one morning a week, on William's day off from the theatre. Lucy agreed that her handmaid would never leave the room, and William told Lord and Lady Montgomery that Mistress Witherington would also be present at every lesson.

William walked back into the Rose and found Russell Northcutt waiting for him. "What was that all about? Did you let her down easy?"

"She is no longer interested in me. She just wants me to teach her how to act."

"William, I fear she is already a good actress and has fooled you."

"I hope not," William said. He knew the risk was there, but he didn't know what else to do to avoid offending the Montgomerys.

Unbeknownst to William, three men from Stratford had attended the same performance as the Montgomery family. They were waiting in the theatre after the play hoping to have a word with their hometown playwright. They watched with interest William Shakespeare's heated conversation with the beautiful young woman clad in a light blue gown with jewels at her neck. When the young woman's servant walked past them, they asked her to whom William Shakespeare was talking. "That's his girlfriend, Lucy Montgomery," Heather teased. The men watched with amazement as William escorted the young woman from the theatre.

Three days later, John Shakespeare was at the Black Swan in Stratford enjoying a cold drink when he overheard three men at a table near him say, "That Shakespeare sure moved fast. Not in London two months, and he has a beautiful girlfriend. I never thought he had it in him. They say Lucy Montgomery's father is as rich as the Queen."

John Shakespeare hurried to his son's house on Chapel Street to warn Anne of the latest ridiculous gossip about William. He thought it best that Anne hear about it from him rather than in the street or at the market.

Anne was busy making beeswax candles and singing to the children as they drew pictures at the table when John arrived. He greeted his daughter-in-law warmly and kissed each of his grandchildren while admiring their latest artwork. "Could you children go find me a nice juicy apple from the tree while I visit with your mother for a minute?"

The children happily raced each other to the garden, and Anne pulled out a stool for her father-in-law. "What has happened, John?" Anne asked with concern.

"It is nothing, Anne. Just the latest gossip in town. I don't know where people come up with these fanciful stories."

"What have you heard?"

"Over at the Black Swan a couple of fellows were saying that William had a girlfriend in London. It's completely ridiculous, Anne, but I didn't want some busybody to catch you unaware at the market."

"What? Why would they make that up? Did they see William with someone?"

"No, no, Anne, calm down. They didn't mention seeing him with her. They just stated that he had a girlfriend. They must have made the whole thing up. They even invented a name for her: Montgomery. They said she was some rich man's daughter."

Anne gasped in shock, covering her mouth with her hand.

"What is it Anne? What is wrong?"

"That is not a made up name, Father. That is the name of the Lord that asked William to spend the night in Windsor. I have to go to London!"

"What? Anne, dear, calm down. You can't go to London."

"Yes, I can. Will you watch the children for a few minutes? I have to talk to Judith Sadler." Anne did not wait for John Shakespeare's response. She hurried out the door and ran down the street towards the bakery. By the time she arrived, the tears had started to flow down her cheeks.

Hamnet was alarmed when he saw the look on Anne's face and the tears in her eyes, "Judith!" he called to the back of the bakery, and then he gently put his arm around Anne and guided her to where Judith was kneading dough.

Judith quickly wiped her hands on her apron and went to Anne. "What has happened, Anne. Talk to me please."

"Hamnet was right" Anne sobbed. "William got drunk and forgot himself in Windsor, and now he has a girlfriend."

Judith looked daggers at her husband, "Hamnet has no idea what he is talking about most of the time. Why on earth would you believe anything he says?"

"She's right, Anne. I don't know anything," Hamnet added.

"You were right this time, Hamnet. William's father overheard men talking about William at the Black Swan.

They said William has a girlfriend named Montgomery. Remember how strange you found it that William stayed in Windsor instead of returning to London with the rest of the company. It's not strange if you are having an affair with the young woman of the house!" Anne resumed crying while Judith and Hamnet looked hopelessly at each other.

"It's not true," Judith said more to herself than to Anne or Hamnet. "It's just not true."

"Hamnet, will you take me to London?" Anne asked through her sobs.

"London? I've never been to London. I don't think that's a good idea. The roads are awful this time of year, and we don't have a carriage that could make the trip."

"I will ride Dobbin," Anne declared.

"No, that's not a good idea," Hamnet said.

"Hamnet," Judith said, "You are taking Anne to London so she can see for herself that William has not forgotten her."

"Really?" Hamnet said incredulously, "I'm taking Anne to London?"

"Good! That is settled. Now Anne, I can help with the children, but do you think they could sleep at your in-laws? I'm sure Beatrice will help as well. I think you should take four days for the journey, Hamnet, so Anne doesn't get too worn out."

"I'm taking Anne to London? We are going to take four days to get there?" Hamnet could not keep up with his wife's plans.

"You can stay in Oxford with Sarah Spencer. Hamnet, stop staring at me and help me think. Where can you stay between here and Oxford?"

Hamnet seemed to realize for the first time that the women were serious about this crazy trip to London. "There's my cousin, Rose, in Banbury."

"Yes! She would be happy to see you and that is about half way to Oxford. Now, where is a good place to stay between Oxford and London?"

"Is your Aunt Minnie still in Loudwater?"

"Hamnet! Aunt Minnie has been dead at least five years, but I think her son Andrew still lives there. I will send a letter today, and hopefully, it will get there before you do. If Andrew is not there, you will just have to get two rooms at an inn in Loudwater."

Anne was grateful that Judith saw how important it was for her to confront William now before she let the specter of an affair fester in her imagination. The odds seemed against William. His failure to explain his stay at Windsor. The men at the pub knowing the Montgomery name. Now that she had time to calm down, she wondered if she had reacted too strongly to John Shakespeare's news.

Anne hugged Judith and Hamnet and thanked them for their help. "I will let you know when I can leave. I just need to talk to my father-in-law." Anne tried to convince herself that she was wrong as she walked back up Henley Street toward her little cottage on Chapel. When she arrived, she found John and the children happily playing in the garden.

"Are you okay, Anne?" John asked with genuine concern.

"Yes, I just need a favor. Could you return to the pub and ask those men for more details on the story they heard about William? If they aren't there, maybe someone at least knows their names."

"I can do that, Anne. One of the men was the son of Stanley Harris. I can find him if I have the need."

"Thank you, Father. I don't want this to be true, but I must know."

Once John Shakespeare was gone, Anne went to her room, took a small valise and as if in a dream, started to put things into it. She soon realized that riding Dobbin to London was a daunting task. William had often told Anne that Lord Strange's Men met very few women on the road during their travels because it wasn't safe. The company had strength in numbers and didn't have to worry as much about the cut-throats and highway men who made their living robbing in-nocent travelers. Anne sat down heavily on her bed and sighed.

It wasn't long before John Shakespeare returned to Chapel Street a dour expression on his face. "It seems bad, Anne. Ross Harris, the son of my friend, was in London at the Rose. He and two of his companions were waiting for William after the play hoping to speak to him, and they saw him in deep conversation with a richly dressed young woman with dark hair. They asked a servant accompanying the mys-terious woman what her name was, and she said, 'Lucy Montgomery, William Shakespeare's girlfriend.' They watched William leave the theatre with her, and then they lost sight of them both."

Anne listened in shock to her father-in-law's story. It was even worse than she had allowed herself to imagine. "I have to go to London," she managed to tell John Shakespeare. "Hamnet will escort me, and I will ride Dobbin."

"Anne, do you really think that is a good idea?" John Shakespeare asked gently.

"Yes, I must fight for my marriage. Can the children stay with you and Mary? Judith and Beatrice will help with them during the days."

"Let's go talk to Mary. Come here," John called to the children in the garden. "We are going to see your grandmoth-er."

Thankfully for Anne, John Shakespeare explained everything to William's mother while William's younger brothers, Richard and Edmond, played with the children. Anne thought that Mary Shakespeare would scold her and tell her to stop overreacting. She did no such thing.

"Come with me, Anne," Mary demanded.

Anne followed her mother-in-law up the narrow stairway to a loft room at the top of the house. Mary knelt in front of a wooden chest and drew forth a pair of blue breeches and a brown doublet. She stood and held the breeches up to Anne. "Richard has outgrown these, but I think they will fit you. Pull the breeches on under your dress and put the doublet on as well. Let's see how they fit."

Anne was confused but did as Mary asked. The clothes fit quite nicely. "Those will do," Mary said. "Now we need a sturdy hat to hide your hair. You cannot ride Dobbin to London as a woman. You and Hamnet must be two male travelers, and it will be better if you can join the post rider or other men for your journey. The children will be fine here. You are not to worry about them."

So it was accomplished that Anne and Hamnet set off for London the next morning.

Chapter 30

Lucy Montgomery's first acting lesson was going remarkably well. William had pushed the heavy furniture in Mistress Witherington's parlor to the side and had formed an open space to represent the stage. Lucy's handmaid had fallen asleep almost immediately after taking a chair by the fire, but ever vigilant Mistress Witherington watched William and Lucy intently while her knitting needles flew at their work.

William walked toward the front of the house, "This is upstage." He walked toward the dining room, "This is downstage. Stage right is always your right, not the audience's right. Stage left is always your left."

"I understand," Lucy said.

"Good. You have been an attentive pupil. Let's finish with a simple exercise. Walk down stage left."

Lucy started to move toward William as he had instructed, when suddenly, a man burst into the parlor from the hallway shouting, "Get away from him! Leave him alone!" The man flung himself at Lucy.

Lucy screamed and covered her face while the stranger in blue breeches, a brown doublet, and a brown woolen hat pummeled Lucy with his fists. William grabbed the intruder around the waist and pulled him from Lucy. "What is the meaning of this?" William demanded.

"Finally, we get some action around here," Mistress Witherington said letting her ball of yarn drop from her lap and unravel across the parlor floor.

"Get away from my husband!" the man shouted and tried to get out of William's grasp.

William turned the angry man towards him and pulled down the woolen scarf which covered his face, "Anne!" William could not believe his eyes.

Lucy was sobbing and hugging herself in the corner. Anne melted into William's chest and sobbed. Hamnet came quickly into the parlor and said, "Hello, William. I tried to tell Anne that a surprise visit was not the best idea."

"I don't understand. How is it possible that you are in London?" William addressed Hamnet as he seemed to be the only sane person in the room.

"It's not my fault, but Anne learned about your girlfriend here, and she . . ."

"My girlfriend!" William groaned.

Suddenly, Lucy stopped crying and wiped her eyes with the backs of her hands. "Is this young man your wife?"

This rekindled Anne's tirade, "He is my husband. You must go! Get out!" She pointed to the door.

William removed the hat from Anne's head and let her hair cascade down her back. Lucy realized in amazement that she had been attacked not by a man but by a woman. No wonder she didn't feel battered. Anne had frightened her more than hurt her.

William held Anne by the shoulders and said firmly, "Lucy is my student, not my girlfriend. There is nothing between us!"

"Well, there could have been something between us," Lucy regained her voice.

"Lucy!" William said sharply. "Tell my wife the truth."

"Truth be told, your husband warned me that you would beat me senseless if I tried anything with him. I thought he was just blustering."

"Tell her the rest," William insisted.

"Sad to say, I used all my charms and wiles to woo your husband, and he turned me down. You are one lucky woman."

Embarrassment began to replace Anne's anger and she whimpered, "But they saw you together at the Rose. You left together, and your servant said you were William Shakespeare's girlfriend."

Heather had awakened abruptly when Anne rushed into the room, and she was following the action with interest. "I have no idea what she is talking about," the conniving handmaid said.

"Don't listen to her," Lucy said. "She is an incredible liar. That's why I keep her around. My parents believe everything she says."

"Oh no, I have made a mess of things. William, I am so sorry. Miss Montgomery, I hope I didn't injure you," Anne was horrified at her actions.

"I told William that I looked forward to meeting you. It didn't happen exactly the way I hoped, but it is good to meet a woman who stands up for her rights!" Lucy told Anne.

Lucy and Heather prepared to leave, and much to Anne's surprise, Lucy gave her a hug before she left and said, "Glad to meet you Mrs. Shakespeare. Your husband is safe with me."

Hamnet unpacked the horses, and Mistress Witherington's kitchen boy lead Dobbin and Hamnet's horse, Grey, to the stable where Barbary was under the watchful care of Tom Knox.

"You can stay in the ante room near the kitchen," Mistress Witherington told Hamnet. "Take a couple of hours to rest and freshen up," she told Anne, "and I will have a proper meal prepared. I want to hear all about your journey to

London. A fine young woman astride a horse for four days dressed as a man. This easily beats shipwreck stories."

Anne and William walked quietly up the stairs to William's room. Once they were alone, Anne attempted to explain, "I thought I was losing you."

"Shh!" William put his finger to Anne's lips. "No talking. It is marvelous that you are here. I have dreamt of this every night for two months. Come to bed, Anne. Save your tale for later, I want to hold you and never let you go."

****

William and Anne walked into the dining room where Hamnet was seated enjoying a plate of cheese and bread. "Did you have a good rest?" Hamnet asked, winking at William and Anne.

"Hamnet!" William clapped his good friend on the shoulder. "I have barely said two words to you since you arrived. Thank you for bringing Anne safely to me. How did you ever arrange everything?"

"It was a bit of a logistical nightmare," Hamnet shook his head. "I had to figure out where we could stay along the way, and I came up with the ingenious idea of dressing Anne like a man so she would be safer."

Anne couldn't help but giggle as she listened to her dear friend weave the fantastical tale.

"What?" William looked at Anne and then at Hamnet. "Why is Anne laughing?"

"Your wife believes in honesty above all else. The truth is that Judith arranged everything. I didn't even want to come," Hamnet joined Anne in her laughter, and the three friends embraced each other warmly.

"Judith was amazing, William. When she saw how upset I was, she just sprang into action, but she is not the only one who helped plan this amazing trip."

"If Hamnet wasn't a willing conspirator, who was?" William asked.

"Your mother!" Anne said with delight. "The boy's clothing I was wearing were things that your brother Richard had outgrown. Your mother dug them out of a trunk for me. It was her idea for me to arrive as a man."

"My mother thought that I was having an affair, and she helped you come here to clear things up? This is a day of one inconceivable event after another."

"Don't you three start with your tale before I am seated at the table," Mistress Witherington scolded. "Anne, help me bring the serving platters to the table."

Mistress Witherington had outdone herself for Anne's welcome to London. The table was laden with roasted potatoes and onions, pork shoulder, Yorkshire pudding, kidney pie, and fresh rolls. Anne and Hamnet were unable to continue their story for the first few minutes as neither of them had realized how hungry they were.

Finally, Anne sat back in her chair and said, "Thank you, Mistress Witherington. This food is delicious. And thank you for taking such good care of William. He raves about you, your cooking, and your lovely home in his letters. I recognized your house right away from his description."

"Why thank you, dear. This is the best house in Bankside. My husband demanded only the best. That's why he married me. Tell me what you think of London," Mistress Witherington said with a twinkle in her eye.

"Well, I," Anne hesitated. "I have hardly had time to see the city."

Mistress Witherington burst into laughter. "You hate it as much as your husband! You two are like peas in a pod."

Anne relaxed, "I don't know which is worse: the smell or the noise. I had to wrap a scarf around my face to be able to breathe. Please tell me about the children in the street. Are they all orphans?"

"Most of the poor creatures are all alone in this world. It's the plague that takes their parents. Those that have parents are worse off than the orphans because they have to steal enough food to feed their drunken mothers or fathers as well as themselves. London is a big city, and she can't deal with all her troubles."

"I thought I saw human heads on stakes as we crossed London Bridge. They aren't real are they?" Anne asked curiously.

William gave Hamnet a hard look, and Hamnet shrugged his shoulders and said, "As soon as I spotted the grotesque things, I told Anne not to look up. Just as I warned her, she looked up."

"It's not Hamnet's fault, William. I was so excited to see the great London Bridge, and I was thinking about our fantasies of living there. I was gawking every which way, and I saw the heads before Hamnet could rush me past them. Who are they?"

"The heads are primarily political enemies of the Queen. Some plotted to kill her; others committed high treason. William could have a place of honor up there if he includes any negative propaganda in his plays. The Queen runs a tight ship."

Anne shuddered. "I've always admired Queen Elizabeth, but I didn't realize she was capable of such cruelty."

"She *has to be cruel to be kind*," William said. "She sacrifices much to protect her country and her people. Her own mother, Anne Boleyn was executed for treason when Elizabeth was only three. When she was twenty-one, her half sister Mary imprisoned her in the Tower of London. They say the back of her head is totally bald from sleeping on the stones of her cell. She wears elaborate collars and high ruffs to hide this fact."

Mistress Witherington continued the discussion, "She is a woman ruling in a man's world. Everything she does is scrutinized. She will never marry because she is engaged to Princes from every kingdom which threatens England. Those countries don't dare attack their Prince's fiance, so she keeps peace."

Mistress Witherington continued, "William, Anne shouldn't have to see those heads from afar. You should take her to the Tower of London for a beheading. They happen frequently. Then you can take her to St Paul's Cathedral to pray for their poor departed souls. The Cathedral is magnificent."

Anne could feel Mistress Witherington's food roil in her stomach as she listened to the friendly woman's idea of good sight-seeing in London. "I would love to see St Paul's," she said quietly. "Must I travel in London as Andrew or can I return to Anne?"

"Don't be silly, girl," Mistress Witherington said. "As long as you are with Hamnet and William and you never go out after dark, you are perfectly safe in our fine city."

"Andrew?" William inquired.

"Yes, my Judith thought of everything Will," Hamnet explained. "I was suppose to refer to Anne as Andrew when we were riding in the company of other men. She knew I would not remember, of course, so she said I could just explain that Anne was my nickname for Andrew."

Anne laughed, "Several times he called me Annnneeee-drew. The men just thought he had a stammer!"

Chapter 31

The sun had not gone down when the friends finished their good meal and conversation, so William, Anne, and Hamnet went for a stroll along the Thames. Hamnet was amazed at the huge barges and the cargo they carried. William explained that as the largest city in Europe, London received goods from the entire European continent. "The most amazing thing about the Thames is that it is heavily influenced by the tides. When the tide is out, the larger boats are unable to navigate, so the ship captains must schedule their arrivals and departures accordingly."

William led them to the Rose, and they stopped along the way to visit Barbary, Dobbin, and Grey. The horses were well-groomed and content. Anne liked Tom Knox immediately and would have taken him and his little brother home to Stratford with her if she could. The two boys were orphans, but they had each other and jobs, so they did not have to steal to survive.

Anne was astonished by the size of the Rose. "That huge theatre fills up with people to watch your plays?"

"Yes," William said proudly, "some afternoons over 2,000 patrons crowd into the theatre. Tomorrow afternoon, you and Hamnet can watch *Henry VI, Part Three.* I will secure the best seats in the house and provide cushions for you."

"I am excited to see the completion of your Henry VI plays," Anne said, "but I really want to watch *Capturing of an Angel.*"

Hamnet was confused as he hadn't heard of this play, "Is this a piece you have written since you came to London?"

William laughed and said, "No, Hamnet. Anne has mistaken the title of our romance. It is called *The Taming of the Shrew*."

"William you are either a very stupid man or a very brave man. I think it is the former. Did you not see Anne beating poor Lucy Montgomery? She will do the same to you, and I don't want to witness the carnage," Hamnet warned his good friend.

Both Anne and William laughed. "Truth sometimes has to be sacrificed for art, Hamnet," Anne explained. "William has exaggerated our personalities to make audience's laugh."

"We are performing the comedy at locations outside the Rose. Russell Northcutt has scheduled us to play at the Inns of Court next week and at Lord and Lady Winters the following week."

"I trust the Winters have only sons," Hamnet said and raised his eyebrows.

"I have learned my lesson, Hamnet," William said contritely.

"I have learned my lesson as well, Hamnet. I promise I will not drag you away from your family and bakery every time William meets an engaging young woman of the upper class," Anne apologized to Hamnet.

The three friends walked happily back to Mistress Witherington's for a well deserved good night of sleep. Hamnet went off to his little ante room, and William and Anne climbed the stairs to William's loft room. As they entered the room, William took Anne in his arms and kissed her neck, her cheek, and her waiting lips. The two felt like newlyweds as they hurriedly removed each other's clothes and fell to the bed in each other's arms. William's caresses sent warm shock waves through Anne, and she nestled closer to the man she loved with all her heart.

Soon they were content to simply hold each other and marvel at the good fortune of being together. "William," Anne said tentatively, "I have a confession to make."

"Have you found someone in Stratford?" William asked.

"William!" Anne scolded and lightly punched him on the arm. "I wanted to tell you about my nightmares. Remember when I was expecting Susanna, and I was disturbed by dreams of a green-eyed monster?"

"Yes, that has been a recurring nightmare for you. Several times I thought you were angry with me," William said.

"I finally figured out what it means. When Hamnet and I were on our way here, every time I fell asleep, I was awakened by that nightmare. Then when we arrived, and I rushed at Lucy, I realized that it was about me. I was the green-eyed monster! I was so jealous that you might be seeing someone else, that I turned into a monster. I'm so sorry, William. I have behaved badly," Anne began to cry softly.

"My sweet, Anne. Please don't take all the blame upon yourself. I was less than honest with you. I should have told you about Lucy. I should have told you about the ugliness of London. I justified my actions by thinking that I was protecting you, but you know me so well, you knew there were things I wasn't telling you." William held Anne close.

"William I can't bring Susanna, Hamnet, and Judith here. It is too horrible for them to endure. I'm afraid we can never live together as a family in London, but I miss you so when you are away," Anne confessed.

"I know sweetheart. That's why I haven't written about London or even thought about having you here. You and the children are much better off in Stratford."

"The Rose is amazing, and your opportunities here are the very best. Can our family survive living in two different places?" Anne asked hopefully.

"I think we must," William said sadly.

"Are we a burden to you?" Anne asked.

"What? Why would you even suggest that?" William was appalled. "You and the children are the best things that have ever happened to me. I will help Hamnet bake bread to support you if I have to move back to Stratford to keep you."

Anne laughed. "You would make a dismal baker, William! You are a playwright. We can manage with letters and visits. I will keep my monster on a leash if you promise not to drink too much wine when beautiful young women are in your presence."

"Russell Northcutt is helping me save and invest my money. Soon, perhaps in five years, I will have enough to support us without acting. I can continue to write from Stratford and just come to London occasionally," William promised Anne.

Though the young couple needed the clarification of speaking face-to-face that Anne's visit afforded them, they needed physical closeness with each other even more. They fell asleep with William's arm around Anne holding her tightly while her head rested on his shoulder.

The next morning, Anne, Hamnet, and Mistress Witherington visited over fried potatoes, eggs, tomatoes, and sausages. "I must tell you, Anne. You gave an old woman quite a thrill with your attack on that spoiled rich girl. I only wish you would have knocked her teeth right out of her head. She is an arrogant little pup," Mistress Witherington laughed at the memory of Anne rushing into the parlor.

"I am so embarrassed," Anne said. "I'm not really a violent person."

"No, she isn't," Hamnet contributed, "but her alter ego Andrew is one tough cookie."

"You make a fine looking gentleman," Mistress Witherington said seriously. "Now Anne or Andrew, whichever, I must tell you that you have nothing to worry about with your man here. William is the most boring tenant I have ever had. He is like a monk in a cloister. Never comes home late and drunk. Never brings strange friends to the house. He is simply boring."

The three friends laughed, finished their breakfast, and went on a short tour of London before going to the Rose to see William's play. St Paul's Cathedral took Anne's breath away, and she loved wandering through the booksellers' stalls which surrounded the beautiful church. William and Anne found books for each of their children. "You need to take Judith and the children something special," William told Hamnet. "Let's look in the shops on London Bridge."

The bridge had over a hundred shops along its span. Hamnet found a toy shop and said, "Now we're talking. My children would cry if I brought them books." He found a brightly painted top for his oldest son, William; a small wooden doll for his daughter, Anne; and a little wooden horse for his youngest child, Harry.

Hamnet and Anne were both drawn to a Tinker's Shop which displayed its wares in a large window. Hamnet found a large pewter platter that he thought Judith would like. Anne was taken by a set of eight pewter goblets with embossed clusters of grapes and elegant, twisted stems which resembled the sturdy vines of the grapes. "I want to buy you this set of goblets," William said.

"Oh, no," Anne gasped. "They are too expensive."

"These goblets have the exact design as those the Montgomery's had at their estate," William laughed. "They will always remind me of what I could have lost. Hamnet, is there room for them in the saddle bags?"

"We will make room," Hamnet said.

After a quick tour of Westminster and Whitehall Palace, William left Anne and Hamnet and went to the Rose to prepare for *King Henry VI Part Three*.

Hamnet and Anne stopped at Mistress Witherington's to leave their packages, and then they walked together to the Rose. It was amazing to see the crowds gathering near the theatre. Many patrons walked across London Bridge, but others debarked from boats that had rowed them across the Thames.

Tom Knox was waiting for them at the entrance to the theatre holding two cushions in his arms. "Follow me to your seats," Tom said politely. William had saved them seats in the lower tier of seats near the stage. The ground surrounding the stage was already crowded with patrons drinking from wine flasks and shelling nuts while they claimed their prime spots near the front of the stage. Many men leaned against the front of the stage and used it as a table for their jugs of ale.

As the theatre continued to fill with people, Hamnet and Anne were amazed at how closely packed the standing audience, or penny groundlings as William called them, became. They were not a quiet crowd. Much shoving and arguing ensued as the men fought to get closer to the front of the stage. Anne was grateful that William had given them seats above the fray.

Suddenly, a young man walked to the center of the stage and blew a fanfare on a long silver trumpet. The crowd began to quiet and then the groundlings divided like the Red Sea allowing the company of actors to walk through them to the stage. Anne cringed when she saw that one of the men was holding a bloody head high in the air. When the actors mounted the stage, Anne could see that William was the actor holding the head!

The actors were dressed as soldiers holding bloody swords and shields. They each had white roses on their hats or armor showing their allegiance to the House of York. The Earl of Warwick stepped down stage and the rowdy crowd became silent as they waited for the first line of *Henry VI, Part Three*. Hamnet, Anne, and the thousands of other patrons were instantly drawn into the war between York and Lancaster. William as Richard, Duke of Gloucester, threw down the bloody head, and said, *"Thus do I hope to shake King Henry's head."* He then moved up stage to sit in the throne of Henry. With a flourish King Henry and attendants with red roses adorning their costumes entered the stage. Thus the action began and the audience was transported to another time and place away from the vagaries of their daily lives.

Anne found the battle scenes difficult to watch, so she looked out over the faces of the audience and saw their focus rapt with attention to the action on stage. She was amazed when William took the stage alone to deliver a long speech, a soliloquy, which revealed his character, the Duke of Gloucester to be hungry for power and dishonest in his dealings with his brother. Anne sat in awe that her good, kind husband could play such an evil character. Perhaps William was able to be a good person off stage because he put on the cloak of evil each afternoon at the theatre.

The audience erupted in cheers and applause at the conclusion of the play. Lord Strange's Men returned for several bows before the crowd quieted down and started to leave the theatre. Hamnet looked at Anne in amazement, "Our William is a star, Anne. We can't take him away from this, can we?"

"No, we can't," Anne agreed. "William was meant to write and perform plays, and those of us who love him have to learn to share him with the world."

Chapter 32

Anne thought her heart was going to break when she had to say goodbye to William, but the applause at the Rose echoed in her head and the thought of seeing her children again made it possible for her to leave William's embrace and mount Dobbin for the ride home to Stratford. Wearing Richard's clothes at least gave Anne some physical comfort for the long journey home.

"William, you're too famous to be standing in this neighborhood hugging and kissing Anne while she is wearing those clothes," Hamnet teased. "I can hear the rumors running from here to Stratford. Soon your father will leave the Black Swan and hurry to Chapel Street to warn Anne that you are having an affair with a man!"

William and Anne both laughed. "Thank you again, Hamnet, for bringing Anne safely to me, and thank you for escorting her home. Give Judith and the children my love," William said as he shook his friend's hand. William had tears in his eyes as he watched his best friend and his true love ride away toward London Bridge.

Anne's visit helped William regain his drive to write as much as he could each day. The more plays he finished, the more money he could make, and the faster his reputation as a playwright would grow. If he could sell enough plays, he could invest in an acting company and even a theatre. Those investments would make it possible for him to spend less time in London and more time in Stratford with Anne and his children.

His work on *A Comedy of Errors,* the play about two sets of twins and the humorous complications of their mistaken identities, was progressing nicely. It made William laugh, and it was good therapy for him to work on the play to assuage the sorrow of Anne's departure. At the same time, he was writing a historical play to follow Henry VI. He had devoted much energy to creating and acting the part of Richard and wanted to continue that story. King Richard III was the type of character audiences loved to hate. William depicted him as having a hunched back and a club foot with a disposition more deformed than his physical being. Russell Northcutt assured William that audiences who had seen his Henry VI plays would flock to see *Richard III*.

Early one evening, William was sitting at the little table in his room working on *A Comedy of Errors* when someone rapped on his door. William called, "Come in!"

Mistress Witherington swept into the room followed by a handsome young man. "This man claims to know you, William. He claims you want to see him. Do you know him?"

"No, I don't believe I do," William answered tentatively.

"Out with you!" Mistress Witherington grabbed the young man by the arm and started pulling him toward the door.

"Excuse me, Mr. Shakespeare," the young man could not contain his mirth. "Your lovely guard. . .err landlady misunderstood what I said. I was trying to tell her that I know you by reputation and though we haven't met, you know me as well. I'm Christopher Marlowe." He shook himself free from Mistress Witherington and walked toward William with his hand extended.

William was thunderstruck and reached out to take Christopher Marlowe's hand. "It is a real pleasure to meet you, sir," William said while pumping Marlowe's hand.

"Do you want this miscreant to stay?" Mistress Witherington asked in disgust.

"It's fine, Betty. Christopher Marlowe is a playwright, and I am very happy to meet him," William tried to reassure his landlady who had taken an instant dislike to Marlowe.

"I don't trust him," Betty Witherington said with a sneer.

Marlowe laughed and said, "I have that effect on all women. Men too, come to think of it."

"We will be fine. Thank you for showing him to my room," William told Mistress Witherington as he put his arm around her and showed her to the door.

Betty Witherington looked Christopher Marlowe up and down and said quietly to William as she was leaving, "Cry out for me if he tries anything." William closed the door behind her as she headed down the stairs.

Marlowe was still chuckling when William turned to face him. "They didn't tell me you brought your mother with you to London."

"How did you find me?" William asked in wonder.

"I've been watching for you in the pubs around the theatre and finally a member of your company, Henry Adams, told me that you spent your evenings writing, not drinking. Sounds like a horrible life. He gave me this address. I hope you don't mind that I looked you up."

"Mind? No, I have been hoping to meet you since I arrived in London. Here, take my chair, and I will sit on the bed. I am a great admirer of your work," William said sincerely.

"That's obvious. I see you have copied my blank verse."

William felt himself turning red and said, "Now look, I started writing my Henry plays in blank verse before I even saw *Dido, Queen of Carthage*."

Marlowe laughed merrily, "I don't own the English language nor her meter. I just naturally pick fights. It's what I do."

"Oh, well I'm sorry. I'm nervous meeting you this way. The thing I love about your writing is the way you vary the meter. You make the language interesting by switching away from blank verse. How do you know when to do that?" William asked curiously.

"You do the same thing in your plays," Marlowe countered.

"You've seen my plays?" William was shocked.

"Just four of them so far. Do you have more?"

"Wait! *Taming of the Shrew* has only been performed once."

"Yes, I was at the Montgomery's estate for that performance. I wasn't asked to stay to dine. An unfortunate incident with their daughter, Lucy, put a bit of a tarnish on my name with them. She is something, isn't she?"

William's head was spinning and he couldn't keep up with the conversation. Finally he asked dumbly, "Do you like my plays?"

Marlowe laughed again and said, "No. I think you have absolutely no talent. That's why I took the time to look you up, so I could tell you to give up the theatre and leave the writing of plays to the university men who clearly know what they are doing."

William was speechless and just stared at Christopher Marlowe until Marlowe burst into his loudest laughter yet and said, "You are even duller than the gossips claim. I love your plays. I thought you could only do battle scenes and histories, but I liked your comedy even more than the Henry plays. And you act. I am petrified on stage. Not with fear. No by two o'clock on any given day, I am petrified with drink. No way could I get through a performance as myself, much less playing a role with lines I had to memorize."

William took a deep breath and looked around the room to ascertain whether he was dreaming or awake. He thought Christopher Marlowe had just complimented him on his writing.

"What are you working on now?" Marlowe asked as he looked at the pages strewn on William's table.

"It's a comedy," William said weakly. When Marlowe nodded encouragement to him, he continued, "I have a set of twin children at home in Stratford, and even though they are different sexes, sometimes they manage to trick my wife and I. They have this amazing communication with each other, without speaking, one knows what the other is thinking," William trailed off.

"So this is a comedy about your children," Marlowe said.

"No. It was just inspired by them. I'm using Plautus' play *The Brothers Menaechmus* as my source, but I am including two sets of twins to increase the confusion and humor."

"Sounds good. I'm working on an autobiography," Marlowe laughed yet again. "It's about a man who sells his soul to the devil. A German tale about Faustus is my source."

Finally, William was catching on to Marlowe's absurd sense of humor, and he was able to laugh along with the playwright he had admired for so long. The men talked for over an hour, and when Marlowe stood to leave, William was disappointed to see him go.

"It has been an honor meeting you," William said as he shook Marlowe's hand.

"Likewise," Marlowe answered. "I've got to go about the devil's work now. I hope to see you again someday."

William sat in shock for several minutes after Marlowe left. He didn't know which was more amazing: that Christopher Marlowe had come to see him or that Christopher Marlowe liked his plays. He started a letter to Anne immediately to share his incredible news.

Chapter 33

The holiday season in London was a busy time for theatre companies, and William was unable to be with his family in Stratford to celebrate the twelve days of Christmas. He was grateful for Anne's unexpected visit to London, but he hadn't seen his children since September of 1590.

He traveled home in time for the twins' sixth birthdays on February 2, 1591, and stayed with the family for a fortnight. He was amazed at how much the children had grown, and he never tired of listening to their stories and having them read to him.

One evening as the family was sitting together around the table, Anne said, "Now that Hamnet is six, we should enroll him at the Stratford Grammar School. He can teach Susanna and Judith what he learns each day as my brother, Bartholomew, did for me."

"His reading is excellent," William said. "I think you might be the best teacher for him."

"I have so many gaps in my knowledge," Anne said. "I want our children to have complete educations."

The Shakespeare children had been taught from their earliest days that they were not to interrupt adult conversation, but six-year-old Judith could not contain herself. "Please don't make Hamnet go to school all day," she said with tears in her eyes.

"I know you will miss him, dear, but he will be with us every evening. He won't forget you while he is at school," Anne tried to comfort her sad little daughter.

"He doesn't have time," Judith said with tears streaming down her face. "He has so little time left with us."

Cold chills went down both Anne and William's spines. They looked at each other and then looked at their children.

Hamnet had gotten off his chair and walked to his twin. They held each other tight as Hamnet tried to console his broken-hearted sister.

"We will hire a tutor if you feel you are out of depth in any subject, Anne," William said quietly. "I think one person absent from this family is enough. Come here sweet Judith."

Hamnet released his sister, and she went to her father and climbed up on his lap. "Thank you, father," she said and kissed him on the cheek.

William hugged his little girl close as he looked around the table at the people he loved most in the world. "I have to return to London next week for two months, children. Then I will be home with you for a full month before I have to join Lord Strange's Men for our summer tour. I am never very far from you when I am on tour, so if you need me, I can be home in a day." William tried to reassure the family that all was well, but Judith's plea, "he has such little time left with us" cast a dark shadow over the Shakespeare home.

"I think the people who live in London are not very smart. They go to plays when it is cold and miserable outside, but when it is warm and sunny, they stay home," Susanna said trying to lighten the sad mood at the table.

William was relieved to be able to laugh. "Good observation, Susanna! Londoners are not any less bright than we are. They know about disease and understand that in the heat of the summer, they are more likely to get sick from being crowded together in the theatre. Those Londoners who can afford it, leave London in the summer and move into the country where they can grow gardens and have fresh air."

"Remember when I returned from London and told you about the magnificent things I saw--St Paul's Cathedral, the Tower of London, London Bridge, and the Rose?" Anne asked the children.

"Yes!" the three children nodded their heads enthusiastically.

"I also told you how sad London was for me. Little children living on their own because their parents and grandparents were dead. Disgusting smells from too many people emptying their chamber pots onto the streets because they have no gardens. Too many people, living too close together makes London an unappealing place to live. That's why your father and I agree it is better for us to stay here in Stratford rather than be with him in London. Can you understand that?" Anne asked hopefully.

As the oldest, Susanna answered first, "We miss father so much, but he is a famous playwright and famous playwrights live in London. Children with parents who love them live in Stratford."

Judith and Hamnet nodded their heads in agreement. "He brings us things when he comes home," Hamnet said laughing.

"Oh, I see, Hamnet. You like it when I go away because I bring you presents when I come home!" William teased his only son.

"The Sadler children got toys from their father. We only get books, so you might as well stay home!" Hamnet winked at his father.

William jumped from the table grabbed his son, and flipped him upside down holding him by the ankles. "Take it back! Take it back!" William cried as Hamnet laughed so hard he could barely catch his breath.

William gently placed Hamnet on the floor and then gathered him into his arms for a long hug. "Six-year-old boys should get bows and arrows, not books! I will try to do better."

"Can I have books and a bow and arrow?" Hamnet asked.

****

By William Shakespeare's twenty-seventh birthday on April 23, 1591, he had completed both *Richard III* and *The Comedy of Errors*. Through dedication to his craft, he had written and helped produce six successful full length plays. Lord Strange's Men decided they would perform four of Shakespeare's plays on tour: *Henry VI, Part Three, Richard III, Taming of the Shrew*, and *The Comedy of Errors*. Through William's friendship with Christopher Marlowe, they obtained his permission to perform *Dido, Queen of Carthage* as their fifth play.

William found his second tour to be very taxing, both physically and mentally. The summer of 1590, everything had been an adventure. He saw new places, heard large audiences applaud his plays, and enjoyed the camaraderie of his fellow actors. The summer of 1591, William had no patience for his low-ceilinged lodging and his snoring roommates. He found it difficult to write in the noisy pubs and found the endless packing and unpacking of the prop wagon pure drudgery.

The only positive part of the summer tour was the opportunity to polish and perfect his two new plays. Both plays were well-received, and Russell Northcutt and William felt they would assure a good crowd in London in the fall. William informed Russell in late July that he would not be joining the company the following summer. His time would be spent in Stratford with his family writing as much as he possibly could. Northcutt said, "Touring is not for everyone. Thanks for giving me early notice, so I can find someone to take your place next year. We can still use your plays, I hope?"

"I'm counting on it," William said. "I'm not ready to give up my entire income for the summer."

"When we return to London, let me introduce you to some possible patrons. You have developed so quickly as a playwright, it should not be difficult to find someone to support you."

"Thank you," William said, appreciative of his manager's confidence in his talent and understanding of his desire to be home with his family during the summer.

Chapter 34

William walked off the stage in Cambridge after a successful performance of *Richard III* and was shocked to find Christopher Marlowe waiting for him. "Hello old chap," Marlowe greeted him, "do you have time for a drink with a fellow theatre rat?"

"Chris! It's great to see you! What brings you to Cambridge? Are they bestowing some honor on you?"

Marlowe laughed merrily, "Not likely. I've done nothing to make this university proud."

"Not true," William countered. "Your plays are a huge success. I wish I could take credit for *Dido, Queen of Carthage,* then this tour would be an all Shakespeare extravaganza," William teased.

The two playwrights left the Guild Hall, crossed the River Cam on Clare Bridge, and entered the Eagle Pub. Marlowe lead William to a table in the back and signaled to the barman that they needed ale. William noted that Marlowe had started his drinking earlier in the day, and that his friend's effusive talk was partially driven by intoxication.

"What have you been up to, Chris?"

"I just returned from the Netherlands."

"What? How are you able to travel so much? I dream of seeing France, Spain, and more of the continent, and you casually mention that you have been in Holland. How do you manage it?"

"I think I told you when we first met that I sold my soul to the Devil. The Devil requires me to travel a great deal. It isn't all pleasant. This trip I was actually arrested on a false charge of counterfeiting Guilders."

"Why would they take you for a counterfeiter?" William asked in amazement.

"Perhaps it was because the Devil financed my entire trip using counterfeit Guilders," Marlowe drained his ale and shouted for more.

"I'm not following. For whom do you actually work?"

Christopher Marlowe seemed to ignore William's question. "I have a great plot for your next play. Start with an evil spirit, a ghost or a witch, and have this evil character charm your hero."

William decided to go along with his friend's line of conversation. "Just how does this evil spirit tempt my hero?"

"That's as classic as man himself. The spirit flatters your hero. The spirit tells your hero that he has the keenest intellect, the shrewdest leadership skills, and that he alone can perform the tasks that must be performed to save his country. Yes. I fell for the oldest trick in the Devil's repertoire."

"Are we still talking about a play I should write?" William asked with concern.

"Yes, friend. I would like you to write the tragedy of Christopher Marlowe when I am dead," Marlowe said sadly.

"What have you gotten yourself into, Chris?"

"I told you. I sold my soul to the Devil, and the Devil always gets his due."

"Is there anything I can do to help you? Do you want to join the tour, so you have friendly faces around you?"

"I'm not like you William. I have no moral vision. I am reeling from my close call in Holland right now, but by morning when I have slept this off, I will be back on my course of self destruction. I'm just asking you to remember me."

"I could never forget you. The world will never forget you. You are a genius," William said sincerely.

Christopher Marlowe smiled gently at William and raised his mug to him in a toast, "To the best playwright in England."

"To the best playwright in England!" William clunked his mug against Marlowe's.

Christopher Marlowe did not return to his dark conversation but continued to consume ale at an alarming rate until William intervened and offered to help his friend to his lodging. "I'm fine! Leave me alone, you fool!" Marlowe shouted.

The barman came to William's aid, "His room is at the top of the stairs."

Marlowe was incoherent and nearly dead weight as the two men placed his arms on their shoulders and muscled him up the stairs and onto the bed in his small room. Soon, Marlowe was snoring loudly. William thanked the barman for his help and sadly walked away from the Eagle and toward the Royal Stag where Lord Strange's Men were lodged.

William struggled to fall asleep even though it was much later than was his custom. He couldn't shake the intensity of Marlowe's conviction that he would not live long. Surely the young playwright was just suffering from the shock of his arrest in Holland and the excessive drink he had consumed.

William must have fallen asleep because he awakened in a cold sweat with the words, *"Fair is foul and foul is fair"* echoing in his ears. He looked around his room half expecting to see the hideous hags of his dream chanting the phrase over and over again.

The next day, William looked for Christopher Marlowe at the performance of his play, *Dido, Queen of Carthage,* but the crowd was large, and he could not find his friend among them.

He hurried to the Eagle after the performance, but the barman told him that Marlowe left at about three o'clock that afternoon. William was disappointed as he hoped to see Marlowe in a better mood after a night's rest. He would just have to hope for the best for his friend.

Chapter 35

When the summer tour was over, William happily rode Barbary home to Stratford and his family. Unlike his grand welcome upon returning from the previous summer's tour, no one was at the gate to greet him. William feared that his eight-year-old daughter and the six-year-old twins had grown so accustomed to his absence that they no longer missed him.

He quickly walked through the cottage door on Chapel Street and thought he could surprise the family, but when he entered, no one was home. He had written to Anne and told her when he hoped to arrive, so he was very disappointed that even she seemed to have forgotten him. He sadly turned to go back onto the street to lead Barbary to the stable when he was attacked from behind by giggling children. Susanna leapt on his back while the twins threw themselves at his legs.

"Did we surprise you, father?" Susanna shouted.

"We were hiding in our room!" Hamnet exclaimed.

Little Judith simply clung to her father's leg and said, "I am so glad you are home, father."

"Mother has planned a party for your arrival!" Susanna explained.

Just then Anne came in from the garden her face red from working in the sun, "Children, let your father breathe! Besides it's time for my hug!"

The children laughed and stepped away from William so Anne could receive a proper hug from her happy husband.

"I thought all of you had forgotten me," William said softly.

"Us, forget you? That will never happen! We are so happy to have you home that we have done nothing but talk of this moment for days. The Sadler family, your family, my family, and Beatrice and Howard Martin with baby Elizabeth are all coming over this evening to welcome you home! We have been baking and cleaning all week for our little celebration!"

William could not believe his good fortune in life. He had a wife and family who loved him. He hugged Anne so tightly that she had to nudge him away just enough for her to breathe. "Are you okay, William?" Anne asked with concern.

"I am more than okay, Anne. I am overcome with happiness. I have missed you so much." William's eyes filled with tears, and he quickly wiped them away so the children would not see them. "Children, will you help me with my saddle bags? Poor Barbary is standing in the street worn out from his long trip."

"I have apples for him!" Hamnet shouted, and he ran to the garden to fetch them.

Susanna and Judith each took a hold of their father's hands, and proud William walked out the door of the little house on Chapel Street with a huge smile on his face and his little girls by his side.

Once William and the children had brushed and fed Barbary, they returned home where Anne had cold cider and honey cakes waiting for them. They sat at the table, and the children told their father all of the things they had been doing. Hamnet had gone fishing with Grandfather Shakespeare and caught a large trout. Susanna had been helping Beatrice with baby Elizabeth, and Grandmother Hathaway was teaching her to sew. Judith showed her father the sketches she had drawn of flowers from the garden. William was interested in every detail and was very happy to announce, "Next summer, I will be here with you, and we can do things together!"

The children were overjoyed with the news. Hamnet asked quietly, "Is that the present you brought for us this trip?"

"Yes! Isn't that a good gift?" William winked at Anne.

"Oh, yes, father," Judith answered brightly. Susanna and Hamnet sat quietly.

William reached under the table and brought out a parcel wrapped in brown paper. "You're not the only ones who can make surprises!" The children clapped their hands.

William unwrapped the package carefully and handed Judith a beautiful illustrated book on flowers. "Your mother told me that you were making your own book on flowers, but I thought you might enjoy looking at this one."

"It is beautiful!" Judith clutched the book tightly.

"Hamnet, I found an adventure book for you. It is all about soldiers and their battles."

"Thank you, father," Hamnet said trying to hide his disappointment.

"Susanna, this book has pictures of the latest dresses the fashionable women in London are wearing. Perhaps you and your grandmother Joan can find something you would like to make."

"They are beautiful! Thank you father," Susanna gave her father a quick hug and went back to paging through her new book.

Though the girls were absorbed in their new books, Hamnet had not yet opened his. "I thought you would like that book, Hamnet," William said with hurt in his voice.

"Hamnet!" Anne said sharply. "Don't be an ungrateful child." But when Hamnet looked at her with his sad eyes, she could play the game no longer. She laughed, "William, you must put this poor boy out of his misery!"

Hamnet wasn't sure what his mother meant, but he didn't want to be put out of anything, and he was about to cry, when William reached under the table once again and placed a longbow complete with a full quiver of arrows in front of his son.

"Is this a better gift for a growing boy?" William asked.

Hamnet could not get out of his chair fast enough to run to his father and hug him around the neck. "I love it! I love it!" he shouted with glee.

"I'm glad! This gift comes with some rules which you must follow, however. Can you obey them?"

"Yes, father. I will listen to what you say. I promise."

Judith said quietly, "Can one of the rules be that he can't shoot birds or rabbits?"

"Your sister is right, Hamnet. This bow is for shooting targets, okay?"

"Yes, but someday I want to shoot a deer."

"When you get a little older, we will see about that," William said, and he glanced at Judith who quickly looked down at her book.

Though Susanna and Judith seemed perfectly satisfied with their books, William reached once more under the table and then placed dolls in front of each of his daughters. They squealed with delight and smothered their father with hugs and kisses.

"Now I know why Hamnet Sadler buys toys for his children! The generous hugs I just received for giving toys are much more rewarding than the polite thank you I received for giving books!"

That evening, the little house on Chapel Street over-flowed with laughter, good food, family, and friends. Every-one wanted to know about William's latest tour and his new-est plays. William wanted to know about all the news in Stratford. It was late by the time the guests left, and the chil-dren were settled into bed for the night. Finally, William and

Anne were alone in their little bedroom, "Have I told you to-day how much I love you?" William asked Anne.

"I'm sure I would have remembered that if you had," Anne teased.

"I love you more each day, my dear, sweet Anne."

"I love you, Will. I'm so glad you have come home to us." Anne put her arms around William and pulled him to her. They melted into each other's arms as their kisses became more passionate and their need to be with each other grew. They enjoyed the bliss of being completely secure and at home in each other's arms.

Chapter 36

The month at home in Stratford refreshed William, and when he left for London in October of 1591, he found himself looking forward to returning to the Rose. Nothing could replace his time with Anne and the children, but finding time for his writing was nearly impossible when he was on Chapel Street.

Mistress Wiitherington greeted him like a long lost son, "It's about time you came back to me. You abandoned me for months to nothing but tedious conversations about high seas, unpredictable tides, and surly ship captains. My insipid tenants forget that I lived with a difficult captain for twenty odd years. Your room is ready. Get settled, and we will have a meal by the fire."

William went up the stairs to his attic room with a smile on his face. Christopher Marlowe was correct in his assessment of Betty Witherington, living with her was rather like living with his mother. The one big difference was that Mistress Witherington was a fabulous cook. William did not tarry in his room as he could smell wonderful aromas coming from downstairs.

"The children are growing up so quickly," William answered Betty's inquiries about his family. "Anne grows more beautiful every day."

"I'm glad you are a man who recognizes that women are like fine wine and only improve with age. Anne is only thirty-five. I'm a finer vintage, but I saw her attack Lucy Montgomery, so I hope you will not turn to me for comfort in your lonely hours."

William nearly choked on his meat pie but managed to say, "Your virtue is safe with me."

"Ha!" Mistress Witherington replied. "I lost my virtue about the same time Anne Boleyn lost her head."

William's reunion with Lord Strange's Men was as sweet as his homecoming at Mistress Witherington's. The entire company was at the Rose when William entered, and they gave him a round of applause. "Our family man has come back to us," Rat proclaimed.

"Have you written some new plays for us, William?" Russell Northcutt inquired.

"I'm afraid I spent most of my time in Stratford teaching an over-eager lad the fine technique of shooting a bow. I think I have convinced him to aim at apples and pumpkins rather than cats and his sisters, but I'm still a bit nervous that I made a bad purchase."

"Sounds like a great idea for a play. You can adapt the William Tell story and have Hamnet shooting apples off his sisters' heads," Rat laughed.

"Rat! Now I will be unable to get that image out of my head! However, I have started writing a bloody historical play which involves rivalry among siblings. It's set in Rome and called, *Titus Andronicus*. It's the bloodiest play I've attempted, and I think London audiences will love it."

"Good!" Russell said. "Anything else cooking in that head of yours."

"You know me well, Russell. When I write too much violence, I have to counter it with a comedy. I've started a fun caper in which a Lord and three of his company forswear women for three years so they can focus on scholarship. Three years without women's company for four healthy men can only lead to confusion and humor. I think I will call it *Love's Labour's Lost*."

"Excellent! That sounds like the perfect play to perform for Queen Elizabeth!"

"What?" the actors looked at Russell in amazement.

"I haven't worked out the details, but William is gaining quite a reputation here in London, and one of the Queen's emissaries contacted me about performing for her in the spring."

William could not believe what he was hearing. He began to laugh quietly.

"That's a strange reaction, William," Russell said.

"I can't believe it. When I was courting my wife, I boldly told her that I would perform before Queen Elizabeth someday. We both had a good laugh, and fortunately, she still married me. Now my wildest ambition appears to be coming true."

"Just make sure the play is worthy of her majesty," Russell said.

That comment sobered William, and he swallowed hard and thought, *just the pressure I need to write successfully.*

Russell Northcutt continued outlining the business of the company. "Henslowe has granted us five days a week here at the Rose. We will perform three of William's plays, *Richard III, Taming of the Shrew,* and *Comedy of Errors.* I have arranged a contract with Thomas Kyd to perform his *Spanish Tragedy,* but I'm not sure what we should do for our fifth play."

"Has Robert Greene written anything since *Friar Bacon and Friar Bungay?*" Henry Adams asked.

Russell shook his head sadly, "I'm afraid Robert is in a bad state, both mentally and physically. Last time I saw him, he unleashed a torrent of swear words on me for performing William's plays. He kept ranting, 'the man doesn't even have an education' and I said, 'Have you seen how good his plays are?' That really made him angry."

"Our audiences seemed to enjoy Lyly's *Mother Bombie*," Richard Clark suggested.

"Lyly is under contract this year with a rival company, so he is not an option," Russell said.

"Christopher Marlowe is finishing a play called *Dr. Faustus*," William offered.

"I'm glad you brought him up, William. Young Marlowe has gotten himself into a mess it seems. Rumor has it that he is a spy and isn't long for this world. We must distance ourselves from him as a company and personally. I know he is a friend of yours, William, but I advise you to steer clear of him. Did he ask you to do anything for him when you saw him in Cambridge on tour?"

"Do anything? What do you mean?"

"Did he ask you to take a message or package to anyone in Oxford or any of the other towns on our circuit?" Russell asked.

"No," William said softly, "He just asked me to remember him. I thought he had too much to drink and was overcome with melancholy."

"He always has too much to drink, but he has real trouble to worry about, I fear," Russell said sadly. "I will continue to look for a fifth play, but if I can't secure anything, can we do your *Henry VI. Part III*, William?"

"Yes, of course," William nodded his head in agreement, but he was thinking about his last conversation with Chris Marlowe. Had the devil convinced him to be a spy?

"Hurry up with that Titon Android play, William," Russell prodded William.

"*Titus Andronicus,*" William corrected. "I will have time to work on it now that I am back in London."

Rat and Robert Andrews laughed merrily at William. "No, nights out at the pub for our William. He'll have his nose to the grindstone as usual."

"You two would do well to be half as committed to your work as William is," Russell said brusquely. "Now let's prepare the staging for *Comedy of Errors*. The play will naturally improve with room for us to exaggerate the confusion the twins create."

The actors got down to business, and it felt to William that there had been no month hiatus from the plays they rehearsed. As usual, Russell was correct about the humor increasing as the actors had room to run about the stage and exaggerate their entrances and exits in *Comedy of Errors.* The small platforms in the guild halls on tour had forced the actors to compress their stage business.

William loved his routine of sleeping late in the morning and having breakfast with Mistress Witherington by the hearth. He hardly saw the other lodgers and was assured by Betty that he was missing nothing. "Their dull tales could never find their way into your plays unless you want to talk about shipwrecks and mysterious islands. Your made up stories make more sense then their supposed factual adventures."

After his filling breakfast with Mistress Witherington, William stopped by to check on Barbary and then spent the rest of the afternoon at the Rose rehearsing and once November arrived, performing. The evenings were all his. After a good dinner, he retired to his room and wrote well into the night.

Russell Northcutt had been unable to find a fifth play for their repertoire, so the company was once again performing four of William's plays. He assured Russell that *Titus Andronicus* would be ready for production in early 1592. *Love's*

Labour's Lost would be done soon after that, so they could perform it for Queen Elizabeth in early spring.

One afternoon in November after playing *Comedy of Errors* to a packed house, Russell said, "William, an important person was in the house today. I didn't want to make you nervous, so I didn't tell you before the play started. He is Lord Henry Wriothesley the Earl of Southhampton, and he would like to meet you. I told you that I would help you find a patron. The Earl of Southhampton would be an excellent choice."

"Good," William said enthusiastically, "should I hurry and get dressed?"

"No," Russell laughed. "The Earl is not someone to be kept waiting while you change into street clothes. He has invited us to dine at his estate this evening. I will hire a carriage to collect you at seven."

"I can't ride Barbary?"

"It is better if we arrive in style," Russell said.

William hurried home to Mistress Witherington and said, "I won't be eating dinner this evening."

Mistress Witherington immediately put her hand to William's forehead. "Are you feverish?"

"No, I am flushed with excitement. Russell Northcutt is introducing me to an Earl tonight. I'm to ride in a carriage to his estate."

"Glory be! I'm glad I just laundered your best white shirt and spruced up your black leather doublet. Get those boots off, and I will give them a polish while you are washing up. Your beard and mustache need trimming."

Promptly at 7:00 that evening a shiny black carriage with a driver perched on a high seat behind matching black stallions arrived at Mistress Witherington's door. Betty had been watching out the parlor window and hurried to the door to meet Russell Northcutt before he could knock. "Good evening, Mistress Witherington. You are looking lovely as usual."

"I don't have time for your drivel tonight, Russell." Mistress Witherington cut Russell off and yelled up the stairs, "William! William! Your carriage awaits!"

"William, you look great!" Russell said when Shakespeare came down the stairs.

"Don't you mean 'he's looking lovely as usual?'" Mistress Witherington said sarcastically.

Russell blushed, took William by the arm, and they were off. The carriage driver seemed to be a madman as he whipped the high stepping horses around slow moving carts and shouted at women and children to get out of the way. William hung on and tried to enjoy the bumpy ride over the cobblestone streets, but he longed to be on Barbary or better yet, on his own two feet.

Their route took them to a part of London that William had never seen. The roads were quieter here and lined with tall trees. Suddenly they turned into a lane and stopped while two men in uniform spoke to the driver. Then one of the uniformed men stepped to the side of the carriage where William sat and said, "What's your name?"

"William Shakespeare."

"What's the name of your acting company?"

"I'm a member of Lord Strange's Men. It's not exactly my company."

"Just answer the questions," the man said firmly. "Where does this company of yours perform?"

"At the Rose."

"Open the gates. He's okay," the uniformed guard shouted to the other man.

They rolled through the gates, and William saw a magnificent palace. It was larger than the Montgomery's estate, smaller and more ornate than the castle at Kenilworth. He had never seen anything like it. As the carriage swept around the circular drive, William saw brilliant light shining from all the windows of the three story structure. "How many candles does it take to light this whole house?"

"Don't ask, William. Try to pretend that you are used to dining in this type of setting," Russell said. Then he looked at William who was frozen at the sight of so much beauty. "Forget that, William. Please, just be yourself."

The two men were greeted at the door by a gentleman in formal attire and were guided to the drawing room. The drawing room was all gold and drapes and heavy furniture. William expected to be joining a large group of people, but only two people occupied the room. A slender, pale young man was seated at a large harpsichord in one corner of the room, and a dour woman dressed in heavy gold and maroon brocade was sitting stiffly on a red velvet chair. The gentleman announced, " Countess of Southhampton and Earl of Southhampton, your guests Russell Northcutt and William Shakespeare have arrived." He then turned on his heel and left the room. William had expected the Earl to be a much older man and was amazed that the pale young man was his potential patron.

William stood perfectly still by the door and watched as Northcutt went to the seated lady and bowed slightly. She raised a limp wrist, and he kissed the back of her hand. He then moved toward the boy at the harpsichord, and William went to the lady and mimicked Russell's actions. William did not observe Russell's manners with the young man as he was busy kissing the sour woman's hand. He bowed slightly to the young man, and when he offered his hand, William was about to kiss it, when Russell said, "No!" much too loudly. William dropped the young man's hand like it had turned into a snake, and the young man broke into merry laughter. "A simple handshake is fine, Mr. Shakespeare."

Dinner was served in an elaborate dining room with seating for thirty. The Countess of Southampton sat at one end of the long table, and the young Earl of Southampton sat at the other end. William was nervous that he would be held captive by the intimidating mother of Henry Wriothesley, the young Earl. The Countess had not said a word to him so far, and William hoped his luck would hold.

Strangely, two place settings, one on either side of the Earl of Southampton were the only places set on both sides of the table. The Countess could have been eating in Scotland she was so far from Russell, William, and young Henry. William could not have been happier with the arrangement. He liked the Earl of Southampton from the moment he lightly laughed at William's stumble when he first greeted him. Though he was an Earl, William could talk to him as easily as he could his best friend, Hamnet, back in Stratford.

"Mr. Northcutt told me that *Comedy of Errors* was a tribute of sorts to your own twin children. Can you tell me about them?" Henry Wriothesley asked William.

"My twins are Hamnet and Judith, and they are six years old. They have an eight-year-old sister, Susanna, and the three of them are the light of my life. The twins look very much alike, but Judith is very quiet and a remarkable artist while Hamnet is a loud, boisterous little boy who is currently learning how to shoot a bow and arrow. One of the most interesting things about the twins is that they can perceive what each other is thinking without having to say anything. It's almost like they can read each other's minds or thoughts."

William finally came up for air and realized he had probably said too much.

"Don't get him started on his family, Lord Henry," Russell said. "He doesn't know when to stop."

"No, no," young Henry replied, "I find it fascinating to hear a father speak so lovingly of his children. My father died when I was six, and I was sent to boarding school until I was twelve when I went to Cambridge. I graduated from there at age sixteen and was forced to return here to live with my mother. I can't imagine what it would be like to have a family like yours."

William's heart ached for this wealthy young man who by all appearances had everything in the world. He was missing the most important ingredient in life, a family to love him. William looked down the table toward the Countess of Southampton whose expression made her look as if she had just sniffed a three day old chamber pot.

Russell Northcutt was able to enjoy every bite of the wonderful six course dinner while the Earl of Southampton and William enjoyed delightful conversation. Russell was very relieved that he had come to his senses and just asked William to be himself. After all, it was William's natural love and understanding of people which made him such a good playwright.

In the carriage on the way back to Bankside, William said, "Thank you for introducing me to the Earl, Russell. I think he is a fine young man, and I know it is probably not appropriate for someone of my social standing to say this, but I feel very sorry for him."

Russell nodded in agreement. "I would love to live in that house, but with that woman in the house—what a nightmare."

Chapter 37

On December 17, 1591, William Shakespeare and Betty Witherington were enjoying their morning meal and a pleasant conversation when a loud rapping was heard at the door. Mistress Witherington's kitchen girl went to see who was knocking and returned to the hearth with a rich parchment envelope with a bright red wax seal embossed with a large S. "This has come for you Master Shakespeare."

William could not imagine who would send such an official looking letter to him.

"Well, open it! Don't keep me in suspense, William," Mistress Witherington said.

William carefully worked his finger under the seal trying to preserve the wax and finally the flap was free, and he was able to remove a folded letter. William carefully unfolded the heavy parchment and read:

To the masterful playwright William Shakespeare,

Your visit to my home last month gave me great pleasure. I did not think it possible to enjoy meeting the man behind the plays as much as the plays themselves, but you proved yourself a worthy dinner guest. Since our visit, I have attended all your plays at the Rose and was thoroughly entertained and edified by your poetic language.

I would be honored to play a small role in your future endeavors by providing you an allowance of £50 a month or £600 a year whichever fits your budgeting needs.

I am hopeful that easing your financial pressure will allow you to both spend more time writing and more time in Stratford with your young family. I hope to visit you one day at your home and have your son Hamnet teach me how to shoot a bow.

Henry Wriothesley, the 3rd Earl of Southampton

Mistress Witherington gasped and held her breath when William read that he would receive £50 a month, and her hand still covered her mouth when William finished the letter. "Is this Earl married? You must introduce me!"

William did not respond. He was studying the letter, rereading it slowly to himself. It certainly looked to be written by a gentleman's hand and the wax seal seemed to be authentic. Could Rat be playing a practical joke on him? No, Rat would not know that he had spoken to Lord Henry about Hamnet's bow. Only Russell heard their conversation, and Russell did not engage in practical jokes.

"Well, is he?" Mistress Witherington shouted.

William recovered from his stupor and said, "Is he what?"

"Is this crazy Earl married? He sounds just my type!"

William laughed, "He is an eighteen-year-old and lives with his over-bearing mother. No, I'm afraid he is not your type."

"I still want to meet him! You are rich William Shakespeare. I must talk to Northcutt about increasing your boarding fee. After all, you do eat more than any two skinny sailors, and you have plenty of money. Congratulations!"

"Thank you. I'm sorry. I can't think right now, Betty. I must talk to Russell Northcutt. Goodbye." William hurried from the house to the Rose hoping Russell would be there. He had the letter safely tucked inside his doublet. Fortunately, Russell was meeting with Gilbert Bly, the tailor, making adjustments to some of the costumes for *Comedy of Errors*. When he saw William stride into the theatre and noticed how pale he was, he stopped what he was doing and rushed to him.

"What is it William? Has something happened to Anne or the children?"

"No, no. They are fine. Something has happened to me!"

"What? What has happened?" Russell asked with concern.

"It's marvelous. I can't believe it yet, but I think it is true. I think he really means it."

"Who means what? William, you aren't making any sense. Come over here and sit down." Russell lead William to the first tier of seats, stage right and the two men sat down on the bench. "Now, start from the beginning, William."

William simply reached into his doublet and handed Russell the Earl's letter. Russell opened it carefully and read it. When he was finished, he threw his arms around William and said, "I knew he liked you! This is fantastic news. You won't have to worry about missing your income from the summer tour. You can even reduce your acting schedule here. You can focus on your writing. This is the best news ever!"

William asked slowly, "You think this letter is genuine, and he really wants to be my patron?"

"Yes! Smile William. Relax! I'm not the only person who sees your talent. You deserve this assistance to help you pursue your writing."

"I'm afraid it is going to cost you."

"What? How can it cost me anything?"

"Mistress Witherington plans to raise my board and room fees."

Both men laughed and clapped each other on the back. "Russell, I will need you to help me manage my finances now. I never had any extra money to worry about before. I just sent everything I could to Anne, so she could take care of the children. Now I might be able to invest for our future."

"Absolutely, William. I think eventually you might want to invest in a theatre or in a theatre company of your own, but let's move slowly. First, you need to send a letter thanking Lord Henry and accepting his generous offer. A monthly stipend might be most useful right now, but I'm sure he would be flexible if you needed money for a good investment."

"I will write him immediately. Russell, thank you so much for introducing me to him. I am obviously excited about his generosity, but I am also grateful that we can now continue our budding friendship. I really like that young man! I hope he will come and visit us in Stratford."

"I need you back here by one. Your windfall doesn't release you from your current contract," Russell laughed and sent William on his way.

Chapter 38

By January of 1592, William had completed *Titus Andronicus* and *Love's Labour's Lost*. Russell Northcutt replaced *King Henry VI. Part III* with *Titus Andronicus* at the Rose. William was not exaggerating when he said it was the bloodiest of his plays. The young errand boys at the theatre were kept busy every morning going to local butcher shops and collecting buckets of sheep blood for the afternoon productions.

Northcutt did not want to perform *Love's Labour's Lost* at the Rose before the company presented it to the Queen, so they planned five performances at estates outside London to test it with live audiences. They were to perform for the Queen on March 7th.

William hated to miss Christmas with his family, but with the Earl of Southampton's stipend, he knew Anne could afford to spoil the children with good food and treats for the holiday. William sent a package of books and toys home for the children. His present for Anne would arrive after Christmas and was a grand surprise.

After discussing it with Russell Northcutt, William arranged for Anne to attend their performance for the Queen. He spoke to the company's tailor, Gilbert Bly, and asked him to create an appropriate gown for Anne. Bly met Anne when she came to London to confront Lucy Montgomery, and he had not forgotten her. "It will be a pleasure to create a gown for such a lovely woman instead of the flat-chested boys I usually have to clothe," Bly said.

William was kept busy writing letters to organize the surprise for Anne. First, he wrote to Beatrice and Howard Martin and asked if they would be willing to move into the house on Chapel Street for ten days and care for the children.

He told them the plan was a secret, and they should not mention it to Anne.

Second, he wrote Hamnet and Judith Sadler and asked if Hamnet would be willing to escort Anne as far as Oxford. He would meet them there and take Anne the rest of the way to London. Hamnet would be away from Stratford for only four days as William would bring Anne home to Stratford after the play because his season in London would be over. He asked them to keep his secret.

Third, he wrote to his mother and asked if she would provide Anne with Richard's clothes again, so she could ride to Oxford in the same disguise she had used on her last trip to London. "It's a surprise, mother, so please don't tell Anne what I am planning."

Fourth, he wrote Sarah Spenser to ask if they could stay with her in Oxford. "Anne will be on her way to meet the Queen, but she doesn't know it. I am going to tell her that she is coming to see my latest play, which she is, but the play will be performed in the Royal Palace with the Queen in attendance. Will you help me keep it a secret?"

By the middle of month, William had received positive replies to all of his letters, and his plan was coming together very nicely. Lord Strange's Men had performed *Love's Labour's Lost* four times, and William made a few edits and some stage adjustments to strengthen the play. Russell encouraged him to write *Love's Labour's Found* as his next comedy, and William laughingly agreed.

William was not acting in the play, so he would be able to sit with Anne and watch both the play and the Queen. William feared that Anne would be so uncomfortable in the restrictive corset Gilbert Bly had created for her that she would not enjoy the play, but he knew she would be the best dressed woman in the room—except for the Queen of course.

He knew how excitable Bly was, but he was not prepared for the man's enthusiasm about Anne's gown! Last week, Bly had rushed into the Rose his arms full of clothing, with three assistants following him with their arms full of white garments. He called William over and showed him each piece he had created for Anne. "This is her linen smock which she will put on first. It has a low square neck, so it will fit nicely with her gown. These are her silk hose, and these ribbons are her garters to hold them up. This is her corset. It is very close fitting and is stiffened with whale bone,"

"Wait!" William interrupted. "Anne does not wear corsets."

"Of course, she doesn't wear corsets in Stratford, but every woman who enters the Royal Palace will be wearing a corset, and your wife should be no exception."

William felt the stiff corset and wondered whether his gift would be a blessing or a curse to his dear wife.

"It's one night for pity's sake! She will still be able to breathe." Bly continued down the line of items spread out on the front of the stage. "This is her farthingale. Notice the fine cone-shape I have achieved through the use of willow bent. She ties this around her waist to puff out her skirt and give it shape."

"She can't possibly sit down in that thing," William protested. "She will have to stand the entire play."

"All the fashionable women sit in farthingales. You may have to help her when she first sits down so her skirt doesn't fly up over her face, but she will be fine. Next she ties the bumroll around her hips for more shape."

"No! The bumroll is absolutely not necessary. I refuse to buy that," William shouted.

"Okay, but she will appear flat in the back. Don't blame me when she is sniffed at by the other women." Bly tossed the unwanted bumroll to one of his assistants. "This is her white silk partlet or blouse. Notice how I have embroidered it with gold thread which matches her gown. The ruffle will accent her neckline. And this," Gilbert Bly said with a flourish, "is her gown!"

Finally, William was impressed. This was what he thought he had asked for to begin with. He only wanted Anne under the gown, not the stack of items Bly had shown him. The dress was beautiful and seemed fit for the Queen herself.

"It is made of yellow Italian silk with a gold leaf pattern, a square neck, and long slashed sleeves," Bly caressed the gown while he described it. "These yellow leather latched shoes tied with gold ribbons complete her outfit."

"She will be gorgeous!" William said. "Will she know how to put all these things on?"

"I will be glad to stop by and dress her before the play," Gilbert Bly said with a hopeful smile.

"Mistress Witherington will give her all the assistance she needs, Bly," William said sharply, "but I do thank you very much for all the work you have done. I must owe you a small fortune."

"If you are willing to pay for the gown and the shoes, I will not charge you for the under garments as I can use them for our plays. Can you bring them back to me?"

"The corset and farthing thing will definitely come back to you. I will ask Anne about the other items. Thank you again, Gilbert."

The dress was a success, now William needed Anne in London to wear it. Early on the morning of March 3rd, Anne was fixing breakfast for the children when after a light knock on the door, her mother-in-law entered the house carrying a bundle of clothing. "Put these on, Anne. You are going to London today."

"Mary! Has something happened to Will?"

"No, he is fine. He simply wants his wife to attend his newest play. Please go and get ready. I will finish up the children's breakfast."

"Can we come along?" Hamnet asked.

"Not this time. You will have more fun staying home. Beatrice, Howard, and baby Elizabeth are coming here to stay with you."

"Hurrah!" Susanna said, "I love helping with Elizabeth."

"I can show Howard my bow and arrows," Hamnet said.

Anne was still standing by the table listening incredulously to the plans going on around her. "Scurry in there and get ready, Anne," Mary Shakespeare urged. "Hamnet Sadler will be here soon with Dobbin, and he will expect you to be ready."

Anne was mystified but did as Mary told her. When she came out of the bedroom, she was met by wild giggles from her children. "Mother looks like a young man," Judith laughed.

"Why are you wearing boy's clothes, Mother?" Hamnet asked.

Mary Shakespeare did not want her grandchildren to worry about their mother's safety, so she quickly said, "It is much more comfortable to ride a horse in breeches than it is in a dress, and it is a long way to London. Your mother is being very practical."

The children wanted to ask more questions but just then the Martins arrived, and they forgot about Anne's strange appearance as they greeted baby Elizabeth and her parents. Directly behind them came Hamnet Sadler, and in a whirl, Anne was on her way to London.

The trip was much the same as Anne's last adventure to London, but Anne was in much better spirits, and Hamnet even remembered to call her Andrew when they met other travelers on the road. They enjoyed visiting with Hamnet's cousin Rose in Banbury the first evening of the journey. Hamnet and Anne left at sunrise the next day, so they could arrive in Oxford by late afternoon. Hamnet did not tell Anne that William would be in Oxford to meet them. Anne was so happy and excited to see Sarah Spencer, she never thought to question why Hamnet wanted to set out so early.

They arrived at Sarah's daughter's house in Oxford in very good time, and Sarah greeted them both with warm hugs and invited them in. Hamnet and Sarah hung back and let Anne enter the house first. As her eyes adjusted to the dim room, Anne gasped, "Will! Is that you?"

William crossed the room to Anne and took her in his arms, "Andrew, it's so good to see you again!" he teased. The happy couple kissed.

"How is this possible, Will? Shouldn't you be at the Rose? What about your play?" Anne was full of questions.

"We are finished with our season at the Rose. The play that you are going to see is at a private residence."

"You are not taking me to the Montgomery's estate!" Anne asked in horror.

"No, no," William laughed. "Lucy Montgomery is safely in France pursuing an acting career. This residence is in the city of London, and I think you will enjoy it very much."

"Don't you have to be in rehearsal?" Anne asked.

"I wrote the play, and I am going to sit in the audience with my beautiful wife and watch the play performed by the rest of Lord Strange's Men. They are doing a brilliant job without me!" William said proudly.

"Oh, William this is the best surprise I have ever had! I can't believe you planned this all for me!" Anne threw her arms around her husband and hugged and kissed him.

Helen E. Burton

"I hate to break up this love fest, but I just rode a cranky horse for two days, so I could see my old friend, and he hasn't even given me a cursory glance," Hamnet said.

Anne giggled and said, "Sorry, Hamnet."

William embraced his dear friend and said, "Hamnet, you are the only man on this earth that I would trust to deliver my wife safely to me! Thank you so very much! You look fabulous, by the way. I think the ride was good for you. That horse must have shook a whole loaf off you, at least a whole bun!"

"By the time I get home to Stratford, Judith will have to force feed me honey cakes, so I can regain my manly figure!" Hamnet laughed merrily.

The old friends had a wonderful evening catching up on each other's lives and enjoying each other's company. Sarah's daughter Betsy found a place for the three guests to sleep, and they retired early, knowing they had a long day of riding the next day. Hamnet would be going back to Banbury and then home to Stratford. Anne and William would ride a bit further than Loudwater where Anne and Hamnet had stayed on their trip to London. They would stay at the Coach House Inn at High Wycombe.

Anne and William were delighted to be riding together on Dobbin and Barbary. It reminded them of their courting days when they were carefree and raced across the meadows. Since Susanna and the twins birth, they had few opportunities to enjoy horseback rides. They talked about the children and Lord Strange's Men as they rode. They spent many hours talking about the Earl of Southampton and his great generosity. The more William described Lord Henry, the more Anne wanted to meet him and bring him home to Stratford to join their family.

Anne accused William of extravagance when they arrived at the Coach House Inn. It was not a pub; it was a lovely, quiet inn with large rooms. The innkeeper was rather surprised when William asked for their nicest room. "What about him?" he asked looking at Anne.

"Oh, he's staying in my room," William said boldly.

In the stairway on the way to their room, Anne said, "You are well-known now, William. That innkeeper will start rumors about you and a mysterious young man."

"Anne, I have learned a great deal living in London. People will say and think what they want. As long as we know the truth of our love, nothing else matters."

When they got into the room, it did not take long for William to transform "Andrew" into Anne. Richard's old clothes were strewn about the room, and Anne and William enjoyed an evening of privacy in each other's arms in the large comfortable bed.

They left the Coach House Inn very early the next morning. The route from High Wycombe to London was well-traveled, and the Shakespeares made good time. Anne was prepared for London this trip and tied a scarf securely around her face to help block the foul air and smells of the busy streets. She did not look up as they crossed London Bridge; she looked straight ahead, except when they passed the Tinker's store where William had bought her pewter goblets!

Mistress Witherington was delighted to welcome Anne to her home. "I haven't laid a finger on your man," Betty joked, "so please don't hit me!"

Anne was embarrassed until the older woman pulled her into a tight embrace and said, "I'm a tease, Anne. It takes awhile to get used to me, but you'll love me forever once you do."

"I'm so glad to be here, Mistress Witherington. Will has outdone himself in surprising me. I can't wait to see his play."

"That's not all you'll see!" Mistress Witherington said. William gave her a stern look, and she added, "I imagine there will be many fine ladies at the play for you to admire."

Anne gasped, "William, I don't have anything to wear to your play. I only brought my cotton dresses."

"Don't worry about it, dear. I'm sure I have something in my trunk that will work fine." Mistress Witherington said. "I was even better looking at your age than I am now."

Anne shuddered, and William put his arm around her waist. "Betty, thank you for the fine welcome. We are both worn out from our ride, and I think we will retire for the evening."

"I figured you two would head straight for bed, so I put some cheese and bread in the room. There's a jug of wine as well. Have a good evening."

"Goodnight!" William and Anne said.

Chapter 39

Anne and William always slept soundly wrapped in each other's arms, and they woke refreshed and ready for an exciting day. "Anne, dear, are you ready for another surprise?" William asked.

"I don't know if I can take many more surprises. I'm afraid the surprise of what Mistress Witherington pulls out of her trunk for me to wear today may kill me. The woman is four inches shorter and eight inches wider than I am. How can I possibly wear any gown that fit her?"

William laughed. "I think she may have something you will like."

Mistress Witherington hurried William and Anne through their breakfast, "We have a lot of work to do, Anne. Don't touch that second biscuit. Go to your room and wash. I will be up there soon."

Anne looked plaintively at William, but he just shrugged his shoulders. Anne did as she was told.

Anne used the pitcher of warm water and basin in their room to wash herself, and then she sat on the bed to brush her long, auburn hair. She heard a light knock on the door, and Mistress Witherington marched into the room, her arms full of white linen undergarments.

"Put this linen smock on first," Mistress Witherington commanded.

"Thank you, Betty. This is very thoughtful of you, but I think my own undergarments are just fine."

"You've got to stop doing your own thinking. Hurry. We have lots to do."

Anne could see that trying to resist Mistress Witherington would be like trying to hold back the tide, so she sadly pulled the smock over her head.

"Perfect fit! I knew it. Now put on these white silk hose, and I will tie the yellow ribbons that hold them up."

Anne had never felt such lush stockings, and she looked inquiringly at Mistress Witherington, suspecting that these were new and had never been worn before. "Did you get all of these garments out of your trunk?"

"Yes," Mistress Witherington answered without looking directly at Anne.

"Really?" Anne pushed.

"They have been in my trunk for a week when your husband put them there! Now I am in trouble for telling his secrets. Could you just do what I ask?"

Anne pulled on the lovely hose, and Mistress Witherington tied a ribbon around the tops of the stockings at her thighs and folded the tops of the stockings down to keep them in place.

"You must stand up straight and tall while I lace your corset."

"What? Now I know you are not being honest with me. Will would never want me to be squashed into that thing."

"I'll admit, I was surprised that William agreed to this torturous garment, but his tailor insisted that it was the only way to show off your gown. He also said all the other women at the play would be wearing one which, of course, made me think that was all the more reason for you not to wear one."

"William's tailor? My gown?" Anne asked in confusion. "You mean William had a tailor make all of these undergarments and a gown just for me?"

"Yes. Please don't spoil his surprise by being a sensible woman."

Anne stood and raised her arms as Mistress Witherington pressed the whale bone corset to her chest. "Now hold it in place while I lace it as tightly as I can."

"No wonder you didn't want me to eat another bite of food this morning. You are cinching me so tightly nothing else could fit in my stomach."

"That's good. Now let's tie your farthingale around your waist."

Anne burst into laughter, "That looks like a tent the children would love to play in, not a piece of clothing." Betty's scathing look caused Anne to quickly step into the farthingale and turn around so Betty could tie the contraption around her waist.

"Now, we are almost finished. Look at this beautiful while silk partlet!"

Anne examined the delicate gold embroidery and sighed, "My sister Jo would love this."

When the ruffled blouse was in place, Mistress Witherington went to the top of the stairs and called down to William, "Bring up the gown!"

Presently, William entered the room, and Anne was astounded by the beauty of the gown he had draped over his arms. "It's too beautiful!" Anne gasped. "I can't possibly wear that!"

"You will be the most beautiful woman at the performance today, Anne dear, but you will not be the best dressed. One woman will have an even more magnificent gown than this."

"That isn't possible," Anne said as she ran her fingers over the beautiful yellow silk of the gown.

"It is, Anne. The Queen is always the best-dressed woman in the room," William said as he watched Anne's face for her reaction.

"What?" Anne's knees went weak, and William and Betty had to hold her steady to keep her from falling. "Will Shakespeare, what are you telling me?"

"I'm telling you that my dream of sharing one of my plays with Queen Elizabeth comes true today, and I want my queen by my side to share the moment."

Anne felt dizzy and tears came to her eyes. "No crying!" Mistress Witherington commanded. "Red, puffy eyes will not look good with this gown. Now let's get it on you and see what you look like."

Anne bent forward at the waist with her arms extended, and Mistress Witherington slid the sleeves onto her arms and then lifted the bodice over her head. Anne straightened up, and Mistress Witherington pulled the skirt of the gown down over the farthingale.

Now there were tears in William's eyes as he looked at his darling, Anne. "You are stunning!"

"You look quite different than the young man who charged into my parlor on your first visit to London," Betty Witherington quipped.

William's tears turned to laughter, and Anne said with concern, "What is wrong?"

"Nothing is wrong, dear. I was just thinking how funny it is that Gilbert Bly usually makes gowns for young men so they can play fashionable women. He made this gown for a beautiful woman who came to town dressed as a young man! This could be a scene out of one of my comedies!"

Anne laughed and then looked down at her dress and twirled around. William had only a small hand mirror in his room, and she couldn't see the full effect of the gown. "I have a large mirror in my bedroom, Anne. Let's go down so you can admire yourself. I have a young neighbor coming to fix your hair, and she should be here soon."

William tried to hug Anne, but he couldn't get close enough with the stiff farthingale in his way. He managed to get his arm around her waist, but he felt stiff corset, not soft

Anne. "These clothes look amazing on you, Anne, but they certainly take the fun out of cuddling." He gave Anne his arm and walked her to the door, but there was no room for the dress and William to pass through.

"I don't think I can walk downstairs in this," Anne said. She started to panic and said, "I don't have shoes to wear!"

"Stay calm, Anne," Mistress Witherington said soothingly. "Your shoes are downstairs. Let me get your far-thingale." She reached up under Anne's dress until she found the ribbon which tied the hooped petticoat at Anne's waist. "Now, lift your wife up, William, while I pull the farthingale down."

With the stiff form removed, the gown fell around Anne, and she could gather the extra material in her arms while William helped her walk down the stairs.

Gilbert Bly told William that Anne did not need a headpiece to go with her gown because her beautiful auburn hair should not be covered. He was correct. Betty's neighbor swept Anne's hair up to accentuate her lovely neck and de'-colletage. She placed a few flowers in just the right places to create a beautiful and elegant hairdo.

When Bly told William to allow three hours for Anne to prepare to meet the Queen, he thought he was greatly exag-gerating. However, it took nearly four hours of dressing, fix-ing hair, and buffing fingernails before Betty called for William's help to get Anne back into her farthingale. When Anne slipped on her yellow leather shoes and William tied their gold ribbons, Anne was ready to meet the Queen. William could not stop looking at her, and he could not stop smiling.

Anne thought William looked very handsome in new black leather boots which reached above his knee, a matching

black leather doublet, and a white silk shirt with puffy
sleeves and ruffles at the wrist.

The couple admired themselves in the mirror, took deep
breaths, and went out to the carriage William had ordered to
take them to the Royal Palace. William wasn't sure there
would be room for him in the carriage once Anne was seated,
but he found that he could force the stiff skirt over a little and
squeeze in beside his dear Anne.

William had hired the same carriage and driver that
Russell Northcutt had employed to take them to the Earl of
Southampton's home, so William grasped Anne's hand tight-
ly and suggested she close her eyes and hold on to him.

When the carriage arrived at the ornate gold gates of the
Royal Palace, William handed a guard his official invitation
which was adorned with the Royal Seal. The guards opened
the gates and the carriage rolled through into a lane lined
with roses and cherry trees. Anne clutched William's hand
tightly and tried to breathe. When the palace came into sight,
she gasped. The gray stone building was accented by long
windows trimmed in white with gold draperies pulled back,
so Anne could see the huge chandeliers inside cascading light
from hundreds of candles. Too soon, William lifted her from
the carriage, and they walked on a red carpet up the steps to
the grand doors which stood open with uniformed guards on
each side. Anne wanted to memorize everything she saw and
felt, so she could tell the children later, but they were moving
too quickly.

Anne tried to remain calm and sophisticated, but she
couldn't see things fast enough. The floor was red marble
with swirls of gray; the ceiling was of inlaid oak and walnut;
the walls were covered in red embossed wallpaper and mir-
rors. They were walking down a grand hallway which lead to
a magnificent ballroom where the play would be performed.

Anne studied the men and women around her. They were beautifully adorned and radiated a regal demeanor. She was grateful to William and Gilbert Bly; her gown rivaled any in the room. Many women in the room wore heavy jewels around their necks and at their ears, but Anne did not mind the simple line her square-necked gown gave her.

As the playwright, William had been given seats at the front of the ballroom, and Anne felt the eyes of the guests on them as they slowly walked to their places. She would have thought she was dreaming, but her corset was cutting into her ribs so tightly that the pain let her know she was very much awake.

William seated Anne, carefully holding the front of her skirt, and then said, "I need to check with Russell to make sure everything is in place. Will you be okay here without me for a minute?"

"Yes," Anne said as she looked around the magnificent room. Anne could hear whispers behind her:

"Must be his mistress."

"His wife is a simple country girl, he couldn't bring **her** here."

"I heard he was with a young gentleman in High Wycombe two nights ago."

Anne smiled. William was right. People would say what they wanted to say. She knew her husband loved her so much that he wanted to share one of the most important days of his career with her and only her.

When William returned, Anne was still smiling. He sat beside her and held her hand. "Are the actors ready?"

"As ready as any actor can be to perform for Queen Elizabeth!" William answered.

Just then three men in red uniforms appeared on each side of the stage with long trumpets. They lifted the trumpets in unison and played a flourish. The crowd stood in hushed silence as Queen Elizabeth came slowly onto the platform. She was attired in a rust, silk, tufted gown covered in pearls. A stiff lace collar fanned out from the nape of the gown. She was escorted, nearly carried, by two large, uniformed men. Anne thought the gown must have weighed more than Elizabeth. She vowed to complain no longer about her simple corset.

The guards helped Queen Elizabeth to a high throne which allowed room for her heavy gown but gave her some relief from its weight. She was seated down-stage right, facing the stage, so the audience would have their eyes on the Queen even as they watched the play. Once she was seated, she gave a little wave of her hand, the guards stepped to the side of the platform, and when they were seated, the audience was seated.

Love's Labour's Lost began. At first, Anne could hear William tensely mouthing the words with his actors, but as the Queen laughed and the audience laughed, William relaxed. Anne also relaxed and breathed deeply. She was enjoying every moment of this memorable experience.

At the end of the performance, the Queen shouted, "Bravo! Bravo!" and the actors came out and bowed to her. They left the platform, and the audience stood as the Queen was escorted out a side door.

For Anne, it was all over too soon. She reached up and gave William a kiss, and he put his arm around her waist. "This was the most magnificent surprise you could have ever given me. Thank you."

William was very happy with the performance and the Queen's response to it. He could barely believe what had just happened. He had not yet reached his twenty-eighth birthday, and his play was performed for the Queen of England.

As William and Anne were gathering themselves to follow the crowd out of the ballroom, Russell Northcutt came hurrying from the platform toward them. "William and Anne, come this way quickly," Russell said out of breath.

"What's wrong?" William asked.

"Hurry! The Queen wants to meet you. Follow me."

William and Anne looked at each other and blanched. They followed Russell to an ante-room off the ballroom where several uniformed guards milled about. "These are the Shakespeares," Russell said a bit too loudly.

"Come with us," two of the guards said.

Anne whispered to William, "I don't know what to do or say?"

"Nor do I," William answered.

Suddenly they were in what they assumed was a throne room, and they were standing in front of a somber looking Queen Elizabeth who was seated in a large gold chair with red velvet cushions. Anne curtsied as best she could in her gown, and William bowed.

"You make me laugh, William Shakespeare. I need to laugh. This country and its problems are not funny, but you are. Thank you. Please write more plays. Is this beautiful creature your wife or your mistress?"

William's mouth was so dry he could barely speak, but he squeaked, "This is my wife, Anne." Anne once again attempted a curtsy.

Queen Elizabeth laughed! "Farthingales will lead to the destruction of us all. I once flipped over backward off a stool in one of those contraptions. Here's some advice, Anne Shakespeare. Stay in Stratford. William Shakespeare, spend as little time in London as your career will allow. This city is more deadly than farthingales. Good day."

William and Anne both managed to say thank you before the guards took them by the arm and backed them out of the Queen's presence.

On the ride back to Mistress Witherington's, William said, "We met the Queen, and she spoke to us. I would like that moment to be ours alone. Let's not tell anyone about it. Are you okay with that?"

"Yes, it is ours alone." Then Anne laughed, "No one would believe us anyway."

Chapter 40

"Good morning, you upstart crow!" Mistress Witherington greeted William as he and Anne entered the dining room the morning after *Love's Labour's Lost.*

"Good morning!" William and Anne said puzzled by Betty Witherington's strange greeting.

"Look at this disgusting thing," Mistress Witherington threw a small pamphlet on the table in front of William.

William picked it up and studied the cover, "Groatsworth of Wits" by Robert Greene. "I have never met Greene, but Lord Strange's Men have performed his plays. Henry Adams suggested we add one of his plays to this season's repertoire, but Russell said that unfortunately Greene was physically ill and mentally unfit. What is this pamphlet about?"

"I'm not interested in reading the whole thing, but my neighbor was glad to circle the part about you. Unlike the Queen, Robert Greene does not like you!"

Anne and William turned to the page of the pamphlet that was folded down, and William read, "An upstart crow, beautified with our feathers, that. . . supposes he is as well able to bombast out a blank verse as the best of you: and being an absolute Iohannes fan totem is in his own conceit the only Shake-scene in a country."

"That's just mean," Anne said. "I have a few words for that man!"

"Put on your men's clothing and let's go over to his house and punch him," Mistress Witherington encouraged.

William laughed. "I suppose this is good news in a way."

"What?" Anne shouted. How can it be good news to be insulted and called 'an upstart crow?'"

"It means that I am being noticed by the other playwrights in London. I think the poor man may even be jealous of my accomplishments. He wrote this before he knew that my play was performed for Queen Elizabeth. Imagine how he will feel today when he hears about the success of *Love's Labour's Lost!*"

"What's this 'Iohannes fan totum' nonsense?" Betty asked.

"It's Latin for Jack of all trades. I guess Greene doesn't like the idea that I am a playwright and an actor."

"And a husband and a father," Anne added.

"And a friend and a hungry boarder!" Betty Wither ington's mood lightened when she realized that William Shakespeare was not going to let a sour playwright spoil his day.

She served Anne and William a huge breakfast as she knew they had a long journey ahead of them as they returned to Stratford and their precious children. Anne described for Betty, in great detail, the Royal Palace and the Queen. She did not tell the dear landlady about their private meeting with the Queen and her advice that they avoid London as much as possible.

The Queen's words seemed prophetic. William thought he was leaving London for the summer and would return in October. However, the plague changed everything. The theaters in London closed in the fall of 1592, and William would not return to London until two years later in the fall of 1594. When he did return, everything would be different.

Anne and William thanked Mistress Witherington profusely and hugged her tightly. "Won't you come to Stratford this summer and get away from the heat in London?" Anne begged.

"I'm too old for a journey that far. I couldn't possibly ride a horse, and I would be jounced and battered about in a coach. No, I will stay here and wait for your husband to return in the fall. Why don't you and the children come along?"

Anne laughed. "I'm afraid I'm too old to tote three children all the way here from Stratford!"

The Shakespeares were so anxious to see their children, that they made the journey in two days rather than four. When Anne learned that William had ridden Barbary to Oxford in one day to meet her, she said indignantly, "Did you break the trip into four days because you didn't think a woman could make the trip in two?"

William stuttered a bit and said weakly, "Dobbin and Barbary are not used to such long days."

"Don't blame this on our worthy horses! They are as anxious to be home as we are!"

"Remember, your first trip to London, Hamnet Sadler broke the trip into four days," William said, and the couple looked at each other and laughed. "We both know that was for Hamnet's benefit, not Andrew's!"

****

Home never looked so beautiful as it did that spring. The wild flowers were in bloom, and the water of the Avon was sparkling. The Martins had taken good care of the children, and Howard Martin said, "Beatrice and I hope to give Elizabeth fine brothers and sisters like your children. It was a pleasure to watch over them."

After many thanks and hugs, the Martin family left the little house on Chapel Street, and the Shakespeare family was officially reunited. William was given a guided tour of the garden by Susanna and the twins, "We have two more hens, and they are the best layers in Stratford. We sell our extra eggs at the market every week."

"We have three skeps of bees now, father," Judith said. "We sell honey at the market too."

"Look how many apples we will have, father," said Hamnet proudly pointing out the blossom laden tree. "I use the rotten ones for targets, and we sell the extras at market."

Anne remained silent as the children showed William the expanded garden spot and described how they would use all the vegetables they could and sell the extra at market.

"Anne, have you become a full-time business woman in my absence?" William asked.

"She's the boss, and we are her assistants," Hamnet answered. "She will assign you work before you can even unpack." Hamnet laughed and ran into the house to see if his parents had brought him something from London. Susanna and Judith joined him.

"Anne, have you used any of the money Lord Henry has been providing for us?" William asked.

"That's your money, so you can write. We are fine without it, Will. I have been saving it all."

"Thank goodness!" William said. "I need a loan from you?"

"What?" Anne asked.

"I still owe Bly for your gown!" but he winked at Anne and swept her into his arms, and she knew he was only teasing her. It was wonderful to be home and to be a family again.

William read to his children every evening and kissed them good night. He would then write late into the night. Anne and the children had a quiet breakfast and let their father sleep as long as he needed in the morning. They knew their father would spend the afternoon and evening with them.

This schedule agreed very well with William, and he found he was able to write as much as he had in his quiet room at Mistress Witherington's. One evening as he was shuffling through a pile of manuscripts, he came across his long poem *Venus and Adonis*. When he read it, he was pleased to discover that with just a little revising, it could be a good poem. He decided that he would complete it and dedicate it to Lord Henry as a modest thank you for his patronage. He wrote Lord Henry and once again invited him to visit Stratford.

The Shakespeare family spent the pleasant days working in the garden, fishing, going on picnics, and enjoying their family and friends in Stratford. At the end of May, right after Susanna's 9th birthday, a heavy parchment envelope was delivered to the little house on Chapel Street. This time William was not puzzled by the red wax seal embossed with an S.

To William and Anne Shakespeare,

I will be traveling to Kenilworth Castle in early June and would like to take this opportunity to visit you in Stratford. My attache has arranged accommodations for me at the Stratford Inn for June 5 thru 8. If these dates are satisfactory, I will be pleased to see you at that time. I hope your family is well. Mother is the same.

Yours,

Lord Henry, the 3rd Earl of Southampton

Anne was thrilled that she would finally meet the young man who had been so generous to her family. William now had a firm deadline for polishing *Venus and Adonis* and writing a dedication to Lord Henry.

Chapter 41

Early on the afternoon of June 5, 1592, William heard a sharp rap on the door. He peaked out the window and then shouted, "Children! Come here please. Be polite and courteous to our visitor. Remember, he has been very kind to us." The children lined up by their mother and waited for William to open the door.

A very officious gray-haired man walked into the house and said in a commanding voice, "Honorable Henry Wriothesly, Earl of Southampton, and Baron of Tichfield." He stepped to the side and gestured to the door.

Lord Henry walked into the little house on Chapel Street. He was dressed in a rust velvet doublet and matching breeches. His blouse had large puffy sleeves and a high lace collar. Though he was a young man, his presence was impressive.

The Shakespeare family did not know whether they should speak or let him speak first, then little Judith walked to Lord Henry, offered him her hand, and said, "Would you like to see our chickens, Henry?"

Anne reached to pull Judith back, but Lord Henry took Judith's hand, and said, "I would love to see your chickens." All awkwardness was gone. Lord Henry turned to the man who had so formally introduced him and said, "Jeeves, I will be fine. You may return to the Inn. Anne Shakespeare, I am very happy to finally meet you." He continued to hold Judith's hand and also grasped her mother's. "This must be Susanna," he gave her a little bow. "And you must be the great archer, Hamnet!" Hamnet nodded his head vigorously. Lord Henry then turned to William and said, "I am very happy to be in your home. Thank you for inviting me."

"We have been looking forward to seeing you since we received your letter. My children have planned your entire visit. You must feel free to tell them that you need peace and quiet if they become annoying."

"I have had enough peace and quiet to last a life time. Let's go see those chickens, Judith."

Judith lead Lord Henry to the garden, and the rest of the Shakespeare family followed them. When they reached the little fenced area which contained the chickens, Lord Henry crouched down to look more closely at the funny birds who turned their heads to the side to look at him. Judith pointed, and Lord Henry reached into the coop and came out with an egg in his hand and a huge smile on his face. "I've gathered my first egg!" Henry exclaimed.

Susanna showed him the skeps for the honey bees, next. "My mother weaves the skeps out of tall grasses and the bees love their shape and warmth, so they swarm to their new home to give us honey."

Lord Henry listened intently and said, "Aren't you afraid the bees will sting you?"

"No, they are afraid of us. If we accidentally step on them, they might sting us, but after they sting, they die. Mother uses a smokey torch to calm them while we remove their honey and beeswax. I made some honey cakes for you. Do you like honey cakes?"

"I'm not sure. I may not have eaten a honey cake."

"When mother passes the basket to you, take two or three the first time," Hamnet encouraged, "because father loves them so much that he might eat them all."

Lord Henry turned to look at William, and William just shrugged his shoulders, "I'm afraid my son knows me too well."

"I set up some targets for you over here if you want to shoot my bow," Hamnet pointed to a line of pumpkins on stumps in front of a high stone wall. Some of the pumpkins had apples on top of them. "I'm sorry we can't go hunting for rabbits or squirrels." Hamnet pulled Lord Henry down towards him so he could whisper in his ear, "It makes my twin sister sad to think of animals being shot, so I pretend the pumpkins are deer and the apples are rabbits."

Lord Henry stifled a laugh and said, "I think that is a very wise solution."

"If the men are going to practice their archery, it is time for us to prepare dinner. Come on girls," Anne said.

Before they could shoot any arrows, William had to drag an old burlap bag of straw out of the garden shed. He pounded the bag down into a rectangle about five inches thick and four feet long. With Lord Henry's help, he placed the straw pad against the stone wall and secured it with burlap straps. "Hamnet is getting stronger, and he broke an arrow when it hit the wall, so I made this to stop the arrows before they hit the hard surface!"

Lord Henry shook his head in wonder at the amount of thought and effort, William put into pleasing his seven-year-old son. This was what it was like to be a child growing up in the countryside with parents who loved him. Hamnet was not served breakfast on a silver platter, nor did he dress in fine clothes like Henry had as a child, but Hamnet was happy, an emotion Henry had rarely experienced.

William had another surprise for Hamnet. He returned to the shed and brought out a long bow for Lord Henry.

"Oh, father that is perfect!" Hamnet exclaimed. "Your bow should be the same height as you are," Hamnet explained. "My bow is too short for you, and father's bow is too tall. I was afraid you would have to kneel down to shoot my bow which would make it hard for you to aim. Where did you find the perfect bow for Henry?" Hamnet asked his father.

"I haven't always been this height, Hamnet. My bow was passed down to my brother Richard, and now he has outgrown it, so he let me borrow it for Lord Henry. You need to be respectful and call him Lord Henry, Hamnet, not just Henry."

"Rubbish! I want your entire family to call me Henry. I quite like it!"

"Thank you, Henry," Hamnet smiled brightly at his new friend.

Hamnet carefully instructed Henry on how to hold the bow, set the notches of the arrow, and pull back the string as far as he could. "Don't pull it back so far that you can't hold it steady or you will miss your mark. You must be able to hold the arch in the bow for at least a count of ten and take a deep breath before you let it fly."

William smiled as he listened to his son. He was never sure whether or not Hamnet was listening to him. Hearing his words echoing back to him from his son gave him a great deal of satisfaction.

Henry's first shot went high over the left-hand pumpkin and into the burlap guard. His second shot was high and to the right, but his third arrow struck the middle pumpkin dead center. "You got a deer! That was a perfect shot, Henry."

Henry could not believe how exhilarating it was to hit a pumpkin! He laughed and clapped Hamnet on the shoulder. "You are an excellent teacher, my friend!"

Hamnet beamed with pride and proceeded to shoot two rabbits and a deer with his first three arrows!

After a dinner of delicious food with constant chatter and laughter, it was the children's bedtime. "Can Henry read us our goodnight stories, father?" Judith asked.

"That's up to Henry, Judith. I'm afraid you children may have worn him out today." William said.

"Henry is not old like you are father. He's not too tired, are you Henry?" Hamnet asked.

Henry laughed. "Your father is not exactly ancient, Hamnet. He is only nine years older than I am."

"You are only ten years older than I am," Susanna said in surprise.

"Your math skills are excellent, Susanna," Henry said.

"Father, could Susanna marry Henry? Please." Judith entreated.

Before William could respond to his young daughter, Hamnet said, "Don't be daft, Judith. Women must marry men younger than them. Mother is much, much older than father."

"Hamnet!" William scolded. "Apologize to your sister who is most certainly not daft and apologize to your mother as well."

Henry had burst into laughter at Hamnet's comments and said to Hamnet, "It is never wise to mention a woman's age."

"Sorry, mother. Sorry, Judith," Hamnet said softly.

Henry turned to Judith and tapped his finger on her button nose, "Susanna will make any man a wonderful wife, but I might just wait for you to grow up." Susanna and Judith both smiled brightly. "Now, to your earlier question, I am not tired, and I would be delighted to read to you this evening."

So the young Shakespeare children were read to sleep by a member of the British aristocracy! Henry joined William and Anne by the hearth after he finished reading. "I fell asleep each night reading boring English history. I would have enjoyed some of Aesop's fables. They are quite fun!"

"Henry, thank you for being so patient with our children. I'm afraid we are not traditional parents. We haven't taught our children to listen and remain silent. They embarrassed me tonight, and I may have to rethink their social training!" Anne said.

"Don't change a thing! They are delightful, and I don't remember a day I have enjoyed more!" Henry said. "What have they planned for tomorrow?"

William and Anne both laughed with relief. "We are going fishing and on a picnic with William's father, John."

"Wonderful! I should go so you can get some rest."

"Before you go, I have something I would like to give you," William said. He walked to his little desk and retrieved the manuscript for *Venus and Adonis* and presented it to Henry.

Henry looked carefully at the first few pages and then he said, "You have dedicated this to me?"

"I know it does not compensate you for your patronage, but I want you to know how much I love and respect you," William said. "It is my first attempt at a long poem, so I hope you won't be too disappointed."

"I now have better reading material for my evening than Aesop could ever hope to create!" Henry said with enthusiasm as he clutched the manuscript to his chest.

"I have something for you as well," Anne said with a smile on her face. She handed Henry the bundle of Richard's clothes that she had worn as Andrew. "It is not a good idea to fish in velvet!"

Anne, William, and Henry laughed together and hugged each other goodnight.

Chapter 42

Lord Henry sat in a chair at the Stratford Inn and read William's manuscript by candle light.

To the right honorable Henry Wriothesly, Earl of Southampton, and Baron of Tichfield.

Right Honorable, I know not how I shall offend in dedicating my unpolished lines to your lordship, nor how the world will censure me for choosing so strong a prop to support so weak a burden only, if your honor seem but pleased, I do count myself highly praised, and vow to take advantage of all idle hours, till I have honored you with some graver labour.

Lord Henry continued reading late into the night and fell asleep happier than he had ever been in his life.

The Shakespeare family taught Henry to fish, introduced him to the Sadler's fabulous buns, and took him on a tour of Stratford, showing him William's grammar school and the sheep platform where his plays were first performed. Judith showed Henry her sketches and presented him with a drawing she had done of him catching his first trout.

Hamnet and Henry became fast friends; the little boy's enthusiasm for life made Henry laugh, and he loved being around him.

Susanna wanted to know all about Henry's life in London and what it was like to live in a huge house and have servants. "It's lonely, Susanna," Henry answered simply.

"But you have such lovely clothes, and you can travel wherever you want," Susanna persisted.

"Yes, that is true. I am very lucky, and I don't mean to disparage the privileges I have been given because of my father's station in life. I guess I am lonely because I haven't yet found my purpose in life. I think your father is helping me figure that out though."

"How has father helped you?" Susanna asked.

"I don't have artistic talent like your father or your little sister, Judith, but I love the arts. Theatre, music, art, and literature are what make this life worth living. I want to help artists pursue their craft. I can use my money to help them."

"By helping others, you will help yourself? It's rather confusing isn't it, but I always feel better when I help mother and father," Susanna said.

"Yes. That's exactly what I mean," Henry said.

Lord Henry's days in Stratford passed quickly, and soon it was time for the Shakespeare family to tell him goodbye. Before he left, he took William aside and said, "*Venus and Adonis* is beautiful poetry. Thank you for dedicating it to me. May I have your permission to speak with publishers in London? Your poem should be read and enjoyed by all. I will make sure the terms are fair and honest, and I will have you approve the proofs before it goes to print."

"Do you honestly think someone will want to publish it?" William asked.

"Absolutely. It's a matter of finding the printer who will do the best job. I hope you were serious in your dedication when you said that you would 'take advantage of all idle hours' to write more. You are an elegant and passionate writer."

"Your faith in me is extremely humbling, Lord Henry. I am working on another long poem, *The Rape of Lucrece* and if it proves worthy, it too will be dedicated to you."

"Please send me a draft as soon as you have completed it. I may not be in London, but my secretary will see that I receive it. William, I am glad you are not on tour this summer. A sickness has fallen on London, and the officials there fear the worst. If it is the plague, it will spread to other large cities. Stay here in Stratford and care for your family. If you need anything, please write me. My mother has asked me to meet her in Spain and avoid returning to London."

"Thank you, Lord Henry and may God bless you for your goodness," William said.

"God has already blessed me by allowing me to be a part of your family," Lord Henry said sincerely.

Susanna and Judith both cried and clung to Henry when he had to leave, and Henry had never felt such a tightness in his chest as he told them goodbye. Hamnet was trying to be a man and not to cry, but he could not look at his now best friend without crying, so he turned his back to everyone and started throwing rocks at every bird foolish enough to fly near the Shakespeare home.

Henry went to Hamnet and crouched down by the boy and put his hand on his shoulder. "I have never met a finer young man than you Hamnet. I refuse to say goodbye to you because I know I will see you again soon. Please take care of your sisters for me." Henry tried to make Hamnet smile, "I may want to marry one of them some day." Hamnet turned to Henry and hugged him.

Anne said, "I hope you realize how much you have done for our family, Henry. Thank you. We love you."

"I hope you realize how much you have done for me! Thank you, and I love you all." Lord Henry Wriothesly, Earl of Southampton walked down Chapel Street toward the Stratford Inn with tears streaming down his face.

Chapter 43

After Lord Henry's visit, William returned to his routine of writing late into the night. The young man had inspired him to work on *The Rape of Lucrece,* the second long lyric poem that he had put away when the pressure to produce plays had demanded all of his writing hours. He continued his habit of working on two plays at once, so now his head was full of *Two Gentleman of Verona* and *Richard the II* as well as the long poem. The variety of writing tasks motivated him rather than exhausted him.

A fortnight after Lord Henry left Stratford, a messenger delivered a brown paper package to the Shakespeare home on Chapel Street. When William removed the string the heavy paper fell away to reveal a small bound volume of *Venus and Adonis.* Beneath the volume was a contract for printing one thousand copies of the poem. William was to receive a very generous 50% of the proceeds from the sale of the book.

William and Anne, with their heads close together, read the volume carefully checking for printing errors. Susanna and Judith happily shared the brown paper wrapper, and Hamnet absconded with the string. Surprisingly, there were very few changes to be made to the manuscript. William made note of those for the printer, signed the contract, and looked for the paper and string to rewrap the volume to return it to the printer. Susanna had used her half of the paper to create a pattern for a new dress for her doll; Judith had already started a sketch of a robin on the other half. Hamnet had no idea what his parents were talking about when they asked him about the string.

William and Anne could only laugh at their industrious children, and William gathered up the signed contract and lovely volume of poetry and headed for his parent's home on

Henley Street. His father had sent many a package of gloves in the heyday of his business, and he would help William with this project.

In the middle of August, an even larger package arrived at Chapel Street. This time the children asked their parents before it was opened if they could have the paper and string. Anne and William laughed and said, "Thank you for asking."

The entire family was surprised to find five individually wrapped packages inside. Each package was labeled with a family member's name. "Judith, you are the youngest. Why don't you open your package first?" Anne said.

Judith carefully slid the string from her package and handed it to her brother. Then she folded back the paper and gasped when she saw a set of ten pastel pencils. The soft pencils were in an array of colors, perfect for her flower sketches. Judith read the attached note, "For my favorite artist. Love Henry."

"Lord Henry has sent us presents!" Hamnet exclaimed. "I get to open mine next." Hamnet's package was small, yet it was heavy. He hurriedly removed the string, and a beautiful walnut handled pocket knife fell into his hand. It had three blades which folded out of the walnut and metal casing. The biggest blade was nearly three inches long, the second was two inches, and the third was a delicate inch-long blade. Hamnet read the note, "Hamnet, I imagine your father will have some rules for you to follow with this knife, and I know you will listen to him. Perhaps you can sharpen your own arrows. Love, Henry."

"Father, I love this knife. Can I keep it?" Hamnet asked with worry in his voice.

"Let's start with the rule that you can only open the blades when I am with you. When you show me that you respect its sharpness, we can expand your use of it. Does that sound fair?"

"Yes!" Hamnet exclaimed.

Susanna had a large soft package, and when she opened it, a delicate pink silk blouse was inside. A matching pink silk ribbon was folded on top for her hair. "A beautiful girl deserves beautiful clothes. I hope you like the color I have chosen. Love, Henry."

Susanna held the blouse to her face, and said, "It will be like wearing a rose petal! It is so beautiful."

"Father is next!" Hamnet shouted.

"No, Hamnet, ladies go first, so it is your mother's turn."

"You said we were going by age, so you are next!"

"Hamnet, what did Lord Henry tell you about a woman's age?" William asked firmly.

"Never mention it," Hamnet said quietly.

Anne's package was the largest and heaviest of all the packages. When she untied the string, she found more brown wrapping. She unwrapped the first item carefully and found a delicate china plate with gold trim around the outer edge and hand-painted pink roses in the center. When she removed the crumbled paper which had acted as protection for the plates, she discovered six plates in all. "Honey cakes as sweet as yours should be served on china. I have enclosed six plates, one for each member of your family and one for me on my next visit to your home. Love, Henry."

"I don't trust myself with those, Mother. Can I still have my honey cakes on pewter?" Hamnet asked.

Anne laughed and said, "Yes. That is a very good idea."

William opened his package last and found five leather-bound copies of *Venus and Adonis*. "I hope you are happy with the way your poem was printed. I know you have many family members and friends you will want to share these with, but these five volumes give you a start. Sales are already brisk in London, and I am sure we will need to publish another 1,000 by fall. Love, Henry."

Anne and William each took a copy of the poem and carefully turned the pages. "You are a published writer, William Shakespeare!" Anne declared. "Now get back to your desk and keep writing," she teased.

****

It seems in life great happiness is often followed by great sorrow. In September, as William prepared to return to London, he received a letter from Russell Northcutt which broke his heart.

William,

I hope both your family and you are in good health. It is very bad here in London. The plague is raging through the city and has decimated Lord Strange's Men. Our founder and patron, Ferdinando Stanley, passed in April. This month we lost two fine actors from the company, Henry Adams and George Wilson (I think you only knew George as Rat, but he was a fine man and good friend. He thought the world of you.)

I just returned from a service for Betty Witherington which prompted me to write this sad letter. I cannot believe the dear woman is gone, and her incessant chattering is silenced forever. I know this news will be hard for you, but life is hard.

I purchased a copy of *Venus and Adonis* and am proud to tell everyone I meet that you and I are friends.

The theatres are closed until this vicious disease has done its damage and decides to leave those of us remaining in peace. Stay healthy and safe in Stratford and continue writing. With no theatre to attend, folks

will eagerly buy all the poetry you can provide.
       With love and respect,
       Russell

When William finished reading the letter, he put his head in his hands and cried. Anne came to his side and took the letter from his hand. She gasped when she came to the tragic news of Mistress Witherington's death and tears filled her eyes. "Oh, William. I am so sorry. I know how much you loved Betty. I only met her twice, and I loved her."

William and Anne held each other and wept for all those who had lost their lives in London, but most especially they wept for Betty Witherington who had taken such good care of William. William wept for Rat, and he wept that he hadn't even bothered to learn his friend's Christian name.

Once they dried their eyes, they were able to comprehend the rest of Russell's letter. William would not be leaving Stratford to perform in London. He could stay with the family. They sent a prayer of thanks to Lord Henry for his patronage. They were financially secure without William's income from Lord Strange's Men, and hopefully, they would remain safe from the plague in Stratford.

William spent the fall writing and in November, he sent Lord Henry the completed manuscript of *The Rape of Lucrece*. His dedication to Henry was more effusive as he felt a closeness to the young man that had not yet developed when he presented him with *Venus and Adonis*.

    To the Right Honorable Henry Wriothesly, Earl of Southampton, and Baron of Tichfield,

The Love I dedicate to your lordship is without end; whereof this pamphlet, without beginning, is but a superfluous moiety. The warrant I have of your honorable disposition, not the worth of my untutored lines, makes it assured of acceptance. What I have done is yours; what I have to do is yours; being part in all I have, devoted yours. Were my worth greater, my duty would show greater; meantime, as it is, it is bound to your lordship, to whom I wish long life, still length- ened with all happiness.

Your lordship's in all duty,
William Shakespeare

Chapter 44

Christmas of 1592 was especially sweet for William because he had missed the last two holidays in Stratford. He set his writing aside for the twelve day celebration and joined in all the festivities. The plague had not reached Stratford, and its residents were very grateful for that. The Shakespeare family was not alone in spending more time at Church services this year. Holy Trinity Church was overflowing with thankful parishioners. Susanna, Judith, and Hamnet took part in a Christmas pageant and were, of course, the best little actors in the production.

William especially enjoyed his time with the Hamnet Sadler family. Hamnet's bakery was thriving, but that meant he was working early in the morning while William was sleeping. Once William was awake and had played with the children, Hamnet was fast asleep. The two friends missed each other.

"It's as if you are still in London," Hamnet said after giving his friend a huge hug. "We don't see enough of you and your family. We were beginning to think you no longer associated with lowly bakers now that you are a published poet." Hamnet teased William when the Sadler family came for a holiday party at the Shakespeare home.

"William would never consider a baker to be lower on the social scale than poets," Anne said. "He can't live without your bread, but I imagine you could do just fine without his poetry!"

"I don't know about that. *Venus and Adonis* did something for the love lives of the poor working class in Stratford. We heard that Beatrice and Howard Martin are expecting their second child, and Judith and I are proud to announce that our fourth is due in the spring!"

Anne hugged Judith and said, "Congratulations! I thought you might have some wonderful news for us when I saw how pale you were the other day in the bakery."

"This little one," Judith laughed and patted her stomach, "doesn't like the smell of yeast. It could be a hard life for the child of a baker."

"Your baby can come and live with us!" Susanna offered and little Judith nodded in agreement.

Hamnet laughed and said, "We're not quite ready to part with the dear thing yet, but we will certainly be looking for baby tenders of your high quality once the tiny creature arrives."

The Sadler children joined the Shakespeare children in their bedroom to play, and the adults sat at the table to catch up on the news. "What do you hear from London, William?" Hamnet inquired.

"The theatres remain closed, and Russell Northcutt says I should plan to stay here in Stratford at least through the summer of 1593. He is hopeful they will reopen in November of '93, but he says it could be another full year before the threat of plague is gone. So many people have died in London that the cemeteries are full. They dug a huge pit in a meadow north of the city, and they are burying the victims of the plague there in one massive grave."

Judith shuddered and said, "Anne, I am so grateful you and the children didn't move to London to be close to William. I remember how hard it was for you to be here alone with the children, but I can't imagine you living in that city now."

"I know. William wanted us to stay here as soon as he saw the horrible sanitary conditions in London. He knew it was no place for our children."

"It didn't take a genius to know that," Hamnet said. "I hated the place from the moment we rode in. Remember how I had to wrap a scarf around your face to keep you from choking. William probably pretended that his meeting you in Oxford on your last trip to London was part of his grand surprise for you. Wrong! He had to ride to Oxford and meet you because I refused to go back to London!"

The friends all laughed together and William said, "Hamnet was as uncomfortable in London as Anne was in her whale-bone corset! I fear he will never take you to the city, Judith."

"I am fine with that," Judith said, "especially now. I will wait until this horrible plague goes away and then I will make Hamnet take me to Paris! I want to learn how to bake their rich croissants."

Hamnet rolled his eyes and said, "First, you need to find a rich baker before you can make rich croissants!"

"William has had one piece of good news from London," Anne said. "The same printer that created *Venus and Adonis* has printed a beautiful volume of *The Rape of Lucrece*."

"The what of Lucrece?" Hamnet asked. "If I heard you correctly, that doesn't sound like much of a love poem!"

"You heard correctly, Hamnet. It's a rhymed narrative poem of a more serious nature than *Venus and Adonis,* and it is quite tragic. I'm not sure that it will be an aphrodisiac for the men of Stratford, but I think it is well-written."

"It made me cry when I read it," Anne said, "but it contains a good warning of what happens when men turn their backs on morality."

"I guess you taught William that lesson when you came to London and beat poor Lucy Montgomery to within an inch of her life!" Hamnet teased.

Anne playfully punched Hamnet and said, "You will be my next victim if you don't stop exaggerating my escapades!"

****

William's Christmas present arrived in mid-January 1593 when he received a package containing ten volumes of *The Rape of Lucrece*. It was the same size and had the same fine leather binding as *Venus and Adonis*, but the printer had put "William Shakespeare" in a much larger font. Anne thought it was perfect; William thought it a bit much. *Venus and Adonis* had already sold over 3,000 copies, so the printer started with a printing of 2,000 copies of *Lucrece*. Lord Henry had negotiated the same fine financial contract for William's second volume of poetry. William and Anne had been pleased and surprised at the amount of money the sales of *Venus and Adonis* had generated.

William hoped that fate would allow him to return to London and perform more plays, but if it was not meant to be, he had at least two published volumes of poetry. He was a writer, and he was supporting his family. He felt a genuine sense of satisfaction.

****

In early April, William was in the garden hoeing peas while Anne and the children planted corn when a man walked into the garden and said, "Has my uneducated rival finally given up his foolish ideas of being a writer and turned to farming?" Anne faced the man with her hands on her hips and was about to share a piece of her mind with the stranger when William tossed the hoe down and strode toward the man.

"Christopher Marlowe! What are you doing in Stratford?" William extended his hand to the writer.

"Wash your hands and come with me to the pub where we can talk."

Anne gestured for William to go on, and he hurried to the bucket of water at the edge of the garden space and washed his hands as thoroughly as he could. He shook the water from his hands, pounded the heels of his boots together to remove the extra dirt caught in them, and strode off with Christopher Marlowe.

Once the men were seated at the Black Swan and Marlowe had consumed his first glass of ale, he said, "You live a very peaceful life here, don't you William?"

"Yes. I imagine it is quite different from your life of high adventure."

"Surviving in London is an adventure these days."

"Are you living there?" William asked with concern. "I imagined that you went elsewhere when the theatres closed."

"I've been abroad and about. Wherever the Devil sends me, I go."

"Chris, level with me. What are you doing?"

"I think that's why I'm here, William. I want to tell at least one person what I've gotten myself into. You are the only honest man I know, and I know my secret will be kept by you."

"You are correct. I will tell no one your business."

"When I was a young man at Cambridge, I came to my professors' attention not only because I had a quick wit but because I seemed to lack a moral compass. I was intelligent but unafraid to lie or cheat to accomplish my goals. I possessed the perfect character to be a spy. I could befriend someone, clap him on the back, and stab him in the same motion. Not many men are that duplicitous." Marlowe drank deeply from his ale.

"You have always been honest with me, Chris, and I don't fear you."

"Ha! I hear you are rewriting *The Jew of Malta!*"

William blushed, "I am working on a play that I call *A Merchant of Venice,* but it is much different from your play."

Marlowe laughed loudly! "You can rewrite all of my plays. I don't care. *Doctor Faustus* has been successful. You should do that with witches. My *Edward II* will pale to whatever you decide to make up about him. I won't live to see any of them." Marlowe drained his ale and called for another.

Marlowe continued, "My only regret is that I couldn't act the great roles I created. That blasted Edward Alleyn gets credit for Tamburiane, Faustus, and Barbabus. It should have been me on that stage, but I let drink dictate what I did and didn't do in life. I made the Admiral's Men who they are, but Alleyn gets all the credit."

Shakespeare knew Edward Alleyn was a very large man and a very good actor. "Has Alleyn threatened your life, Chris? Is that what this is all about?"

"No, no. Alleyn is an actor not a killer. This has nothing to do with the theatre or acting. It has everything to do with espionage. When you agree to spy for someone, it doesn't matter if you think you are working on your country's behalf or against your country, your usefulness is finite. When they are done with you, they have to clean up the evidence that they stooped to spying to begin with."

"For whom were you working, Chris?" William asked.

"Your new best friend, Queen Elizabeth."

William was shocked and stammered, "I'm not sure she is my friend." He remembered her warning to leave London. He thought she was concerned about the plague, but now her warning seemed more ominous.

"She befriends anyone she can manipulate. Her only goal in life is to stay on the throne. Haven't you wondered how she has ruled our country for so long and kept the constant invaders away. She had help from the weather when the Spanish Armada failed, and I suppose she would call that divine intervention. Her main weapon against the continent is to stay unmarried—I don't buy the Virgin Queen title. She brokers her marriage as a peace treaty with vying countries. She holds the hounds at bay because they believe she may make an alliance with them."

"Is she really an evil woman?" William asked incredulously.

Christopher laughed loud and long. "Did I make her sound evil? She is simply a good politician. Politics is all about image and who has the power. I went for the power, but I was too reckless to realize that I had no status to prop me up when they were through using me. I am certainly not of royal blood, and I have no army to defend me. The vultures are circling, and I will be their evening meal soon."

"Isn't there anything you can do?"

"When they arrest me, I can go peacefully. Perhaps the courts will take pity on me."

"Would it help if I testified for you?" William asked.

Chris laughed quietly, "I wish I possessed your naivety. What would you say? 'He's a great guy and doesn't mind that I steal his plays.' I sincerely appreciate your willingness to help me, but I've come to the end of a good run, and I need to bow out gracefully. Actually, you have helped me a great deal today. I just wanted to talk openly about my situation. I think I can face my future now whatever it holds."

William searched for something positive to say to his friend, "If the courts send you to prison, at least you can still write. They can't take your talent from you. I will visit you there."

"Of course you will. You'll be trying to steal anything I write!" Christopher laughed loudly and ordered yet another ale.

"Would you like to stay with us tonight?" William asked.

"No. I'm not fit to be around children. I'll stay here and drink until I pass out. The barman will drag me up to a room. I'm used to it."

William didn't know what else to say or do, so he stood and said, "It was good to see you again Chris. Thank you for confiding in me. I will tell no one. I hope you are wrong about the vultures." He shook Marlowe's hand, and Marlowe staggered to his feet to embrace William.

"Farewell you upstart crow," Marlowe cracked.

Chapter 45

On June 5, 1593, William received a letter from Russell Northcutt.

William,

It seems it has fallen to me to be the bearer of bad news. On May 18th Christopher Marlowe was served with a writ of arrest for libel and heresy. He did not resist or flee. He presented himself at the court on May 20th which was the date he was to appear. No one was at the court, so he went back to his lodging thinking the guards would come for him. They did not.

On May 30th he was drinking in a local pub and was involved in an argument and brawl. It may have been about an unpaid bar tab. No one seems to know for sure.

I am sorry to tell you this, William, but Chris was stabbed and killed in the fight. An investigation is under way, and I will let you know if I learn any more details.

I hope you and your family are safe and healthy in Stratford. The plague continues to rage here. Please do not come to London.

Yours in friendship,
Russell

William cried for his friend and rival, for the plays that would never be written, for the mystery that would surround Christopher Marlowe's death forever. The vultures came for him, and they were fed.

Chapter 46

William turned to his family and his writing for comfort as he came to terms with Marlowe's death. He took pleasure in remembering his friend's *The Jew of Malta* as he worked on *The Merchant of Venice*. Its opening line, *Forsooth, I know not why I am so sad* was William's commentary on all the lives lost in the past year. Marlowe would never write again, but William could and would.

The comedy *Two Gentlemen of Verona* was finished as was his historical play *Richard II*. Though Russell had informed William that Lord Strange's Men was in disarray after their patron's death and the loss of William's friends and fellow actors, William still wrote with the company in mind. He felt sure that he would return to London and the stage, and he wanted to have as many plays ready for production as he could.

To balance the dark mood of *The Merchant of Venice*, he was writing a comedy, *The Merry Wives of Windsor*. The great public support for his narrative poems, *Venus and Adonis* and *The Rape of Lucrece* should have inspired William to write lyric poetry, but he found each time he tried, he fell into a melancholy mood and could not write. Instead he turned to a new type of theatrical production. *A Midsummer Night's Dream* contained fairies, star-crossed lovers, and common players dreaming of the stage. It made William smile as he wrote it and was the best medicine for relieving his fear of an uncertain future.

William did not return to London until the fall of 1594. The plague had taken 10% of the city's population, but those who survived were ready to be entertained again. They wanted to see plays. William was delighted to be reunited with Russell Northcutt.

"William, it is wonderful to see you looking so well!" Russell embraced his young friend.

William was shocked at how thin Russell appeared. "Are you well, my friend?"

"I have struggled this last year as has everyone in the city. I've come to the realization that I can no longer maintain the heavy schedule of actor and manager of a theatre company. Conveniently, I have no theatre company to manage," Russell coughed out a hollow laugh.

"Has Lord Strange's Men been abandoned?" William asked in concern.

"Yes. Our patron's widow thought she would keep the company alive in memory of her husband, but as the plague continued and the theatres were shuttered, she gave up the dream."

"I'm not sure what I should do," William said.

"I hope you don't mind my boldness," Russell said, "but the one activity I do have energy for is continuing to be your friend and advocate. I have spoken to James Burbage on your behalf. Of course, your name is well known in the theatre world. That pathetic Greene and his tirade about you has made your name very recognizable. Your plays, obviously speak for themselves. By the way, did you hear that Robert Greene is dead?"

"No. I haven't given him much thought. Tell me about James Burbage."

"Oh yes. Burbage has built The Theatre in Shoreditch. It's outside the walls of the city to the north near Finsbury Fields. He has a company of actors including his son Richard who is a marvelous performer. It's a huge company, fifteen actors, sponsored by George Hunsdon, known as Lord Chamberlain and thus they are called Chamberlain's Men."

"Fifteen players! Do you think they would perform my plays?" William asked.

"They are counting on your plays, William! I meant to write and ask you about this, but Burbage approached me, and I acted on your behalf. They want you to be the 16th member of the company, and they want exclusive rights to perform your plays. The money is better than with Lord Strange's Men, and the actors are more versatile."

"I don't know what to say. Thank you, Russell. This sounds like the best place for me. I wasn't sure I could face going back to the Rose and Bankside. My memories of Henry Adams and Rat are so vivid, and I can not endure seeing Mistress Witherington's house."

"I thought that was how you would feel. The Theatre is in Bishopsgate, and you can lease your own chamber there. The neighborhood does not have bear-baiting and brothels, rather it has several churches and two pleasant inns, The Bull and The Green Dragon. I think you will feel at home there."

"Thank you for arranging this for me, Russell. I have come to depend on your wisdom and advice. Even though you are retiring from the theatre business, could you still be my manager?" William asked hopefully.

"I was hoping you would suggest that," Russell laughed, "since I've already made so many decisions for you! Of course, I signed no contract with Burbage. If you meet the company and see the Theatre and decide you do not want to join them, you are free to look at other acting companies."

"I trust your judgment, Russell. When can I meet the players?"

"I've told Burbage we would be at the Theatre later today, but before we go, I have another suggestion for you."

"What is that?"

"If you like Burbage and Lord Chamberlain's Men, I think you should buy a share in the company. It will cost you £50 up front, but you will have a share in all of the profits. Of course, the expenses of the company come out first, but I expect Lord Chamberlain's Men to do very well this season and into the future. You will have your salary as an actor, payment for your plays, and a share of the company's profits. You could retire to Stratford a wealthy man!" Russell laughed.

"An excellent plan!" William toasted his dear friend.

William liked the Theatre. It was much like the Rose, but the open yard in front of the thrust stage was cobbled where the Rose had a dirt yard that was stirred up by the milling audience and blew onto the actors' costumes and into their eyes and noses. The stones may make the noise of the penny groundlings louder, but William preferred noise over dust.

The Theatre's roof was tile rather than thatched. William thought it was wise of Burbage to use tile in the construction. Thatch was highly flammable, and the actors at the Rose had to be very careful with the flaming torches they carried to exemplify night scenes.

William had met some but not all of the actors in the Chamberlain's Men, and when Russell Northcutt introduced him, they made him feel welcome. He was glad to see Will Kempe, a fine comic actor, was a member of the company. William could picture him playing Bottom in *A Midsummer Night's Dream.*

By that evening, William Shakespeare had signed a contract with Lord Chamberlain's Men and paid £50 for a share in the profits. Russell helped him find an airy chamber with lots of light and a view of Finsbuy Fields. He would have no Mistress Witherington to cook him fabulous meals and make him laugh, but he had many pubs and inns nearby when he needed food or company.

The people of London had indeed missed the theatres, and Lord Chamberlain's Men played to sold out crowds during the 1594-1595 season. William enjoyed the summer of '95 in Stratford and returned for another successful season at the Theatre in 1595-1596. Russell's financial advice and William's prudent spending and investments were making him nearly as successful as a businessman as he was as a playwright and actor.

The summer of 1596 started as a happy one. Susanna was a young lady of thirteen, and the twins were eleven. William and Anne couldn't believe how much the children had grown, not just in height but in intelligence and compassion for others as well. Anne continued to teach the children at home, and they were glad they had not enrolled Hamnet in Stratford Grammar School as he was becoming a good little student at home. He still couldn't sit still as long as the girls, but Anne could not fault him for his energy!

The children were old enough to have their own ponies, and the Shakespeare family could often be seen riding over the meadows toward Wilmcote and the little cottage where Anne and William started their lives together. The children never tired of hearing the story of their courtship and marriage. They wanted to see the falcons that Richard Spencer had trained, but Anne explained that Richard had passed away, and his wife Sarah now lived in Oxford. The trained birds of prey were no longer in Wilmcote, but the children could lie on their backs in the meadow and watch the birds soar above them. "That's how birds are meant to be," Anne said. "Free to fly where the breeze takes them."

****

Very early on the morning of August 9, 1596, Judith came into William and Anne's room, "Hamnet is hot, and he is red," Judith said fearfully.

William and Anne rushed to the children's room and found Hamnet bathed in sweat and covered in a fine, red rash. "Susanna and Judith, go climb into our bed while your father and I care for Hamnet," Anne tried to sound calm. "Hamnet will be fine, you girls go back to sleep."

Anne removed Hamnet's bed clothes while William went to the well for fresh, cool water. "My head hurts, mother," Hamnet moaned.

"I know, dear. Your father has gone for water. You will be fine."

William cradled Hamnet in his arms while Anne bathed the boy with cool water. His skin cooled as the water touched it, but as soon as Anne moved to bathe another part of his body, the heat returned. "I'm thirsty," Hamnet said.

Anne brought cool cider from the crock in the buttery, but Hamnet had difficulty swallowing it.

"He's burning up, Anne. I am sweating from holding him. We have to break his fever."

Judith and Susanna were unable to go back to sleep when they saw how sick their brother was, and Susanna came to the bedroom door, "Father, may I ride to Claire Bates' home and see if she will come to help, Hamnet?" Susanna asked.

William and Anne looked at each other and nodded at Susanna, who grabbed a dress to put over her nightclothes. She flew out the door and down the street to the stable where the horses were kept. Dobbin was faster than her pony, and she slipped a halter over his ears and climbed on his back by standing on the stable fence. Then she was off on a gallop to summon Claire Bates, the midwife who had brought her into this world.

Judith stood in the bedroom door with tears streaming down her face. "I can't live without my twin. He is part of me. What are we going to do without him?"

Anne took Judith in her arms and held her close. "Your brother will be fine. He is not feeling well now, but he will be fine."

"No," Judith said sadly, "he won't be fine."

Anne looked at William with fear in her eyes and continued to hold Judith. William clutched Hamnet in his arms and rocked him gently to ease his pain.

Susanna returned with Claire Bates by midmorning. The dear, midwife was aging and moved arthritically to Hamnet's bedside. "There's me fine wee lad. You've gone and gotten yourself a blessed fever. Anne, grind up some of your dried dill and mix it with honey for his rash. William, place your dear lad back on the bed. He likes your nearness, but you are making him even hotter by holding him so tightly."

All that day, they put cool compresses of honey and dill on Hamnet's rash. They had him drink as much cider as he could. They watched with prayers and vigilance, but his fever didn't break. He was awake and could still say a few words. He asked for his bow and his jack knife, and they put them in his bed beside him. He asked for his sisters, and they held his hands until he fell asleep.

The next day he was worse and Claire said with great sorrow, "I don't know what else to do for the sweet lad."

Early the next morning, August 11, 1596, young Hamnet Shakespeare, William and Anne's only son passed away with his sisters and parents at his bedside. The family could not bear the silence that enveloped the little house on Chapel Street. They held each other and sobbed.

They had a simple service for Hamnet at Trinity Church, and the chapel overflowed with well wishers including Lord Henry Wriothesly who felt he had lost a dear, younger brother.

The Shakespeare family dealt with their grief in different ways. Susanna took on the burden of caregiver, fixing meals, washing clothes, and tending to the chores that Anne could not find the energy or desire to do. Little Judith became even more introverted and spent her time drawing and gazing sadly at the garden where she and her brother had spent so many happy hours together.

Anne wanted to talk about Hamnet, to replay the three days of his illness and figure out what they did wrong that caused them to lose their son. "What could we have done differently?" she asked William repeatedly.

William had no answer for her. He spent his time writing. He didn't cry at Hamnet's funeral. Anne thought he was going on about his life as if Hamnet had never existed, and it was breaking her heart and making her feel as if she was losing her husband along with her son.

One day as Anne was sitting idly at the table, Susanna placed a piece of manuscript paper before her on the table, "I found this while I was straightening father's desk. I think you should read it."

Anne picked it up and read:

> *Grief fills the room up of my absent child,*
> *Lies in his bed, walks up and down with me,*
> *Puts on his pretty looks, repeats his words,*
> *Remembers me of all his gracious parts,*
> *Stuffs out his vacant garments with his form;*
> *Then, have I reason to be fond of grief?*
> *O Lord! My boy, my [Hamnet] my fair son!*
> *My life, my joy, my food, my all the world*

My . . . comfort, and my sorrows' cure!
<u>King John</u>, (3.4).

  Anne put her head in her hands and cried. Susanna rubbed her mother's back, and said, "Father misses Hamnet very much. We all do, but somehow we must not let our family die with him. We all love each other so!"

    That night Anne held William close and said, "I love you."

    William kissed Anne and said, "I love you! I always have, and I always will. You are my one true love!"

Author's Notes

Shakespeare's True Love is a fictional work; however, I have followed the historic timeline of Shakespeare's life as closely as possible. When I use his exact words, I indicate I have done so by using italics and note the source at the end of the passage.

The following books were helpful in the creation of this novel: Russell Fraser, *Shakespeare a Life in Art* (New Brunswick: Transaction Publishers, 1988); Jonathan Bate, *Soul of the Age: A Biography of the Mind of William Shakespeare* (New York: Random House, 2010); Bill Bryson, *Shakespeare: The World as Stage* (New York: HarperCollins, 2007); Hannah Crawforth, Jennifer Young, and Sarah Dustagheer, *Shakespeare in London* (London: Bloomsbury/Arden Shakespeare, 2015).

I found helpful information about 16th Century England on the following websites: www.elizabethancostume.net; www.galway-beekeepers.com/skeps/; Children & Youth in History, www.chnm.gmu.edu; Sports and Pastimes in Popular Use in Shakespeare's Day, www.shakespeare-online.com, and List of Christmas carols and Yule Log on en.wikipedia.org.

CPSIA information can be obtained
at www.ICGtesting.com
Printed in the USA
FSOW04n2154121117
41101FS